*Them*

ALSO BY NATHAN MCCALL

*Makes Me Wanna Holler*

*What's Going On*

# Them

A NOVEL

Nathan McCall

**ATRIA** BOOKS

NEW YORK   LONDON   TORONTO   SYDNEY

**ATRIA** BOOKS

A Division of Simon & Schuster, Inc.
1230 Avenue of the Americas
New York, NY 10020

First Atria Books hardcover edition November 2007

**ATRIA** BOOKS and colophon are trademarks of Simon & Schuster, Inc.

For information about special discounts for bulk purchases, please contact Simon & Schuster Special Sales at 1-800-456-6798 or business@simonandschuster.com.

*Designed by Kyoko Watanabe*

Manufactured in the United States of America

10   9   8   7   6   5   4   3   2   1

Library of Congress Cataloging-in-Publication Data
  McCall, Nathan.
  Them: a novel / Nathan McCall—1st Atria Books hardcover ed.
    p. cm.
    1. African American men—Fiction. 2. Printers—Fiction. 3. Atlanta (Ga.)—Fiction.
I. Title.

PS3613.C34514 T47 2007
813'.6—dc22                    2007020627

ISBN-13: 978-1-4165-4915-4
ISBN-10:    1-4165-4915-3

*To Paula*

"And there are those who have the truth within them,
but they tell it not in words."

—KAHLIL GIBRAN

# Them

# PART I

# Chapter 1

April 15th, four thirty-six.

Barlowe Reed drove down an Atlanta parkway, heading south toward North Avenue. The car, a battered old Plymouth with sagging pipes, had seen its best days ten years before. Barlowe drove it slowly, like he halfway didn't want to go in the direction he was moving in. He chugged along, a twinge of irritation tugging at him. (It had nothing to do with the young boy riding his bumper.) Barlowe was always annoyed about one thing or another—usually some item he'd read in the paper. The source of this latest vexation, though, was more personal than headlines in the daily paper. Ever since he'd gone downtown that afternoon to pick up his income tax returns, his mood had soured.

Barlowe hated paying taxes. He couldn't explain it in fancy words, but the reasons were clear enough inside his head. Most folks didn't know the half of what the government did with all the tax money it collected, but Barlowe had his suspicions. He figured a lot of that cash financed dirty work: vast conspiracies, domestic and foreign; secret plots and counterplots; greedy, underhanded, fiendish stuff.

He glanced at the tax documents in the seat beside him and the vexation seemed to magnify. When he'd gone into H&R Block that morning, the accountant, a white man dressed sharply in a crisp shirt and tie, had smiled a big smile, like he had produced some financial masterpiece.

*Accountants*, Barlowe thought now, slugging forward. *Charge an arm and a leg for doin nothin.*

His taxes couldn't have required heavy lifting, and not for what that accountant charged. *Please.* He was a printer; an underpaid printer at that. In fact, he was so flat broke he had considered doing his own returns. In the end he decided to pay white folks to assume the risk. Let the government, the almighty Caesar harass *them* if some decimals and zeroes got mixed all up. Let Caesar go after *them*—not him.

Barlowe wondered how Caesar would use his money against him this time around. He hated that feeling: not knowing the particulars about such things; giving his hard-earned coins to Caesar, and in the blind.

But what could a man do? You had to render unto Caesar what Caesar claimed as his. Either render or break the law and foolishly deliver yourself into Caesar's hands.

He drove along, mulling Caesar. One day maybe he'd hit the number and get Caesar's foot off his neck.

He slouched down in the seat a little, the top of his bushy head peeking just above the steering wheel. He covered two more city blocks and spotted a car that made him sit up straight. Barlowe couldn't see the driver clear; it was the make of the vehicle that he took notice of. It was a Caddy, a gleaming, bright blue number with shiny rims and whitewalls scrubbed clean as a baby's butt. A Caddy. When it came to hogging the road, Caddy drivers were the worst.

The Caddy pulled out in front of him and settled into a lazy crawl. For several blocks the driver loafed along like the street was named for him. Barlowe pressed in closer, to send a message. The Caddy kept gliding steady, like maybe the driver was masturbating behind the wheel.

There was an American flag sticker pasted, dead center, in the car's back window. Barlowe grunted. "Um." Even more than taxes and Caesar, he hated flags. Ever since the planes struck, the things had sprung up everywhere. Houses, buildings, clothes, you name it; flags were attached some way.

He thought about that now as he trailed the Caddy. The patriot finally flashed a turn signal, swung a sharp right and disappeared.

Barlowe reached the post office and glanced at his watch. That Caddy had thrown his timing off. Every tax season he waited until the final day, April 15, and for good measure he got to his neighborhood post office only minutes before they locked the doors at five o'clock.

Inside, a white man, the supervisor, greeted him with a stale smile. He pointed toward a line that snaked to the cashier counter. People stood limply in a single file, their faces empty or tired or contorted in agony at the idea of having to wait in yet another line, with so much more *stuff* to be done in life.

Barlowe opted for the shorter line, the one leading to the stamp machines. There were only three people ahead of him, and five minutes left before closing time. He reached the front of the line and scanned the display window. He leaned in close and turned up his nose. Hovering behind him, a tall, spindly fellow in a Hawaiian shirt shifted impatiently on his heels. Barlowe studied the display again, to see if maybe he had missed something.

He hadn't.

American flag stamps lined nearly every row! Only two rows, B-3 and B-4, offered other choices. Of those, one stamp hailed the invention of the Model T. (It may as well have been a flag.) The other stamp featured the bust of a brown-skinned woman. Barlowe didn't recognize the face right off, but the color suited him just fine.

He slid a five-dollar bill into the slot and paused before pressing the selection button. An announcement floated from somewhere off in a corner. "Post office closes in one minute!"

The man behind Barlowe shifted again, making a show of his impatience. Barlowe leaned down closer, concentrating on stamps. The man behind him clucked his tongue and stomped to the longer line.

Seeing the anxious shuffling, the supervisor approached. "Sir. Sir. Is there something I can help you with?"

Barlowe nodded at the stamp machine and pointed at the stamp bearing the brown woman's picture. "I wont *her*."

"The Marian Anderson stamp is sold out, sir. We don't have time to restock the machine. If you want regular stamps for mailing returns, you'll need to get the flags."

"I don't wont flags."

"What?"

"Naw. Don't wont em."

The supervisor frowned as his Homeland Security training came to mind. He gave the customer a good once-over, for information-gathering sake. Barlowe was a big-boned, corn-fed country boy. His face, the shade of cocoa, bore a slightly weathered look, like the faces you see on faded photos of people toiling in cotton fields. With thick, kinky hair, and lips full and broad, he looked a bit like Otis Redding before he'd made it big.

What stood out most about Barlowe, though, were the hands. The hands were rough as sandpaper. The hands were clean but harsh and stained with ink: red, blue, brown, yellow and black ink from the print shop where he worked.

Another postal worker, seeing his supervisor's frustration, sidled over to investigate. "Everythang all right here?" A short, dumpy man with jet-black skin and thick white hair, he brought to mind Uncle Remus storybook tales.

The supervisor turned to Remus and whispered: "This man says he wants stamps, but he won't buy *flags*."

Barlowe pointed again at the likeness of the brown lady. "I wont *her*." He nodded toward the supervisor. "He say he ain't got time to get some more."

Remus shrugged. "We bout to close up shop now, partner. You gotta do *somethin*." He turned and waddled off.

That gruff response wouldn't have seemed so off-putting if the two men hadn't met before. Some time back, Barlowe had come in that same branch to mail a package. He asked for a book of stamps, and the way old Remus acted you would have thought Barlowe handed him the winning lotto ticket. Remus slapped a vintage book of Duke Ellington commemoratives on the counter and hooked his thumbs around his suspenders, which stretched taut across his big belly like a pair of rubber bands about to snap. He poked out his chest, as proud as if he'd designed the things himself.

The stamps were so beautiful a full month passed before Barlowe could bring himself to mail a single one.

Now Remus headed to the front counter and pulled down the steel cage, to close up shop.

Barlowe turned to the supervisor. "I think I'll jus get my money back, then."

"The machine doesn't give refunds, sir."

Barlowe pressed the change button anyway, but nothing happened. He nodded toward the counter. "Then I'll get it there."

"The counter is closed . . . I'm telling you, sir: You *have* to get the flags."

There was no persuading Barlowe Reed once he made up his mind about something. When he made up his mind about something, pressure of the sort now being applied only served to stiffen his resolve. When the supervisor finished saying his piece, babbling on about what Barlowe *had* to do, he calmly shook his head. "No."

The red light on the stamp machine began blinking.

"You're gonna lose your money."

Shortly, the blinking stopped.

"Toldja. Now we're officially closed." The supervisor walked away.

Barlowe took a few steps back to collect himself. He stood there a moment, his eyes flitting around in disbelief. He cursed, charged forward and rammed a knuckle into the machine. *Whack!* He banged it again, determined to knock his five dollars loose. *Whack! Whack!*

The third punch shattered the glass. The few Model Ts, and all the flag stamps, tumbled out. Barlowe stood back, surprised that the glass had caved so easy. He hadn't intended for it to break.

The supervisor returned when he heard the noise. He homed in on all the stars and stripes lying on the floor, desecrated. His lips quivered, like he wanted to speak, but no sound spilled out. He glared at Barlowe and wagged a finger, then turned and rushed from the room.

Within moments—seconds it seemed—the post office door flung open, and three police officers burst inside. The postal supervisor pointed downward. "Look! Right there!"

The cops panned the shattered glass and scattered stamps. They eyed Barlowe standing there, nodding slowly, like he knew how the thing might play out. The cops unsnapped their gun straps and started forward. "Aw right, buddy! Aw right! This is it!"

It wouldn't be so easy for them this time around. Barlowe Reed was experienced at this sort of thing. He came from a long line of people who were experienced at this sort of thing.

Before the police could get the whipping going, he calmly turned his back to them. Without being told, he placed both hands behind him and held the wrists close together, inviting the cops to clamp on cuffs.

The officers stood there looking dumb, trying to think this one through. Finally, one cop, the only woman among them, stepped forward and slapped on cuffs. Her partners shot her a disgusted look.

While the post office employees looked on, the officers escorted Barlowe through the double doors. They shoved him into the squad car and sped him off toward jail.

Along the way, the city whizzed by in a lightning blur. Barlowe sat handcuffed in the backseat, a mixture of sadness and triumph gripping him.

*I have survived this one*, he thought. *I have survived this one.*

Survival or no, he had also done the very thing he always took pains *not* to do. He had delivered himself to Caesar. And, too, he would be late filing his tax returns.

# Chapter 2

Barlowe stayed locked up in the city jail for three whole days before Nell came downtown to spring him out. She went to the Free-At-Last bail bonds agency, one in a string of dubious enterprises crouched like hyenas across from the jail. Barlowe was lying faceup on his bunk, daydreaming, when the sound of jangling keys rustled him to. He rose on his elbows and spied a tall white man heading in. The jailer opened the cell and stepped aside.

"Caesar." Barlowe muttered it again as he passed through the gate. "Caesar."

The jailer cut him an evil eye. He led Barlowe down a long hallway, through several doors, to the inmate release area. The room was filled with people, mostly dark, hapless friends and family of hapless loved ones locked away.

Barlowe spotted Nell sitting in a corner, off to herself, on a long wooden bench. He approached her smiling, cautious. "Nell."

She sucked her teeth. "Les get outta here." Looking past him, she pointed to a glass partition across the room. "You need to go to that window to claim your stuff."

Barlowe retrieved his belongings and trailed Nell to her car, a Nissan Altima that she'd bought six months ago. Six months, and she had left the price sticker plastered to the side window, like some brash announcement to the world that she had *arrived*.

They got his car from the impound lot and zipped to Nell's condo in Clayton County. She went straight to the back of the house. Barlowe slouched on the living room couch, waiting for a sign. It was still early; they hadn't eaten yet. He wondered if she'd be up for a quickie on an empty stomach.

He sat tight and listened for the birdcall. Nell usually saved her come-hither voice for the birdcalls, those low, husky moans that relayed her moist yearning. She often sounded that call late at night, when she came in from working at the salon. She'd put her six-year-old son, Boo, to bed and point at Barlowe, bending an index finger at the joint, in a gesture that said, "Come with me." He would grab two cold beers from the fridge and hurry to the bedroom before she managed to change her mind. Once in bed she'd spread her wings and melt into him, screaming and flailing in orgasmic fits. Afterward, she'd light a cigarette, blow smoke rings at the ceiling and come up with an excuse to get an attitude.

For the most part, that was how they carried on, even in the year they tried living together. Theirs was a mad, moody affair: sheer fire under the sheets; conflict and chaos otherwise.

Barlowe waited patiently now while Nell fumbled around in her room. From where he sat he could hear the gentle rustle of clothing. He pictured her slipping into something soft and sheer.

Minutes later, Nell appeared in the living room, fully dressed. She sat down across from him and jump-started the conversation she had been rehearsing for some time now.

"We need to talk, Barlowe. Somethin's not workin here."

The words didn't register at first. Barlowe's eyes flitted around the room and settled on Nell's shapely thighs, which were framed in black tights. She lit a cigarette and crossed her legs, to shift his attention above the waist.

He sighed. "Okay, Nell, whas the matter? Whas wrong *now*?"

"I jus got you outta *jail*, thas whas wrong."

"They tried to make me buy flags, Nell. What you expect from me?"

"Yeah, well, *your* li'l crusade cost *me* time and money. I ain't got money for that . . . And I definitely don't have time to be goin down there, minglin with ghetto folk."

He resented the tone and sound of that, the way she distanced herself from her own people.

Nell, unfazed by his resentments, pressed on with the attack: "You too cozy, Barlowe; you too laid-back for me. You go to work and lay round a house that ain't even yours. It wouldn't bother you none if things stayed that way."

"That ain't true, Nell. You know it ain't true."

"All I can go by is what I see. I been waitin a long time for you to show me somethin. But you ain't showin me nothin I can use . . . Barlowe, I wont things . . ."

*Things.* That was the problem, far as he could tell. If he had been willing to overlook it before, it was apparent now: Nell was content to be one of the sheep.

*Things.* She didn't give a squirrel's butt about *people*; she didn't know diddly, and couldn't care less, about Caesar wreaking havoc everywhere.

Barlowe was hip to Caesar, all right. He had never cared much for school, but he'd always studied history, even after dropping out. He'd read *Before the Mayflower*—fourteen times—and he had devoured stories about the '60s, tales about how Caesar used black people's tax dollars to train the police dogs they sicced on them.

Times had changed some, though not as much as people liked to pretend they had. The white folks in Milledgeville had proven that.

*Things.* He had met Nell years before, when she came into the print shop and ordered flyers to advertise the salon. After the printing, she slipped him a number and asked him to call. He phoned, they talked and later dated. Eventually, he even moved in with her.

Barlowe was so taken by her fine looks that it took a while to notice who she was. Now, sitting in her living room, it was clear: The two of them were like mismatched socks.

All of a sudden he felt weary. "I ain't sure I'm what you wont, Nell. I ain't even sure I wanna be."

She leaned forward, almost eagerly. "I guess this is it, then. You can't say I didn't try."

She got up and went to her bedroom and returned minutes later with her hands full. She had gathered his belongings—a shaver, toiletries and two crisply ironed uniforms that he kept there for overnight stays.

"I'm sorry, Barlowe . . . I got plans."

He stood up and gathered his *things*. "You got plans? I got plans, too."

He had plans, all right. He planned to buy his lottery tickets; he planned to get himself a nice, cold beer; he planned to go home and relax on the porch and listen to the pigeons coo.

Barlowe started for the door. Nell walked behind him, keeping a safe distance in case he moved to grab her around the waist. On the way out, he stopped in the doorway. She stepped back and folded her arms tight, like a sudden chill had rushed in the house.

Nell said good-bye and Barlowe left, half-hoping she would stop him like she'd done before.


Barlowe took the back way home, down Memorial Drive. He cut through Cabbagetown, with its shotgun houses and narrow streets. The few days in the dungeon had inspired in him a fresh appreciation for natural air and light. He took it all in, every bit, as his clunker rattled down the street, the windshield wipers swishing every time he hit the left-turn signal switch.

He whizzed past the ash-brick factories now being converted into trendy lofts to make way for the chi-chi Yuppies swarming in. The poor white trash in Cabbagetown despised chi-chi Yuppies a tad less than they hated niggers. They had more in common with the blacks, but you could never convince them of that.

He crossed onto Edgewood Avenue and entered the Old Fourth Ward, where the people's faces were mostly dark and unsure, like his own. He tapped on brakes and waited as Viola and The Hawk shuffled forward and stepped unsteadily off the curb, in front of his car. Viola and The Hawk were two neighborhood drunks. As usual, they had taken the shortcut through the trampled dirt pathway between the house Barlowe rented and the place next door. They were headed to Davenport's place to toast another day of sunshine, another day of living, another day of anything to justify another drink.

Barlowe parked in front of his house, got out and looked around. He could see the horizon in the backdrop of downtown Atlanta, its towering skyscrapers standing pompous and smug.

He went indoors and passed a pair of dirty sneakers on the living room floor and whiffed pork chops frying on the stove. He went through the kitchen and opened the back door, which led to a partially enclosed porch.

A voice, speaking low, gentle, floated to the doorway. "There ya go, baby. C'mon, do this for me. Thas it. Ri there. Riii tthhheerre . . ."

Barlowe stepped onto the porch, flopped in a chair and studied his nephew, who was feeding his three pigeons.

"Ty."

Tyrone jerked around. "Yo, Unk. I din't hear you come in."

Barlowe didn't say anything to that. He stared blankly at the birds.

Tyrone released the pigeons into the backyard, to let them stretch their wings a bit. As usual, the birds flew into the big oak tree in the yard next door. They sat there awhile, then returned to Tyrone, who gently placed them back in the cage.

Barlowe watched, marveling at how hands that handled animals with such loving care were so quick to shed human blood.

Tyrone picked up a beer and took a chug. "Where you been the last few days, Unk, bangin some honey on the sly?"

Barlowe ran a hand wearily through his knotty head, using the fingers like an Afro pick.

"Yeah. I been bangin."

"Nell?"

"No," Barlowe said. "No."

"So what honey kept you on lockdown for three whole days?"

Barlowe thought about the brown lady on the post office stamps. "Jus a gal," he said. "You wouldn't know her."

"What you wanna bet?"

"Make it light on yourself."

Tyrone chuckled. He went into the kitchen, grabbed a pot holder and took the pork chops off the stove. He placed them onto an ugly platter, then turned to Barlowe.

"C'mon, Unk. Les grub and go ride."

"Ride?"

"You got a birfday comin up, right? The big 4-0, right?"

"Thas still a few weeks off yet. Ain't no point in rushin that."

"So what?! Les celebrate early! C'mon. On *me*."

Barlowe liked a good time as much as the next man, but it was too early in the day for that. Besides, he didn't hang out much with Tyrone. There was a solid fifteen years between them, and in their heads— their ways of looking at things—they were at least more than twice that far apart. And right now he craved a little peace and quiet. He needed time to bathe and chase the sights and smells of the dungeon from his head.

"I'ma stay home and chill."

"Suit yourself. Me, I gotta git in the wind."

"Then git, then."

Tyrone laughed. He had a funny, *chee-hee-hee* laugh that made you want to laugh, too, just because he was laughing. Tyrone had a bright, baby-face smile and a mustache that never seemed to grow more than a wisp of fuzz. With smooth, olive skin and jet-black curly hair, he could pass for East Indian at least three days a week. He was quick to tell anybody who needed to hear that he was black, pure black, "A hunnered percent!"

After he and Barlowe finished talking, Tyrone went to his room. He came out a few hours later, scrubbed and sharply dressed.

Barlowe didn't care much for clothes. Except for very special occasions, he wore his khaki uniform every day. Now he studied Tyrone, giving him the up and down.

"Where you goin all dressed up?"

"Gotta git wit this honey I jus met."

"You gonna poke her, or what?"

"Gawd willin." Tyrone paused. "I gotta play this one smart, though. She a house girl. She ain't never had no *real* trash like me."

"How old is she?"

"Don't know for sho. I can tell she got some mileage on her, though. When she talk, you can see that silver shit in back of her mouf."

"She good-lookin?"

"Phatter than a Bojangles biscuit wit butter."

When he said Bojangles, Tyrone dragged out the first syllable for emphasis. *Bo*-jangles. Barlowe got the picture.

Soon, a car horn sounded. Tyrone headed for the door. Barlowe followed, hoping to steal a peek at tender flesh. When Tyrone and his date drove off, Barlowe scanned casually up and down the block. He spotted one of his neighbors, Miss Carol Lilly. She was bent over, working in her flower bed, her wide butt sticking straight up in the air. Barlowe waved at old Mr. Smith across the street, then something bizarre caught his eye. It was a man—a white man—standing on the sidewalk near the front of the house. Dressed in a shirt and tie, the man looked Barlowe dead in the face, then turned and hurriedly walked away. He walked about ten yards along Randolph Street and got in a black Lincoln Town Car parked at the curb. Another white man waited inside.

Barlowe watched them closely, thinking, *Surveillance!* Maybe it had something to do with him refusing flags.

Ever since the planes struck, there was all kinds of surveillance going on. He had read in the papers how Caesar now sifted through folks' e-mail and eavesdropped on private phone conversations. They even checked people's library records, to see what kinds of books they read.

Barlowe considered that as he studied the two white men. They sat there a moment, taking notes and talking. Finally, the car cranked and drove away.

It was odd, Barlowe thought. Long before the planes struck, he had felt like he was under surveillance. His whole life he'd felt people— *them*—watching like they expected him to do something violent or strange. In a weird way it would seem almost fitting if the suspicion that had dogged him so long somehow got formalized.

The boys at the store swore Barlowe was paranoid, and to a certain extent he agreed. He was born here but he couldn't recall a time when he felt he belonged. He had never been outside the country, yet he didn't feel safe inside it, either. In fact, he felt downright vulnerable. And now all the public hysteria had left him even more on edge.

Later, Barlowe ate some pork chops and macaroni and cheese and washed the dishes. Afterward, he sat down in the living room and picked up the newspaper. As he read, a pang of loneliness whipped through him. After all the musty manliness in jail, he craved a woman's scent and softness. He thought about Nell:

"You too cozy."

Normally, Nell's words would have rolled off his back like so much rain, but her timing—and Barlowe's history—made them stick. He would be turning forty soon, and he had begun to ponder what that meant, or what it was *supposed* to mean. Somehow, forty seemed miles apart from thirty-nine. At forty, he figured, a man should be firmly established and grounded. He was approaching the fourth decade of his life and the truth was, he hadn't yet figured out how to live.

Still, Nell had no right to put him down the way she'd done. It proved she wasn't right for him. He might have seen it before now if his two heads hadn't collided so.

Now he shifted focus back to the strange white men he'd seen earlier, and he was reminded that Nell wasn't his only problem. His court case was scheduled two months out. Then he'd have to face Caesar. His court-appointed attorney predicted he'd likely get off with a lightweight fine. All he had to do, the lawyerman said, was go before the judge and explain why he busted up that stamp machine. He made it sound easy as pie, but Barlowe feared otherwise. How could he explain to a judge, a *judge*, the way flags affected him?

Ever since the planes struck, he couldn't get away from them. People hung flags—the biggest ones they could find!—on porches and trees in front of their houses; draped them from buildings in every big city and poot-butt town. Folks wore flag T-shirts, sweatshirts, jackets and hats; plastered them across the sides of garbage trucks. TV newscasters wore flag pins on their freakin coat lapels! Flags screamed from

huge billboards and fluttered from gigantic poles in front of car deal-
erships. One day, Barlowe passed a bunch of long-haired bikers—a
motorcycle gang!—with flags pasted across their sleeveless leather
jackets.

*Is crazy.*

Barlowe wasn't sure how other folks felt. Maybe they felt the same
as him and just weren't saying. Who knew these days? The trip to jail
had taught him one thing, though: He would have to exercise more
self-control. He would have to, or he wouldn't last long, not with all
the paranoia since the planes struck.

He got up to go take a leak. It would be nice, he thought, standing
over the commode, if he had someplace safe to go. Not someplace far
or foreign or isolated, like jail. He never wanted to go back there. It
might be nice to live beneath the radar and, at the same time, be free
to move about in the open air.

He flushed the toilet and returned to the living room, chewing on
that idea. Then he considered something: He actually felt halfway safe
on the ragged patch of land where he now stood. He cherished having
his own dark, separate corner of the world, where he wouldn't be
judged or watched or pushed around.

Funny; that notion hadn't come to him like that before. It came
now as a kind of dawning, an epiphany. He was at least partly insulated
in the neighborhood, nestled among people who looked like him.
These were *his* people. They were all he had. These were *his* people.
These were the people of the Old Fourth Ward.

# Chapter 3

Nearly two months to the day after the arrest, Barlowe stepped outside the courthouse, where blistering sunlight bore down hard. It was a searing June heat, a bit like the anguish burning inside his chest.

Driving home, he sighed and contemplated the verdict: Guilty. Disorderly conduct and destruction of property. The judge ordered him to pay for the broken stamp machine, then pointed a crooked finger and lectured him about the sanctity of the law.

"... You understand?"

"Fug you." That's what Barlowe had a mind to say. "Fug you *and* the law."

He would have loved to say it and storm from the courtroom, leaving the words dangling in the air to marinate. But he kept quiet. With an elbow prod from his lawyer, he shot His Honor a stony stare and nodded, yes. The gavel struck, and it was over.

Now the strain of holding back, of not speaking his mind, sloshed around in Barlowe's stomach like sour milk. That judge had lectured him like he was a child. He was a man, a grown man deserving of a man's respect. He was a man, yet he had been unable, unwilling maybe, to pay the steep price to demand that Caesar properly reverence him.

He didn't feel good about that. He didn't feel good at all.

Beyond the verdict, though, there was one small comfort to be had. He had been doing some thinking lately. He had been thinking that a man don't always have to eat what he's fed in life. If he wants, a man can fix a meal of his own choosing. Barlowe planned to get to work on that; he planned to get on it soon.

For now he craved distraction, something to help him get past the public lashing he'd endured in court. For starters, a pair of lotto tickets might boost the spirits some. And then, maybe, the camaraderie of friends.

He reached home and stepped across the street. Nearby, a group of children played along the curb. They uncorked a fire hydrant and squealed gleefully as bursts of water cooled them off.

Barlowe went to the corner store, the Auburn Avenue Mini-Mart. The size of the average matchbox house, the one-story, wood-frame store was stocked from floor to ceiling with everything short of bicycles and auto parts. Among the mini-mart's most loyal clients were three men (Barlowe called them the elders) who lived as boarders in the shotgun rooming house next to the store. On most days, they hauled rickety kitchen chairs outside and held court in the shade of a maple tree. They came out early mornings to critique the rush-hour traffic and retreated indoors at noon to escape the smog or sun. Like clockwork, they returned in the cool of evening time.

Grizzled old coots, the elders were the self-appointed eyes and ears of the Old Fourth Ward. Nothing much escaped their notice. They were quite nosy and, they thought, keenly perceptive, too. Rough-edged and straightforward as rumbling trains, these were men Barlowe could talk with and be listened to in the way he most needed to be heard. Which is to say, without judgment, and sometimes, without reply.

All his life he had preferred the company of older men. People back in Milledgeville had said it was because he was an old soul himself, a change-of-life baby, born when his mama was going through menopause. So he joined the elders around flameless campfires, where they spoke, sometimes through gritted teeth, about matters that pertain to life and men. They shared fantastic stories, about good, pretty women they'd conquered and lost, or fistfights or poker games they'd managed to win. And sometimes, if the liquor loosened their manly restraints, they even shared deep regrets—over jobs quit, rejected or yanked away; over words spoken too hastily, too harshly or not at all; over what might have been if not for roadblocks thrown up by *them*.

At the moment, the one called Ely had gone inside the mini-mart for liquor, thanks to a newly arrived Social Security check. His comrades, Amos and Willie, sat outdoors waiting with plastic champagne glasses.

As Ely browsed, the door swung open, and a brooding Barlowe came plodding in. He was trailed a few steps behind by Lucretia Wiggins, the neighborhood diva. Barlowe said hey, but Ely didn't hear. He cut a sharp eye at Lucretia, who drifted quietly down the second aisle. Ely could have bought his whiskey and left right away. Instead, he scooted to another aisle and pretended to consider some sardines and soda crackers on the shelf.

He often saw Lucretia switching her pear-shaped bottom through the neighborhood on the way to and from her mama's house. But Ely rarely got a chance to get close up on her.

While he spied, she glided to the last aisle, her trim hips bouncing softly on flat-heeled shoes. When she breezed past Ely on the way to the register he noticed she held a pack of hair extensions in one hand and clutched something tightly in the other fist. Ely moved in closer and stood near the crates of bottled water as Lucretia paid the store owner, Juliette. When she left, Ely's eyes trailed her firm bottom through the door.

He bought a pint of Wild Turkey, then rushed outside to his friends. He sat down and prepared to pour himself a drink, rolling his big false teeth around in his head.

"Eh! Y'all see Eye Candy come through heah?"

No response. The boys resented that he'd taken so long to bring the spirits. Ely downed a few swigs and peered at Amos, who blithely waved at the mailman across the street.

"That gurl oughta be shamed a hurself." Ely leaned forward, pushing his teeth outward from the gums. The teeth were uncomfortable, mainly because they weren't fitted for him. Ely had bought them from a low-rate dentist who'd had them made for another client. When the client died unexpectedly, the dentist offered them on sale to Ely, no extra charge for installation, of course.

Now Barlowe came outside, carefully studying his lotto sheets. Amos and Willie prepared to start a game of checkers.

"Barlowe," Amos called to him while Willie set up the pieces. "How did yore court case go?"

"It went."

They all took that to mean the topic was shut down for the day. Willie moved a checker piece and changed the subject.

"What that gurl oughta be shamed for, Ely, wearin them britches tight like that?"

"I ain't studin the britches. I'm talkin bout what she *bought* in there."

"Wha she buy?"

Ely sipped from his glass and let the warm liquor glide down real slow. Then he winked at Barlowe, who was pouring himself a drink.

"Don't look at me," said Barlowe. "I didn't see nothin to speak about."

"Ely, go on and tell us, gotdammit," barked Amos. "You done started now."

Amos had a scraggly beard and a shock of salt-and-pepper wool that looked like an Afro but lacked enough symmetry to call it that. He topped it off with a baseball cap, which he now removed and used to wipe his round forehead.

Ely rolled his eyes and set his glass down easy, taking his sweet time.

"Come on, Ely. Wha she buy?"

When he could no longer stand his own suspense, Ely leaned forward and whispered: "Rubbers."

The men's eyes widened bright as full moons. "*Rubbers?!*"

"Yeah. The spensive kind."

Willie grinned. "I ain't got no problem wit that. I jus wish she was buyin em for *me*."

Ely reared back. "You cain't do nothin wit that. Young gurl like that would bust yore heart. You'd haveta turn her over to ol Barlowe there."

Barlowe beamed, thinking that might not be such a bad idea. By now, the liquor had soothed his torment some. He flung the court case from his head and turned his attention to all the rusty bravado being tossed around. He threw down another drink and talked awhile, then left the elders and started home.

Heading up the sidewalk, his thoughts were jarred by something he picked up from the corner of his eye. There was a white man knocking at the house next door. When no one answered, the man left and paced up and down the sidewalk, carrying a legal pad. He appeared to be writing down house addresses.

"*Who is he?*" Barlowe wondered, "*A salesman? A detective stalking somebody on the run?*"

He watched the man a moment longer, then tossed it from his mind and rushed on home. He had an important meeting coming up.

William Crawford stepped into the living room and stood by the doorway like he intended to keep the conversation short.

"Sit down, Mr. Crawford." Barlowe waved an ink-stained hand toward the couch and set a bowl of stale peanuts on the coffee table. "Have a seat right there."

It seemed strange saying that to the man who owned the house he rented. Still, he needed practice. This was how you did business with white people.

Crawford sat, reluctantly, and slid a thumb and forefinger under his chin. He had no real chin to speak of, which made his face look like it was hanging on the edge of a cliff, or of a thought, perhaps pondering a way to squeeze an extra dime from some person or circumstance. A retired air traffic controller, Crawford dabbled in real estate. He owned a few houses in the Old Fourth Ward.

"Now, son," he said, "what can I do for you today?"

"I asked you to come over cause I wanna talk."

Crawford said nothing. He took off his tinted gold-wire-rimmed glasses and wiped a sweaty brow. He didn't really need the glasses. He used them to shade his eyes, much like a poker player. The eyes moved all the time, like he was thinking hard, always plotting ways to add a few more coins to his pockets.

"I'm forty now," Barlowe declared. "I been thinkin is time to start settlin down."

"Good." Crawford waited, certain there was more to come.

"Thas why I wonted to talk—about the house."

"The house?" Crawford slid forward and clasped his fat fingers. "What's wrong with the house?"

"Nothin. Nothin's wrong with the house. I like livin here. I like this place a lot. In fact, I like it so much that I wanna buy."

Crawford studied him closely. Barlowe guessed he was calculating, maybe crunching numbers. After a moment, Crawford shook his head.

"To be honest with you, Barlowe, I don't know. You're a good man and all, but I don't know about breaking up my property. See, that house is parta my portfolio . . . I don't think you understand how much a house like this is worth nowadays."

*Worth?* Barlowe looked into the old man's eyes with the certain conviction that Crawford couldn't possibly grasp the gravity of his desires. Crawford may have known the assessed value of the place he owned, but Barlowe doubted that he knew, or even cared to know, its history, which could hardly be quantified in dollar bills.

Such was the case with the Old Fourth Ward. When the neighborhood was first built, whites lived in most of the area, especially up on the northern end of Randolph Street. In the 1920s, blacks following factory jobs moved down on the opposite end, near Auburn Avenue. To keep the boundaries clear, whites changed the name of their end of Randolph to Glen Iris Drive. When blacks kept coming, white folks hauled tail out of town. Blacks moved into the fine Queen Anne cottages, bungalows and shotgun houses and claimed the place for themselves. The main drag on Auburn Avenue eventually came to be widely known as "the richest Negro street in the world."

In time, though, the ward suffered as black tax dollars were steered to the white areas in Atlanta. City neglect and more integration gradually siphoned middle-class blacks from the neighborhood. As the single-family homes, duplexes and apartment buildings fell into disrepair, the Old Fourth Ward declined.

In the late '80s, a smattering of blacks began trickling back. By the time Barlowe Reed showed up, twitchy and desperate, a decade later, blacks had begun a sturdy push to revive the ward.

Barlowe moved onto Randolph Street. Randolph was a classic street, with sidewalks that people actually used each day, and modest yards and even some driveways leading to cozy houses owned by families with long ties to the ward.

Through generations, they worshipped at churches, frequented bars, celebrated births and mourned deaths; they raised children who sprouted tall and were sent off to colleges and wars and penitentiaries; they fed their dogs, attended parties and wept at weddings—all in a swatch of land spanning less than one square mile.

With the few pesky crack and liquor houses operating, the ward remained a work in progress. Still, in his years living there, Barlowe had found it to be a fine retreat. In fact, it was more than a retreat. It had become a need. It was the kind of place where a man could get genuine conversation and a sincere smile.

These were *his* people; these weren't the pretenders, the self-absorbed buppies, puffed-up over fancy houses and big-shot careers. These were *his* people. He liked talking with them, exchanging notions about life and the world. And their dreams; he especially liked hearing them talk about their dreams. Their dreams were simple and straightforward, like his own: They wanted to get along in life and do all right.

For Barlowe, there was something else special—something mythical—about living in the Old Fourth Ward. In Atlanta, where Martin Luther King sits in glory on the right hand of God, the neighborhood boasted a prominent claim to M.L.K. He was born there; his birth home and tomb were there, preserved for the stream of tourists who came daily in double-decker buses and Bermuda shorts to gawk, snap pictures and reflect on "The Dream."

Living amid all that rich history and driving past King's crypt on his way to and from work every day inspired in Barlowe a sense of hope sometimes.

Now hope was the thing he clung to as he sat in the living room, meeting with William Crawford.

"How much money you got saved?" the old man asked.

"Well—" Barlowe had exactly $138 in his bank account. With his shaky credit, no mortgage banker in his right mind would extend him a loan. But he had read in the papers that you could sometimes lease a house with the intention to buy.

"You got enough for a good down payment?"

*Whas a good down payment?* Barlowe had to be careful. If there was a way to cheat a man in this world, then a man would be cheated, and William Crawford was just the one to do the cheating.

"Well. Right now I'm startin mostly with an idea, and then I thought, dependin on what you said, I'd work from there."

"An idea? An idea won't get you nothing but another idea. You need money, *cash,* to make anything happen in this doggone world."

Crawford stood, signaling he was ready to leave. He had no more time to waste. He turned to the door, then something happened that gave him pause: Tyrone appeared from the back bedroom. He had showered and gotten dressed in a spiffy outfit, accented by shiny things. He wore a Kangol cap and a blue suit, with a matching shirt. He wore a fake-diamond-studded ring in one ear, and a thick gold chain around his neck. He had on a pair of black alligator shoes, shining so bright you could see your face in them.

He smiled broadly. "Hey, Mr. Crawford!"

Crawford's face lit up like a big marquee. "Hey, Scooter!"

Crawford fondly called him "Scooter." He liked to hear Tyrone brag about the young women he had bedded. He liked to soak up stories about wild adventures in the fast lane, which, being old and married with grown children, Crawford could visit only in his dreams.

"Where you on your way to, Scooter?"

"Me and a dude goin over to the nekkid club."

"Oh, yeah?"

"Yeah, they got a new girl dancin there now . . . Albino!" He whistled and rolled his eyes around in his head.

The two men chatted a moment, then Tyrone rushed out the door. Crawford prepared to follow. Before leaving, he stopped and turned to Barlowe.

"Tell you what, son. Let me get back to you on this business about the house. I'll think about it and let you know what's on my mind."

"Thas all I can ax, Mr. Crawford. Sounds fair to me."

When the old man left, Barlowe sat down and crossed his legs. He crunched a few peanuts and considered the way the brief talk had gone. Crawford had made no promises, true. Nor had he flat-out turned him down. Which meant he could be persuaded.

For a long while, Barlowe sat there and stared up at the ceiling, thinking. He had turned forty, and it had occurred to him that in all his life he had never been committed to much. He'd always known what he was against: He was against Caesar and taxes and stuff like that. But up until now he hadn't given much thought to what he was *for*. He had latched onto something concrete now.

If Crawford cooperated, this place would be his; he would become a property owner, an official resident of the Old Fourth Ward.


Tyrone came in later, staggering a bit. His eyes were glassy, and his hat was cocked so far to the side that it looked like it would fall off if he moved an inch. His right hand was wrapped in a bloody rag.

Barlowe was relaxing on the back porch. He had taken a nice, long bath. He had spread newspaper on the floor, beneath his bare feet. He was bent over, clipping his toenails, and lost deep in thought about something he had seen earlier, after he let Crawford out the door. He'd seen another white man. Dressed in nylon shorts and a T-shirt, the man came jogging past and trotted down Randolph Street. Barlowe had studied him closely. The white man turned left onto Edgewood Avenue and disappeared.

Except for tourists who were lost or turned around, white people rarely ventured on foot to that end of Auburn Avenue.

"What you thinkin bout so hard?" Tyrone disrupted his train of thought.

"Nothin," said Barlowe. "What happened to your hand?"

"Got in a scrap with that punk Black Sam, down at the Purple Palace. We was shootin dice and the nigger tried to say I cheated. Had the nerve to act like he wonted some a me. We took it outside, and everybody stood back and let us go, heads-up."

Using his good hand, he inspected the birdcage, checking the food and water. The pigeons fluttered against the cage, clamoring to be set free. When he released them, they flew straight next door and settled in the big oak tree. He had taped red I.D. tags to their legs, in case they got lost.

Moments later, the birds returned, their heads bobbing as they scooted in the cage. Tyrone closed the door, then held up his bloody knuckle and examined it some more, thinking about Black Sam.

"I dusted im off, good. Gave im a *country* stompin . . . Made me hurt my damned hand, though."

Barlowe kept on clipping nails. After a while he sat up straight and faced Tyrone.

"Listen. I had a li'l talk with Mr. Crawford."

"What fo?"

"Bizness."

"What kinda bizness?"

"House bizness," said Barlowe.

"It gonna mean payin mo rent?"

"Hope not."

"Me, too. I'm po as a broke-dick dog."

Barlowe regarded his nephew pensively, as if trying to decide whether to let him in on a secret. Then he started: "I axed Mr. Crawford to sell me the house."

He felt a surge of pride when he said those words. Tyrone, however, was unimpressed.

"You wanna buy *this* ol thang?"

"Yeah. This ol thing."

"Why you wanna do that fo?"

Barlowe's face sagged with the weighty impatience of having to explain something that should already be understood. He looked squarely at his nephew. "Ty, I'm forty."

That was all he said. It was all he could *think* to say.

Tyrone responded with a blank expression. Living with Barlowe he'd learned to keep harmony, mainly by tuning his uncle out when the need arose. Whenever Barlowe started talking high-minded or paranoid Tyrone would simply blast away; he'd send his mind racing right through the door.

Barlowe recognized the vacant look and instantly discerned its meaning. He went back to clipping nails.

With the foolish house-talk abated, Tyrone casually reached in his waistband and pulled out a gun. It was a gleaming .38, an old-school standard, with a white pearl handle. He held the gun aloft, admiring it like it was a pretty girl.

"I started to pistol-whip Black Sam."

Barlowe looked up from his toes, wondering how long he could keep his nephew away from trouble. "Be careful, Ty. Be *real* careful with that. Remember. You still on parole."

Tyrone stuffed his gun away. "Don't worry, Unk. I got everthang under control."

He went toward his bedroom and disappeared.

Barlowe balled up the newspaper with the clipped toenails and threw it in a trash can near the door. Sitting there, he weighed the potential for things to shape up some. If he got that house, he thought, he would dig right in. He would find a good woman—maybe a "house girl" like the one Tyrone described—and build a real life for himself.

That's what he wanted: Something he could put his hands on.

# Chapter 4

A month after the talk with Barlowe, William Crawford showed up at the house to oversee delivery of a new refrigerator. After sputtering and groaning and hanging on for years, the old fridge had finally given up the ghost. Crawford replaced the thing with one he'd picked up from the Sears scratch-and-dent sale. It would be ages before he'd come out of his pocket to upgrade anything else. So the visit doubled as a dedication without a ribbon cutting, a chance for Crawford to publicly commend himself.

When the deliverymen left, Crawford jangled his car keys, signaling that he, too, was about to go. Barlowe stopped him. "Wait a minute, Mr. Crawford. I wanna pick up where we left off before."

Crawford furrowed a thick brow, feigning puzzlement. "Huh?"

"The house," said Barlowe. "You said you were gonna think about the house."

"Oh, *that*." The old man sat down and wiped his forehead. He hadn't come here for that. Which meant he hadn't prepared a suitable lie. He wiped his head again. "This neighborhood is historic, you know, with Martin Luther King here and all."

*There it is,* Barlowe thought. *There's the play to jack up the price.*

Crawford wiped his forehead once more. "I just dunno . . . I'm fine having you as a tenant . . . That refrigerator in there"—he pointed at the kitchen—"I don't do that for everybody. But I like *you*. You pay on time. You keep things quiet. I kind of like the way things are."

Barlowe stuffed his hands deep in his pockets and tried not to let his disappointment show. But it was there. It was there, and it ran deeper than he cared to admit. Since the idea of buying the house took hold, cravings had bubbled up inside him from places he hadn't even known about. He had become vaguely aware of being swept along by desires rooted deeper than his capacity to control. So he had progressed from *wanting* that house to *needing* that house. He hadn't considered the distinction before.

For a moment, he held that need inside like a man holding his breath underwater. Finally, when he couldn't hold it anymore, he let go:

"Mr. Crawford. *Please*."

He hadn't known what else to say, but as soon as he uttered that word, *please*, Barlowe instinctively knew he had gone too far. He knew he'd breached some barrier, built up over years with painstaking care; he'd flung open mighty gates to some deeply private, sacred fort.

It wasn't the word alone that bothered him. It was the slight inflection in his voice, the hint of a subtle pleading, and to a *white* man, that left him shaken. He hadn't intended that at all, at least not consciously.

The word spilled out on its own and whisked him back some thirty years. He was a young boy, maybe ten, when the "officials" of Milledgeville came to the house to talk to his daddy. His daddy was a lease farmer who had taken over from *his* daddy, a sharecropper before him.

Barlowe and his four brothers were weeding the field when the white men showed up. The men rode in an official car, with an official city seal on the side door. A picture of the flag shone beneath the seal.

The men got out, leaned against the car and folded their arms, waiting for Barlowe's daddy to come to them.

He went. They talked.

Barlowe couldn't hear what was being said. He figured it was serious, because his daddy mostly listened. He listened and nodded now and then as the men addressed him in hushed, paternal tones.

Their business done, the white men politely tipped their hats and turned to leave. His daddy took one step forward and raised his voice after them in a desperate plea.

"Sir. Please!"

The man standing closest to him whipped around. He jabbed a finger in his chest and sharply chastened him. That done, the men climbed into their official car, with the official seal and the red, white and blue flag painted on the side door. They drove away, sending a cloud of dust swirling high as the treetops.

When Barlowe's daddy turned around, his face was ashen. He looked like he'd aged fifty years.

He plodded over to his sons. "They say we grown too much crops. We gotta burn half the field."

The boys, stunned, destroyed the family's good yield like they were told. In the years that followed, the family struggled, hard. Barlowe's daddy was never the same man after that.

*Please.*

Now having used that word, Barlowe hated himself. He hated himself and Crawford, too. In fact, he hated the whole world. He hated the world and everybody who had ever lived in it since the beginning of time. He wished like hell that he could take back that word. He wished he had never allowed it to slip from his tongue:

*Please.*

Sitting there, he reminded himself that, above all else, he was a man. He was a man, just like Crawford was a man. Either they would do business man-to-man, or not at all.

As if to restore what morsel of manhood that might have been diminished by his clumsy slip, Barlowe resolved, then and there, to drop the issue of the house. *Fuggit.* That's what he thought. *Fug the whole damned thing.*

He extended an ink-stained hand, signaling to Crawford that he would let it go. "Fine," he said. "Fine."

He held his head high, even as he saw his dream fading like leather exposed to too much sun.

"Fine." He said it once more, for good measure.

Crawford appeared both confused and relieved. He prepared to go, to take the opening and run on through.

Then something almost magical happened—magical only in the sense of its quirky timing: Tyrone came to the front door and fumbled with the lock. Just as Barlowe moved to open it, he turned the knob and stumbled in. His eyes were glazed, and the smell of reefer clung heavy to his clothes. He took one glance at Barlowe and Crawford, looking all serious, and he broke into a wicked grin.

"Hey, Mr. Crawford!"

"Hey, Scooter! How you doing?"

"If it got any better I'd have to go jump off a cliff!"

"Yeah?"

"Yeah. Bet y'all don't know where I been!"

Crawford grinned. "Off juking somebody's daughter, I'm sure."

"Been over to the titty bar on Piedmont Road."

"That right?"

Tyrone whistled. "They got gals can do thangs make you stand on your toes!"

Crawford's eyes rolled around in the sockets like steel balls in a pinball machine. The look of the voyeur spread across his face.

"I never been to one a those places before, Scooter. Can you believe it? Been in this town more than twenty years, and never set foot in a single one."

Tyrone gazed upon Crawford with sincere pity. "Aw, c'mon, Mr. Crawford. Don't tell me that. Fitty thousand nekkid bars in Lanta, and you ain't never been to *one*?"

Crawford held up his right hand, like he was being sworn into public office. "The God's honest truth."

"You don't know what you missin."

"Pretty gals, huh?"

"Pretty!?" Tyrone reared back unsteadily on his heels. "They got eighteen-inch waists and big, ol jellyroll butts!"

Crawford swallowed hard, like there was a lump in his throat. He sat back on the couch, eager for more.

"On Tuesdays," explained Tyrone, "you get the first table dance for *free!*"

"Free?" Crawford appeared embarrassed and excited, all at once. He slapped his knee hard, signaling that he'd reached a firm resolve.

"Okay, Scooter. You win. I'll go."

"Bet."

Crawford waited for him to propose a date. Tyrone tilted slightly to one side and slapped him five. Then he waved good-bye. He staggered to his room and closed the door.

Crawford took out his handkerchief again and wiped his neck. He was sweating pretty heavy now. He looked at Barlowe and nodded toward the bathroom.

"Yeah," said Barlowe. "Help yourself."

Crawford returned minutes later, walking slow and wide-legged, like he had peed in his pants. He sat down again and faced Barlowe.

Selling a house was a bit much to ask, but there was no need telling his tenant that; not now, anyway. No point in crushing the man's motivation.

"Tell ya what, son," said Crawford, leaning forward. "Tell you what I'm gonna do . . ."

# Chapter 5

Wat good is life if a man can't aspire to a thing well beyond his reach, with the heady faith that determination, sheer force of will, can close the gap? Following the talk with Crawford, Barlowe wasted no time preparing. If he was going to become a homeowner, he figured, he should begin acting like one.

For starters, he thrust himself more deeply into the mundane affairs of the house. With creaky floors, and paint peeling from the walls, the place had its share of problems. Overall, though, it was stacked with potential; all the potential in the world if Crawford would put a little money in it. But Crawford wasn't one to invest money into his houses unless there was promise of a quick return.

Rather than wait on his chintzy landlord, Barlowe used his own funds to fix up the place. He mended broken appliances, and decorated, too. Although he had lived here for several years, it was still sparsely furnished, even in the living room: There was a salt-and-pepper couch (fairly new); a Mama-San chair (old, but acceptable for a single man); a nondescript floor lamp, a scatter rug and a coffee table.

To fill some of the empty spaces, Barlowe bought big plants with sprawling leaves. And after he had paid the rent, he bought some cheap black art at the Auburn Avenue street festival. Standing in the center of the living room one day, he noticed that most of the art carried likenesses of women: On the wall, a tall, slender African woman in multicolored beads; a batik with two jet-black women sipping from separate drinking gourds; an abstract mahogany wood carving that, on closer inspection, turned out to be a pair of bouncy tits.

Somehow, the female theme had escaped him before.

Tyrone thought he was acting strange, obsessed, but Barlowe didn't care what his nephew thought.

Barlowe also joined the Old Fourth Ward civic league, and signed on to its public safety committee. As a committee member he and three other men regularly patrolled the neighborhood on alternating days. The others shirked their duties now and then, but Barlowe showed up, on time, whenever scheduled. He grew to enjoy patrolling the ward. He felt proud walking those streets.

That occurred to him one day as he stopped by the mini-mart to pick up his lotto tickets. The elders were lounging outside the store. Barlowe hung around and chatted awhile, then started his patrol down Randolph Street. He strolled along the sidewalk, his hands clasped contentedly behind his back as a cluster of children, wild-eyed and giddy, zoomed past on brightly colored bicycles. He passed houses where people worked in gardens. He waved toward a porch, where chatty teenage girls sat listening to music and braiding hair.

Bright and bustling, the neighborhood seemed to finger-pop to its own soulful tune.

The season was changing to fall. The trees had begun to shed, bringing the dazzling downtown Atlanta skyline into clearer view. The remaining leaves on some trees, a rich green just a month ago, now appeared muted, while others had already turned a deep golden brown.

Barlowe noticed the neighborhood was changing, too. A new family had moved in recently, further down on Randolph Street. They'd bought a weedy lot and built a fine split-level with a wraparound porch. Next to the new house was a run-down shanty, one strong wind from tumbling down. On the other side stood a shaky one-story firetrap in need of an expert handyman.

The mishmash of old and new houses, sturdy and run-down, was fairly common in the ward.

Ambling along, Barlowe spotted sleepy-eyed Randy Simpkins sitting on his front porch, staring vacantly into space. Actually it was Randy's mama's house, but he had lived there with her for all of his forty years. When Barlowe approached, he and Randy each tilted their heads back, in the silent greeting that black men do.

Barlowe pressed on, heading to the lower end of Glen Iris Drive, toward the Purple Palace. That's what folks called the run-down rooming house down that way. It was a mystery why they called it purple. Actually, the house was bird-shit yellow, with pale trim around the window frames. The owner, an old white man from Cobb County, had slapped on a fresh coat of paint the year before, after community leaders complained that it was an eyesore.

For years, the Purple Palace had been a half-respectable shot house. Barlowe used to drop in sometimes to buy chicken dinners and socialize. He'd hang around and have a drink or two; maybe watch Tyrone play blackjack or roll the dice. Then he'd move on before things got rowdy.

Now that he was a member of the public safety committee, it didn't seem proper to go in there. Besides, the buzz on the street held that the Purple Palace was diversifying. According to the wires, a dude called Henny Penn was nudging the establishment into drugs and prostitution. Now a parade of glaze-eyed zombies drifted in and out like it was the main post office downtown. Now flashy women strolled the strip, searching men's eyes for desire as they waved at passing cars. And the men's wives, if they happened to be riding along, commented for the thousandth time: "Somethin oughta be done bout that place."

Traipsing along, Barlowe studied the Palace, where the front door was left ajar. That front door stayed open all the time, even in winter. He passed the place and made his way on down the street.

By the time Barlowe finished his rounds, the Sunday sun had set. The neighborhood had begun hunkering down for the evening. Children were called home for supper. Working folks scuttled in to prepare for the next day's grind. They ironed their work clothes or packed their bag lunches, or simply tried to gear their weary minds for another week of hard labor and routine insults on low-paying jobs.

As Barlowe reached home, a huge dump truck rumbled past, barreling toward Edgewood Avenue. One of its wheels sank into a pothole and bounced up noisily.

Barlowe had started up the walkway, when a familiar raspy voice floated his way.

"Hey dere, young man!"

He turned and saw Mr. Smith, his elderly neighbor from across the street. Mr. Smith and his wife, Zelda, were both retirees who had lived in the Old Fourth Ward for thirty years. A short, bald, bow-spined man with banjo eyes, Mr. Smith was out front, leaning under the open hood of his broken-down Chevrolet. It was an old convertible with a tattered rag top that had been peeling back like dead skin on a shedding snake.

That rusty car hadn't moved in years. Still, he spent his spare time out there with a huge red toolbox, tinkering with the thing.

"How you doin taday?" he asked cheerily as Barlowe approached.

"I'm fine, Mr. Smith. Workin hard, thas all."

"Aw, don't worry bout that, son. Hard work ain't never kilt nobody." Then he reconsidered. "Well, not lately, no way."

Mr. Smith liked Barlowe. He didn't care much for that fish-eyed Tyrone, but he liked Barlowe a lot. He liked that Barlowe read newspapers and history books and seemed to search into the heart of things.

Barlowe liked Mr. Smith, too, mostly for the same reasons. He liked him so much, in fact, that he used variations of Mr. Smith's house address, 1023, for good luck when he played the numbers.

"Mr. Smith," said Barlowe, "I gotta idea."

"A idea?" The old man leaned over his toolbox and exchanged a wrench for a pair of pliers.

"We should do somethin bout them heavy trucks comin through."

"Somethin like whut? Whut you gon do?"

"We should petition the city to ban em from takin shortcuts through here. Maybe I could call that councilman, Cliff Barnes."

Mr. Smith stood up straight. "Uh-huh. You go right head, and see what happens."

"What you think will happen?"

"Abslutely nothin. When you call Barnes, he'll check his books to see how much money niggers out chere give to his last campaign. And that'll be the end a that."

"Nooo," said Barlowe. "We gotta hound em. We gotta bring pressure, like white folks do."

"Okay, Mr. Pressure. You go right head. Come back and lemme know how it went."

As usual, the talk turned to sports. There was a big boxing match coming up. They bet a six-pack on the fight. While they talked, a white man came strolling up the walk. Dressed in shorts, a T-shirt and flip-flops, he led an expensive-looking dog on a leash.

Barlowe and Mr. Smith stopped talking and gazed at the troubling sight. Lately there had been rumors, all kinds of wild rumors, about *them* coming through the neighborhood, snooping around for who knows what.

The white man stopped at the edge of Mr. Smith's yard. The dog sniffed a stocky shrub, squatted beside it, hunched its back and took a hefty dump. It sniffed its waste and scratched the ground, kicking up dirt and grass.

When the dog had finished, its master tugged the leash and moved on, walking slowly toward the two black men. Both owner and animal studied them warily. Likewise, Barlowe and Mr. Smith sized up the intruders, but with a different dread.

As the stranger drew nearer, Barlowe noticed his eyes were blue as water in a swimming pool. The man spoke, cautious, as he walked by.

"Hello."

Mr. Smith nodded, only slightly. Barlowe didn't nod at all. When the man was beyond earshot, Barlowe craned his neck and whipped around. "You see *that*?"

"Yeah. I saw it."

"He let that dog shit, *right* there in your yard."

"I know. The dirty bastard."

They watched as the white man disappeared around the corner.

For a long while, Barlowe and Mr. Smith stood there, drawing into themselves. Finally, Barlowe broke the silence.

"I think we better get ready, Mr. Smith."

"I know," the old man said. "*They* comin."

# PART II

# Chapter 6

Sean and Sandy Gilmore walked into a large office and sank before a mahogany desk so massive it made them feel small. Once seated, they leaned in close together and held hands, as if lending each other emotional support. They appeared anxious, like young newlyweds in for the first sex therapy session.

Actually, the issue was real estate.

Their agent, a wily veteran named Joe Folkes, leaned forward, slightly annoyed that they had shown up at his office unannounced.

"Well. What brings you two in today?"

Sean and Sandy exchanged furtive glances, to see who would be the first to speak.

"To tell you the truth," said Sandy, "we're a little frustrated."

"Oh?"

"Yes. We've spent forever house-hunting in-town, and so far, well, nothing."

"Actually, it's been only two months," said Joe.

"Whatever. When we started, you assured us we'd at least be able to find a fixer-upper, or even a two-bedroom bungalow. We've scoured Buckhead, Virginia-Highland and Morningside. It's crazy what they're asking for these places."

Joe smiled, confident the Gilmores' frustrations were no reflection on *him*. Joe was considered one of the best, an ace in the urban market, and from the looks of him there appeared to be some truth to that. He was partial to fancy gabardine suits and two-toned starched shirts—the kind favored by the high-end lawyers who bill you by the hour for every fraction of a minute's conversation.

This day, Joe also wore an American flag tie, with the stars and stripes merging majestically at the knot.

"We've invested a lot of time." Sean felt the need to pitch in now. "We're wondering if maybe we should give this up."

"Give up?" Joe winced. He had no intention of letting loan-approved clients slip away. He stood and paced the floor.

Tall and trim for a man of fifty-six, Joe had a salon-tanned, angular face and a high forehead that sloped into a crossover comb. He sprayed and teased his precious hair, so that it appeared to stand on its own. The hair looked magical. It meant a lot to Joe.

Joe liked to boast that he was successful because he understood human nature. He had an instinctive feel for home buyers, especially the sophisticated ones. The sophisticates were an easy sell. They understood housing trends and market forces. They were aggressive, too.

So when Sean and Sandy showed up, complaining about in-town housing costs, Joe made his patented Plan B pitch. The commissions were smaller, but what the hell?

"Why not go black?"

Sean's jaw dropped. "What?"

Joe casually filed his nails from behind the gleaming desk. "There are lots of solid houses in neighborhoods that are ready to flip. And you can get em for the cost of a ham sandwich."

In the silence that followed, you could hear a mouse pissing on cotton.

The Gilmores felt firmly grounded in their social stands, mind you. They were Philadelphia transplants, and lifelong Democrats. But as for Joe's proposition, naturally there were practical considerations to weigh.

After a long pause, Sean finally mustered the nerve to think out loud. "What about, you know, values?"

Joe dabbed his do. "Mr. Gilmore. *We* drive values. *You* know that." Rearing back in his high-backed swivel chair, he beamed brightly and tugged at his tie. "Is this a great country, or what!?"

He pulled out a Cuban cigar and examined it, front to back, to give them time to get the point.

Instead, Sandy's spirit stiffened, and Joe picked up the vibe. He put away the cigar, wondering if he'd somehow misread these folks. He hoped to God they weren't bleeding hearts. Normally, he could spot the bleeding hearts right away. They usually pranced into his office, walking all feather-footed in their Birkenstocks and tie-dyed shirts. They came with their snooty airs and liberal ideas about saving the world.

They were different. Or at least they *thought* they were. Joe knew how to handle them.

Now he leaned forward and pasted on a sober look. "Listen, I don't want you to think I'm pressuring you. I understand if you tell me this is not the way for you to go. Really, not everybody has the stomach for, you know, mixing . . ."

"Yes," said Sean. "We were more interested in—"

Before he could finish, his wife cut him off. She was not about to let some citified hayseed imply she shared his backward views.

"Mr. Folkes, we would *very* much like to see the neighborhoods you're recommending. We have no problem with that; none at all."

Joe moved quickly, before Sean could object. He slammed a palm down on the desk.

"Good! Good! I'll take you to an area that's just starting to show some signs of coming to life." He winked. "The prices are still real low, but I'm telling you, it's about to explode. It's got awesome potential, and marvelous skyline views . . ."

Less than four miles away, Barlowe came home from work and lurched to the curb. A tire sank into a huge, crater-sized pothole that rocked the car. He got out and checked for punctures. In the past few years, he'd lost two decent tires to potholes. It led him to join a feeble community push to force the city to patch the neighborhood's ragged streets. During election time, promises flowed like confetti from City Hall, but nobody ever came afterward to make repairs. So drivers around there learned to zigzag and swerve, like police trainees on an obstacle course. They dodged potholes and waited for change that they doubted would ever come.

Barlowe had checked the tires and started toward the walkway, when a faint screeching noise sounded from a distance up the street. Everybody in the neighborhood knew that sound. It was the squeaky wheel on Ricky Brown's Winn-Dixie grocery cart. Coming from the end of Randolph near Irwin Street, Ricky walked casually in the middle of the road, with that squeaky wheel vibrating in a spastic fit.

Ricky wore dingy tennis shoes, Air Jordans, with no laces. As he walked, the long tongues of the sneakers flopped from side to side, like the distended tongues of thirsty dogs.

*Flop, flop, flop, flop.*

Barlowe wasn't exactly sure where Ricky lived. He often saw him pushing the cart through the streets, collecting bottles, cans and anything else that helped him scrape up enough money to buy a sandwich and a pint.

Like Viola and The Hawk, Ricky was a drunk, but he didn't rate high enough to drink with them. At some point in their cloudy pasts Viola and The Hawk had been respectable citizens, with driver's licenses and jobs that carried insurance benefits. But Ricky had never held a go-to-work-every-day job, so he was deemed a lower class of drunk.

Ricky parallel parked his cart like an automobile and sidled up to Barlowe. Call it insight or just plain intuition, but something told Ricky there was money in that man's wallet, and maybe even some cash for *him*.

"S'cuse me!" He spoke loud, like he was yelling at somebody up the street. "I rake your yard for few dollas!"

"Naw," said Barlowe. "I'm gonna do it myself."

"I do a good job! You'll love my wurk!"

When Ricky spoke, two rusty teeth peeked out from between ashy lips. Barlowe studied him closely and reconsidered.

Ricky wore dirty blue jeans, a grease-stained shirt (with an ink pen hung proudly in the breast pocket) and a thin, oversized nylon jacket. A black-and-white do-rag covered his shaggy head. The do-rag was ringed by an elastic band, with words printed in italics: *Jesus Saves.*

He also sported mod sunshades, one of the many gems he'd come across rifling through garbage cans.

Ricky and Barlowe were about the same age, but Ricky appeared a full ten years older. His face, a medium brown, was sallow, with pock-marked skin. Patches of coarse hair were scattered across his mug like sagebrush blown over a dusty plain. He looked like he'd been shoved through a meat grinder, twice, and left for dead.

Barlowe finished the sly inspection and thought to himself: *There's a thin line between me and him.*

He steered Ricky up the walk. "Now, Ricky. If I let you do the work, how much you gonna charge me?"

Ricky peered toward the sky, as if consulting some heavenly pricing chart. Then he glanced down at Barlowe's work shoes. The shoes looked pretty sporty; had a nice shine, too.

"Gimme thurty-five!"

He glanced at Barlowe over the top of his sunshades and quickly looked away.

"Ricky. I know you can do better."

"I do a good job!" He smiled, flashing his dirty teeth.

"Yeah," said Barlowe. "I got somethin that might help us out. Wait right here."

He hurried around to the back of the house and returned carrying a leaf blower and a red gas can. He handed them to Ricky.

"You can use this blower on the light stuff in front. You won't have to do much rakin at all . . . *Now* how much you gonna charge?"

Ricky concentrated hard, making mental computations for a price adjustment—allowing for use of the man's leaf blower, of course.

"How bout les do thurty!"

"Ricky. Is *my* blower."

"I'ma do a good job! You gon love my wurk!"

Barlowe weighed the counteroffer. For him, such negotiations amounted to a kind of charitable game. The goal was to donate and inspire, without giving handouts. The intent was to be tough but fair, to avoid being taken advantage of and, at the same time, taking care not to wound the recipient's pride.

The recipient—in this case, Ricky Brown—had his own simple goal: to maximize profit. That required a certain rough-hewn shrewdness, the ability to spot the angle on a negotiating edge. Ricky was very experienced at this, ever watchful for signs of fear, a bleeding heart or, best of all, profound guilt. On a good day, any one of those factors could bring a full ten dollars more than the asking price.

But Ricky could see right off that Barlowe had been a few times around the block. This dude was not one to be intimidated or fooled.

"Tell you what, Ricky. Les do twenny and call it a day."

"Okay, twenny! I'ma do a good job! You gon love my wurk!"

Ricky unscrewed the leaf blower cap, then opened the gas can lid and looked at Barlowe with surprise.

"Ain't no gas in dese! You need gas!"

"I know. I'll go get some."

"Thas all right! I git it! I git it! Gimme fi dollas and I run up the street and git it right quick!"

Barlowe paused. He thought that *he* should go, but he was tired. He had run four big jobs at the print shop that day. Looking at the front door to the house, he pondered: There was a six-pack in the fridge. He could almost hear it calling. And there was a claw-foot tub waiting, too, with outstretched arms.

He reached in his wallet, pulled out a five-spot and reluctantly handed it over.

Ricky grabbed the money and glanced above the top of his sunshades. "I be right back!" He tossed the gas can onto the trash heap in his cart. "I'ma run up the station and fill this up!"

"Ricky. Is easier if you leave the cart . . . I'll guard it. I promise."

Ricky hesitated. "Oh! Yeah! I leave it here! I leave it here!"

He pushed the cart into the bushes, then walked to the middle of the yard and studied the shrubs, making sure it was out of sight. He didn't want to risk losing all his fine trash collections to competitors or thieves.

Once he felt assured of the safety of his garbage loot, he scooted off with the crisp five-dollar bill clutched in his fist.

He rushed up the street, the tongues of his sneakers flopping from side to side.

Later, Barlowe stood in the living room, peeping through the open blinds. He caught sight of pretty Lucretia Wiggins. She had left the Auburn Avenue Mini-Mart, and now switched up the sidewalk, toward her mama's house. He studied her backside as she went indoors.

Tyrone came into the living room and saw his uncle staring outside. "What you lookin fo?"

"Ricky Brown." Barlowe quickly shut the blinds. "He was sposed to clean up the yard."

"You paid im first?"

"Gave him five dollars to get gas for the blower."

Tyrone rolled his eyes. "Damn, man; why you do dat? Why you pay that nigger fore he did the job?"

Barlowe kept quiet, thinking.

"You won't see him no mo til he spend it up. Then he gonna come back wit a long story . . . You watch."

Tyrone set down two packages on the kitchen table. Barlowe peeked at the goodies. One bag contained a bottle of expensive cognac. The other held a box of Kentucky Fried Chicken.

"What you got goin here?"

"Gonna git wit this gal I know," said Tyrone. "We goin to Piedmont Park for a li'l bullshit picnic. Then is off to her place to knock some boots."

When the horn sounded, Tyrone rushed outside, taking giant strides like a person scaling a stairway, two steps at once. Barlowe closed the blinds and sat down in the living room. That night, when he went to bed, a familiar jolt of loneliness shot through his bones. He hadn't been on a date in a while. He wondered if maybe he should start going out on the town, putting himself in places where he might meet some women.

He considered phoning Diane, a redhead he'd met a while back. Diane would come over in a heartbeat, if it wasn't her night for choir rehearsal.

But Diane was too tame. Barlowe craved someone edgy, wild—like Nell.

The image of Lucretia Wiggins returned to him. He fluffed the pillows, stretched out on his back and closed his eyes. He softly touched himself. He touched himself like he would want to be caressed if Lucretia or Nell was lying beside him now.

In time, he drifted off to sleep. He was roused later by a noise outside. It sounded a bit like rustling brush. When it sounded again, he lifted his head, straining to hear. He rested his head back on the pillow. His eyelids felt heavy. He needed sleep. He had a busy printing schedule the next day.

He finally drifted off to the sounds of the night: the sound of an old hoot owl's mating call; the sound of a freight train rumbling by; the sound of floppy tennis shoes, and a squeaky grocery cart being pushed, fast, down Randolph Street.

# Chapter 7

Sean and Sandy Gilmore met at Joe Folkes's Midtown real estate office on a Saturday morning. They got in his Cadillac and cruised to the Old Fourth Ward. The first house Joe pointed out was a recent sale.

"One of *our* clients. Happy as can be. No children; no worries about crappy schools." He looked at Sean. "You don't have children, do you?"

"No. No children," said Sandy, speaking from the backseat. (She had told Sean before they left home, she didn't want to sit near that man.)

The house was impressive, a freshly painted, two-story, columned Victorian. Huge bay windows and a wraparound porch. Two flags hung out front. One, a large American flag, somehow struck Joe Folkes as out of place. Hanging from another column, the smaller flag was fluorescent orange, red, yellow, blue and purple. Over the next half-hour, they ran across two other houses decorated with multicolored Gay Pride flags.

"A good sign," observed Joe. "I hear there were two more recent sales around here."

He drove on, reciting the history of the Old Fourth Ward, emphasizing its ties to Martin Luther King. After a quick strategic pass by The King Center, they swung around to a vacant house on Randolph

Street. Joe drove slowly, making sure the Gilmores got a good look at the Atlanta skyline peeking just above the treetops from where they were. When they pulled in front of the house, Sandy's eyes brightened. It was similar to the one they'd just seen. The yard was unkempt, and the roof clearly needed repairs, but overall, the structure appeared sound.

Joe smiled and toyed with his suit lapel. "A good paint job and some cosmetic work, and she'll be good as new."

Sandy noted the nice, long porch facing downtown, providing a fantastic frontal skyline view.

"This one's a gem," said Joe. He leaned over, whispering as though sharing a secret. "And the owner is very motivated, actually *pressed*, to sell."

Sandy wasn't sure why, but a wave of guilt passed over her.

They got out of the car and scanned the block, as a stray dog crept past along the walk. Across the street, several men sat out next to the Auburn Avenue Mini-Mart. Off in the distance, Ricky Brown pushed his cart up the block.

"How safe is the area?" asked Sean.

Joe beamed. "Safer than a fat bank on payday." He ushered them a few steps along the walk, to the point where Randolph Street intersected with Auburn Avenue. He pointed down Auburn.

"There's a police precinct less than five blocks away, and the area is crawling with federal park rangers. They protect The King Center and live right here in the neighborhood.

"Now." He dabbed at his do. "Let's take a look at this gorgeous house."

At the moment, Barlowe was lounging out back, on the screened-in portion of the porch. He had gone to the mailbox earlier and gotten his mail. As usual there were piles and piles of paper from advertisers vying for his attention. One brochure featured the smiling face of some clown running for a city council seat. Then there was a letter addressed personally to Barlowe, from the president of Chase Manhattan Bank.

Did Barlowe know, the Chase president asked, that he had been approved for a new credit line? Fixed introductory APR, for up to 15 months!

There was harassment from others, too: Home Depot, Sears, a lighting store; a whole useless, overwhelming pile of paper.

But that wasn't the thing that bothered him most. The thing that bothered him most was the time devoted daily to ripping up every piece of junk mail sent his way; it was just one of the many time-consuming rituals that wear on the soul.

But he did it, dutifully. He tore up paper ads, one by one, making sure to rip his name and address apart lest somebody sift through the garbage and use his information to buy a computer, furnish a house or go on the vacation Barlowe had always wanted to take.

When he was done shredding, he drank a beer. He had begun dozing off, when three white people appeared around the side of the vacant house next door. At first he thought he might be dreaming. Then he heard the tall, funny-looking man talking loud, pointing this way and that, as though conducting a tour.

*Whities!* Barlowe ducked indoors and out of sight. He went to the kitchen window and peeked through the blinds. *Whities! Right next door!*

The seventy-year-old house next door was owned by an old woman named Hattie Phillips. It was a solid, spacious place, a once-fine Victorian that had fallen into disrepair. When the bills and burdens of living there became too much, Hattie Phillips went to live with her daughter and put the house up for rent. Lacking funds to renovate, she rented it to tenants as it was: with a few doors hanging loosely on squeaky hinges, and a leaky roof that required a rain bucket on the kitchen floor. The maintenance problems kept rents low and limited Hattie's tenants to people like Vincent and Irene Benton—the last family to lease before it would be placed on sale.

Unlike some of the more rowdy clans that had lived there, the Bentons were pleasant, hard-striving folks who always seemed one day late in life and two months behind on rent. Irene, a mousy woman, worked as a cook at Deacon Burton's soul food spot. Vincent, who was muscular and quiet, worked as a laborer. The family enjoyed brief periods of near-stability whenever Vincent got steady work.

Barlowe sometimes saw Vincent leave home early mornings, dressed in heavy industrial boots and camouflage fatigues. He wore a red bandanna tied around his head, which bobbed as he trudged with his lunch pail toward the bus stop on Irwin Street.

The Bentons were peaceful people, except in those anxious periods when Vincent was unemployed. Then things got stormy. Irene would get so uptight that she could be set off by most anything—a stray ball landing against the flimsy front screen door, or a broken window they couldn't afford to replace.

She'd explode, attacking their three children. "Git in this house fore I kill you, boy! I tole you to be careful with that stupid ball!"

The children would disappear inside, amid Irene's profane bursts. The commotion would die down until Vincent came home. Then a second wave of attacks would follow, more fierce and sustained than the first.

Barlowe could tell whenever Vincent was out of work. That's when the children came knocking at the door. "My mama said can we borrow some bread and milk till nex week?" Too young and naive to feel ashamed, they begged casually, as though asking for the time of day.

To offset the parents' humiliation, Barlowe sometimes knocked on the Bentons' door to borrow eggs or butter he didn't need. Irene showed her appreciation by playing along.

One winter evening, Vincent himself showed up at Barlowe's door, wearing a dingy T-shirt and that red bandanna.

"The lectricity been cut," he said, plainly. His eyes dropped to the ground as he struggled to hold up under Barlowe's gaze. "I went downtown to pay the bill, but the lady tole me I had to ketch up the udder months, too. My money was a li'l short, so they cut off the power till I git the rest."

It was dark outside. The winter moon, full and bright, looked like a great big lantern in the sky. Standing in the doorway, Barlowe felt a chilly breeze whip across his face. He glanced at the side window to the Bentons' house and thought he saw the glimmer of a candle. He imagined Irene and the children huddled in a single room around that single candle, trying to keep warm until the weather broke.

He looked at Vincent and thought to himself: *There's a thin line between me and him.*

"What you need me to do?"

For weeks, an orange industrial extension cord ran from one house to the other. Barlowe provided electricity to the Bentons until well after Vincent got another check.

The Bentons lasted a full three months after that. Barlowe came home from work one day and found their furniture and other belongings tossed along the curb. The family was nowhere in sight. Two street urchins had come upon the crumpled heap and begun patiently sorting the secrets of the Bentons' lives. The men worked in silence, stopping now and then to appraise a clock or try on a sweater. Sifting through the possessions, they looked like eager scavengers feasting on fallen prey.

And so it went with the house next door. People came and people went. Tenants hung on as long as they could before a frustrated Hattie Phillips was forced to drive them off.

The Bentons were gone. Now there were white people walking around outside the house, peering into windows like nosy ghosts. They headed back to the front, where the tall man used a key to open the door.

Barlowe studied the strangers as they went inside. "Huummmph!" He couldn't count the number of times he'd walked through *their* neighborhoods and had cops roll up on him. "Huummmph!"

He went to the phone and picked up the receiver, then put it down. He picked it up again and put it down once more. It occurred to him that he had never called the police before. Police had always been called on *him*. It felt weird even thinking about it the other way around.

He picked up the receiver a third time and dialed. A woman's voice came across the line.

"Yes, 911 emergency."

Barlowe said nothing.

"Hello, 911."

"Is this the po-lice?"

"Yes. Do you have an emergency to report?"

"Yeah."

"Sir, speak quickly if this is an emergency."

"There some spicious lookin people walkin round the house next door."

"What are they doing, sir?"

"Look like they scopin the doors and windows to see if is locked."

"What?"

"You need to send somebody, fast."

"What's that address, sir?"

"What?"

"The address."

"Mine or the one next door?"

"The house next door. I need the address?"

"I don't know that address."

"Okay, sir, what's your address?"

Barlowe hesitated. *She askin too many fuggin questions.*

"Sir, I need you to speak quickly."

"I'm at 1024 Randolph Street."

"We'll send someone over right away."

Barlowe hung up. He went back to the porch and peeked around the corner. He spotted The Hawk trudging through the pathway. Viola staggered two steps behind, carrying a brown paper bag, which she cradled like a newborn child. The two drunks disappeared around the corner.

Minutes later, the white people came outdoors and went around back again. Barlowe withdrew, making sure to keep out of sight. He checked his watch. Ten minutes passed, and still no cops.

*Damn!*

Meanwhile, Joe Folkes pressed on, pointing out features of the house and yard. The Gilmores listened intently, nodding in unison.

Barlowe peered out the window again. It appeared the white people were preparing to leave. They stood chatting at the corner of the house, partially hidden by the big oak tree.

Barlowe rushed to the front window and peeked outside. Still no sign of cops. He returned to the rear window and peered some more, then rushed back to the living room again. He paced back and forth, antsy, trying to decide what to do.

He concentrated, hard. For the first time in his life he actually *wanted* the police to show up somewhere. He went back and dialed again.

"Yes, 911."

"I called about burglars damn-near a half-hour ago."

"Yes, sir. Are you at 1024 Randolph?"

"Thas right. You already *got* that information." His voice was tight, hostile.

"Well, sir—"

"Y'all gonna mess around and let them fuggin people get away!"

"Sir. Sir."

"Y'all ain't—"

"Please, don't cuss at me, sir. We've already sent a car."

"Where they at, then?! Where they at?!" He was shouting now.

"Sir, they should be there any minute."

Barlowe slammed down the phone and growled. "Caesar!"

Outside, the white people strolled casually toward Joe Folkes's car. Finally, a police cruiser pulled in front of the house. Barlowe peeked from behind the living room blinds as two officers approached the trio. The officers tipped their hats.

"We got a call about prowlers."

Joe Folkes stepped forward, smiling. "Prowlers? I'm a Realtor. These are my clients, and I'm showing this house."

He wore a natty double-breasted suit, a silk-wool blend, Hugo Boss. As usual, his hair was meticulously teased.

One cop smiled, apologetic, and glanced at his partner. "Sorry . . ." He tipped his hat again. "Have a good day."

Barlowe watched the policemen leave. Likewise, the Gilmores climbed in Joe Folkes's shiny Cadillac and disappeared.

When the cars glided out of sight, Barlowe left the window. He flopped down hard onto the couch and sat staring emptily into space.

"Caesar!"

He picked up a glass from the coffee table and shattered it against a wall.

On the drive back to his office, Joe Folkes stopped at a light and turned to Sean, who was seated beside him. "Isn't it a dandy?"

"Yeah, nice." Sean was surprised at how much he liked the house. "And it has more space than the place we're in."

Oddly, he thought of Sandy's father; the old man would have conniptions if he were here.

Sandy was lost in her own thoughts, about landscape ideas and furniture placement. Her enmity toward Joe had receded some. *Maybe he's not so bad after all.*

Joe sensed he had the Gilmores hooked. He had them wriggling like striped bass on a bamboo rod. Now it was time to reel them in.

"It will officially go on the market in another week or so. *We're* listing it so you've got a chance to beat the rush . . . Better get it now, though. This baby won't last long."

He didn't really have to work the sale. Sandy had already made up her mind. Without saying it in front of Joe, she knew they wanted that house. The spacious rooms and the skyline view were clearly major plusses. But just as impressive was the strong sense of community there.

*Imagine. Someone actually cared enough to call the cops.*

That settled it for her. Sean and Sandy were moving to the Old Fourth Ward.

# Chapter 8

Barlowe stepped through the double doors of the Auburn Avenue Research Library and dumped an armload of books into the front seat of his car. He rushed around to the driver's side, feeling giddy as a child with a new batch of toys. It was Friday evening, and he had his weekend all laid out. He would spend much of it on the back porch, soaking up those books. He had gone to the library to find a book that explained the workings of mortgages and loans. Then he'd drifted to the history section.

From there it was on to the travel books. He liked to look at pictures of faraway places and read about the backgrounds and cultures of different people. He planned to go to some of those places one day. He intended to see for himself how other people got along.

Some folks traveled to faraway places on their own, but Barlowe hadn't seen a way to do that yet. When was there ever time and money to venture out *there*, to journey to exotic places just for fun?

When he was younger he had tried to figure out a way to see the world for free. Three of his brothers joined the army and navy and were shipped to Germany, Korea, places like that. But he hadn't wanted to travel that way—serving Caesar's causes for reasons he could never trust.

He almost joined the merchant marine once. He'd thought that he might join the merchant marine and travel the world while getting paid to do decent work. Then life got in the way: His mama got sick; a girl named Joan said she missed her period (it turned out to be a false alarm); one thing or another kept him pinned down and stuck at home.

Moving to Atlanta had been a major deal, though not nearly enough to satisfy. So he went and got a library card and started reading about the rest of the world, which sometimes seemed about as out of reach as a pearl buried on the ocean floor.

Now he had a routine down. On most Friday evenings after work he'd buy his lottery tickets, pick up a six-pack and head to the Auburn Avenue Research Library downtown. He went there so much now the librarians knew him by name. They'd see him come in, shambling slow and tired in his ink-stained khakis. They'd watch him browse the shelves, sometimes for hours.

When he first began going there, one librarian, a high-yellow, cheeky girl named Rachel Worthman, studied him closer than anyone else. She wondered if he was actually reading books or merely gazing at pictures on the pages.

When she could no longer stand the suspense, Rachel tested Barlowe one day. He had come to the front desk with an armload of books that he planned to skim that week. She scanned the books and lobbed a question, framed as an offhand compliment.

"My. With all these travel books you're reading, I'll bet you know all the continents now."

"I guess I do," he said, matter-of-factly. He rattled them off, one by one, in alphabetical order.

In other brief exchanges, Rachel Worthman discovered he knew a little bit about many things. He could tell you the seasonal rituals of Africa's Dahomey people, and he knew the main industries in Nigeria and Brazil. He had memorized other trivia, such as the average annual rainfall in Zurich, Milan and Johannesburg.

Rachel was taken by Barlowe's raw intelligence. She also thought he was kind of cute with his thick, untamed hair and pearly whites. With no ring on his finger, she wondered if he might not be spoken for.

Now she looked forward to seeing him come through those tall, ornate doors on Friday evenings. She began wearing her special sweater on Fridays, just for him. It was a pink sweater, made of angora wool, the one her mother gave her for Christmas.

Rachel wasn't sure if Barlowe had noticed her in a certain way. She straightened her sweater and flashed an inviting smile whenever he approached the desk. Lately, she had started trailing him into the aisles sometimes, to ask if he needed help finding anything. He would politely say, "No, thank you," then move on to another row.

This day, though, Rachel had hung shyly behind the desk, careful not to scare him off. Barlowe browsed the shelves for a full hour, until he found the mortgage guide and other books he was looking for. In the travel section he had searched for a book that told the story of the Gullah people. He had met a wild Geechie girl somewhere once; she was black as coal, and so pretty the sight of her made his armpits moist. She told him her people descended from slaves who had escaped to the islands off the South Carolina coast. She said the Gullah people held an annual festival, in a place called Beaufort.

Barlowe promised himself that one of these years, when his money was right, he would go to the Gullah festival, and maybe even look up that fine Geechie gal.

As usual, he took the books up front and plopped them down on the desk. Rachel Worthman smiled and poked out her chest, which was quite qualified to be poked out that way.

"Find everything you were looking for?"

"Yeah. I did all right today."

He leaned over to slide a book beneath the scanner. He felt Rachel's eyes bearing down and could hear her breathing hard, like she had a mild case of emphysema.

Rachel glanced at one of the titles: *Bo Rabbit Smart for True: Folktales from the Gullah*. Then she held up the book below it: *The Legacy of Ibo Landing: Gullah Roots of African American Culture*.

She smiled. "Oh. The Gullah people. They have a festival every year."

"Yeah. I heard about that."

"I'll bet it's nice."

She fixed on his face with a hopeful look and cocked her head slightly to her good side. In her own homely way she tried to look delicious. It didn't wear right on her.

Barlowe dropped his eyes, first to the full breasts poking against the angora wool. Oddly, he thought of Tyrone. No doubt, Tyrone would declare that Rachel Worthman had promise. She had strong headlights. Tyrone insisted strong headlights were always a good place to start in a relationship.

Barlowe's gaze shifted from Rachel's headlights to her eyes. That was when he realized there could be no future there. The eyes were dull, lifeless. They suggested she might be one of the sheep, one of those drab and dreary people who play life by the numbers. That seemed mildly confusing, considering she was a librarian, with access to all those books.

And another thing: The eyes were awfully tame; tame as a cat curled up on a fluffy couch. He studied Rachel closely while she assisted a patron across the desk. As she turned to a computer, he noted again the languid movements and depthless gaze.

He thought: *She'd require brown liquor to loosen up.*

It would be just his luck that Rachel didn't drink. And even if she did indulge, it might be tough getting to sleep after a good romp with her. Barlowe imagined himself lying in the dark, waiting for sunrise while Rachel snored. He was sure she snored.

So what did he want, then? If not a decent house girl, a librarian like Rachel, what did he want?

In the daytime, he swore he wanted substance, a woman who thought serious thoughts and followed current events. At night, it was different: He craved debauchery, full-tilt; someone wild—like Nell.

He recalled how Nell used to lose herself in lovemaking. Sometimes she'd lose herself so completely that she'd wrench free of his clutches and bolt from bed to catch her breath. She'd flop against a wall, furiously fanning her face with her hand, whispering, imploring herself to settle down.

Sometimes she would . . . Now Barlowe stopped himself. He didn't want to think about Nell.

In the neighborhood, he'd found himself paying more attention lately to Lucretia Wiggins. Some days he stood in the front window and watched her switch up and down the walk. He liked the way she strutted—sassy and light, like she was gliding barefoot. Without having to be told, he knew what she was like. More and more, the idea of her excited him.

It was settled, then, in the library that day. Barlowe would leave Rachel Worthman to tend to her books and seek his pleasures in other places. He said, "Thank you," to Rachel and turned and walked out the door.

Heading to the car it occurred to him that he should maybe find another library branch. He drove away, glancing every now and then at his new stack of books, especially the ones about the Gullah people.

Who knew? Maybe he would go to Beaufort one day and find that big-leg Geechie gal.

Barlowe reached home and came across a sight that brought a triumphant smile to his face. Ricky Brown stood in the front yard, raking leaves. More than three weeks had passed since Ricky disappeared. Now he'd returned, and even brought back the red gas can he took away.

When Barlowe approached, Ricky spoke fast, like he'd memorized the words. "I came to do what I promised long time ago!"

"I been waitin on you," said Barlowe. "One more week and I was gonna come lookin. That wouldna been a pretty sight."

Ricky raked faster. "I woulda been back fore now but I got hung up on some thangs. Don't worry. You ain't gotta pay me nothin. I'ma do it anyway. I always do what I say. So I'ma do it, whedder you pay me or not."

He glanced over his sunshades.

"All right, then, Ricky. All right, do what you promised." Barlowe headed to the curb to check for mail.

If he had paid closer attention to Ricky's mouth, he might have guessed the reason for the sudden reappearance. There was a front tooth missing, separated from its owner just the day before. Ricky had collected some aluminum and glass from the streets and pushed his grocery cart to the satellite recycling station on John Wesley Dobbs Avenue. He and his friends went there at noon each day and waited for a white man in a pickup truck, who paid for the scraps and cans they gathered.

Ricky was waiting in line to be paid, when a hand—strong, forceful—grabbed him from behind. The hand squeezed his shoulder blade so hard he collapsed to the ground.

"Oooowwww!!!"

He looked up and caught a fist, flush in the mouth. *Whack!*

It was Tyrone. He had been walking up the street and spotted Ricky.

"Nigger, ain't you got some work to do?"

"Who, me?"

"You was sposed to rake my yard!" *Whack!* Tyrone pummeled him. Ricky's buddies drew back, repulsed by the violence.

When the dusting was done, Ricky leaned over and coughed up blood. "I'ma do it! I'ma do it!"

Tyrone smacked him. *Whack!* "I *know* you are! And you gonna do it soon!"

Ricky spit more blood and examined a loose tooth, half-wondering if he could push it back into his bleeding gums.

The next day, Ricky, his lip still slightly swollen, hurried to Randolph Street and rang the bell. Tyrone escorted him around back and handed him a rake and garbage bags. "Now do what you promised. You sposed to live up to your obligations, nigger."

Ricky was anxious to finish the job, mainly because Tyrone threatened to deliver a "fresh ass-whuppin" each week it went undone.

All that drama was lost on Barlowe now as he emptied the mailbox and strolled back toward the house. He stopped and watched briefly while Ricky gathered leaves and stuffed them in the bloated bags. Ricky worked hard, like he didn't mind doing the chore at all.

Heading into the house, Barlowe felt a surge of pride. That's what he liked about living in the Old Fourth Ward. He had given a man a chance to make an honest dollar, and after all that time the man had been moved to come back and prove himself.

# Chapter 9

The closing on the house at 1022 Randolph Street took place on neutral ground. It was held in the conference room of a real estate lawyer's office, down on Peachtree Street. The attorney, a short, jowly man in a dull gray suit, was there with his secretary, who was already glancing impatiently at her watch.

Flanked by her selling agent, Hattie Phillips showed up at the closing dressed in her Sunday best—white gloves, a shiny blue dress and matching heels, with little fake diamonds sprinkled at the toe. Her head was crowned with a bold, bright blue hat, feathered and furred all around.

The Gilmores were much more casually dressed, in blue jeans and sneakers. They looked like they'd run out to pick up bread from the grocery store.

Joe Folkes, his usual dapper self, sat with his long legs crossed and monogrammed pen ready.

The parties took seats on opposite sides of the table and tried not to look adversarial. They all smiled politely, nodded and, as much as possible, avoided eye contact. The attorney handed the parties a thick packet of closing documents and launched the process in earnest with formal introductions around the table. Amid the introductions, Hattie Phillips turned to acknowledge Sandy Gilmore, eye-to-eye, which was only fitting with so much money changing hands.

Sandy blinked hard when their eyes met. A flash, a memory forced her to look away. The old black woman before her bore an eerie likeness to the longtime family maid, Ethel Fields. Ethel was the only true superwoman Sandy had ever known. Ethel had been there proudly looking on when Sandy took her first baby steps. Ethel taught her to ride a two-wheel bike and pulled her first shaky tooth. She rocked her to sleep on countless nights when Sandy's parents were out socializing.

It seemed Ethel had always been there. And while she nurse-maided Sandy and her older brother, Jared, she somehow managed to raise her own five children, and later, took in a stranded grandchild or two.

Sandy had always wondered what became of Ethel. She was haunted by her likeness everywhere. In college she saw Ethel in the faces of the old black women who cleaned the toilets in her dorm; she saw Ethel in the sassy school cafeteria cooks who stood in the serving lines in crisp white uniforms and black hairnets. She saw sleepy-eyed likenesses of Ethel on early mornings, peering from bus stop shelters in the drizzling rain, waiting to be whisked to crosstown jobs.

Now Sandy saw her sitting across the table in white gloves, preparing to sign over the only house she'd ever owned.

A flood of memories gushed through Sandy's head:

*Returning home with her mother from a shopping spree . . .*

Sandy figured Ethel must have been close to fifty, though she looked much younger. Ethel was an attractive woman, especially when she wore her hair pulled back tight against her face. She had skin the color of chestnut, and dark, alert eyes, set above full lips that required no coloring at all.

*A can of furniture spray, a woman's shoe and a crumpled dust cloth, strewn curiously across the living room floor . . .*

The resemblance to Hattie Phillips was so strong Sandy could hardly concentrate when the attorney referenced the closing documents for their review. "I'm going to ask each of you to take a minute to read over the contents on page eight. As you can see . . ."

*Ethel had been there when they left home. Now she was nowhere to be found . . .*

The words on the pages of the legal document in front of Sandy faded into one big blur.

"As you'll notice," the lawyer was saying, "the property's boundaries are specified on page seventeen. According to the original deed, the property . . ."

Sean nudged Sandy to see if she understood the point about the property boundaries. She ignored him. She couldn't focus.

*"Mom, where's Ethel?"*

*Her mother's response was one of practiced calm. With pursed lips, she steeled herself as she had often done through the years when confronted with damning evidence of her husband's sloppy indiscretions.*

*A week later, Ethel was quietly let go, dismissed. Just like that, she disappeared . . .*

The lawyer droned on, but Sandy didn't hear. She was upset now, all over again. She pushed her chair back from the conference room table and stood up straight.

"I . . ."

The lawyer stopped in midsentence. All eyes shifted to her.

"I . . ." Blood drained from her face. "I'm not sure I can go through with this."

Suddenly, and without explanation, she stormed outside. Sean followed, trailed by a puzzled Joe Folkes. The others looked on in surprise. Moments later, Joe returned, sheepish and pale. He smiled nervously and tugged at his tie.

"I'm really sorry. My client is not feeling well. She needs a minute to collect herself."

Hattie grunted. "Hunh."

"I wonder," Joe said, "if we could take a brief unscheduled break."

Hattie grunted again, took off her gloves and plopped them on the table. She clutched her shiny pocketbook close to her chest and cut an eye at her agent. The agent, a young black man in bifocals, whispered something and patted her reassuringly on the wrist.

Outside, Sean tried to comfort his wife; he trusted he'd learn the reasons behind her outburst later. "You all right?"

"I'm fine. I need a drink of water, that's all."

Joe Folkes, nearly sick with the thought of losing his commission, came back and tried to rally his clients. He whispered low, like he was scared the people inside the building could hear through walls.

"You can't pass this up! Trust me! It's a *steal*!"

Sandy whipped around and hissed, "Please! If you don't mind, I'd appreciate it if you didn't use that word!"

She bolted to a restaurant next to the lawyer's office. She went in the ladies' room and vomited. Moments later, she returned to the front parking lot and fell into Sean's embrace.

Ethel came back to her once more:

*"Mother, why?!"*

*"Shhhhhh! Sandy, you know your father's heart is not that strong. He doesn't need anything to upset him now."*

Yes, her father. Sandy recalled her father's dismissive response, the brash cluck of the tongue, when Sean first told him where they'd decided to move. "Well," her father had said, gently shaking cubes in a glass of sherry, "you can kiss that investment good-bye."

Sean held his ground. "Well, Mr. Peterson, this is not just about the money. It's something Sandy and I feel we need to try . . ."

Her father folded his fat arms and assumed his usual smug expression. "And just *what* is it you intend to try?"

Sean fumbled around for the right comeback. Finally, he said: "Hell, nobody even *tries* anymore!"

Sandy had been so proud of her husband in that moment. It was the first time he'd actually stood up to her father. So many times, her father had tried to make Sean feel like less than a man for failing to insulate her from the harshness of the world. This time, Sean stood up to him. She was pleasantly surprised by that.

At the closing, a half-hour passed before Sandy could bring herself to return to the conference room table. During that time, Sean reminded her of their mission, which *she* had defined: a commitment to building bridges. He also reminded her, twice, of what Joe Folkes had said about the black woman selling the place. "Remember? He said she badly needed money."

That said, Sandy took a deep breath and went indoors. She sat down slowly and scanned the room, searching the bewildered faces until she met Hattie Phillips's stinging gaze.

"I'm very sorry. I was feeling nauseous. I needed some fresh air."

When the documents had been reviewed, Sandy took a pen in her trembling hand and signed her name on the dotted line.

# Chapter 10

For Sean and Sandy, the actual move was preceded by a small army of painters, plumbers, carpenters and electricians, who stormed in to prepare the way. The workers began restoring Hattie Phillips's once-dilapidated house into a solid, well-built home. They added a new roof, replaced old pipes and fixed whatever else needed repair.

The Gilmores moved in a week after the work was done and happily began settling in. They had moved there from Forsyth County, a rural area some thirty miles north of Atlanta. They were thrilled to be stationed in the heart of a bustling city, only a five-minute drive from downtown, with quick access to the interstate. They were close to restaurants, parks, theaters and concert halls—all in short supply in rural Forsyth.

But there were trade-offs, too: In that first month, the Gilmores met none of their new neighbors. When they'd first moved to Forsyth from Philadelphia, folks paraded over, welcoming them with freshly baked cakes and cookies. Nobody came to the door this time. There were no bright smiles or "How do you dos" when they saw neighbors out and about.

During dinner one day, Sean and Sandy noted the cold reception they'd received so far. They agreed some initial distrust on the part of the locals was to be expected. So they took it upon themselves to initiate acquaintances with the people of the Old Fourth Ward. They printed flyers and stuffed them in mailboxes all along Randolph Street:

WE'RE YOUR NEW NEIGHBORS!
COME MEET AND MINGLE
WITH LEMONADE AND A SWEET!

SATURDAY 2–3:30 P.M.
1022 RANDOLPH STREET
SEE YOU THERE!

The doorbell rang at exactly 1:59. Sean answered and greeted an elderly woman, dressed to the nines, high heels and all.

"Hi!" She smiled. "My name is Lula. Lula Simmons. Welcome to the neighborhood!"

Lula had plastered on a layer of makeup thick as pancake batter. Her hair was tied back in a spinster's bun, and she wore big-framed glasses that looked like car windshields.

She stepped in and feasted her eyes on the Gilmores, their faces aglow. Lula clasped her hands together, barely able to contain herself.

"This is wonderful! Just wonderful!"

"Yes," said Sean. His eyes darted to Sandy. "We're glad to meet you, too." He stepped back. "Come in. Come in and make yourself comfortable."

Lula glided past Sean and Sandy and inspected the living room. With apparent disappointment, she eyed the plain blue couch and simple scatter rugs. She'd obviously expected better from *them*.

"Well." Sandy took in a deep breath, "We're glad you're here. Won't you have something to eat or drink?"

"Why, thank you."

Lula floated into the dining room and scanned a table filled with light refreshments. Stepping closer, she mumbled something under her breath about "rabbit food." She plucked a homemade oatmeal cookie from a batch and took a dainty nibble.

For the next half-hour, Sean and Sandy listened as Lula raved, a bit too much, they thought, about how happy—*thrilled* was the word she used—she was to have them in the neighborhood.

It was weird. The lady even spooked Sandy.

Speaking perfect textbook English, Lula recounted her whole life story. She was a retired elementary school principal, she said; a transplant from Washington, D.C. She moved to Atlanta after her fourth husband died. She went on like that in endless detail, even reciting the French names and peculiar habits of the various poodles she'd owned over the years.

With Lula's story complete, they small-talked—about weather, traffic, anything to fill the awkward pauses. All the while, they pretended not to notice that no one else had shown up yet.

Sandy was relieved when it ended. On the way out, Lula stopped in the doorway and clasped her wrinkled hands again.

"Let me know if there's anything I can do to help with your transition. Anything. I mean that, too." She patted Sandy's arm, reassuringly. "And don't worry. Folks will get over it. You'll fit in just fine."

When Lula had gone, Sean and Sandy went into the dining room and began wrapping leftover food. They worked in silence, keeping their disappointment to themselves.

For the rest of that day, they both wondered, what had they gotten themselves into? A month had passed and they hadn't exchanged so much as one hello, not even with neighbors on either side of them. On one side was an old woman. (Joe Folkes said she was in her eighties and hardly ever showed her face.) On the other side were two young, mysterious men. The Gilmores saw them come and go, but they never got a chance to say hello.

The day after the fruitless meet-and-greet, Sandy happened to peek out the kitchen window while washing dishes. She spotted Barlowe out back, unwrapping a water hose. She watched as he sprayed the patchy lawn and watered the base of the tall oak tree.

At one point, he turned around and looked her way, intuitively sensing he was being watched. Sandy dropped her gaze. A moment later, she looked up and met Barlowe's studied glare. Awkwardly, they both turned away, neither acknowledging the other.

Sitting on the front porch later that day, Sandy told Sean about the uneasy moment with their next-door neighbor. "I like our house," she said, simply.

"Yes, me, too."

They fell silent. Then, from out of the blue, Sean muttered, "I wonder what that old lady meant when she said, 'Folks will get over it.'" He turned to Sandy. "You think it'll be all right?"

"I'm not worried," she lied. "People are people. You wait. Before long, we'll make new friends and have them over from time-to-time to share a glass of chardonnay."

From their new porch in front of their new house they played Chinese checkers, marked time and took in that gorgeous skyline view.

# Chapter 11

In the decades before the Gilmores showed up, the people of the Old Fourth Ward had remained fairly anonymous. Not by design, mind you. Barring routine forays to other parts of town, they were simply too consumed by life's unyielding grind to be concerned with much of anything else. If life was running on most cylinders, which it seldom did, they counted themselves blessed to make frayed ends meet and avoid the sudden shadow of the repo man. A job lost or some hoped-for ship that failed to dock could result in a steep plunge off one of life's brutal cliffs. Except for neighbors living close enough to eyewitness the fall, the descent went largely unnoticed; anonymous.

Such was life for the people of the Old Fourth Ward. For years, they tended their business, gave what their government asked of them and learned to expect little back from that same government, which noted their existence mainly during tax collections and census counts.

So it came as some surprise when they began to notice a sudden outside interest in the neigborhood. It had long been accepted as undisputed fact that white folks had forgotten they were there.

■ ■ ■

Another month passed, and nothing changed. Nobody came to the Gilmores' house. Nobody said hello when they passed in the street. Nobody made eye contact, if they could help it. It was enough to make a body feel downright isolated.

Sandy hated that feeling. Lounging in the living room one day, flipping restlessly through *People* magazine, she suddenly stood up straight. She felt jumpy. She needed to do something, at least to *try*.

Earlier, she'd seen a few men playing dominoes outside the Auburn Avenue Mini-Mart. She had never gone into the store before. It seemed like some fraternity house or private club she was not yet a member of.

Her instinct about the store was more on point than she might have imagined. The mini-mart was one of the most revered institutions in the Old Fourth Ward. The store was founded by a man named Cornell James. As a young buck coming up, Cornell was a sharp crapshooter who could roll sevens and elevens, almost at will. After being dragged kicking and screaming to Vietnam, he made good use of his gambling skills. He ran the rounds to soldiers' barracks on payday every month. Often rolling with fixed dice, Cornell would clean out the troops before they tramped off on weekend leave to blow their money on booze and whores.

Cornell had the presence of mind to send his substantial winnings home to his young bride, Alberta, who promptly socked it away in keeping with their future plans. When Cornell returned from war in 1975, he and Alberta were set to start. They didn't have to beg white folks for what they needed, and surely wouldn't get: a business loan. They bought a home in the Old Fourth Ward and opened the mini-mart.

Cornell worked hard to get the place going, then died of a heart attack two decades later. Alberta ran the store for a short while and turned it over to their eldest daughter, Juliette. Juliette James proved to be a better business manager than both of her parents put together. She served patrons with a friendly smile, but when managing customers and accounts she was as hard-nosed and savvy as they came. On the day after she took over, in 1999, she posted a sign in big red letters on the cash register at the front of the store:

## IN GOD WE TRUST
## ALL OTHERS MUST PAY

Thanks to Juliette's business knack, the mini-mart became a marvel in efficiency. It could compete head-to-head with most any grocery chain in town. There was another store just around the corner, but the mini-mart claimed most folks' loyalty. The people viewed it as a special point of pride that it had been black-owned and -operated for so many years.

Of course, that bit of history had preceded Sandy. Whenever she needed things for the house, she usually drove to the Winn-Dixie, less than a mile away.

Standing in her living room now, she told herself that this might be the time to take some symbolic step toward establishing herself in the community. Then it hit her: Shampoo! She was out of shampoo! She would run over to the mini-mart.


Barlowe had gone to the store to buy the lottery Quik Pik and shoot the breeze. The boys were all there, standing around, socializing outside. Amos had a kitten that he'd found wandering through an alleyway. He'd cleaned it, fed it and claimed it as his own. The kitten was female but he named it Caesar, just to get a rise from Barlowe.

With Barlowe looking on, laughing, Amos held little Caesar in his lap and explained the complexities of the creature's mind. Ely and Willie insisted normal black people didn't own cats.

"I don't give a shit," Amos declared, "what black people own."

Just then, Lucretia Wiggins sashayed around the corner. Barlowe was the first among the men to spot her. She wore a snug lime-colored midriff top, with her dark, flat belly peeking out.

One day, about a week before, he had bumped into her coming out of the store. When they collided, she looked up at him and smiled. Barlowe fumbled in his head for something to say; something witty that might jump-start a conversation. But nothing came to mind. The moment passed, and Lucretia went inside. He determined to be quicker on his feet next time around.

Now Ely saw Lucretia head into the store. He poured himself a soda chaser and held the Coke bottle aloft.

"Um! Eye Candy! She shaped like this here bottle ri chere."

Willie chuckled. "She wouldn't want you, Ely, wit them dead man's teef . . . What you gonna do wit a gal lak that?"

"Shoot," groused Ely. "Them young boys don't wanna do nothin but hump up-and-down on her alla time." He beat a knotted fist against his flat chest. "*I* know wha to do . . . I'd treat her lak a real woman; take her out to a movie, buy her a hot dog and stuff like that."

"Lemme tell y'all niggers somethin," said Amos. "That gal ain't worf all that slobberin over."

"Buulllllshhhiiiit!" Willie snorted. "Thasa perty piece a sculptin dere!"

"She might have a fine shape now," Amos countered, "but I can look at her and tell that won't last."

"How *you* know what ain't gon last?"

"Easy." Amos pointed in the direction of Lucretia's house. "All you gotta do is go over there and look at her mama."

"And?"

"And that'll tell you how the daughta gonna look down the road!"

He launched into some winding theory about how, using a woman's current age, weight and bowel habits, you could compute the amount of fat she'll accumulate over time.

"I can look at that gurl's bones and tell she gon be heavy. She healthy as a grown woman *now!*"

The others kept quiet on that point, which did seem to bear a certain strength of logic.

"Sides," added Amos, "she cain't do nothin no other woman cain't do . . . Y'all niggers don't know nothin bout no woman!"

"Huummph. Sound to me like *you* don't know."

Amos turned and faced Willie. "I ain't gonna argue wit you, Willhime . . . What the hell kinda name is that, anyway? *Will*-hime!"

Willie's Christian name was Wilheim, but he was called Willie for short. It seemed simpler to pronounce, even though it was the same number of syllables.

"Lemme show you somethin," Amos said, returning to his theory. He snatched a Coca-Cola bottle from Ely's hand, just as he prepared to mix himself another drink. He poured some Coke into a plastic glass and handed it to Willie.

"Taste dis."

Willie eyed it suspiciously. "You wont me to put some likker in it?"

"Naw, man! Jus taste the soda like I axed you to!"

Willie sipped warily and put it down. "Okay. Now what?"

Amos handed him the Coca-Cola bottle. "Now taste dis; drink it straight from the bottle."

"I jus drank some soda . . . Whas yo pernt?"

"Taste it from the bottle, man, then I'll tell you my gotdamn pernt!"

Willie tasted, again reluctantly. "All right. So whas your pernt?"

"Which one taste better? The soda in the glass, or the soda in the bottle?"

Willie grumbled: "Wha you ax me that stupid quer-stion for? The Co-Cola in the bottle the same as the Co-Cola in the glass!"

"Thas jus my pernt. It don't matter what *shape* the containa come in; Co-Cola is Co-Cola! And it don't matter what shape a woman come in, neither. Is whas *inside* the containa that count."

That said, Amos reared back in his seat and folded his arms across his chest. For him it was one of those rare moments when his innate wisdom seemed crystal clear to him. It was moments like this when he regretted he had not become a lawyer or something in life.

He showed his satisfaction by reaching over and pouring a drink for each of his friends. He wanted them to go undisturbed as they pondered the sheer profundity of his analogy.

Amos would have basked in his brilliance some more if Barlowe hadn't interrupted with a question that flung the debate far afield.

"Have y'all wondered why the only white people to move on this street moved next door to *me*?"

They all looked at one another, puzzled.

"Don't y'all think thas strange?"

Willie took a deep, exasperated breath. "Barlowe, I hear they used to pay twenny dollars a head to turn in crazies to the loony farm in

Milledgeville. If I was to wrap you in a tater sack and take you back to yo hometown, I blieve white folks would gimme enough for a fif a scotch."

They all laughed.

Barlowe waved him off and went in the store. The boys followed. As they walked behind, they glanced at each other with raised eyebrows that said, *That Barlowe got a real problem. He might need to get some help.*

When Sandy approached, the mini-mart was filled with people and chatter. The men now stood off in a tight corner, laughing and knee-slapping at some private joke.

"An he said that ooman had a mustache thick as his!"

"Hahahahahahahahahahahahahahahahaha!"

When Sandy appeared in the doorway the place fell deathly quiet.

Barlowe had gone to an aisle looking for the shelf where the oatmeal was kept. Like everybody else, he stopped and appraised the white lady coming in. He saw the long stem of a neck that ran up to dirty blonde hair, cut short at the nape. He noted the slender, athletic build. She was feminine, but with a bit of a rugged mountain look.

Met by burning eyes, Sandy advanced just beyond the first row of canned goods. She gathered herself and rushed down one of the narrow aisles. She could hear her own footsteps as she moved. She could feel the eyes trailing her.

She stopped in the hair care section and scanned the shelf: Dark and Lovely; Bronner Bros Super Gro; Smooth'n Shine Polishing Curl Activator Gel.

Strange. Nothing there for *her.*

Assuming she'd landed in the wrong spot, she moved down further and scanned some more: African Pride Braid Sheen Spray; TCB Naturals No-Lye Relaxer; Comb-Thru Texturizer.

She paused. All of a sudden a simple search for shampoo felt complicated. She went down the row again, certain she had overlooked something. All the while, she felt the eyes. She had the sense of walking through a dense forest at night, with twenty owls peering down from surrounding trees. The owls could see her but she couldn't see them, and she dared not look their way.

Sensing a tension mounting in her store, Juliette James called to the white lady from up front. "May I help you, ma'am?"

The owls fastened onto Sandy's lips, to see what she would say.

"No. I'm fine, thank you."

She could feel it: Every hint of a motion she made was scrutinized, especially by the women. Their eyes cut like razors, peeling back her skin and clothes. With withering contempt, they noted the shoes: *Humph! Dusty, dowdy sandals.* Then on to the shorts: *Too wide at the legs; goofy looking, if you ask me.* And the blanched skin: *Chalk! No color at all!* Finally, the hair: *A mop, really—lopped at the base of a bony neck and left to fend for itself.*

The men took stock of more basic things: *She look flat-chested in that blouse; nice ass, though, for a white girl.*

Sandy wondered what those people would say when she left the store. Would they share a laugh at her expense?

For the moment, nobody said anything. Not a meek hello. Not *Hi-my-name-is-so-and-so.* Nothing.

The whole affair wore on Sandy. She decided to get out of there. She needed to buy something and get out, now.

She absentmindedly snatched up some personal item she didn't need. She started the long walk toward the register, and her thoughts shifted, oddly, to Arkansas. Little Rock, she believed it was. In a college history course she'd once taken, she had seen grainy newsreels of a black girl walking amid a hostile crowd. The poor child was headed up a long sidewalk leading to an all-white school in Little Rock. White people, their faces brimming with hate, lined each side of the walk, shouting obscenities as they were restrained by state troopers. They screamed and taunted and shook their fists. They didn't want her there.

Accompanied by a few other black kids, that girl went in anyway.

Now walking through the mini-mart with the spirit of that girl's courage nudging her on, Sandy knew what she must do. With owl-eyes tracking every step, she steeled herself. She walked and stared straight ahead.

To avoid confronting the muddled gazes, she fixed her sight on the cash register up front. She read the curious red-lettered sign pinned to the back:

IN GOD WE TRUST
ALL OTHERS MUST PAY

She zeroed in on the bottom line, vaguely wondering if it somehow applied to her:

ALL OTHERS MUST PAY

For the first time in her life, she felt like "other." She was overcome with the sudden urge to scream, to announce to everyone in the room how awful and otherly she felt right then.

She reached the front counter, the owls still watching, waiting to see what she would do. She held her package aloft and forced a sheepish smile.

"Just thought I'd pick up a few things, that's all."

The people stared, first at the package: Stayfree pads. Then they looked at her.

Sandy paid Juliette James and rushed to the door. On the way out she heard snickering. From the far corner a woman's voice spat an ugly curse: *Beeeiiiitttttccccchhhhh! Beeeiiiitttttccccchhhhh!*

Sandy scooted across the street and reached her front porch, panting. She went indoors and flopped on the couch. For a long while, she stayed indoors and kept to herself.

Sean noticed her downcast mood and asked what was the matter.

"Nothing. I need to think, that's all."

For the rest of that day, she couldn't stop thinking. She kept thinking about that poor girl in Arkansas.

# Chapter 12

Barlowe sat at the table at Martha's Kitchen and wolfed down a plate of fried chicken, collards and candied yams. On most days, he took a bag lunch to work, but on payday he usually rewarded himself. So he ate at Martha's at least once a week, and always alone.

The boys at the print shop often went out together for lunch and beer. In some awkward gesture of kindness, or sympathy about him being the odd man out, they invited him sometimes. He joined his colleagues a few times, but found it a strain talking with them for more than ten minutes, unless the talk centered on work or sports. So Barlowe usually turned down their invitations. It made them happy, too.

Now he finished his meal, took up the tray and said good-bye to Martha, who owned the place. The weather outside was nice; bright and sunshiny, with a bit of a chill.

He took another route back to the print shop. He often took a different route, to see what he could see. This time he went up Walker Street. Eventually, he came upon a strip of businesses nestled between an ice cream parlor and a clothing store. Before reaching the end of the strip he nearly bumped into a wooden sign in front of another shop.

Come In!
Make Your Own At
The Pottery Place!

He stepped to the huge plate glass window and pressed his mug against the pane, cupping both hands tight around his face. The place looked cluttered, like an elementary school art room. There were several long tables spread out over an open floor, topped with clay pots and porcelain figurines. Pots in various states of completion filled rows of shelves lining the walls.

There were about twenty people inside. Some sat at tables and sculpted wet mounds of clay placed on spools and twirling around. Others painted on pots that had already been shaped and dried.

Barlowe stood there and studied them. Deeply absorbed in their clay creations, the people seemed unaware they were being watched.

It occurred to Barlowe that in the normal course of things it wouldn't cross his mind in a thousand years to go inside a place like that. What would he do in a place like that, a place where people went to make clay pots? He wouldn't know where to begin. How had those folks started? How had they come to spend their free time making pots?

He stood there a moment and tried to think that through. After some reflection he concluded that making pots was clearly about the activity itself. He'd read somewhere that it was therapeutic. Still, he wondered how people found space in their heads to indulge in the sheer pleasure of making a thing, especially if that thing was an item they could easily find at Kmart or Lowe's.

It seemed odd. Then again, maybe it wasn't odd, for *them*. Maybe it was the most natural thing in the world.

He came back full-circle in his head. So why had he never been inside a pottery? He didn't know. And he wondered if his not knowing was yet more proof that other people knew so much more than him. It always seemed to come back to that: knowing or not knowing how to live. Something about that notion left him vaguely unsettled.

He scanned the room again and noticed a white woman eyeing him. She sat at a table in one of the corners. A spool of wet clay twirled in front of her. When their eyes met, she shifted her gaze back to her art, every now and then glancing his way, a curious expression etched on her face.

He wondered what she was thinking.

He checked his watch and noted that it was time to go. He had scheduled a meeting with his foreman. He left, heading back toward the print shop. Along the way he thought again about The Pottery Place. When he had time again, maybe next week, he would go back and watch some more.

He doubted he would go inside. Still, he was curious. Who knew? It might be fun making pots.

The Copy Right Print Shop was located on Marietta Street, up on the northwest end, near the industrial area. Barlowe got there and headed straight to the foreman's office. The office was a glass-encased partition that enabled the foreman to keep a watchful eye on shop operations.

When Barlowe showed up, a Tennessee boy named Drew Wallace was inside, knee-slapping and cracking jokes. Barlowe waited outside the office until they were done. When Drew left, the foreman waved him in.

The foreman was a man named Billy Spivey. Billy was born and raised in Louisiana, where they still had plantations in modern times. A tall, lean, hard-boiled man with deeply stained teeth and a crew cut, Billy had his jaw puffed with a wad of tobacco stuffed inside. He carried a scratched-up tin cup to catch tobacco when he had to spit.

Billy's office was just like Billy: spare, straightforward. The desktop was piled high with ink-stained paper, sheets he'd snatched off presses to ensure quality control. Besides a few pens and paper clips, that was about all Billy kept on the desk.

Several printing plaques lined a side wall. The back wall was nearly fully covered—with a huge American flag. It had been nailed into the Sheetrock like some glorious crucifixion.

Barlowe sat down, crossed his legs and tried his best to ignore that thing.

"Billy."

"Barlowe."

The two men had an unspoken pact. They looked at each other no more than they had to, and spoke to each other even less. They got along well so long as they kept their exchanges confined to work.

This day, Barlowe needed to talk with Billy about something vital, so he'd asked the foreman to set a time.

Billy raised the tobacco spit-cup to his mouth. "What can I do you for, Barlowe, m'boy?"

Barlowe shifted in his seat a little. He could see that flag—he could *feel* it—out the corner of his eye.

"I came to talk to you bout a raise, Billy."

"A raise?"

"Yeah, Billy. A raise."

The foreman's mouth puffed out, blowfish-like. "Raises not due fore next year, Barlowe."

"I know. But I got a special need."

"You wanna tell me bout it?"

Barlowe glimpsed that flag and veered back at the man sitting beneath it.

"Actually, is personal, Billy. Is personal."

"Well, raises not due fore next year."

Barlowe fixed on his boss with a level stare. "I work hard for this company, Billy. You know I work hard."

"Yeah. I know that, Barlowe."

Billy sat there, stiff as wood. No doubt, Barlowe was a good worker; one of their best, actually. In the years he'd worked there he'd established himself as a real pro, the top man in the house on four-color jobs. He had a way of setting the press register just right, slapping the colors on top of each other so straight the images popped up and out, camera-perfect. Billy liked that he had an ace four-color man he could depend on, especially for the most important jobs.

And Barlowe was a bit of a press mechanic, too, which was vital in a shop that used such old machines. Whenever his press broke down, Barlowe would come in on weekends and fix it himself, rather than wait on outside maintenance people. Barlowe saved the company money. The bigwigs at Copy Right liked that a lot.

Billy sat there thinking, his face blank, impassive. There was no need trying to make Barlowe feel guilty. Unlike some of the other boys around there, always bitching about this and that, Barlowe never asked for anything he didn't rightly deserve. He did his work and minded his business, which was all a boss could ask of any man.

Still, with men like Spivey a certain deference was required to get real cooperation on anything. After working there for several years, Barlowe didn't seem to know that yet. Either he didn't know or didn't care. He made that clear when he uncrossed his legs, leaned forward and pounded an ink-stained fist on Spivey's desk.

"I work *hard* around here, Billy. And all I'm askin is for a raise."

Billy's face flushed the deepest red. He would have loved to fire Barlowe on the spot, and, for general principles, have him tossed out on the sidewalk—on his head. But Billy was in a bit of a pickle here. Print shops around town were always looking for good four-color men. He couldn't risk losing Barlowe to another shop. If he lost Barlowe, Billy would likely have to answer to the higher-ups, the big shots in the white cotton shirts who paraded through the pressroom, assessing production costs and employee waste.

Billy didn't want to be hassled by them. He hated people like them, just like he hated Barlowe's kind. They were all shit to him; just different shades of crap, that's all.

The foreman sneered and spit in his cup. The sour look on his puss said it all: It said Spivey didn't like the direction this country was moving in. There was a time in the country when life was straightforward. Now things were complicated. Times like this, Billy longed for Louisiana. Things there were still pretty cut-and-dried. Certain people in Louisiana knew where they stood, and knew where they were damned well *supposed* to stand.

Billy leaned back in his swivel chair. He leaned back so far it looked like he might spill over. He was daydreaming now; daydreaming about the good ol days in the bayou, when a man like Barlowe wouldn't dare barge into the boss's office, making demands. In Louisiana, a person like that might be known to disappear. At some point he might be found hanging among sprawling Spanish moss, maybe with a note—a reminder to the living—clipped to his big toe.

But times had changed, too much, if you asked Billy Spivey. Leaning forward in the chair now, he regarded Barlowe coldly and thought to himself: *A man can take only so much abuse in life. Even a dog will bite if it gets pushed too far.*

Billy Spivey was nobody's dog.

"Tell ya what, Barlowe." A thick vein throbbed in his temple now. "I'll go and tawk to the big boss bout your raise and see what we can come up with."

"I'd preciate that."

Billy ground his teeth a little.

Barlowe rose from his seat. In spite of himself, he glanced again at that flag and tugged his belt, hitching his pants up a bit.

"I'd also preciate if you lemme know somethin soon as you can."

Billy spit hard in the cup and clenched his jaw. "Will do, Barlowe, m'boy. Will do."

That said, Barlowe left. Billy sat there swiveling in his chair. He swiveled and stared dreamily off into space, wishing he was back in Louisiana.

Later, Barlowe sat on the back porch with a cold beer, listening to the pigeons coo. He sat there and pondered the meeting with Billy Spivey. Would Spivey do what he'd promised? Would he push for that raise like he said he would?

Who was he kidding? Billy was no friend of his. Spivey was no friend at all.

Barlowe pulled out a newspaper and began reading. The front page featured an article about the president, mouthing off again about democracy and war. *Democracy and war. Huummmph.* Barlowe felt so alone in his outrage sometimes.

He crumpled the paper and tossed it in the trash.

He took another swig and, out of the corner of one eye, picked up a movement in the yard. He turned and saw Viola stagger from around the side of the house. A dark, haggard woman with a cheap, fluffy wig and bloodshot eyes, she flung an irritated glance his way. She trod through the pathway and disappeared. Minutes later, The Hawk trailed behind, trying his best to catch up to his woman. He wore wrinkled pants and a sports jacket with one flap of the side pocket tucked in and the other hanging out. The jacket was snug and short at the sleeves. Its single split in the rear rode up his backside.

The Hawk made it as far as the pathway and fell down near the house next door. He rolled over and stretched out on his back, resting on his elbows. The pigeons cooed. He stared in Barlowe's direction, straining to track the sound of the birds. Exhausted from the short hike from Davenport's house, The Hawk closed his eyes and keeled over in grass left damp from a recent rain. He fell into a deep sleep, right there between the two houses.

Watching the drunk, Barlowe smiled, warmed by the thought of something his mama said years ago, when he was a child. Once, when she'd caught him throwing rocks at two staggering winos, she scolded him.

"Boy, don't do that."

"They just drunks, mama."

"No, baby. They not just drunks. They *people*, just like you and me."

"Then why they drink alla time?"

"They drink cause they hurtin. They cryin inside."

Every time Barlowe saw drunk people after that, he looked for the tears. Then, when he grew older he learned better how to spot the pain. He searched for the sadness in the eyes, or the deep stress lines etched onto the faces.

Now that he'd done some living himself, he understood how life could break a man down. He had seen enough in life to know: There was a thin line between them and him.

He stared again at the man passed out on the ground. Though he never would admit it out loud, he envied The Hawk in a certain way.

The Hawk had the courage—or whatever you wanted to call it—to live the way he damn well pleased, even if it meant doing nothing but staying tore-down-pissy-drunk. As wasteful as that life seemed, it carried a certain appeal. It seemed a kind of perverse liberty. That was it; a form of freedom. Barlowe didn't feel anything close to that.

Eventually, The Hawk woke up and rose to his feet. He brushed dirt and grass from his clothes, then unzipped his pants and leaned against the side of the house next door. Stretching a hand above his head to support himself, he peed against the wall.

"Hey!" Barlowe barked. "Take that somewhere else!"

The Hawk glanced nonchalantly over his shoulder and kept on peeing. When he was done, he zipped his pants and raked his fingers through his hair. Taking his sweet time, he stuffed his shirttail halfway inside his pants. He squared his broad shoulders and, with some ceremony, hocked up a glob of phlegm from his whisky throat.

He spit, then turned on his scuffed heels and resumed his journey, staggering down the pathway toward home.

# Chapter 13

A full month passed before Barlowe got word on his request for a raise. He was preparing to run another print job, when Billy Spivey appeared in the doorway to his office and waved him in. Barlowe got there and stood before Spivey, who sat half-sideways on top of his desk, that big bright flag hanging behind him like some hulking bodyguard.

"Hey, Barlowe, m'boy."

"Billy."

"Got some good news for ya."

Barlowe waited.

"I got you that raise you ast for."

Billy smiled. Barlowe waited.

"Boss said they'll give ya two percent."

Barlowe frowned. "Two percent? You serous, Billy?"

Spivey nodded. "You know they been raisin hell tryin to cut costs round here. Nobody but you is gettin an extra raise."

"Two percent. That don't seem like much, Billy."

"Hell, it's better'n nothin. Right?"

Barlowe tried to do the math in his head. After Caesar took his cut off the top, he figured, there wouldn't be much to speak about. William Crawford had said that if he was inclined to sell he would require at least five thousand down. With a two percent raise it would take a million years to raise that much.

When he got ready to sell, Crawford wouldn't likely wait too long. When it came to his money William Crawford was not a patient man.

Now Spivey spit in his cup and shrugged. "Best we can do, Barlowe. What can I tell ya?"

Barlowe stared at Billy. Spivey had very close-set eyes, so that if you looked at them a long time, the two began to look like one great, big Cyclops eye. That's what he looked like to Barlowe then. A Cyclops.

Worse still was Billy's facial expression. The expression was close to a smirk. Actually, it appeared he might bust out laughing any second now.

"What can I tell ya?"

Barlowe stared at the Cyclops. Again, the smirk. After a moment, Barlowe turned and walked away, thinking, *This man from Lousana. What can you rightly expect from Lousana?* Then: *And I'm from Georgia. Same difference as Lousana.*

Barlowe went back to his press thinking about how much Billy Spivey reminded him of some of the white folks he'd come across in Milledgeville. It didn't make him homesick any.

Milledgeville was a small and small-minded town, a place where a dark man's dreams—if he had managed to muster any—were best tucked away, lest they be stomped on, ground out like a cigarette butt, by men like Billy Spivey.

For Barlowe it had been that way from the beginning. It had been that way since *before* the beginning, starting with his mama and daddy, and theirs before them, and running on up for several generations. In all that time, the only distinction his family achieved was a tragic footnote in the city's dreadful history: His daddy's oldest brother was the last man known to be lynched in those parts.

"Had somethin to do wit a white gal is all I know."

Barlowe's daddy recounted the sketchy details a thousand times, taking care to ensure due warning was stamped in his boys' woolly heads: *White girls, off limits. No eyeballin, greetin, embracin, shunnin, kissin, or otherwise touchin the fruit.*

"Seems is always a white gal," his daddy would say.

His daddy told them other things, too: about how his family were called sharecroppers but were driven like slaves; about how his days as a young boy felt happy, only because he didn't know any better; about how the nicer white folks nearby, descendants of a plantation family (and likely undeclared kin to the Reeds), would stop in on their way to town and give his brothers and him a ride to the movies. They'd buy their tickets at separate windows, enter the theater through separate doors and watch the same film from separate sections.

Afterward, they'd all meet up on Nigger Street. Officially listed as Mckintosh Road, Nigger Street marked the section in town where black folks cavorted. They played washboards and harmonicas on corners, sometimes with smiling white folks looking on; they sold chitlin dinners and ran numbers, round the clock.

By the time Barlowe came along, the Jim Crow signs had been grudgingly removed. But since time stood still as daybreak in Milledgeville, Jim Crow's ghost carried on.

For decades, Nigger Street remained a vital nerve center, a place where furtive glances said more than spoken words; a place where white men searched out black flesh, undercover; a place where moonshine money was muscled out by crack cocaine.

Among black folks, those who could find a way bailed out of Milledgeville. You didn't leave as much as you *fled* that place. Those fortunate enough to muster the gumption to escape were considered a success in life, even if they moved no more than two counties away.

When he came of a certain age, Barlowe weighed a future dangled between two options that ran jagged as the dirt road leading from his family's house: He could leave, abandon that wretched town, or like so many others, remain and watch his spirit rot.

For those who stayed there were ways to earn a subsistence living: backbreaking farm work or crushing labor down at the local chalk mines. People who shoveled chalk onto railroad cars stumbled home evenings, dead tired and flour-faced, smothered in the yellow dust. It blanketed their clothes, polluted their lungs, burned their eyes, clouded their brains.

If not farming or chalk mining, there was sometimes work to be had at the state mental hospital. It appeared most patients at the crazy house had either fled, were fleeing or were plotting escape. They seemed to possess more get-up about them than many of the locals who spent whole lifetimes mired in the muck that was Milledgeville.

Somehow, Barlowe always knew he would leave. Even as a child he'd sensed there was something horribly wrong with that town. He saw it in the stooped shoulders and rutted lives of the black people he knew. Saw it in the haughty air of well-doing whites. He saw the outline of something broad, amorphous, yet rigidly structured, that no one in Milledgeville could honestly justify or explain—not the shouting preachers who spread outrageous myths about a vengeful God; not the half-taught teachers who dispensed glorious Old South fabrications; and certainly not his parents, who were too busy living the wrongness, too steeped in it, to wrench free of its stubborn hold.

Despite its power to grind ambition, Milledgeville lacked the force to contain Barlowe Reed. He possessed in him a spirit of dogged rebellion, passed down perhaps from dark cargo shipped from a continent he might never see.

Besides, there were too many big questions churning in him. What sense would it make to seek answers to big questions in the same damned place that had dredged them up?

Yes, Barlowe left Milledgeville long before his bags were packed. The actual going was merely ceremony. Having learned a printing trade, he worked at a small shop and saved his money. When he'd stashed enough to float for six months clean, he visited his mama's grave, then trudged five miles to the bus station and caught the gray dog to Atlanta.

In one month, he'd landed his first printing job. In three months, he moved from a rooming house to a small apartment. He bought used furniture and an old piece of car and scoured the big city on his days off work.

He liked Atlanta for all it offered, though some of the well-doing black folks puzzled him. They seemed too contented, too busy celebrating a victory that was still incomplete. Some appeared deliriously relieved simply to have found a hell at least cooler than the ones they'd left behind—in Tuscaloosa, Alabama; in South Bend, Indiana; in Boston, Massachusetts—or wherever else they had fled.

*A cooler hell.* Standing at his printing machine, Barlowe reminded himself that he had come to Atlanta seeking more than that. He thought again about what his boss had said. *Two percent.* Billy Spivey wanted—no, expected—him to make peace with a cooler hell.

Barlowe cleaned the rollers and wiped a printing plate for the next run. He switched off his press lamp, wiped his hands and tossed the ink cloths into a nearby laundry box.

*A cooler hell.* The thought of that was too unsettling. Barlowe left work early and went on home.

As he stepped up the walkway leading to his place, a car crept slowly up Randolph Street and stopped in front of the house. A late-model Lexus, the car had a Coldwell Banker sign attached to the door. There were four white people inside. Barlowe stopped and waited to see what they wanted. The white folks peered past him and studied the house; *his* house. He could see them talking inside the car. A woman sitting behind the wheel appeared to be pointing. Barlowe guessed she was a real estate agent. While she spoke, the passengers, a man and a woman with a toddler in her lap, listened, nodding every now and then.

The people eventually noticed Barlowe. The woman behind the steering wheel waved.

Barlowe shot them a hostile glare.

After a brief moment, the driver pulled slowly away.

# Chapter 14

"Go home!"

"What?!"

"I gotta go to sleep. Go home!"

"You go to hell, Davenport!"

Nobody said Davenport's name like Viola. She seemed to spit out the name, especially when she was drunk. Actually, his first name was Paschal. Paschal Davenport. But he had dropped the first part since his days in the navy, when his superiors called enlisted men by their last names. He had heard his last name barked so many times during the course of service to his country that he kept using it long after his military discharge.

Davenport's house had long been the neighborhood watering hole for a select few drunks that included Viola and The Hawk. It was Davenport's house—and the promise of steady drink and social exchange—that kept them marching back and forth through the pathway next to Barlowe's place.

This latest visit had started the day before, a Saturday, and gone on through the entire night. The pints and quart bottles of liquor they'd consumed had taken their usual toll. Everybody was blind-high, paralyzed.

Davenport could drink with the best of them, so he wasn't the least bit ashamed when his body began shutting down after daybreak. The floor seemed to be rising up to meet him, which meant it was time to pack it in.

"Y'all ain't gotta go home, but you gotta get the hell outta here!" He had heard somebody say that somewhere once. He liked the way it sounded. "Y'all ain't gotta go home, but you gotta get the hell outta here!"

"I ain't goin nowhere!" A sliver of drool ran down Viola's lip. "Play Ray Charles!"

Davenport wanted to cuss Viola, but he took care not to offend The Hawk. He and The Hawk had been fast friends since their navy days.

He didn't want to offend the other guests, either—two women and a man who had dropped in to visit. Slouched in worn-out chairs around the room, the visitors listened to the testy exchange. They wanted to hear Ray Charles, too, but as relative outsiders in the drinking clique, they weren't qualified to make special requests.

Besides, Davenport was a big man. He could get rough when he wanted. So the visitors kept quiet and waited patiently for the next round of drinks to flow.

Still, Viola was in a nasty mood. She craved a sad song to match her spirit. "Dammit, play Ray Charles!"

Only The Hawk seemed to hear her now. The others reclined in various states of semiconsciousness. The Hawk roused himself from a sunken chair with the stuffing busting out. He went to the old turntable and placed the needle on the record. The scratchy needle grated his peace, but Ray Charles calmed him down:

*It's cryin time again, you're gonna leave me . . .*

The drunks all sat quiet, listening, thinking back to more coherent days. When the song ended, Viola waved to her man, signaling it was time to go on home. The Hawk got up and followed her to the door.

The other visitors got up, too. They took Viola's departure as a sign that the party was winding down. They all shuffled through the doorway and scattered across the yard.

On the way out, nobody bothered to shout good-bye to the host. Dead tired and sick of Viola's disrespect, Davenport had stumbled back to his bedroom and collapsed onto his bed.

A few blocks away, Barlowe sat on the back porch, drinking his morning coffee and listening to the pigeons coo. He had the day's newspaper and a bunch of books, along with a big dictionary, spread across a table.

Lately, he had been thinking. He'd been thinking that his life didn't reflect everything going on inside his head. So he had gone to the library and gotten some books. He thought he would read a few biographies this time, to learn about other people who might have stumbled through a chunk of their lives, then somehow come upon their intended path.

He didn't expect to get religious about it, but there was a religious aspect to his yearning, just the same. From time to time he went to the Ebenezer Baptist Church on Auburn Avenue. He went partly because the place was tied to Martin Luther King, and partly to see what the preacher had to say. The preacher seemed to talk a lot about purpose. Purpose and direction. From what Barlowe could gather it all came down to this: Whether God was your compass or whether you relied on your own internal lights, which, according to the preacher, was no more useful than a two-dollar street map from a foreign land.

As for maps and life, Barlowe was disturbed by the notion that a man could lose his way and veer off his path. He was troubled by the idea that a man could spend a whole lifetime traveling down somebody else's road.

What a shame if he, Barlowe Reed, had taken a wrong turn somewhere and was one or two streets over from where he should be. Or what if he was in the wrong city, state or even country? It seemed a definite possibility that he had wound up in the wrong country. America didn't seem a natural fit.

He reared back, reading, sipping coffee and reflecting on life. He considered a phrase he had seen on a poster somewhere:

**Life. Be in it.**

He wondered, *How can a man be in life if he can't figure out how to live?*

**Life. Be in it.**

He went back to reading.

There was a cool morning breeze blowing through the backyard. It was the kind of breeze that rustled the trees and made you feel at peace, even if there was nothing going right in your life. Barlowe was sitting out there reading and feeling rather peaceful when his new next-door neighbors came outside. He studied them a moment as they smiled at each other and slipped on gardening gloves.

He hadn't yet figured out what to make of *them* moving into the Old Fourth Ward. Last he'd heard they'd vacated the cities and fled to the woods. He thought they were happy out there. Now it appeared they'd changed their minds.

*White folks.* He shook his head. *Crazy as they ever wanna be.*

Now one of the neighbors appeared to look his way. He hoped they hadn't noticed him on the porch. He didn't care to be seen by them. If they saw him they might say hello. Then he might have to say hello back. They might even come over to the edge of the yard and try to start a conversation.

He wasn't feeling up to that. He dreaded the thought of getting trapped in one of those strange exchanges where everybody feels uneasy and nobody knows exactly what to say, so they walk on eggshells and talk around the edges of things until they can't stand it anymore.

He got up and went into the house, leaving his coffee and books with the birds.

■ ■ ■

Sean and Sandy stood outside and inhaled the fresh Sunday morning air. They both saw their next-door neighbor get up and leave the porch—and without even saying hello!

No matter. The morning was too beautiful to let anything bother them. They looked into each other's eyes, full of the sense that, already, the move to the Old Fourth Ward was impacting their lives in ways they had not imagined. In some ways, their new lives—sharing a neighborhood among the strangest of strangers—was like an adventure drawing them closer. They now spent more time together and talked more about their experiences and observations.

In other ways, the adjustment drew them further inward, each one chewing on private doubts. Sometimes Sean worried about his wife, especially since she got home from work before him most evenings. Why shouldn't he worry? There were two weird-acting men next door, and neither of them seemed very friendly.

Sean had run into them both by now. One refused to even acknowledge him. The other, the one with the bushy hair, had exchanged greetings at the mailbox once, but that hadn't seemed to go so well.

Sean felt vaguely concerned that there were no women living in that house. Having grown up in Pittsburgh with two sisters, he knew how females could take the edge off a place.

Sandy nursed her own set of private fears. The move seemed to have raised more questions than she had answers for. Since the experience at the mini-mart, she'd wondered if she could ever feel at ease in the neighborhood. What if she'd made a bad decision about the move?

She was too proud to admit her doubts to Sean. Besides, it was too soon to tell, anyway. They had to give it a real chance, if for no other reason than the most practical one: They had bought a home; they were committed. They were here—right in the heart of the Old Fourth Ward.

And so that lovely Sunday morning, they decided to work in the yard. The weather was charming. There were rosebuds blossoming, and crab apples and dogwoods sprouting everywhere.

By 9 A.M., they had cleared all the weeds from around the flower beds and planted begonias out front. They planned to go to Pike Family Nursery later to buy more bales of pine needles and pick up some tulips to plant on each side of the house.

"They'll be pretty when they bloom," said Sandy.

She wore bib overalls, which made her appear young and playful. Looking at her made Sean feel young and playful, too. That was exactly what they needed these days—to lighten up a bit.

Sean got down on all fours, then stood up straight. "We need more potting soil." He tossed off his gloves and bounced indoors.

Sandy followed, fresh with an idea to surprise her husband: The occasion called for an early morning mimosa toast.

Except for a shaggy mutt lying lazily beside the Auburn Avenue Mini-Mart, the streets of the Old Fourth Ward were fairly deserted. The only sound to be heard was the raspy voice of Viola, who fussed at The Hawk about the frustrating pace of their progress on the five-block walk from Davenport's house.

"C'mon, man! You too slow!"

"Hole up, woman. I'm comin."

The Hawk was too drunk to accelerate. He took a few shaky steps, then stopped and carefully lowered his lanky body to the curb, near Barlowe's house. He dropped his head between his legs, in a feeble attempt to clear his mind.

Viola was drunk, too, but not so blind-high that she didn't know what time it was. In another half-hour or so, people would start showing up at The Way of the Cross Baptist Church at the end of Auburn Avenue. Viola had seen them before; mostly prim old ladies in patent leather pumps and elaborate hats with those stupid flowers propped on top. As they headed to church to praise the Lord, they'd turn their wide noses up at "sinners" they passed in the street.

Viola looked at least as bad as she felt. There was no need to let those snooty people make her feel worse. So she pressed her drinking partner, and sometime lover, to push on.

"C'mon!"

But he couldn't. Being drunk and prone to grave miscalculations, it was a wonder The Hawk had made it that far. He rose to his feet and tried to follow, but every time he stepped too fast, Jim Beam commanded him to "halt!" And being experienced enough to know his limits, The Hawk obeyed. It was either obey or vomit. After twenty-five years of hard drinking, he still hated that feeling—the violent convulsions that made him feel like his high-yellow skin had just turned seaweed green.

So he gave in to Mr. Beam. He knelt down on one knee, as though offering up a Sunday prayer. Then he cursed his woman. "Damn you, Viola."

Problem was, she heard him. She doubled back and smacked him once. *Whack!* "I'm sick a waitin on yo sorry ass!"

She adjusted her wig and staggered off through the shortcut between Barlowe's house and the Gilmores' place.

The Hawk raised his head and squinted, barely able to make out the fading outline of her skinny frame. "Thas all right! Go on and leave me if you wont! You gonna miss me when I'm gone!"

He got up and stumbled to the huge oak tree and unzipped his pants to take a leak.

Meanwhile, Sean came back outside and set down the bag of potting soil.

Standing on opposite sides of the big oak, neither man noticed the other right off. Sean knelt to open the bag and stood up to stretch his legs. At that moment, The Hawk turned to leave. Zipping his pants, he took a few sloppy steps forward.

That's when it happened: The two men's eyes met, each staring at the other through the grim prism of history.

Sean reached down and grabbed his garden hoe, standing ready to defend his life. "Don't move! . . . I don't have any money!"

The Hawk squinted. "Me, neither."

Sean tried to run inside to dial 911, but found he couldn't move. The Hawk tried to dash away, but found *he* couldn't move. So they each stood there, frozen, staring.

The Hawk finally broke the stalemate. He took two slow sideways steps, like a child tipping cautiously across a wet kitchen floor. Moving with all the dignity a drunk can muster, he picked up the pace, heading speedily toward his place, one street over.

Sean watched and waited, still gripping the hoe. When he was sure the intruder was a safe distance away, he dashed into the kitchen and slumped heavily against a wall.

Sandy was busy pouring drinks. She swung around.

"Sean. What's wrong?"

He let out a great, big sigh. "Thank God! I made it! I was almost mugged!"

"What?!"

"A man! He sneaked right up on me! I chased him off with the garden hoe!"

Meanwhile, The Hawk scurried around the corner and stopped near a neighbor's house to catch his breath. He leaned against the house and considered that he could have been arrested for something.

The brief, harrowing encounter left both men shaken and wondering what unknown dangers lurked ahead.

# Chapter 15

On the way past the mini-mart one day, Barlowe bumped into Henny Penn and one of his boys. This day, Henny wore a blue velour jogging suit. (He owned every color jogging suit there was to own.) He sported high-end sneakers, white and new. In one hand he held a toothbrush, used to spruce the sneakers.

Barlowe didn't care for Henny. More and more, during his neighborhood patrols, he had seen Henny scouting out near the Purple Palace, supervising graft and prostitution.

Henny saw Barlowe patrolling, too.

"Yo," he said now, as he brushed past Barlowe coming around the corner. "You wanna be a lawman when you grow up?"

Barlowe fixed on him with a wicked gaze and pointed a finger in his face. "Don't play with me, boy. I ain't to be played with. Hear?"

Henny could see in Barlowe's eyes that he meant what he said. Everybody else around there knew, too. Barlowe was cockstrong. He had knocked a man cold one day, right out there in front of the store.

Still, Henny waved Barlowe off. "Whatever." He and his partner went in the store.

Barlowe continued up the sidewalk on Auburn Avenue, thinking that it wouldn't bother him if Caesar got ahold of Henny Penn.

He headed southwest into the Sweet Auburn district, a compact, quarter-mile stretch of black-owned businesses that flowed from the Old Fourth Ward into downtown Atlanta. He passed places that sold Caribbean music, Ethiopian food and clothes from Ghana. He breezed by the Masonic lodge, where old men in tasseled fezzes claimed to know the secrets of the pyramids. He passed teenagers hanging out in low-riding baggy pants, and he saw old-school hustlers, sporting flashy threads from yesteryear.

Near the corner of Auburn and Bell he stepped into the Black Leopard Cafe, a gritty bar with a hand-painted sign hanging over the door:

**Every Hour Is Happy Hour!**

He hadn't been there in a while. He sat near the window and ordered a beer. He looked around, noting the flimsy tables scattered about. They looked like secondhand card tables, with folding chairs shoved up against each one. All around the room the walls were decorated with black-and-white glossies of blues and jazz greats: B. B. King, Bobby Blue Bland, Sarah Vaughan, Miles and others.

Two pretty young ladies sat at a table nearby. They wore different clothes but somehow looked the same: Spike heels; skirts rising high on shapely thighs; slinky blouses that showed lots of flesh. The women sat with their legs crossed just so, like the clueless beauties used as stage props on BET. They chatted and pretended not to notice the hungry stares from men around the room.

Barlowe considered sending drinks to the table. Then he thought better of taking the risk. Finally, the ladies stood up to leave. Tyrone appeared in the doorway, briefly blocking the exit. He leaned down and peered above the rim of a pair of sunshades, set delicately on the tip of his nose. He whispered something to one of the women. She giggled and slid past, brushing lightly against him as she disappeared.

Tyrone moseyed to Barlowe's table, nodding toward the doorway.

"You see that?"

"Yeah."

"Poke chops, smothered in gravy!"

When the waitress returned, Tyrone gave her the up and down. "Hey, precious."

She almost blushed. Tyrone's eyes rode her backside as she took their orders and slinked away. He reared back in his chair and turned to Barlowe. "Talk fast, Unk. I got thangs to do."

Barlowe looked askance at his nephew. "I hope you not takin somebody to the house."

"I'm straight. This lady got her own crib."

Barlowe studied Tyrone's face. "Where you meet all these women, anyhow?"

Tyrone bent down to tie a shoelace. "You know what they say: Produce, baby."

"What?"

"Produce section in the grocery stoe."

"You serous?"

"Is true. Honeys be hangin out near the fruits and lettuce and shit."

"Produce, huh?"

"Yeah, produce."

"What happened to that gal you were runnin after last month?"

"Who, Lucy?"

"The one you said you could marry."

"Oh, Vicky!"

"Yeah." Tyrone had brought Vicky to the house once. Barlowe wished he had met her first. "She was pretty."

"Nah," said Tyrone. "She weren't my type."

"Why not?"

"Biscuit heels."

"What?"

"Biscuit heels. Ash all on the back of her feet . . . I couldn't work wit that."

When the waitress brought their drinks, the two men sat in silence awhile, each taking a sip every now and then. Barlowe got up to go to the bathroom. Tyrone studied his awkward gait. The khakis, he thought, were a bit too tight. Tyrone would never wear *his* pants that snug.

When Barlowe returned, Tyrone glanced at his watch and leaned forward. "So, Unk. Whas up? Tell me what you wanna talk about."

"I wonted to ax about your job."

"What?"

"How they treatin you?"

"Fine, man. They treatin me fine."

"You workin hard?"

"Hell naw! Me and some dudes got a system goin. We punch the clock and take turns sleepin in the back. Sometimes we go get steak or beer and come back in time to punch out."

Barlowe appeared concerned. "Everything okay?"

"Tell you the truth, I'm spoiled, man. If they made me work eight hours, I'd haveta file a grievance."

"You gonna be all right for a while? You not bout to quit or nothin, right?"

"Uh-uh. Why you axin, anyway?"

"I got somethin I'm tryin to do."

"Nigger, what you tryin to do?"

"The *house*, man. I'm tryin to nail down the house. Mr. Crawford promised that when he sells he'll give me first dibs and a break on the price."

Tyrone scowled. "So, Unk."

"Yeah?"

"Tell me the *real* reason why you wanna buy this house."

Barlowe's lips parted, like he was about to speak, then he stopped himself. It struck him that nobody in his family had ever owned a home. He came from generations of renters; people like his daddy in Milledgeville, who'd leased land from *them* all their lives. There was a great big old world out there, and as long as Barlowe could remember, none of his people had ever owned much of anything in it. And they had accepted owning nothing as simple proof of the way things are.

So how could he convey the depth of his yearning to Tyrone, who was a spitting reflection of such resignation? How could he explain to Tyrone, who really didn't give a rat's ass about such things?

"Is time," he said, after a long pause.

"Is *time*? Thas all you gotta say? Is *time*? What you mean is *time*?"

Barlowe sat up straight. "They say you save on taxes when you own a house."

"Yeah?"

"Yeah. They say you save a lotta money."

"I bet you *spend* a lot, too."

Barlowe glanced out the window. There was an old man out on the walk, begging for coins.

"Ty. I'm grown."

"What you wont, nigger, a trophy?"

"I'm a grown man, Ty."

"So. What you wont?"

Tyrone laughed. Barlowe's mouth turned up in a grin, but no sound came out.

"A grown man gotta settle down."

Tyrone shook his head. "I worry bout you."

"What you worry bout, Ty?"

"I worry you gonna fuck around and make life complicated."

"Life gets complicated when you get grown. Thas jus the way it is."

"That ain't how it gotta be. Take *me*." Tyrone poked a finger at his chest. "Me, I'm happy with the simple thangs: I try to stay outta jail, keep a li'l money in my pocket and git a li'l pussy ever now and then, and I'm set."

Barlowe gulped beer and puckered. "Yeah, but I can't put my hands on that. A house is somethin you can put your hands on. Know what I mean?"

Tyrone looked through him without responding. Barlowe finished his beer and ordered another.

"When you gonna buy?"

"I figure I might have enough saved sometime within the next year or two." He looked Tyrone in the eye. "Thas why I wonted to talk to you. I'm gonna have to raise the rent."

Tyrone clucked his tongue and leaned back hard against the chair. "I *knew* that was comin soon or later. I knew it, I knew it, I knew it!"

"Not much," said Barlowe. "Maybe twenny, thirty extra, thas all . . . You okay with that?"

"Ain't got no choice but to be okay wit it. Do I?"

"You always got a choice. Might not be one you like, but you got one."

After a long stretch of silence, Tyrone said, "You gonna have a mortgage, man."

"I thought about that. Thas why I need to know how is going on your job. I need to *know* we got the money comin in."

"You really thank old man Crawford gon give you a break on the price?"

"Thas what he said."

Barlowe pondered the folly in that remark. It implied some measure of faith on his part. Faith in Crawford's promise required him to vouch for the soul of a white man, which, on its face, seemed a crazy thing to try to do. Besides, his read on Crawford was more intuitive than concrete. His read on Crawford had evolved only in relation to other white men he had come across. Men like Spivey. Crawford was strange in his own way, but Billy was worse than strange. Above all else, Billy was fiercely committed to being white. That was his main source of being and pride. Crawford seemed more green than white. More than anything, he pledged allegiance to the dollar.

Barlowe was pretty sure his instincts about Crawford were on point, but he dared not say that to his nephew.

Tyrone smiled a wry smile. He had always looked up to his uncle. Even in those times when he felt fairly fed up with Barlowe's lectures about Caesar, Tyrone respected him for having the forthrightness to call life the way he saw it.

Now he pitied Barlowe. His uncle seemed now to nurture a desperation so urgent it led him to see what he wanted to see, rather than what he knew, what he must have known, was really there.

Tyrone glanced over the rim of his shades. "You sho puttin Crawford on a high horsie."

"Well, Ty, *you* seem to like him a lot. You even promised to take him out."

"Sheeeiiiitt! I ain't takin that cracker nowhere. I jus tell im that to have some fun. I like to see them big eyes a his rollin round . . . I ain't takin him nowhere. You know better 'n that." He stared into his glass.

"Crawford aight for a white man, but I ain't gon trust him no farther than I can sling him. And *you* bet not trust him, neither."

Barlowe remained quiet. Now he almost regretted raising the issue. He looked around the room again. In the corner behind them was a rusty, dimly lit jukebox that still played three tunes for a quarter on 45s. It blinked a lot, like it was about to cough and die. At that moment, Sam Cooke was moaning through a pair of scratched-up speakers.

Responding to the music, a man in highwater pants rose from his seat with no prompting at all. Drawn back to a time and place that only he could see, the man danced slowly on the floor. His eyes were closed, and he held an imaginary partner close to him.

"Okay," said Barlowe. "Two months, and then we change the rent."

"Aight." Tyrone rose to leave. "Gotta go, man. Gotta go."

Barlowe paid the bill and got up, too. They stepped from the near-darkness of the Black Leopard into the brightness outside. Tyrone headed to catch the bus. Barlowe started back up Auburn Avenue, toward home. He strolled up the street, absorbing the energy around him. There were people walking everywhere; Cadillacs and hoopties parked back-to-back in front of beauty salons, bars and barbershops. Outdoor vendors selling fish sandwiches with hot sauce, and barbecue ribs, cooked on open pits.

*The richest Negro street in the world . . .*

It struck him that on that street a person could get just about anything life had to offer. You could buy groceries, get your teeth fixed or cop a vial of crack cocaine; you could get discount life insurance (term or whole life), take in a foot-stomping church service (AME, Pentecostal or down-home Baptist) and attend to your banking needs; you could get a seven-dollar haircut, a good game of nine-ball and a back-alley blow job, all on the same block.

Even the business of death could be tended to in "Sweet Auburn." Barlowe passed a funeral home with a bright red banner out front:

### COMPLETE FUNERALS
### AS LOW AS $2,795

As he approached the Martin Luther King historic home, a group of tourists stood out front and posed for pictures while they listened to a preacher talking from the top of the steps. Barlowe knew the minister by reputation: His name was Reverend Dr. Owen J. Pickering, Jr. He was a civil rights veteran, part of a cult of old-school preachers who claimed to have marched at the right hand of Martin Luther King. To hear them tell it, they all had been close confidants to "Mah-tin." They called themselves King's "lieutenants" and insisted on being referred to as Reverend Dr. So-and-so, even if they had never been near a seminary.

The boys at the store said that of the many pretenders, Pickering had come closest to being an authentic King disciple. Back in the '60s, he had begun to make a name for himself as a gifted young preacher.

Now he pastored The Way of the Cross Baptist Church and sometimes led groups of people to the King home, where he regaled them with stories about his old friend.

Standing on the sidewalk, Barlowe paused, waiting to walk past a man aiming a camera for a snapshot of the preacher framed in the forefront of the famous house. When the shot was done, the tourists smiled, satisfied they'd captured a precious piece of living history to show off to friends back home.

Barlowe shuddered. He still shivered sometimes when he passed the two-story, brown-and-yellow frame house. Here was Martin Luther King's birth home, and he, Barlowe Reed, lived only three blocks away. He was connected to important history. He added a bit more bounce to his step.

Treading along, he waved at a man named Sanford, who was traveling in the opposite direction, across the street. Then he headed for the mini-mart to get his lottery tickets. He greeted the boys, who stood around arguing about Lena Horne. Willie claimed to have reliable knowledge that Lena had once shacked up with a white man in Europe. Amos accused Willie of telling a bald-faced lie.

Barlowe left before the debate was settled. He crossed the street and waved at Mr. Smith, who was outdoors working on his old rundown car.

Across the way, near the far side of Randolph Street, a blue Volvo pulled up to the curb. Two white men sprang out and took to the sidewalks. One began jotting notes on a legal pad. The other, a short necktie resting on his round belly, walked two steps ahead. They paraded up and down the block, pointing at this house and that one.

As the two men worked their way toward Edgewood Avenue, people stopped what they were doing and zeroed in: Barlowe paused at the end of his walkway; the elders stood stark still in front of the store; Mr. Smith leaned against the hood of his old car, folding his arms across his chest.

Nobody uttered a word, but their eyes spoke collectively. Collectively, their eyes said: *So this is how it happens.* They had heard of far-off regions where dark natives were driven from their land. They had been told about places where people's homes were taken, then gutted and used as kindling for romantic fires. But in all that hearing they never imagined how the process looked day-to-day.

Now they saw. More and more, they laid wary eyes on pale people riding through the neighborhood, scoping. As change swept through the Old Fourth Ward, the people first looked on with interest, then concern. With each passing month, that concern grew in nervous bits and pieces.

There were those who set out early to defend their ground. They noted the beginnings of the trickle—and pondered ways to plug the leak.

# Chapter 16

*A* quick pass-through. That's all it was supposed to be. A quick pass-through, and now it's home.

*Yes, indeed. Life can turn on a dime. A quarter can flip it completely. But life can turn on a single dime.*

Sean sat at home, thinking. Sandy had gone to her evening meditation class, which pleased him because it gave him some time alone. Sean loved spending time with his wife, but Sandy was so forceful in her opinions that it was hard sometimes to separate her thinking from his own. Now that she was gone he could be sure his thoughts belonged to him.

He gazed out the front window into the street and pondered the implications of the new address. This wasn't exactly what they had in mind a few years back, when they were lured from Philadelphia by good-paying jobs. When they first arrived, the Gilmores moved out to Forsyth County. They bought a sprawling, four-bedroom, ranch-style house for $120,000, a bargain unheard of in the pricey North. Their new home rested on a swath of land four times the size of the stingy clump of grass in Philly. They settled in, confident they had come upon the fabled New South they'd read so much about; the New South of sweet tea and magnolia trees (minus the beer-bellied boys in Red

Man caps); the New South of mild weather and warm hospitality, even toward Yankees like them.

In that first year, the Gilmores thought they'd died and gone to heaven. In time, though, flaws appeared in their New South paradise. The sterile suburban streets were one thing; traffic stress was quite another, especially for Sandy, who commuted some thirty miles from Forsyth to the family services agency in downtown Atlanta, where she worked.

After two years of fighting traffic jams, the Gilmores agreed a change was in order. Some urban ambience might do them some good. They signed on with Joe Folkes, who promised to find them the house they were looking for. Now Sean recalled Joe's description of the Old Fourth Ward.

"Awesome potential!"

If it had been up to Sean alone, he and Sandy would never have entertained the idea of moving there. He had nothing against *them*, mind you. He measured himself far more tolerant than the average man. But as for Joe's proposal, there were too many risks involved. That near-robbery in Sean's backyard had proven that.

He had agreed to visit the neighborhood, mainly to appease his strong-willed wife. He'd felt confident in the logical outcome of that exercise: As he'd figured, they would visit the ward and Sandy would see for herself that it was not a sensible option. She'd come away pleased with herself for even considering such a thing. Then they would get on in earnest with the housing search; they'd look some-place that made more sense.

As far as the decision to buy the house, Sean had actually surprised himself. He had been shocked to come upon such a lovely place, and one so affordable, too. It was far more appealing than the overpriced dumps they'd explored in the Yuppie havens.

Now, sitting alone, Sean acknowledged his decision to buy also was influenced by other factors; namely a weekend trip he and Sandy had taken around that time to visit her family in Connecticut. One evening, while they were all having dinner at the estate (Sean called it the Big House), he began lamenting the hassles of house-hunting in

Atlanta. When he mentioned in passing that they planned next to explore an in-town black area, Sandy's father furrowed his thick eyebrows and began to yell.

"Insane!" He insisted that no child of Fulton Peterson's should be "forced" to even consider such a thing. He ranted on, endlessly it seemed, about how his daughter didn't need to live "desperate."

Mrs. Peterson, a doting appendage if there ever was one, ignored Sandy's protests and echoed her husband's concerns.

"Sandy, you weren't raised that way. You just weren't brought up like that."

The old man directed his assault mostly at Sean, as if the house-hunting thing was all his fault.

What a scene! Sean was thrilled when, finally, they got away from there.

He would never tell Sandy, but he actually hated her father. The man was a boorish egomaniac! That was apparent from the very start, beginning with their wedding. They had planned a modest ceremony in the courtyard of a bed-and-breakfast. Sandy's father refused to attend unless the ceremony was relocated to a place more "suitable." The wedding date was changed and the location shifted, all to satisfy *him*.

Everything in that family was done to accommodate the old man. Sean had privately nicknamed him "The Captain."

And then there was the time his father-in-law offered Sean a job working at his big financial management firm. He presented the offer under the guise of being supportive of the young newlyweds.

Sean knew what that was really about. It was about the little problem her daddy seemed to have with Sean's blue-collar bloodlines; the fact that both his father and grandfather had worked in the Pittsburgh steel mills.

Sean also suspected the job offer sprang from some private fear of the old man's that, as a computer repairman, his son-in-law wouldn't earn enough bread to support Sandy in the lavish manner she was accustomed to.

In the end, Sean turned down the offer. He didn't need the old man's money. Ever since he and Sandy began dating in college she'd made it clear that she didn't need it, either.

In the years they'd been together, Sean came close, many times, to telling The Captain what he thought of him. And he would have, too, if not for fear it would cause Sandy undue stress. So Sean usually zipped his lips to keep her happy, even during those times when the old man took maddening potshots, clearly meant to humiliate him.

Sean couldn't tolerate humiliation. Humiliation sometimes sent him into a trembling rage.

During the weekend visit to Connecticut, though, he'd felt empowered by something he discovered. He stumbled upon the one weapon that could be used to counter, and even preempt, his father-in-law's stinging jabs.

The weapon was this: The very mention of *them* made the tiny little hairs on Fulton Peterson's big, bald head stand on end. Hearing the dinner talk about his daughter's considering moving into an urban area, the veins in The Captain's neck bulged so thick it looked like he might treat Sean to an aneurysm.

Now Sean got up to get a drink of water, glancing at the clock. Sandy would be coming home soon. *Yeah*, he thought. *The Captain is a flaming bigot.*

He had to admit, he got a real rush in knowing he had finally hit upon a way to yank the old man's chain. As role reversals went it was downright exhilarating. Standing at the refrigerator, a smile crept across Sean's face. He could hardly wait to invite the Petersons to visit their new home.

He thought again about the recent backyard encounter with that drunken man near the old oak tree. It left him unsettled still. He would hate more than anything than to be forced to admit what he was already beginning to suspect: that The Captain's ominous predictions about their new neighborhood just might come true.

# Chapter 17

The Old Fourth Ward Beautification Committee gathered only once every three months. And it was a good thing, too, because that was about all its members could stand. The group gathered in the community's shining jewel, the Martin Luther King, Jr. Center for Nonviolent Social Change.

On paper the Beautification Committee membership numbered thirty-three. But only about nine people could be counted on as regulars. Others had signed up, not so much because they were thrilled about the prospect of Saturday morning cleanup campaigns and the patient planting of marigolds. They signed up because at one time or another they'd been cornered, collared and asked to join. One year, the committee launched an aggressive door-to-door recruitment drive.

On this Saturday morning, Barlowe was one of two relative newcomers to the group. He'd recently joined out of concern for the improving, but still-patchy appearance of the neighborhood.

The meeting started slowly. They discussed the horticultural implications of the changing season. They debated the need to plant more begonias and tulips in the center of the triangular cobblestone public space at Auburn Avenue and Randolph Street.

The final item to be considered, curiously titled "Selection," promised to be a more delicate matter. It concerned the racial persuasion of two people chosen as finalists for the annual Old Fourth Ward Green Thumb Prize. In the past decade, the award had rotated almost solely among three old women—all retirees with nothing but time on their hands to make their yards look like full-page glossies in *House & Garden* magazine.

But this year, there were two new finalists, both young white couples that had only recently moved to the ward.

"I ain't doin it!" Wendell Mabry bellowed, his arms folded defiantly across a pumpkin gut. "I don't kere if they the last people left on Gawd's urth. I ain't givin no white folks the Green Thumb prize."

Wendell, a stocky stub of a man who always kept a toothpick dangling from his mouth, was born and raised in the Old Fourth Ward. He'd moved away to Indiana some years ago. When his parents died, he returned to look after the family home. The family home meant everything to him.

"I'm afraid, Mr. Mabry, that you have no choice." Lula Simmons spoke crisply, enunciating every word. "Everybody can see as plain as day that those people won. It's only fitting and fair to give them the prize."

"Fair?! Fair?!" That word set Barlowe off. "Don't talk to us about *fair!*"

The committee members nodded in collective agreement. That word had lost meaning centuries ago.

Not content to argue on the basis of history alone, Wendell sought to frame his protest in technical terms: Was it fair, he asked, in so many words, for lay gardeners in the ward, who learned by painstaking toil and error, to compete against the studied skills of trained professionals?

"Them white folks didn't perty up they yards theyselves! They went and hired a archatet!"

"*Landscape* architect," Lula interjected.

"Whatever. The pernt is, them people cheated!"

Lula regretted that her unpolished neighbors failed to grasp the many benefits that could accrue from having *them* in the community.

She understood, if no one else did, that the very presence of whites added prestige and value to a place.

"I'll tell you what," she said, determined to move the process along. "Let's just do the proper thing. And if anyone feels they have a legitimate grievance, invite them to Irwin Street to inspect those people's yards for themselves. If they're forthright they'll have to admit that we did the right and proper thing."

When she spoke, Lula held her nose turned up, as if she had always done the right and proper thing. And it was true, to the best of her knowledge. Even as a teenager she was never one to be caught like other girls, smooching in cars with her clothes all askew and legs flung about. It wasn't right. It wasn't proper.

Studying her tied-back hair and huge eyeglasses, Barlowe guessed Lula had probably always seemed old, even when she was young.

"We must be ethical." She rolled her eyes at him. "Above all, we must be fair."

"Well," said Wendell, "it don't seem fair to let *them* come in and start winnin prizes right away."

That said, Miss Carol Lilly jumped in. As committee chair, she felt obligated to mediate.

"Somebody show me where it says in the rule book that folks gotta do the yard work theyselves."

Wendell drew a spare toothpick from his breast pocket and aimed it at her like a bayonet. "There ain't no rule book, which means there ain't no rules."

"There are *implicit* guidelines," noted Lula. "Implicit guidelines are always useful."

Wendell snorted like an angry bull. "Whasa matter wit y'all!? Dontcha unnerstand? We can make up some daggone rules!"

"No we cain't," Miss Carol Lilly grunted. "Everbody know all we ever jerdged people on is how perty they yards and gardens were. We ain't never axed nobody how they yards got that way.

"And you can see well as anybody that some a *them* got some perty yards. They got 'xotic flowers and plants that I ain't even seen befoe."

She was right. With all the hemming and hawing about the perils of "whitey" coming in, there was no denying that the neighborhood was slowly flowering into a more attractive place. One couple had installed a Chinese water garden, complete with marble sculptures. Out front they'd planted stocky shrubs and elephant ears, and lined each side of their walk with monkey grass.

Another white family had settled on a funky southwestern motif, with cacti imported all the way from the Nevada desert. No question; it was beautiful.

Barlowe had noticed that the people next door to him did their own yard work. But what consolation was that? They were still *there*, weren't they? For weeks after the Gilmores moved in, he would wake up mornings and look outdoors, hoping they had somehow disappeared.

Clarence Sykes, Wendell's friend and poker buddy, had remained quiet throughout most of the debate. Now he weighed in, prompted mostly by a simmering resentment that the women on the committee seemed to be running things.

"What it gon look like if you give *them* that award wit all these black people livin out chere?"

"Hush, Clance," said Miss Carol Lilly. "Ain't nobody stopped other folks out chere from competin. They coulda got out in they yards and planted, just like them white folks done."

Wendell yanked the toothpick from his mouth and snapped it in two. "You know well as me, folks ain't got spare change to be puttin down fertlizer every time the dang seasons change."

"Oh, *reaallly*?" An exasperated Lula clucked her tongue. "Then how much does it cost to bend your posterior down and pick up trash?"

Other committee members kept quiet on that point. They recalled the many Saturdays they'd spent in that very room, wracking their brains to find ways to persuade neighbors to show more community pride. Some people maintained their yards quite nicely, while others seemed not to care at all.

"I don't know why we keep having the dang competition in the first place," Clarence complained. "The same three people win alla time, anyway. We should let somebody else win."

"Mr. Sykes." Lula sounded very weary now. "What part of this conversation don't you comprehend? That's exactly what we're proposing to do—allow someone else to win."

He waved her off. "Oh, woman, you know what I mean."

The debate raged on like that for another ten minutes until other committee members spoke up. After his initial outburst, Barlowe kept quiet and listened. He had definite views, and more to say, but being a renter, he felt less entitled to force debate with people who owned their homes.

Meanwhile, somebody in the middle row raised a hand. "Maybe we need to brainstorm ways of doing a better job getting the word out about the competition."

It was a fine-boned young woman named Marvetta Green. Smart, pretty and confident, Marvetta was one of several single black women to recently buy homes in the ward. Barlowe had met her before, and they'd chatted briefly. He looked upon her with new interest now.

"Clearly, we need to do more to expand the pool of people who compete for the award."

"Been there, done that." Miss Carol Lilly's gruff tone suggested she doubted a woman with a waistline trim as Marvetta's had anything of use or substance to say. Some years back, Miss Carol Lilly had lost her husband to a trim-hipped woman. The only thing she had to show for her ceaseless pain was the house she was awarded in the divorce.

"It—jus—ain't—gonna—work." She uttered each word slowly, as if Marvetta was dim-witted or hard of hearing.

Marvetta shot back. "Have you put flyers on people's doors? Have you offered better prizes than the plaques you normally hand out to winners?"

"Prizes like what?"

"Instead of a plaque we could offer cash prizes or free grass and flower seeds."

"I think thas a good idea!" Wendell was interested to hear what else the pretty gal had to say.

Miss Carol Lilly shot him a look that carried the force of a backhand.

"We ain't got a *dime* in the budget as it is. How we gonna offer somethin we ain't got?"

"Maybe we on the committee could all pitch in somethin extra." When he spoke, Barlowe glanced at Marvetta, but she had turned her attention to Lula Simmons, who raised her hand.

"You can do anything you want to attract more people, but don't be surprised or offended when our Caucasian neighbors start showing up. A few have already approached me and inquired about the committee. So we must be right and proper in our positions. We must be fair in how we conduct our—"

Marvetta broke in. "As the committee that oversees the selection process, we're well within our rights to dictate the criteria for the award. Let's reexamine the wording. Maybe it's time to update the language."

Except for Lula, whose pursed lips signaled she was quite displeased, the committee veterans looked sideways at each other, wondering why they hadn't thought of that.

"Thas right!" barked Wendell. "We'll review the daggone guidelines!"

Lula pouted, acutely aware that she was outnumbered.

With Marvetta's guidance the wording was doctored so expertly that it appeared the award criteria had been left the same.

The original document said: *Winners are awarded the Green Thumb Prize based on the overall beauty of their yards, shrubs and flower beds.*

The committee simply tacked on extra language: *Winners are awarded the Green Thumb Prize based on the overall beauty of their yards, shrubs and flower beds, as a result of work wrought by their own hands.*

For good measure, committee members cast anonymous ballots to select a winner.

In the final vote, one of the old retirees—a black woman who had lived in the Old Fourth Ward for twenty years—won the Green Thumb Prize.

For the time being, all was right again with the world.

# Chapter 18

With the meeting over, committee members mingled briefly, some chatting about the outcome of the vote. Barlowe noticed Marvetta Green preparing to leave. He took a step in her direction but was halted by a voice calling to him from across the room. It was Miss Carol Lilly. She yoo-hooed, waving him over with a flabby arm.

"I ever tell you bout my niece?"

"No, ma'am. You didn't." He glanced toward the door, looking for Marvetta.

"Pretty gal," crowed Miss Carol Lilly. "I want you should meet her."

Barlowe scratched his chin, unsure what to say to that.

"My niece got meat on her bones." Miss Carol Lilly rolled her eyes, glancing at Marvetta across the room. "And honey, that girl can *burn*! I tole her bout you one day, and she bout grinned from ear to ear."

Barlowe suspected what brought on the sudden matchmaking interest from Miss Carol Lilly. She had spied him coming in from church one day, dressed in the only suit he owned. She'd pegged him as a nice man, and eligible, with a steady job. Now there was a bull's-eye marked on his chest.

"Smiled ear to ear, huh?"

"Yeah. I want you should meet her."

Barlowe was hornier than a cat in summer heat. Still, he wondered, what sense was there in getting tangled up with somebody blood-tied to Miss Carol Lilly? If relations flopped, it could mean trouble. And what if the niece was just like Miss Carol Lilly—heavy-breasted and full of Christian cheer?

Glancing at his watch, Barlowe told Miss Carol Lilly he'd love to hear more, some other time, but now he had to leave.

She waddled out the front door, waving good-bye.

Barlowe chitchatted with a few other committee members and tried not to seem so clearly interested in Marvetta Green. At the moment, Wendell Mabry had her hemmed up in a corner, grinning up close in her face like she was some tasty church dinner he planned to devour.

Finally, the remaining committee members shuffled toward the exit. When Marvetta got outdoors, Barlowe rushed to catch up.

"Marvetta, you walkin home?"

"Yes. You going that way?"

"Matter of fact, I am."

They strolled and talked, mostly about the beautification drive and the neighborhood. Up ahead, Viola and The Hawk stumbled past the mini-mart.

"Thanks for helpin us out in there. We were stuck, bad. That coulda gone on for days."

"That Carol Lilly," said Marvetta, "is an effortless ass."

*An effortless ass.* He liked the way she put her words together. *An effortless ass.* He wished he could put words together like that.

"How'd you vote?" asked Barlowe.

"I'm not telling. How'd *you* vote?"

"I ain't tellin, neither."

They chuckled and walked and talked some more. Strolling along, Barlowe stole a better look. Marvetta had a mod, artsy look about her, which he really liked. She wore tinted sunshades, and beyond them he saw deep-set, intelligent eyes. Unlike the librarian Rachel Worthman, Marvetta's eyes revealed light and life, and maybe even a little fire. She wore a cute gray blouse with matching shorts and a straw hat with lit-tle plastic flowers poking out. She wore sandals, and her toenails were painted bright red. She was easy on the eyes, all right. All the pieces right in place.

Barlowe told her about the house that he rented but planned to buy. She told him about her renovation project a few blocks over from where he lived. She was restoring her 1920s Queen Anne cottage.

"I just had stained glass put in the window on the stairway landing and I'm having skylights installed in my bedroom . . . Wanna see?"

"Sure."

Barlowe felt a sudden rush. Just what did she want him to see? Her house? Only her house? Was she being friendly, or what?

He picked up the pace, every few steps sneaking a peek at those bright red toenails.

They reached Marvetta's place on Bradley Street. It was a long, narrow two-story house, unlike his place, which was short and squat. She had decorated her yard with flowers and put in an elegant oak door, with a stained-glass window out front.

Inside, she showed him around, gliding through the living room like a museum guide. She knew the house's history and had even collected gossip about the former owners. She explained in detail the work she'd had done, and outlined other projects she was planning to do.

Barlowe noted that Marvetta's decorating taste was much more sophisticated than Nell's. Nell had furnished her condo with lots of cheap brass and flashy chairs. But Marvetta had classic furniture, and cultured artwork lined the walls. Strolling through, Barlowe glanced at family photos and noted there were no pictures or signs of a boyfriend. She led him to her bedroom upstairs and showed him around. Seeing no lovers' photos in there, either, he guessed again that she had no man to speak of. Maybe she was separated or divorced.

He fixed his eyes on her queen-size bed. It was a tall canopy, covered with a blue comforter and lots of frilly pillows. Barlowe imagined himself stretched out there after making love. He could see himself lying on his back, his hands resting contentedly behind his head.

The room overlooked a backyard surrounded by leafy trees. The trees shielded a view of her neighbor's house, giving it a closed-in, private, courtyard feel.

"I'm gonna have large windows placed here, and a French door leading to a balcony. I wanna be able to sit out there and read the paper on weekend mornings."

Barlowe imagined himself sitting out there reading the paper, too. "This is real nice," he said. "Real nice."

"*Gracias.*"

When they returned downstairs, he felt a mild tension surging through his thigh.

"Can I use your bathroom?"

"It's right down the hall."

He rushed to the bathroom and closed the door. He stood there a moment, eyes closed, and took in a deep breath, trying to force excess air from his chest. He opened his eyes with the sudden awareness of where he was: inside the home of a beautiful woman; a beautiful woman who happened to live close enough for him to drop by from time to time to borrow a cup of sugar.

Marvetta was a few steps up from the young, rough-hewn women he was used to. He wondered what she thought of him. There was no real way of knowing. She was friendly, but there was no *vibe*, no yearning or energy popping from her pores.

Now he looked around. On top of the toilet was a box of pink tissue; an ornamental bowl on the counter, filled with potpourri. The door to the medicine cabinet was slightly cracked. He leaned over and peeked. On the end of the shelf nearest him, there was nail polish and hair remover.

His imagination caught fire. In his mind's eye, he could see Marvetta in this bathroom, doing very private things. He stared at the toilet and pictured her sitting there, her beautiful raw bottom, right there on that seat.

He felt closer to her now. He unzipped his pants and relieved himself. When he was done, he critiqued himself in the full-length mirror behind the door. His khaki uniform was crisp and clean, but the belt and work shoes were a bit worn. He decided he needed to do better.

Suddenly, he heard footsteps. She was headed toward the back of the house. He went into the living room, sat down and picked up *Ebony* magazine. How long had he been gone? Five minutes? Ten? How long?

Marvetta sat down across from him and crossed her legs. "Can I get you anything? Juice or tea?"

"No, thanks." He could see light strands of hair running down her forearms. He tried to avoid staring.

"So, Mr. Barlowe." She homed in on him. "Tell me, what has life been like for you?"

The question struck him as odd. "I ain't too sure I know how to answer that."

"Try answering it straight." She smiled.

"Well." He cleared his throat. "Life is complicated. Seems like it comes at you every day."

"Sometimes you get weekends off."

"Sometimes. Yeah."

"Are you from Atlanta?"

"No. Milledgeville."

"You grew up there?"

"Yep. A country boy. And you?"

"I was born here."

"What high school did you go to?"

"Booker T. Washington."

He wanted to ask her age.

"When did you graduate?" asked Marvetta.

"I didn't."

"You dropped out?"

"Leventh grade . . . Well, actually, they axed me to leave."

"Why?"

"I had problems."

"What kind of problems?"

He found her directness stimulating.

"I didn't like some a the things they tried to tell me."

"Things like what?"

"It was like they tried to pretend the world made sense . . . I guess it made sense for them, but not for me . . . The stuff they taught . . . Crazy. It jus didn't make sense."

"Like Christopher?"

"Yeah, Christopher."

Marvetta leaned back in her seat and nodded, a knowing look spreading across her face. She waited. He paused.

"That was bad enough," he said, "but then they tried to make me write that stuff down on paper . . . It was one thing to *say* it. It was another to have to write it down. It was like writing it down made it permanent. Know what I mean?"

"I see."

He paused again, then: "After a while, I told the teacher I wouldn't write down some a that stuff, and nobody was gonna make me. So they kicked me out. Told me to come back when I was ready to learn.

"I left and never went back. Took up printing in trade school. After that, I got a job. Been workin ever since."

He finished talking and looked at Marvetta, wondering what she was thinking. She appeared concerned.

"In hindsight, do you think that was the best way to handle that situation?"

"It was the best I knew."

"Well." She seemed to be searching for the right words. "You took a stand. Sometimes that can cost you."

He wondered if it was costing him now.

They talked some more. He learned Marvetta was an engineer. She had a mother and three sisters in Brooklyn.

After a while, she glanced at her watch. "My! Time has flown!" She stood up. "I'm afraid I've gotta get ready for an engagement . . . Going out to dinner with friends."

Barlowe strained to think of something to say. He felt embarrassed that he'd stayed too long. Oddly, he found himself thinking of Tyrone. What would Tyrone say right now?

"Would you like to get a bite to eat sometime?" It came out sounding awkward, rehearsed.

"What?"

"Or I could cook. I'm decent at cookin certain stuff."

Marvetta shifted to another foot. Her body language suggested she had suffered the discomfort of the clumsy come-on before.

"Actually, my schedule is pretty intense. I'm not sure I could swing dinner anytime soon."

"Okay, then. Maybe we can do somethin when you're free—a movie or somethin."

"We'll see."

She walked Barlowe to the door and said good-bye. He left. Heading down her walkway he felt lonelier than a Carolina country road.

On the way home, he stopped at the Auburn Avenue Mini-Mart. He greeted the boys sitting outside, then went in and browsed around. He bought his lottery tickets and a soda from Juliette James and stepped back out onto the walk. He sat down to play a few games of checkers. He couldn't get his mind off Marvetta Green. *Nice woman. Pretty, and friendly, but not my type.*

He lost three games straight, then went on home. Barlowe climbed the steps and lumbered to the door, eager to bring the day to an end. He slid the key into the hole, then suddenly froze. He thought he heard a noise. It sounded like a scream. Muffled but shrill, it seemed to come from inside the house. He leaned in, holding his head against the door, and listened again. The screaming stopped. Now there was a low, guttural moan.

His mind ran the range of possibilities. What if it was a daytime burglar? What if it was more than one? He considered dashing across to Mr. Smith's house to call the cops, but there might not be time for that. Besides, cops around there were too slow. They always took their time showing up.

He heard noise again; this time it came in short staccato bursts. He had to do something! He had to do something fast!

He took a deep breath and exhaled hard. Then, in one furious motion he turned the key and burst through the door. A spray of sunlight flooded the room and mingled with a thick cloud of reefer smoke. Instinctively, he checked to see if the stereo and TV were still in place. Then he caught something—a movement—in his peripheral view. It came from the sofa. He turned and his eyes nearly popped from the sockets. Right there on the couch was a naked woman. Tyrone was stretched out lying beneath her and on his back. His pants were pulled down to the ankles. Shirtless and smug, he lay there, eyes closed and hands resting behind his head.

Barlowe went slack-jawed. After a moment, he collected himself. He slammed the door and cleared his throat. "Ahem."

Tyrone opened one eye. "Oh, maann!" Now both eyes opened. He shoved the woman aside. She swung around, startled, then turned away. She yanked her panties from the floor and used them to hide her face.

Tyrone rose and strained to clear his head. "Unk! Oh, man! I ain't know you was comin home!"

Barlowe's face pinched tight. "Ty. You promised to respect the house."

Tyrone sat up straight, struggling to gather himself. "Unk. This here is my, er, friend . . . She came over to see my, ah, pigeons."

The woman kept her face averted, refusing to turn around. She didn't have to. Barlowe knew those Coke-bottle hips anywhere: It was Lucretia Wiggins, in all her naked glory.

Barlowe stood there a long moment, staring in disbelief. Then he realized he'd been watching too long. Once again, he cleared his throat, which was dry as parchment paper.

"Ty. I tell you what. I'm gonna make a run. I'll be back in fifteen minutes . . . Clean up the place, okay?"

"Okay, Unk . . ." Tyrone hurriedly gathered the sofa pillows, which had been tossed to the floor. "Hey, man, I'm *real* sorry. I swear, I ain't know you was comin home."

"We'll talk later." The tone was blunt.

Now Lucretia turned and stared at him. Her lips curled, like maybe she was annoyed about being interrupted.

Barlowe left and slammed the door. His heart pounding, he went to his car. *Now what?*

He needed to get away, to catch his breath. He drove around and stopped at the Caribbean restaurant on Auburn Avenue. Inside, he grabbed a table in the far corner. He ordered a soft drink and stared blankly out the window, thinking.

He and Tyrone would have to have another talk, about house rules and goals and things like that. Barlowe told himself that he might need to remind Tyrone about agreements they made when he first moved in.

Tyrone had been living with him for three years now, ever since he got out of prison. After serving his second bid for assault, he'd gone up for parole, twice, and been denied. Tyrone probably would have been turned down a third time if his people hadn't stepped in to help him out. Parole board members refused to release him without firm guarantees that he could meet two conditions: First, he would have to leave Milledgeville—the police chief didn't want him there. Next, he would have to be released into the custody of a relative. Since Barlowe was the only family member to leave home and remain in Georgia, their people appealed to him for help. "He family." They said it like all of a sudden the word meant so much more to them.

Tyrone appealed to Barlowe, too, in rambling, five- and ten-page letters, sent from the joint. He wrote about the confidence he'd gained from learning an electrical trade. He swore to the high heavens that he had changed for good this time. "I'm family," he'd said, begging Barlowe to take him in. "I'm family."

Barlowe consented, reluctantly, to take in Tyrone until he found work and established himself. It was risky, but what choice was there? He was family.

Except for a few petty aggravations, things had worked out all right with Tyrone, at least enough for his uncle to let him extend the stay. Besides, Barlowe needed help with the rent. Most times, Tyrone could be counted on to come up with his half, even when he wasn't working regular. As long as he paid his share there was no real reason not to let him stay.

So Tyrone stayed. They rotated cooking and washing dishes and, as much as could reasonably be expected of two single men, kept the house presentable. Things between them were going well, until this business with Lucretia.

Now a flash of jealousy surged through Barlowe. He downed a few drinks and left. When he got home, Tyrone and Lucretia were nowhere in sight. On the way through the living room, he stopped and stared at the couch. In his mind's eye he saw Lucretia again. She was *stacked*, just like he'd imagined; firm hips spread smooth as butter on toasted bread.

The shape of her body, the texture of her skin, reminded him of someone he preferred not to think about. Almost against his will, he recalled the time he lived with Nell. It was a luscious memory, until he got to the part when she kicked him out . . .

# Chapter 19

He could tell by the way Nell sounded that day that it wasn't a birdcall. Lying in bed, still groggy-eyed, he suspected something was up when she summoned him from the safety of the living room. It was a Saturday morning, when her son, Boo, was awake, instead of late at night, when the boy would be sound asleep. And it wasn't the singsong birdcall voice this time. It was the flat, almost hostile tone reserved for white folks trying to sell you something you don't *ever* want to buy.

Barlowe got up and stumbled out in his boxer shorts, stubbing a toe on a toy along the way. When he reached the living room, Nell sent Boo outside to play. Then she sat down, lit a cigarette and looked at him.

"I need some space, Barlowe. I need to think about some thangs."

"Space?"

She gazed at him, incredulous, like the question was a prime example of The Problem.

"Yeah, space. You know. Time. Alone."

As usual, they tried to talk things over. As always, it ended in frustration.

"I'm sorry, Barlowe," she said, finally. "You cain't have the milk without the cow."

*You cain't have the milk without the cow.* He had heard her say that so many times it was starting to sound like some kind of Buddhist chant. *You cain't have the milk without the cow.*

Barlowe raked a hand through his nappy head and went to the fridge and popped a beer.

"I'm sorry you feel that way, Nell."

Nell took a long, labored drag on the cigarette. "I'm sorry, too." She assured him she knew he was a good man at heart. But in matters pertaining to women, she said, he still had some distance to cover.

Barlowe got up slowly and went to the bedroom to get dressed. On the way out, he stopped in the living room and took in her face. Nell was pretty in a natural way, without all the manicures and facials, which of course she got for free. She had a mustard-colored silk scarf wrapped around her head. He could see the hair pulled back tight underneath.

"I'll come back later to get the rest a my things."

"Okay." That was all she said. "Okay."

Nell said good-bye, and Barlowe left. It was the first time she fired him.

Barlowe drove to Atlanta from Nell's place in Clayton County. He bought his lottery tickets and stopped off at a newspaper stand, then headed downtown to Mitchell Street. Along the way, he passed clusters of homeless people curled up spoon-like in knots along sidewalks and in the entranceways of department stores. He stopped at a bar where he hung out sometimes. The bar was officially closed, but the front door was ajar. There were two workers inside, cleaning up, preparing to open in the afternoon. One, a tall, reedy man with a vicious overbite and bulging eyes, swept the floor. He took short, slow strokes with the broom like he intended to stretch out the chore for the rest of the day.

The bartender, a man called Roach, was busy taking upturned chairs down from the tables. Roach was a big bruiser with amateur jailhouse tattoos splattered on his fat forearms.

"Wrong place, my man," Roach said, when Barlowe's frame filled the doorway. "Waffle House over on Riverdale Road."

Barlowe took a few steps inside. "Roach, I need to squat a minute and work through some things."

Roach saw the confusion in Barlowe's eyes. He had seen that brand of confusion many times before, and even in his own mirror once.

"Tell ya what," he said in a gravelly voice. "I cain't sell you no likker this early, but you can come in and squat and think for free."

His newspaper tucked under one arm, Barlowe shuffled to a stool down at the far end, near the men's bathroom. He relived the exchange with Nell.

*You cain't have the milk without the cow.*

Being thrown out like that had brought back harsh memories of the time he was kicked out of school. The school thing still ate at him sometimes, even after all these years. And although he had done okay for himself since then, he felt sometimes like a man walking around with a big hole in his chest.

Nell.

As he sat at the bar with his legs crossed, he reminded himself that he had to move forward. Nell was now in the past. And right now the present posed a very real challenge that demanded his full attention: He was homeless—a half-step from the men he'd just seen lying on the sidewalks.

He spread the newspaper across the top of the bar and began studying the classifieds. He studied hard, the sluggish *swish, swish, swish* of the worker's broom the only sound cutting through the quiet in the room.

Meanwhile, Roach finished with the chairs, went behind the counter and began arranging glasses and bottles a certain way. He worked in silence awhile, then made his way down to the other end, close to where Barlowe sat. He leaned over and whispered, though there was nobody around to overhear.

"She got ya by the short hairs, huh?"

Barlowe kept his eyes fixed on the newspaper. "Worse than that, Roach. She put me out."

Roach nodded knowingly and left him alone. He went down to the other end of the bar and started pulling big bottles of liquor from boxes set on the floor. Minutes later, he returned.

"I had a li'l gal did that to me once. Was knock-kneed and slew-footed. Knock-kneed and slew-footed, and still had the goddamned nerve to throw me out." Roach shook his huge head. "Women. Know what I said to myself after that?"

Barlowe looked at him but didn't answer.

"I said, 'Gawd bless the chile . . .'"

The big man left again and returned a minute later. He set a shot of scotch in front of Barlowe and walked away.

Barlowe drank and scanned the paper for apartment rentals. It occurred to him that each listing on that page carried the promise of a different fate. On the less complicated side of things, he knew what he needed. He needed a place close to the print shop downtown, where he worked. His old car couldn't stand another year of long commutes.

And considering the pathetic state of his bank account, he needed a place where the rent was cheap.

He zeroed in on an obscure ad that, in its sheer economy, suggested it might offer what he was looking for:

**Classic house for rent: Affordable!!!**
**Historic in-town neighborhood.**

Later, he checked into a fleabag motel. He stretched out on the sunken mattress and listened to the muffled moans floating through the walls of the room next door. Then he drifted off to sleep, half-thinking he'd wake up in the morning beside Nell.

The next day, Barlowe pulled into the neighborhood and crept along, reading mailbox numbers. He found the address listed in the newspaper: 1024 Randolph Street.

He parked and glanced at the house. It looked nothing like the description in the ad. A one-story frame, it appeared to lean slightly to one side, like it was being propped up by two-by-fours. The gutters drooped, and paint peeled from the siding.

He scanned the lane. As streets went it seemed like a fairly lively place. There was a rowdy card game going on in the front yard of the house next door. A rap tune blared the standard bitch-ho anthem from somewhere a few doors down.

*Not a good sign for starters,* thought Barlowe. *Maybe I should look somewhere else.*

After what he had been through—being kicked out of Nell's apartment, with no forewarning at all—he craved a quiet sanctuary, someplace where he could hear himself think.

He did a broad sweep of the surrounding area. There was a grocery store across the way. A sign out front announced it was the Auburn Avenue Mini-Mart. Several men lounged in chairs outside. A stray dog strutted past, moving casually down the center of the sidewalk, as though headed somewhere important.

Barlowe got out of the car and leaned in to get the classifieds. He turned around and nearly bumped a tall, gaunt man standing there. The man stood so close Barlowe could name the brand of whiskey on his breath.

"Brudderman. Can you hep me out? I jes need somethin to eat."

*What kinda neighborhood is this, where a man can't turn his back without somebody creepin up?*

"Brudderman."

Before Barlowe could dig in his pocket for change, a gray car pulled up to the curb. A white man sprang out. The man rushed up to him.

"You the feller called yesterday?"

"Yeah. This place still for rent?"

"Yep." The man extended a hand. "I'm Crawford. William Crawford."

Crawford pulled a handkerchief from his pocket and wiped his face, which seemed to be sweating for no reason. Then he noticed the beggar standing there.

"Go! Go on way from here!"

Crawford steered Barlowe toward the rental property, looking him up and down.

From the walkway the house appeared empty inside. As they stepped through the front door a dark shadow dashed out back. Feet tramped loudly off the porch, and the kitchen door was left flung wide open.

Crawford pretended not to notice the commotion.

They stepped further inside and were greeted by a potbellied cockroach strolling across the floor. It moved at a leisurely pace, stopping midway to rest a bit. Crawford took two quick steps forward and kicked it, hard. The roach slammed against the baseboard and pretended to lapse into a coma.

"Lemme tell you," Crawford said, wiping his sweaty forehead again. "You called right on time, cause there's a lady wants this place, bad."

Barlowe ignored the hard sell, his thoughts drifting back and forth between now and yesterday. He wondered what Nell was doing. He wondered if she'd met someone.

He noticed the house carried a strong odor. "Whas that smell?"

"Oh, probably just a little mildew from the rain. Sprinkle some charcoal around here and it'll take it right away."

They toured the rooms and soon pegged the source of the fumes. Set in a corner of the back bedroom was a fresh pile of, well, shit. Human shit, to be exact, a full bowel movement, no more than a few minutes old.

Crawford mumbled. "Damn bums . . . Don't worry. We'll take care of that."

*Strike three: A man startin fresh needs to be able to sleep peaceably at night without fear of strangers walkin in.*

The tour ended in the kitchen. Barlowe opened the icebox and the door collapsed onto a single hinge.

"I can fix that," Crawford offered. "No problem. No problem at all."

Barlowe peered through the rear kitchen window. The backyard looked like it was used for cattle grazing.

Now Crawford checked his watch, like he had somewhere vital to be. "Well, son, whatcha think?"

Barlowe walked a few steps away, still inspecting. He thought he should look around at other places. There was still plenty of daylight left. He turned and looked at the front door, thinking again about Nell. *Maybe I should call. Maybe she changed her mind.*

"Tell you what." Crawford appeared nervous, jittery. "You seem like a nice young man. Give me one month's rent, and I'll forgo the deposit for now."

Barlowe pondered.

"Give me half a month right now—one hundred fifty—and we can square the rest later."

Barlowe weighed the second proposition, considering the classifieds in his hand. Three hundred a month seemed about as good a deal as you could get for a house standing on its own.

He looked at Crawford. "I'll take it."

Even as he uttered the words, he wondered if he was making a mistake.

Crawford whipped out a one-year lease from nowhere and produced a shiny key. He got the lease signed, took the man's check and hurried off.

Barlowe drifted back to the living room, where the cockroach had resumed its stroll. He wasn't sure why, but he suddenly felt gripped by panic, flooded with doubts. The whole place felt creepy.

He hated being wishy-washy, but he decided to tell Crawford he'd changed his mind. He would go back to that mangy motel and take more time to think things through.

He rushed to the door and looked outside, in both directions up and down the street. Crawford had disappeared—vanished into thin air, it seemed, without even driving off.

Barlowe sighed. *Now* what had he gotten himself into?

Of course, he had no idea—he couldn't have known. He had cast his lot in a quaint, struggling neighborhood called the Old Fourth Ward.

# Chapter 20

Barlowe stepped outside the print shop early one afternoon and glanced warily up at the cloudy sky. Showers had fallen steadily in the past few days, leaving the city hung-over from too much rain. The sun pushed briefly through stubborn clouds, but it appeared the rain would return. Barlowe wanted to beat the showers and head on home.

Driving home, Barlowe thought about the look on Billy Spivey's face when he told him he was leaving work early. He could see it bothered Billy. There were several more print jobs to be run, but he couldn't stop Barlowe from taking time off. So Billy shrugged, spit hard in his tobacco cup and stormed away.

In the months after he got the news about the stingy pay raise, Barlowe had taken more time off. He'd decided that if his bosses didn't intend to do right by him, he would make sure he took care of himself. From now on he would do no more than was required and he would make sure he got everything he was entitled to. It would start with all that overtime he'd built up through the years. Until now, he rarely missed a day at work. He always went in early and stayed as long as it took to finish the job. Now things would change. He would see to that.

There would be even bigger changes, too, if some of his other plans came through. He was shopping himself around a bit to see if other printing operations in town might want his services.

Riding along a different route, he cut through the southern tip of downtown, past all the government buildings named after dead white men. He rode up Peachtree Street, beyond the towering skyscrapers, which stood as grotesque markers of a city trying too hard to prove its mottos were true. Atlanta had its professional sports teams and its glittering theaters and bustling crowds. But it also had its Confederate past (and present), which no amount of sloganeering could shed.

Likewise, Barlowe tussled with his own nagging doubts. It seemed that no matter how hard he tried to shake it, something inside was flawed, lacking. And the loneliness. The loneliness was there, too, always hovering over his shoulder. More and more, he lay awake late nights listening to disc jockeys play old-school songs that promised love around the bend. And more and more he asked himself, *Around what bend? Where?*

In his desperation, he was even moved one day to borrow a page from Tyrone's playbook. He went to a Kroger grocery store and piddled around, hoping to meet somebody in the produce section. He saw a lone old lady in a blue trench coat and brown stockings, rolled up around the knees. She leaned heavily against a shelf, mulling over a single apple.

Lingering among the fruits and lettuce, he looked up and saw another woman, standing with a big bag of oranges cradled in her arms. He went over and commented about the shortage of apples in stock. She turned and walked away.

All he picked up in produce that day was fruit, and some of it had spoiled.

Before leaving the store, something else caught his eye, which now came back to mind. As he stood in the checkout line he noticed a black lady at the cash register. She had three young children, all shabbily dressed. The lady was dark, and she wore a scarf tied around her head. It was an American flag scarf, knotted in front, so that the ends stood up like bunny rabbit ears.

The white people in line stared hard until their foreheads crinkled.

They searched each other's eyes for answers, then stared at the black lady some more.

It was touch-and-go for a minute there. Barlowe enjoyed every bit of it. It brought a smile to his face as he thought about it now.

When he reached home, he stopped at the Auburn Avenue Mini-Mart and bought his lottery tickets. Then he went outdoors to challenge Willie on the checkerboard.

Tyrone had slipped off the job again, this time to go to some strip club. He phoned to see if Barlowe might want to come along and got the usual rejection.

Tyrone came in from the club earlier than usual and went straight to the back porch to feed his pigeons. He opened the cage. The animals jostled for position and rattled their feeding tray, spilling water onto the newspaper lining the cage bottom. He reached in and stuck an index finger near the guilty bird. The animal strutted forward and hopped on board. Tyrone brought both hands close to his face and confronted the creature, eye-to-eye.

"Vito, whas the matter wit you, boy?" He rubbed a finger over the bird's head, softly stroking. "You got problems? Huh? Huh? Tawk to me, baby. Tawk to me!"

The creature cooed a short reply.

Tyrone picked up a box of seed next to the cage and filled the food tray. When the animals had pecked until their bellies bulged, they hustled toward the open door, the red ID tags dangling from their skinny legs.

He released them. Wings fluttered wildly as they rose up, up, upward and landed in the majestic oak tree in the yard next door. They looked down contentedly on the world below.

Tyrone watched and smiled, then went inside and fussed around in the kitchen, making himself a peanut butter sandwich.

Suddenly, a noise sounded outside. It sounded like a heavy-duty lawn mower revving up. Tyrone drifted toward the living room and away from the noise. Then he remembered he'd let the pigeons loose.

He rushed to the back porch in time to see the birds fluttering, frantic, away from the big oak tree. Two of the creatures flitted to another tree, shedding feathers as they flapped and flailed. The other bird took refuge on the neighbor's roof.

An engine hummed, followed by a cracking sound. It was the big oak! It swayed back and forth, as though battling wind from a heavy storm. Tyrone's eyes dropped from the top, to the bottom of the tree. He saw a man in goggles and work gloves leaning down with a power saw leveled at its base.

It was his new neighbor! He was chopping down the big oak tree!

The birds, more frazzled now, fluttered still farther off and away. They landed on the far end of the Gilmores' roof.

"Shit!"

Tyrone set down his sandwich and bolted toward the neighbors' yard. Sean was so intently focused on the tree that he didn't see him bearing down. At some point, though, he *felt* a presence. Instinctively, he looked up in time to see his neighbor charging, fists clenched and eyes blazing.

Before he could react, Tyrone pounced. He thrust both hands around Sean's neck and shook him until his teeth rattled.

"You stupid sumbitch! You stupid sumbitch!"

Sean dropped the power saw, which cut off, tripped by its safety switch. He tried to pry Tyrone's hands loose.

While the two men wrestled, the tree swayed. It leaned toward Barlowe's house, then appeared to correct itself. It leaned back and away from the Gilmores' place and let out a crackling wail. Its half-cut bark, shredded by the sheer height and weight of the thing, tilted sharply, falling in a slow-motion tumble, crashing to the ground.

Tyrone seemed unaware of the noise and dust and crumbled mass of wood debris. He tightened his grip around Sean's throat, determined to wring his neck.

"You stupid sumbitch!"

"Arrrgggghhhhh!" Sean managed to rip off his goggles. "Arrrggghhhhh!"

"Sumbitch!"

"Arrrggghhhhh!"

He gagged violently, trying with all his might to wrench Tyrone's hands from his throat. He couldn't. Tyrone jiggled his neck some more, eventually cutting off the breathing passage.

Sean let out a wheezing sound. "Heeeeeeeccchhhh! Heeeeccchhhh! Heeeeccchhhh!"

At some point, Sandy peeped out the kitchen window. Seeing her husband dangling in the clutches of the man next door, she dropped the silverware she'd been putting away and ran outside, screaming.

"Stop it! Stop it! Let him go! You're hurting him!"

Tyrone had slipped into a violent trance. He squeezed tighter, even as Sandy began desperately pounding his back.

With one hand clutching his neighbor's throat, Tyrone used his free hand to whip Sean's limp arm behind him. He planned to snap it like a toothpick. He'd broken a man's arm in a fight once. Snapped it right in two. He wanted to hear that familiar snapping sound. So he tightened the pressure, all the while studying Sean's eyes. He liked what he saw: the arm and eyes, bending to his will.

Sandy pounded harder. "Stop it! Stop it!"

Tyrone leaned forward, to get more leverage.

"Stop it! Stop! Pleeasse! Please stop!"

Tyrone prepared to give the arm a final twist.

Suddenly, a hand, firm and heavy, grabbed his wrist. A familiar voice called his name:

"Ty. Ty. Let im go, man. Let im go, Ty."

It was Barlowe. He had come home and heard the screaming out back.

"Let im go, Ty. Is all right, man. Let im go."

Slowly, Tyrone released the white man from his grip. Sean slumped to the ground, like a flimsy burlap sack. With Sandy kneeling beside him, he clutched his throat, gasping.

Sandy rubbed Sean's arm and moaned. "Oh-my-God! Oh-my-God! Sean, is it broken? Oh-my-God! Ooohhh, baby, I'm sorry; I'm sooo sorry, baby!"

Sean didn't move. "I think it's broken."

Sandy gently rubbed the arm some more, then looked up past Tyrone and yelled at Barlowe.

"What's the matter with *him*? He's crazy! He's crazy! He attacked my husband! For no reason at all, he attacked my husband!"

Tyrone spit on the ground. "Shut up, Becky."

"The name is *Sandy*!"

"Same difference, bitch."

Barlowe broke in. "Ty. Calm down, man. Chill."

Two of Tyrone's pigeons came fluttering back. They landed on the ground a few feet away and poked around in the dirt for bugs.

Barlowe turned to Tyrone. "What happened?"

Tyrone pointed at the fallen tree. "Looka what that sumbitch did! The *tree*, man! He cut down the gotdamn tree, and right while my birds was in it!"

Barlowe studied the fallen tree, wondering how he'd overlooked it before.

With help from Sandy, Sean sat up straight. Still holding his throat, he tried to find his voice.

"It's *my* tree! That tree is on *my* property!"

Tyrone balled his fists and leaned down, ready to throw a punch.

Barlowe grabbed his arm. "Ty. Calm down."

Sean was livid, and especially upset that his wife had witnessed his humiliation.

"I had every right to cut down that tree!"

Barlowe shook his head. "No you didn't, partner."

"It's on *my* property."

"No, partner. That tree stood between both our yards."

"I happen to own the part of the yard that held the tree." Sean lowered the volume now, careful not to provoke another attack. "I can prove it . . . We can compare deeds and lot drawings and I'll show you . . . Shoot, I'll show you if you get *your* deed—the tree belonged to me . . . You don't have to believe me; go and get your deed."

Barlowe lowered his eyes as Crawford came to mind.

"We don't have to go through all that . . . It woulda made sense for you to tell us you were gonna cut down the tree . . . That tree kept things cool back here. It gave us shade, and you jus went and cut it down."

Tyrone chimed in: "Stupid sumbitch!"

"You leave him alone!" Sandy shouted.

"Shut up, Becky!"

"It's Sandy!"

Sean grimaced, more from embarrassment than pain. He had been nearly strangled by the neighbor. Now here was his wife stepping in like some protector.

With Sandy's help, Sean climbed to his feet. He was woozy, unsteady.

"Nobody told me I needed permission to cut down a tree in my own yard. I did it for safety reasons." He looked at Tyrone. "I had no idea I'd be attacked!"

Tyrone charged him again. "I'll fuck you up, gray boy . . ."

Barlowe blocked his path and turned back to Sean.

"Safety?"

"That's right. All kinds of shady people creep through here and hide behind that tree."

Tyrone turned and stamped off, disgusted with the whole scene. He went to round up his birds.

Sandy began leading Sean slowly toward the house. Halfway there, he stopped and turned around. "We'll show you the deed and the lot drawings." He shot Barlowe a snotty look.

Barlowe shot him one back. "I don't care bout your deed."

Now he regretted having come home so soon. He wished he had played one more game of checkers—*one* more.

Then maybe Tyrone could have finished the job.

# Chapter 21

According to the emergency room doctor Sean Gilmore was very lucky.

"No broken bones at all, young man; only a minor sprain. A few pills for pain, a sling around the arm; in a few weeks you'll be good as new."

The doctor's cheerful tone irritated Sean. On the way home he remained fairly quiet. Beyond vague references to "the incident," he was in no mood to talk about what happened to him. The humiliation was too fresh, too painful.

Driving along, Sandy tried to deflect her husband's shame. "Let's try to forget about this, Sean. It was a misunderstanding, I'm sure . . . You think we should still try to get those Braves tickets?"

He turned to Sandy. "You know things could get worse before they get better."

She didn't respond.

"You know that, don't you, Sandy?"

She patted him on the knee. "Don't be negative, Sean. Don't release that kind of thinking into the universe."

If looks could kill . . .

Over the next week, Sean moped around the house, still licking his wounds and tickling the edges of shallow exchanges with his wife. When he was home, he stayed indoors, partly to follow the doctor's orders, and mostly because he felt uneasy about returning to the yard.

He was especially self-conscious about the sling. It was an affront to his manly pride. And what if he should run into one of the neighbors? He'd have only one arm to defend himself.

Sandy respected Sean's need for space. She had needs of her own, conflicting emotions she struggled to reconcile. There was lingering guilt, and mostly anger to appease. *How could a next-door neighbor do such a thing?*

Sitting in the living room one day, she turned the incident over in her head, looking at it from different angles. Neighbors everywhere had clashes all the time. They fought over property boundaries, barking dogs, lawn tools borrowed and not returned. They fought and even made up sometimes and became best friends after that.

Whatever the problem, she couldn't give it power to rule her days; she couldn't let one run-in cloud her vision of what the neighborhood could be.

And she definitely couldn't feed into fear right now. Sandy made up her mind. She would refuse to give in, no matter what.

Two weeks after the incident with Tyrone, Sean went to Sandy, who was sitting in the living room, reading. He had slipped into sneakers.

"I'm going to take a walk."

A concerned look splashed across Sandy's face. "I'd better go with—"

"No. I'm going alone."

She gave in. Sandy knew her husband. Sean was a proud man. He had to feel like he was standing up.

She bit her bottom lip as he went through the door. She stood in the window and watched him head up Randolph Street.

Sean started out walking fast, then forced himself to slow down some. *No need to hurry*, he told himself. He lived here now. Like it or not, people would have to get used to that.

He tried to blend in, stopping here and there to admire a garden, or to pick up litter, in a gesture that said: "This is my neighborhood, too." Still, he looked like an outsider, and that was how he was regarded by people he encountered along the walk. Passersby flashed curious sideways glances, like he was some intruder, some wide-eyed tourist who'd strayed too far from The King Center.

Walking along, Sean tuned into the routine sounds of the neighborhood. Laughter flowed to him from a porch nearby. It spilled from dark faces set back too far in the shadows for him to see. Music floated through an open window. A dog barked. Children played in a front yard, chasing each other round and round in silly circles.

Sean spotted Mr. Smith coming in from the grocery store. The old man didn't offer so much as a neighborly nod. A block farther, he passed a woman working in the yard. In a muted response to Sean's cautious "hello," the woman flicked a stingy wave and promptly turned her back.

He wondered, *Are these people actually angry at me, or am I being paranoid?*

Judging from the backyard attack, it seemed pretty clear. A full two weeks had passed and still he couldn't face it head-on just yet, and least of all with his wife. Besides, talking about it might force him to admit what he now felt bubbling just beneath the surface of his skin—full-blown fear, dread and, yes, even resentment: What had Sandy gotten him into?

He reserved a special disgust for the thug next door. If the world were still right-side-up, that man would answer for what he'd done. Sean would personally see to that.

But what could he do? This was sensitive. The man lived right next door.

Maybe it was a freak misunderstanding, out of the ordinary. Then it came to him: Maybe it was just the opposite. Maybe it was *very* ordinary.

So, then. Was the attack a forewarning of more to come? He could hardly bear to think about it, and yet he knew he'd *better* think about it or risk another assault.

He shuddered and suddenly became aware again of his surroundings. He was moving down a sidewalk in the Old Fourth Ward. He was outdoors, out in the open where he was being watched. He looked around in all directions, taking care to be alert.

He tried to appear casual, nonchalant, but it didn't work so well. He fell into a self-conscious stride that made him appear awkward, out of sync with his own feet. He covered another block and was struck again by the sense that he was being scrutinized, more like assaulted, by untrusting eyes.

They seemed to be everywhere. Eyes poured out of windows, squeezed between houses, trailed him up and down the street. Some people, like the nappy-headed man leaning over a rickety upstairs balcony, shot him hostile glares. Others peered intently, not seeming to care that he saw them staring.

It was unsettling. Sean could actually *feel* his whiteness. He felt it in ways he had never experienced before.

Eventually, he came upon a group of teenage boys, about five of them, heading toward him. The boys were dressed in brightly colored clothes, large, outlandish athletic jerseys and baseball hats, with those appalling black stocking caps wrapped around their heads underneath. As they brushed past him, he tensed up some but tried to appear unconcerned. He could hear them talking, casually cursing one another. Why did these people curse so much?

When they passed, a few of the boys turned around and glared. *What a pity,* Sean thought as they bounced jauntily up the block. *Still kids and yet all the innocence gone from their eyes.*

It seemed to Sean that he had looked into their faces and seen their future. He thought of their futures in the singular, as one. He guessed the average age among them was seventeen. By his estimation, each of their lifespans would extend for maybe four more years. Unless they got religion or made new friends, they probably wouldn't make it past twenty-one. Based on what he gleaned from daily news reports, they would all likely come to the same sickening end.

It was hard to know which emotion gripped him stronger: sorrow or disgust.

By the time he reached the middle of the next block, his mood had begun to crumble. Then he came upon a sight that made him smile. It was a little boy heading toward him with a puppy tied to a thick piece of string. A little boy! When they met along the walk, Sean grinned and lowered himself to look in his face.

"Hi. What's your name?"

The boy stared at the white man, then looked curiously at the sling on his arm. "MynameDarrelle."

"And who's this walking with you, Darrelle?"

The boy's face lit up. He turned proudly to the dog. "HisnameKing."

"What?"

"HisnameKing."

Sean had to focus hard on the boy's lips to understand the words. For some reason, he found, that irritated him.

While he stood there talking to the boy, he felt eyes bearing down harder now. He refused to give in to fear.

"And how old is King, Darrelle?"

"Fourmonthsold. Hestillapuppy."

Sean smiled, not really sure what the boy had said. He would have talked longer, but in his self-consciousness ran out of things to say. He bid Darrelle good-bye and moved on, still aware he was being watched.

He made it as far as the intersection of Randolph Street and John Wesley Dobbs Avenue before turning around. Not even a full four blocks from home! He'd covered more than four blocks at a time when strolling in his old Forsyth County neighborhood. At least in Forsyth a man could take a leisurely walk and not be made to feel so self-conscious. He could get out and get some exercise without being made to feel unwelcome. At least in Forsyth he could . . . He stopped. Was he feeling nostalgic? About Forsyth?

Of course not. No need to romanticize that place.

When he reached the sidewalk near his house, Sean spotted Barlowe going to his car. He was sure his neighbor saw him, too. Barlowe kept looking straight ahead. Moving up the walk, Sean watched to see if he would acknowledge him. He wanted to start a conversation, maybe even talk, man to man, about the backyard misunderstanding.

But Barlowe didn't look his way. He started the car and pulled on off, like Sean wasn't there.

A flash of anger shot through Sean. *What kind of neighbors are these?*

In the end, the walk was too brief to claim any triumph of spirit. Indoors, he shared the experience with his wife, maybe hoping for sympathy.

Sandy moved close to him and caressed his face. "I hope that experience helps you better understand what I'm beginning to see."

Sean nodded. "I'm starting to see it, too, Sandy. I'm starting to wonder if this thing is right for us."

He would have continued, but she cut him off.

"No, Sean. That's not what I meant. What I meant is, now we know."

He frowned. "Now we know what?"

"Now we know how it feels being regarded with suspicion all the time."

When he first came in, Sean had sat down next to Sandy on the couch. He abruptly got up and left the room.


After the sun had faded for the day, Viola and The Hawk appeared from across the street. Coming from Davenport's home, they stumbled toward the pathway between Barlowe's place and the house next door.

Viola fussed at The Hawk for walking too slow. "C'mon, man!"

"Hole up, woman! I gotta pee!"

They stood near the front corner of both houses and argued. Finally, Viola got fed up and left.

The Hawk staggered and leaned on the side of the Gilmores' house for support. He unzipped his pants and relieved himself. When he was done, he knelt to the ground and sat with his back resting against the house. He sat there awhile, trying to clear his head. Tired and woozy, he dozed off to sleep.

Shortly, two police cruisers pulled up to the curb. Three cops jumped out and went straight to The Hawk. One bent over and tapped his shoulder.

"Hey. Hey." He tapped again. "Get up, buddy. Get up and come with us."

The Hawk mumbled something incoherent. He struggled to get to his feet and fell back down. Two cops helped him up again. Supporting his arms on either side, they escorted him to the cruiser.

They tossed The Hawk into the backseat and hauled him off to jail.

# Chapter 22

Barlowe slipped on a cap and went to the back porch, preparing to work in the yard. Locked in the cage behind him, one of the pigeons cooed mildly, then sidestepped its way across the horizontal bar. It bumped into another bird. Wings fluttered wildly as conflict ensued over the infringement of space.

*Space. Conflict. The Old Fourth Ward.*

Barlowe went into the yard, leaving the pigeons to work out their differences. He plundered the toolshed and pulled out a rake and garbage bags. Hands on hips, he surveyed the yard. It seemed almost naked back there, exposed with the big oak gone. More light filtered through now, leaving less shade protection from the glaring sun.

He slipped on gardening gloves and went to work. Lately, he'd begun to take yard work more seriously. Members of the Beautification Committee, Miss Carol Lilly insisted, should set a good example. Besides, Barlowe reminded himself, if all went according to plans, he would one day own this house. Which meant he should beautify the land surrounding it.

Barlowe was fairly good at gardening. It was a carryover from the farming he'd done growing up. So he began to go outdoors more often on days like this, days when the skies were clear and the sun was bright enough to make a farmer's son smile and remember the gritty feel of the soil and the salty smell of skin moistened by sweat dripping from the brow. He thought of his daddy in Milledgeville. His daddy who could outwork a Georgia mule. His daddy used to love days like this.

Barlowe piddled around, potting plants and gathering pine needles to freshen flower beds. The needles had fallen like snowflakes, especially on the property next door, where most of the pine trees stood. In past years, when Hattie Phillips owned the house, her tenants gladly let Barlowe collect pine needles. It was one less maintenance worry for them.

White people lived there now. Barlowe wouldn't dare ask them for pine straw, and especially not after what Tyrone had done. From now on, Barlowe would have to make do with the pine needles that fell in his yard.

He busied himself, raking pine straw into neat little piles, sometimes stopping to transfer portions to flower beds around front. After several trips back and forth, he bent down low to scoop the last clump of a pile. He had shifted to another bale, when a voice called out from across the way.

"Why do you hate us?"

It was a woman's voice. It came from behind, just over his shoulder. He turned around and saw his neighbor, the white woman, standing there. With one swift sweep of the eye, he gave her the up and down. She appeared to be his age, maybe older. You never could be too sure with *them*. She wore blue jeans and a shirt. Her arms were folded tightly against her chest, like she was cold. She looked a bit out of sorts, nervous, like she was unsure why she was standing there.

Barlowe leaned on his rake and stared at her. "Nobody hates you, lady."

Sandy took a few steps forward, stopping at an imaginary boundary to her yard. "It would be hard to prove that by my husband and me. We move here thinking we've found the ideal place to live, and he gets attacked by the next-door neighbor."

*Yes*, Barlowe thought. *The husband*. He had met her husband at the mailbox once. The exchange had been a short, awkward one. He could sense the man's uneasiness with him. Now here was his wife giving it a turn.

Sandy stepped a few feet closer. "In all the hysteria over the tree, I never got a chance to introduce myself. My name is Sandy. Sandy Gilmore." She extended a hand.

Barlowe nodded hello, then clenched his rake, signaling he had work to do.

"I wanna thank you," said Sandy, "for what you did for Sean. I still don't know what got into your housemate. But if you hadn't shown up when you did, I think he really would have done some serious harm."

"Thas my nephew," Barlowe said, by way of correction. "He's real protective of his birds."

He wondered, *Why hadn't they called the cops?* For hours after the incident he and Tyrone waited anxiously for the policeman's rap at the door, maybe followed by an arrest warrant and assault charges. They had even tried to estimate how much Barlowe would have to post for bail.

But no one came.

Sandy seemed to sense Barlowe's need to understand.

"Sean and I discussed the whole thing later, and we agreed that you were right about something you said. As a courtesy we should have let you know that we planned to chop down that big oak tree, even if it was on our property."

Barlowe said nothing.

"Anyway. Enough about that," said Sandy. "So. Are you an Atlanta native?"

"I'm from a small town not too far from here."

"We're from Philadelphia. We came here a few years ago."

Barlowe made no attempt to keep the conversation going.

"So." She zeroed in. "You didn't answer my question."

He blinked. "What?"

"Why do you hate us?"

"I toldja. Nobody hates you."

Sandy folded her arms again across her chest. "Well, what is it then, around here, this *attitude* toward us?"

He began raking. He didn't care to talk to her. He bent down to collect another pile of pine needles.

Sandy appeared unfazed by the contempt, which seemed to ooze from his pores. "Well?" She stood there, clearly prepared to wait for an answer, however long it took.

They both kept quiet for a long while. Finally, Barlowe said, "Maybe is what you *do* that people round here don't like so much."

Sandy felt a sudden surge of anger coming on. "And exactly what do we *do*?"

He glared but kept quiet.

A wry smile from her. "I know. 'There goes the neighborhood.' Right?"

"Yeah. 'There goes the neighborhood.'"

"How can you say such a thing? You don't even *know* us."

"Oh, we *know* you." He nodded. "We know you."

"What does that mean?"

He waved, dismissive.

"How do you know me? Huh? How are you capable of knowing me? This is the first time we've even talked."

She was pissed now. He could see it, and he resented that. What right did *she* have to be pissed about anything?

He waved her off again, signaling he didn't want to talk. He dropped his rake and went indoors.

*Knock, knock, knock.*

Barlowe appeared in the doorway with a damp dish towel in his hand, wondering why the visitor didn't ring the bell. There was a white man standing there, with a woman, about an inch taller, hovering behind.

"Excuse me. Are you the owner?"

Barlowe clenched his teeth. "Can I help you?"

Slack-jawed and doofus-looking, the man glanced at his companion, then back at Barlowe.

"We've been admiring your house, and we thought we'd stop by to ask if we could see it inside."

"No," said Barlowe, wiping his hands on the towel. "No."

The woman chimed in. "Are you planning to sell anytime soon? Because if you are, we—"

Barlowe slammed the door and returned to the kitchen. Tyrone stood at the counter making an egg sandwich. He leaned against the counter.

"I don't blieve it."

"Believe what?" asked Barlowe.

"Them same whities come by here a week ago, axin a whole buncha gotdamn questions. I tole em we was rentin." He took a bite from the sandwich. "Cain't blieve they right back agin."

Barlowe hung the dish towel on the refrigerator door and regarded Tyrone with some surprise. "You talked to em before?"

"Yeah. They kept axin questions till I tole em don't ax me nothin else. I ran em off."

"Recently?"

"Bout a week ago."

"You told em we were rentin?"

"Yeah, they was axin all kinda questions bout how much we paid for the house, and stuff like that. I tole em they axin the wrong people, and don't be axin us, cause we don't know."

He took another big bite from the sandwich.

Barlowe sighed. "Ty."

"Yo?"

"From now on, do me a favor."

"Whut?"

"When folks come to the door, don't answer. If you do answer, tell em they need to talk to *me*. Okay?"

Tyrone seemed surprised. "Whasa matter? What I do?"

"Nothin. Jus don't give out information bout this house."

Tyrone sucked his teeth in frustration. "Aight. Aight. Next time they come through, I'll just run they ass on out."

"Whatever. Jus don't talk to em."

"Okay, man. Don't get mad at me. I dint know." He polished off the rest of the sandwich and lingered in the kitchen a moment.

"Hey, Unk."

"What?"

"You still pissed off cause a what happened with that white dude nex doe?"

"Naw."

"You sho?"

Barlowe didn't respond.

"He got off real lucky," said Tyrone. "If you hadna come back there I was gonna eat im for lunch. He was bout to be barbecued."

"Then I'm glad I showed up," said Barlowe.

Tyrone shook his head. "You gettin soft on me, Unk. You cain't be gettin soft on me. We country boys from Milledgeville."

He went to his room, came out a few minutes later and left the house.

Barlowe went outdoors to work in the yard. When he stepped out there, he heard loud rap music. He couldn't tell where it was coming from.

He dropped the rake and went out front. He could hear the music clearer now. He crossed the street and went up the walk. Two doors up from Miss Carol Lilly's place, he stopped at a wood frame house with a short, wooden fence out front. He went in the gate and up six stairs and spotted Jacoby Mott, along with three of his high school friends. Lounging in flimsy wicker chairs, the boys were stretched out on the porch.

Jacoby lived with his mama and older sister. He could be a good boy when he wanted, but he was a boy just the same.

When Barlowe approached the porch, Jacoby and the three boys jumped, startled. The music was so loud they hadn't heard him come through the gate. One of the boys, a buck-toothed kid with hair done up in looping braids, held something shiny in his hands. He quickly stuffed it under his shirt when he saw Barlowe's face.

"Jacoby."

"Yes, sir, Mr. Barlowe?" Jacoby looked nervous, guilty.

"Your mama home?"

"No, sir. She and my sister went to the stoe."

"You think everybody out here wanna hear this cussin music blastin up and down the street?"

"No, sir."

"Don't you think you oughta turn it down?"

Jacoby got mad about being talked to like that in front of his friends. He wanted to sass Barlowe, maybe talk back a little to save face. But something about Barlowe, the sturdy, hard-bodied frame and the quiet fierceness in his eyes, let him know he'd best not try. So Jacoby jumped up and rushed in the house. He turned down the music and returned to the porch.

"Thanks, Jacoby."

"Yes, sir."

Barlowe went back across the street. He rounded the corner of the house and saw Sandy in her yard, working. It had been several days since they first talked. He looked at her and started toward the shed. She came directly over and confronted him, not bothering to say hello.

"I wanna say something about a comment you made the other day."

He picked up a tool and began raking an area near his foot, on ground he'd already combed.

Sandy moved two steps closer. "You questioned our motives for moving here. I think you may have made some wrong assumptions. For all you know, we may have actually come here to help."

No response from him.

"Look. I can't speak for everybody moving here; I can only tell you, there is no ill intent on the part of my husband and me."

Barlowe shrugged. "However it starts out, lady, the endin's the same."

"You don't understand," said Sandy. "We—my husband and me—hate what we see happening to this country . . . I mean, that man in Texas who was dragged to death some years back . . . That was awful. There's still lots of work to be done."

He nodded. "I see . . ."

"What is it you see, Mr.—I still don't know your name."

"The name is Barlowe. Barlowe Reed."

"What is it you see, Mr. Reed?"

"Missionaries . . ."

"Not at all."

"No?"

She ignored the sarcasm. "Things happen for a reason. I believe this is where we were led."

He looked upon her now with a mixture of contempt and pity. She read his face and felt she knew exactly what he was thinking.

"Look, it's a long story. The short of it is that for a lot of reasons this neighborhood seemed like a good fit for us."

"Uh-huh." Barlowe started raking again.

"We know we have things to learn, too, as you can see from the incident with the tree . . ." She leaned forward, unsure he was listening. "But we're also willing to take risks and try. Isn't that what Martin Luther King did? Didn't he take risks? Didn't he try?"

Barlowe whipped around and faced her now. "Please, lady. Don't start with *that*. Don't drag *him* in this."

"He's already in it," replied Sandy. "I mean, what better place to try? I know that may sound corny to you, but—"

"You're right. Is corny."

Sandy threw up her hands, exasperated. "Why is it so hard for people to accept—?"

He rolled his eyes.

"No, it's true. You have to give people a chance."

"You got plenty chances, lady. All the chances in the fuggin world."

"No, we—my husband and me—have been given *no* chance here so far, and that's not fair."

Barlowe stiffened. "Don't—"

"But—"

"But *nothin*. Don't use that word with me."

Sandy was startled, stung by the forcefulness in his tone. She threw up her hands again. "I can't win."

"No, lady. You already won. Don't you know? You already won." There was a long, tense pause, then: "Scuse me. I got other things to do." Barlowe turned around and stalked indoors.

# Chapter 23

Barlowe went on another job interview, at a print shop across town. There was a good chance they would offer him a position, but now he wasn't sure he would take it. The shop foreman was a man named Don Pritchard. Don seemed different from Billy Spivey, which was a good thing. But he'd appeared annoyed that Barlowe asked so many questions during the interview.

Once home, Barlowe went outside to work in the yard and mull over the prospective job. He plucked weeds from around shrubs and yanked at crabgrass in flower beds. When that was done he shifted around back and began rearranging flowerpots. He took a few pots to the porch and lined them up, trying to decide where to place them.

While he worked, he thought about the interview. If he changed jobs, would the new place be any better than where he worked? And what if by some stroke of cursed luck it turned out to be much worse? That thought made him shiver.

If he went to the new place and it turned out to be a big letdown, he could wind up being twice as frustrated as he was now. He would have jumped, as the old folks said, from the skillet into the fire.

He thought about that a long while, posing some tough questions to himself. Like: What's the point in going from one plantation to another? What's the point in taking the risk, changing jobs just to add a few coins to his pockets? Caesar would claim the lion's share of the extra money, anyway.

*Caesar.*

Barlowe continued working, now moving a pile of pine straw to the side of the house. As he worked, Viola came creeping through. She walked gingerly, almost tiptoeing down the path. Viola wore new flats, the kind of cheap, tacky shoes worn by women who no longer care about their appearance.

When she saw Barlowe, she did a half-nod and shifted her eyes like she was unsure if he or the white people would hassle her. Barlowe nodded back and returned to his thoughts. Viola vanished around the side of the house.

He leaned over a few empty flowerpots and poured in soil. As he stood up straight, a now-familiar voice called to him from across the yard.

"Hi, there."

He swung around and saw Sandy. He had seen her several times in the months since those first testy exchanges. The tension between them had eased up some, so much so, in fact, that she sometimes came out to work in her garden just because she saw him outdoors.

The two of them would chat, mostly about the yards. Then she'd return to her work, and he to his.

In spite of himself, Barlowe found Sandy intriguing. She seemed a bit different from most other white people he had run across. Although she'd never said so, he guessed she was college educated. Yet she seemed to understand so little about how the world *really* worked. He found her to be maddeningly naive sometimes. His instincts warned him to be careful.

Still, something about her—maybe the sheer force of her sincerity—led him to second-guess himself.

"Hi," he said, looking at her now.

"I just got back from Pike's Nursery." Sandy moved in closer, stepping across the boundary to his yard. "They have a sale going on. I got some azaleas, cheap."

Barlowe finished filling another pot with soil, then closed the bag. Sandy hovered, waiting for him to face her. She pushed her hands deep into her blue jean pockets and crooked her slim neck to one side.

Barlowe turned around and squatted over another flowerpot.

"I've been thinking about one of our earlier conversations," said Sandy. "I wanna tell you the real reason why I wanted to move into this neighborhood."

He turned to her. "That mean you lied before?"

She looked embarrassed. She always seemed to look embarrassed. "I didn't exactly lie, but it was—"

"A *white* lie." He grinned.

She smiled, half-relieved, thinking, *So he has a sense of humor.*

"No, not a white lie," she said. "It just wasn't the total truth."

"So whas the total truth?"

"The total truth is that my decision to come here was not entirely a selfless one. It's true, I want to help, as I said before, but I also came for other reasons. One reason was convenience. Also I think that maybe I needed to find out some things about myself."

Barlowe waited. He was curious now. What could she learn about herself by moving into *his* neighborhood?

Before Sandy could explain, they were distracted by a shout. It was an impatient, shrill shout. It came from the direction of her house.

"Sandy! Telephone!"

It was Sean. He had come home from work and seen them out there, talking. He stood in the doorway, holding the phone, a puzzled look on his face.

From the distance across the yard, Barlowe acknowledged Sean with a wary nod. Sean nodded back, also warily.

Sandy shouted over her shoulder, "Be right there!"

She turned back to Barlowe. "I gotta go . . . guess I should apologize. I was about to start rambling again."

"Yeah. You do tend to do that."

He didn't know what else to say. He couldn't tell her what he felt at that moment, which, oddly, was disappointment.

In a quick, curious counter to his snide remark, Sandy smiled, then ran off to get the phone.

Atlanta's springtime blew in early that year. The first few weeks of spring were erratic. One day, the flowers, bathing in the warm southern sun, perked up and appeared ready to bloom. The next day, temperatures would plunge into the thirties, freezing flowers stiff as ice. The dying winter hung on, resisting the seasonal change. In that time, Barlowe functioned in a kind of cloud.

Just as he'd expected, Don Pritchard offered him a printing job when a spot came open. Barlowe turned it down. He'd decided that he didn't trust Don. As distasteful as the acquaintance with Billy Spivey was, he *knew* Billy. Even though he hated Spivey, he took a certain comfort in that knowing. However Billy might try he could never catch Barlowe off guard. He could never do more than limited harm.

But Don Pritchard was different. Don was the devil he didn't know. Which meant the particular dangers he posed were unknown, too.

*No,* Barlowe thought. *Too risky.* He would look for another printing job somewhere else.

Meanwhile, he went to work at the Copy Right Print Shop every day and, as usual, said no more than was required to get the job done.

Every now and then Spivey made a point of stopping by his press to say hello, smiling and spitting in that tobacco cup. There was a triumphant air about him. Barlowe guessed it might be linked to that stingy raise. He refused to let on that it bothered him. He was content to bide his time. Besides, there were other matters to think about. There was the issue of the nagging tension in his chest, the result, he was sure, of the long companionship drought. The tension pounded so heavy sometimes it seemed to press against his ribs.

As for the neighborhood, Barlowe wasn't the only person around there feeling stressed. Mr. Smith stopped him coming in one day, and the old man was so mad Barlowe feared he might work himself into a stroke.

"I got a visit from a city inspecta yestiddy."

"An inspector?" *Caesar!*

"Yeah. Gave me some kinda violation notice. Tole me I got thurty days to move my cah from off the street. Said if I don't move it they gonna come and tow and I'll have to pay a big, fat fine."

Mr. Smith stared off into space. "Damn feller wouldn't tell me who called the city on me." He looked toward Sean and Sandy's house. "Betcha I know who it was."

Barlowe kept quiet.

In recent weeks, city inspectors had gotten "tips" that sent them rushing to other houses, issuing warnings for infractions that folks said were news to them. In some cases, harsh words and threats were exchanged. Tensions rose, and names were called.

The threat of inspectors was nothing compared to the aggressive land-grab now going on. It seemed every patch of vacant land in the ward was being snapped up by speculators.

Houses that went on the market usually were bought, fast, and renovated even faster. Construction crews invaded with ladders and saws and big, fat hammers, banging and banging until it left folks' ears ringing long after workers had left for the day.

It got so bad that the people of the Old Fourth Ward went to bed at night and heard the *clack, clack, clack* of those big, fat hammers in their sleep. In their burning restlessness, some had nightmares, too, about battalions of construction crews storming the streets, bursting into their homes, hammering away.

When summer arrived, people's hope of salvation seemed to rest on the crest of an oppressive heat wave, which some folks swore was sent by God. The heat wave lasted most of the summer. It ushered in a wicked drought that wreaked environmental havoc, wilting flowers and scorching land.

The heat wave lasted so long that some folks began to hold out the feeble hope that it might somehow stifle the ravenous grab for land and houses in their midst.

The drought drained lakes and sucked rivers dry. It forced the mayor to impose restrictions on water use. It was decreed from City Hall that people throughout Atlanta could water their lawns only on even-numbered days if their houses ended in even numbers, and odd-numbered days if their home addresses called for that.

The formula seemed simple on paper, but by the end of the first week, it got all confused in people's heads. From day to day, some folks couldn't remember, so they stopped watering their grass altogether, rather than risk being hit with fines. Others watered their lawns in the dark of night, in case they had gotten mixed up and missed their turn.

In the spirit of good citizenship and conservation, some whites in the Old Fourth Ward promptly phoned downtown and reported neighbors who broke the law. Generally, whites could afford to be law-abiding. Almost to the family, they had installed automatic sprinkler systems, which sprayed well water in their yards.

While black folks' scorched yards turned an ugly shit-colored brown, the whites' lawns were lush and full and green.

When the contest for the annual Green Thumb Prize was held, it turned out to be no competition at all. The sprinkler systems prevailed, hands down. Whites won every gardening category that year.

# Chapter 24

The meeting of the Old Fourth Ward Civic League convened at The Way of the Cross Baptist Church, a modest, two-story structure at the southern tip of Auburn Avenue. The meeting normally was held at seven o'clock on the first Tuesday of every month. This time, a special session had been called on a Saturday at noon.

Civic league gatherings were usually poorly attended, but the church was packed this day. Word had spread that there was a crisis afoot. Nothing on the one-page agenda hinted at the nature of that crisis. (Community leaders were too shrewd to put it in writing.) All around the ward the news had been whispered from ear to ear, with a private vow: No white folks were to be told about the gathering.

Practically everybody was there. Clarence Sykes broke a poker engagement to come; Lula Simmons showed up (though some folks regarded her presence with deep suspicion), followed by pretty Marvetta Green. The boys from the mini-mart, who otherwise never set foot in God's hallowed house, also hobbled over. Even Henny Penn and some of the thugs who hung in and around the Purple Palace came to see what was going on.

Barlowe entered the church and joined Mr. Smith and his wife, Zelda, in one of the center rows. Tyrone drifted in minutes later.

The meeting opened with a long-winded prayer, followed by the secretary's report. The secretary read off a detailed summary of proposed zoning changes and announced that City Councilman Clifford Barnes was in the house. With routine civic league business done, Barnes and a group of ministers paraded to the front of the sanctuary. They were led by the church pastor, the Reverend Dr. Owen J. Pickering, Jr. Watching the preacher come forth, Barlowe thought about the last time he had seen him, standing on the steps of King's birth home.

When he had taken his place behind the podium, Pickering paused a moment and scanned the crowd, waiting until all eyes were fixed on him. Before he opened his mouth to speak, Councilman Barnes stepped forward, as though insisting on being the first speaker. The minister, visibly annoyed, hesitated, then gave up the mike.

Standing there in a pin-striped suit, Barnes looked like a displaced king among commoners. Speaking in measured tones, he told the crowd the meeting was called to discuss a neighborhood problem, which he described as an "invasion of sorts."

"In recent months we've seen people moving into the Old Fourth Ward at a shocking rate. Some of the newcomers are black professionals, like myself." (He could barely contain his pride in the comparison.) "Most of the new people, though, you could classify as 'other.'"

That jab drew scattered laughter. Barlowe shifted uncomfortably in his seat.

"We certainly don't mind people fusing new blood into our neighborhoods," Barnes declared. "We're all God's children, for sure. But as we look around the city, we see a curious pattern taking shape. It's happened in Summerhill. It's happened in Oakhurst. It's happening in Kirkwood. It's spreading to East Point, and now we're seeing it with our own eyes, right here in the ward."

A chorus of grumbles flowed forth from the crowd.

"I've got some ideas to share about that matter," said Barnes. "But first we'll have some people come forth and talk about how things are starting to look and feel for them."

He summoned several people sitting in a roped-off section on the second row. First came Dawn Ransom, a pygmy of a woman who shuffled forward and pulled a crumpled piece of paper from her jacket pocket. Doe-eyed and crowd-shy, she stood up straight and cleared her throat, like a student preparing to recite a class report.

"I got a simple story to tell, but I wanna make sho I don't get nervous and forget. I ain't never spoke in front a no crowd befo."

She opened the paper and read: "I was sittin in my livin room one day and some folks came a knockin at the doe. I knew what they wonted. They axed me if I would sell my house. Said they pay me cash.

"I tole em I ain't goin nowhere. I been livin out chere since right after Martha Lutha Kang died . . . I tole em ta git the hell way from me."

"Good for you, sistah!" somebody shouted. "Good for you!"

"And that weren't the last time." Dawn gained more confidence as she went along. "They keep comin back. Not a week don't go by that one a them crack—er, uh, white people—don't come knockin . . . They jus like roaches, comin and comin.

"Now when they come to my doe, I git my butcha knife and run em off."

"Amen, sister!" came the shouts. "Amen!"

Barlowe shifted in his seat again. Something troubling gnawed at him. He struggled to get a handle on what it was.

Dawn Ransom was followed with a similar story by a toothless old lady with rollers in her hair. Then a deacon in Reverend Pickering's church came up and testified after her. It went on like that until several people had shared disturbing stories or lodged complaints.

The people mumbled angrily, as each witness walked back to his seat.

Returning to the mike, Councilman Barnes moaned out loud: "Um! Did y'all hear that?" The word *y'all* sounded awkward, forced, rolling off his privileged tongue.

"It's interesting to see that some people speak of these developments in our community as though it's some brand-new phenomenon. But I'm here to tell you, they've got it wrong!"

Somebody shouted, "We hear you! Yes!"

He paused as the crowd grew quiet, attentive. "I don't have to tell you all what's happened before, do I? Visit an Indian reservation and see for yourself."

"Teach, brother! Teach!"

"People, I'm telling you this so you'll understand. And I'm telling you so you won't sit on your hands, or go treating this like some great mystery! This is no mystery. This is just history—repeating itself!"

Somebody shouted: "I know thas right!" The crowd responded with hearty applause. As Barnes spoke the old preacher took in the young politician's words, studying him with a frigid stare. Pickering listened closely, his heart dripping with disdain. *What kind a leadership,* he wondered, *can the people expect from a man whose breath still smells like baby's milk? And how can that man profess to be qualified to lead when he ain't never paid his dues?*

There was no questioning Pickering's civil rights bona fides. He had marched, been jailed and bled for the cause. He was once a finalist for consideration as a warm-up act for Dr. King. It was said that when Pickering was inspired, his preaching could wrench the devil straight up from hell.

Still, he didn't get the warm-up job. After several interviews, King's handlers noted that, although Pickering was a gifted orator, he took too many shortcuts on the "th" sound. Phrases such as "beneath the cross" came out sounding like "beneet da cross."

"I'm sorry," the selection chairman said, somberly delivering the decision. "The committee has deemed that such linguistic lapses are unbefitting of the crisp doctoral eloquence of Martin Luther King."

The rejection had been a major blow, one that haunted Reverend Pickering to this very day. Now, after years on the front lines, he was tired of being passed over for one thing or another and seeing his contributions to the Movement routinely ignored. He was especially vexed by both the gall and the success of young bucks like Cliff Barnes— Johnny-come-latelies who reaped the bounty of all *his* suffering, and without having to shed a drop of blood!

When Barnes wound down his prepared speech, the audience applauded again. He nodded acknowledgment of their good taste and appreciation and took a few triumphant steps back to hand over the mike.

Now it was Pickering's turn, and he stepped forward. The reverend was a tall, high-bellied man with deep razor bumps and dark skin that had the kind of oily texture you see on the faces of people who drink too much. His hair was thick on the sides, topped with a thin, stringy crown. He wore a shiny beige suit and matching shoes.

As he stood before the civic league gathering, a host of anxieties tugged at him. After four decades in the pulpit, the reverend feared he might be losing his thunder. His church membership was tapering off. His worshippers were being lured away by the new breed of celebrity preachers, clerical capitalists who served up fancy words like candied yams. With their manicured nails and tailored suits, the celebrity pastors preached a gospel of prosperity that appealed to black folks with hefty mortgages on expensive houses and fat bank notes on late-model cars.

One night, as he knelt in prayer, Reverend Pickering told God his ministry badly needed a boost. Now he suspected he was about to come upon God's reply. That was what Reverend Pickering was thinking when he took the mike. He was thinking God was about to speak through him.

Ministry or no ministry, God or no God, he was not *about* to allow himself to be upstaged by some greenhorn politician, some young boy with nothing more to offer the people than a fancy Yale law degree. He intended to show this boy how to speechify.

The preacher stepped forward and started slowly, almost reluctantly, just like King used to do back in the day. Speaking in a thick southern drawl, spiced with low and rhythmic Baptist cadences, he ran off, rapid-fire, a long list of despicable deeds, carried out at the behest of this country's leaders, that had led to untold suffering and hardship throughout the world. These were loathsome, callous leaders, he said, whose salaries they—black people!—helped pay.

From there, the reverend flowed into a freewheeling, half-hour rant against misguided domestic policies, unfettered graft by lobbyists swarming Capitol Hill and rampant corporate greed. Then, with the audience hanging on his every word, he deftly steered the ship back to its local port.

"I don't know bout y'all," he bellowed, "but I'm sick-and-tied a dis! And I'm sick-and-tied a bein sick-and-tied!"

Reverend Pickering took a strategic pregnant pause and lowered his voice to a near whisper. (He used to love the way King did that; it left folks eating out of his hands.) He spoke so softly that people seated in the middle pews had to lean forward to hear.

"There are those who say we should step aside!" He pounded the lectern. "Uh-uh! Uh-uh! *Y'all* might step aside, but I'm not! . . . I'm a fighta from the ooolll school!"

As the preacher went on, Barlowe beamed in hard, trying to get a read on this man's heart. He studied the meaty nose, wide and long, and the bulging eyes—maybe the most fiery eyes he'd ever seen.

"I'm tellin you that, insofar as Gawd is my witness!"—Pickering pounded the lectern again, harder this time—"I shall *not* be moved!"

When it was timed just right, that simple phrase, peppered with a dash of pastoral passion, had worked charmingly during the Movement. It usually got folks all fired up.

This evening was no different. The people clapped heartily, louder than they had clapped for Barnes.

Pickering proceeded to milk the cow: "We must fight like the biblical David, who took on big, ol Go-li-a wit no weapon, save for a flimsy slangshot and a sturn faith in Gawd . . . I'm tellin ya, is time for l'il David to dust off his slang!"

There were more approving shouts, screams and wild applause.

He tilted his head skyward: "I saaaiiiddddd is tiiimmmeee for li'l David to dust off his slang!!"

Before long, the crowd was on its feet. Some folks shoved clenched fists in the air, in a Black Power salute. Others stomped, shook their heads and banged the pews like conga drums.

Still others hissed, "Yeessss! Yeessss! Yeesssss!"

By the time he crossed the midway point, Pickering had achieved what he had set out to do: As oratorical matches go, he thought, he chewed that young boy up and spit him out like a pork chop bone.

Barnes watched and listened with grudging admiration, itching for another crack at the old warrior. But it was too late. The momentum had swung to the reverend now.

As for the people, this was the moment they had been waiting for. They were outraged, restless, ready to attack somebody—*now*.

Even Henny Penn and his hoodlum crew joined in. They were so charged they forgot where they were. Just when the crowd began settling down, Henny rose to be recognized. Everyone turned and studied him.

Henny Penn was a sturdy, handsome man. He kept his hair cropped short and meticulously neat—parted down the middle, New York style. He sported a mustache so thin and straight it looked like it had been drawn by a stylist skilled at eye shadow work. This day, Henny wore a red velour jogging suit.

Henny wasn't shy about speaking his mind, not even in a gathering of decent folks. He shouted, at the top of his lungs: "I say we kick they asses! I say we run them crackers outta here!"

Somebody invoked the ghost of Malcolm. "By any means necessary! By any means necessary!"

A few supportive shouts came from other young people scattered in various corners of the sanctuary. "Yeah! Yeah! Any means necessary!"

Reverend Pickering calmly watched and listened, waiting for the commotion to die down some. Then he signaled for the people to take their seats.

"Hole on. Jus hole on a minute."

When they were settled, he turned and faced Henny Penn across the room, looking him squarely in the eye.

"Tell me somethin, son."

Henny sensed a lecture coming. He rolled his eyes. "Whut?"

"Son, whut make you thank bein ignant is a *political* act?"

Henny tugged his jacket collar and glowered at the preacher.

Reverend Pickering spoke with a patience that bordered on condescension."In the Movement we never stooped to vi-lence. When I was wit Dr. Kang, me and Andrew Young and John Lewis took all kinda beatins upside the head. Whut we did in them times took a kinda courage you young folks nowadays don't know nuthin bout."

Henny Penn cursed under his breath. "Sheeeitt!" He snorted and nodded to his crew. "I thought these niggas was serous. Fug dis. C'mon!" He straightened the wrinkles in his jogging suit and led his minions through the door.

Several other young people, impatient, edgy, got up and followed. Tyrone stood, too. Barlowe tugged at his pants and pulled him down.

Meanwhile, Clifford Barnes glanced nervously at an assistant, who returned a knowing nod. Barnes held up an arm, high enough to be clearly seen checking his watch. Then the councilman politely excused himself—"I have another commitment pending"—leaving the preacher to handle the flak.

When the politician had disappeared, Pickering pointed toward the door. "Dis fight ain't for the faint-hearted, no!"

He took a handkerchief from his pocket, wiped his brow and returned to the mission God had set him to.

"In all this time, nuthin's changed, my friends. Nuthin has changed, and nuthin will ever be the same."

He thought of his good friend Jesse Jackson, and revved up the grandiloquence another notch. "Dese newcomers can't cohabitate! They gonna come in and nihilate!"

Those words charged the crowd again. Applause sailed up to the church rafters. Shouts and screams seemed to rain down from the heavens, as people leapt to their feet and roared.

Elated that he could still electrify a crowd, the preacher stood there recalling days long gone by. He pined for those days again, the days when righteous warriors took to the streets and boldly challenged stubborn segregationists.

Those days would return—he could feel it. The fire in the room was a heavenly sign. It was a sign that he'd come to the right conclusion that night when he knelt down to lay his burdens in God's expansive lap. The Lord was telling him—he was sure of it now—that he needed an old-fashioned civil rights march. Surveying this pumped-up crowd, he could tell the people here needed one, too.

Reverend Pickering hadn't had a good march since 1987, when he and Hosea Williams led 25,000 people up to Forsyth County to face down the Klan. What a grand march that was!

Indeed, Reverend Pickering's whole adult life had been defined by the march. Those marches during the Movement had brought a deep sense of purpose to his life. He missed the camaraderie of walking, arms locked with Martin, Coretta and countless other frontline soldiers, heading to the battlefield. He missed the rapt attention from news reporters and camera crews, who zoomed the eyes of the world on them.

High drama. Excitement. Danger. That was what the march was all about!

He longed for that excitement again. He needed it. Now the challenge was to convince the people that they needed what he needed. He had to lead them to it carefully, like a wife leads her husband to believe *her* idea is actually *his* idea.

Looking around the room, he sensed he was almost there. He pressed forward with a message aimed to close the deal.

"We can't step aside, no matter how powful the forces! We mus stand and fight!"

People shouted: "Yeah! Yeah!"

The preachers behind him flung their arms skyward and did the Holy Ghost dance.

"Yeah!! Yeah!!! Is tiiime!"

"Preach, brother!!"

"Make it plain!!"

"Weelllllllllll!!!"

The people got so fired up that Reverend Pickering was tempted to lead them—right then and there—into the streets for an impromptu, warm-up march. And why not? They were ripe as week-old apples, just plucked from the tree.

But he resisted the urge. People needed to be properly trained, organized. He calmed the crowd and prepared to launch a discussion about what should be done.

Barlowe sat erect, antsy. He suspected the preacher was about to lead the gathering to some frightful course of action that they might regret later on.

Reverend Pickering picked up steam. "I'll share wit y'all somethin Mah-tin tole me yeahs ago—I'll never forget—we were campaignin down in Missippi for votin rights! He came to my hotel room late one night, and he was troubled! He couldn't sleep! We had been beggin ol

Pharaoh to do right by us! And ol Pharaoh—the white mayor in dat Missippi town—told us ta go straight ta hell!"

He paused. "Well, Mah-tin came to my room and we talked thangs through! Finally, after hours a pokin and probin for slutions, we came to the clusion that there was but one thang left to do!

"I'm tellin ya dis evenin that Mah-tin didn't wanna do it, and neither did I! But we knew we had to! And ventially he looked me in the eye—I'll never forget—he looked me in the eye and said dese wurds: 'Owen, I'm fraid we gon have to march.'"

The reverend gazed out over the church gathering and paused to let the idea sink in and mix real nice like a Brunswick stew. Then he stirred the pot a little. He said what they were all waiting, now dying, to hear.

"Now I'm sayin to you people tonight: Lawd knows I don't wanna do it! But I'm fraid we gon have to march!"

There were cheers, and loud, thunderous applause. People standing around the walls pumped their fists in the air and yelled.

"Yeeaaahhh!!! Yeaaahhh!!! Yeeeaaahhh!! We gotta march!!"

Mr. Smith and Zelda and Tyrone all stood and clapped heartily. Barlowe stuck to his seat. Glancing around the room, he could see it coming. This train was starting to move.

He couldn't bear to sit there quietly. He had to speak up, say something that might slow things down and give folks more time to think.

Not knowing exactly what he would say, Barlowe raised a hand. After a few minutes basking in the glow of applause and cheers, the preacher recognized him, reluctantly.

Barlowe stood. He looked around the room, then turned and faced the reverend. He cleared his throat. Then: "You don't know me, but my name is Barlowe. Barlowe Reed. I don't wanna take up much time, but it seems to me that before we go marchin there's some things we need to talk about."

Pickering beamed in, curious, skeptical.

"Yeah. We listenin. Whut we need to tawk about?"

Barlowe shifted from one foot to the other. "Well, I share the concerns bout the neighborhood. But I'm confused: How we gonna protest folks payin their own money to live where they wont?"

People looked at Barlowe, then turned to each other. They really hadn't thought about *that*.

Tyrone tapped him on the arm. "Whut you doin, man? Whut you doin?"

Barlowe ignored him. "And one more question . . ."

"Yeah. Go on." Pickering strained to conceal his irritation.

Barlowe pointed southward. "Right there, just a few blocks up the street, is Martin Luther King's old home. And the next block down is his grave."

Now there was complete silence in the room. Folks were anxious to hear the point.

"I was thinkin bout the fact that we talkin bout marchin to keep folks *out*. King fought so people could get in . . . So if we march, what are we sayin? Are we bein hypocrites?"

When he finished, he sat down, having already gone much further than he'd intended. Oddly, Sandy Gilmore crossed his mind.

The boys from the store looked at each other, mystified. Willie whispered to Ely: "Is dat ol Barlowe—Mr. Conspiracy—up dere changin his song?"

"Maybe the boy fell down this mornin and bumped his head."

This crowd was in no mood for technicalities and complications. Barlowe braced himself for the sure attack.

The first shot was fired by Clarence Sykes, seated two rows ahead. Clarence turned around, twisting his mouth sideways when he spoke.

"C'mon, Barlowe. Be serous. We ain't on no schoolyard here. We playin for keeps, man."

There was scattered applause, and a kind of eager hope among the people that Clarence—or somebody, for heaven's sake—would bail them out.

Clarence went on. "I been livin in the Ol Fo Wode all my life. I'm committed to stayin here. When you committed, you gotta be ready to stand and fight!"

"Yeah! Yeah!" More scattered applause.

The second strike came from Wendell Mabry, who stood straight up from his seat. He had a toothpick in his mouth, and he worked it round and round, beneath the tongue.

"Barlowe, you know you all right with me and all, but I gotta tell ya, you soundin kinda scary. You sound like you moe concerned bout ol massa than your own people."

Barlowe fixed his gaze deep on Wendell's eyes. He raised up slowly, both fists balled in a knot.

"What you sayin, Wendell? What you sayin?"

"You heard me! I'm sayin what I just *said!*"

"Which is what, Wendell?"

"Which is what I just said!"

Barlowe made a move to get to the aisle, but Tyrone held him back.

Wendell didn't shudder or shrink. "So tell us, Barlowe. Whut *you* propose we do? Nothin?"

Barlowe squinted, breathing heavy. He wanted a clean shot at Wendell's throat.

Finally, when he had calmed down some, he spoke through clenched teeth. "I'm not proposin nothin, Wendell. I was just askin a simple question, thas all."

Barlowe and Wendell faced off like that until Lula Simmons interjected. "Why don't we just reach out to the new people? Some of them are really nice."

Wendell didn't even bother to look her way. "Lula, why don't you wake up and smell the coffee?"

"Now, now," said Pickering. "Les remain civil heah." Studying Barlowe, he let out a nervous chuckle. "Son, lemme be the furst to say dis: I give my en-tyre life to the struggle. Got the battle wounds to prove it, too."

He yanked off his jacket and started to roll up his shirt sleeve to show his scars.

"You don't haveta show me nothin," said Barlowe. "All I'm sayin is, this feels a little bit like the kind of meetin *they* used to have to keep *us* out."

Silence again. Heads turned in unison toward Reverend Pickering, waiting for a comeback that would put them back on solid moral ground.

Pickering stepped away from the microphone. He raised an index finger to his cheek, weighing the young man's words. Finally, he said, after some reflection, "Tell me, son. How long you lived in dis neighborhood?"

"Some years," said Barlowe.

"Uh, huh. *Some* yeahs . . . Well, I been livin here a li'l mo then twenny-five yeahs. And dis church been part a dis community for twenny-three. You follow me?"

Barlowe said nothing.

Reverend Pickering continued. "And tell me, young man. Whut is your line a wurk?"

"What?"

"Whut do you *do* to urn a livin?"

"I work at a print shop downtown."

"Uh-huh. Uh-huh. A print shop downtown."

He was getting geared up to take this young punk to the woodshed. And he would have, too, if Mr. Smith hadn't raised a hand. Mr. Smith stood and spoke loudly, addressing the congregation.

"I been livin out chere for thurty yeahs, so I think I have a right to speak on this, too. I ain't happy bout what I see, neither." He pointed at Barlowe. "But I know this main. He a *good* main. Live right cross the street from me. And I can tell ya, he not tryin to be no distraction. He jus tryin to tell us that maybe we gotta be careful, thas all."

Mr. Smith never looked at Barlowe once while he spoke. Although the old man had come to his defense, Barlowe sensed he would have preferred they were sitting farther apart—maybe at separate ends of the earth.

"Okay, okay," Reverend Pickering said, quickly. He had no quarrel with Mr. Smith, who was well regarded in the ward.

"We git your pernt. We git your pernt. We don't wont nobody to misunnerstand whut we tryin to do . . ."

Pickering addressed Barlowe. "Lemme say dis: We share The

Dream. Mah-tin would flip in his grave if he thought we was doin udderwise. Your pernt is well taken, son. But dis here may be a li'l more complicated than you thank.

"Unfortunely, we don't have time to go into it all right now. We'll have to pick up on dis discussion, maybe at the nex meetin."

And there *would* be another meeting, though when the date was set, some folks might conveniently be overlooked.

After a brief discussion, they formed an ad hoc committee to study the matter. Of course, Reverend Pickering appointed himself as chair.

The preacher ended the civic league meeting as they often had done during the Movement: They joined hands crossways, swayed slowly and sang that old civil rights battle song:

> *We shall over-co-ome.*
> *We shall over-co-ome.*
> *We shall over-come, some da-aaa-aa-ayyy!*
> *Deeeeep in my heaart*
> *I do be-liee-eve*
> *that we shall overcome,*
> *Some day . . .*

# Chapter 25

After the meeting, Barlowe and Tyrone went outside and joined a group of people gathered along the sidewalk in front of the church. Mr. Smith grabbed Zelda's hand and led her off without saying so much as one good-bye.

Wendell was talking, holding court about the meeting, when Barlowe approached. He sliced a sentence in half and walked away.

Others followed, leaving Tyrone and Barlowe standing alone.

Tyrone stood there a moment, gritting his teeth. He rolled his eyes, looking up and down the street, away from Barlowe.

Finally, when he couldn't hold it any longer, he turned to his uncle. "Whut you do that fo?!"

Barlowe kept quiet, thinking. After a long moment, he said, "Tell you the truth, Ty, I don't know. Somethin bout that meetin didn't feel right to me."

Tyrone looked off into the distance again. "I cain't blieve it. *You* of all people. Always talkin that *black* shit."

Normally, Barlowe wouldn't have let that one slide. He would have told his nephew to shut his mouth or he would shut it for him. But this day, after what he'd just done, he sensed something was different somehow, yet he didn't know what it was. So he simply repeated:

181

"It jus didn't feel right."

Tyrone squinted, still glancing up and down the block. His eyes danced around in his head like his thoughts were racing.

"I'm tellin ya, man. These whities. They need to be dealt with. Know what I'm sayin?"

"Dealt with how, Ty?"

Tyrone looked down at Barlowe's shoes like he wanted to spit on them. "Never mind, man. Never mind." He said a tight-lipped "Later" and started up the street.

Barlowe stood outside the church alone, disconnected from his own emotions. Why *had* he done that, anyway? He had never done anything like that before.

Well, at least he had made a point. And maybe he had bought some time.

He decided to take a walk. Across the street and catty-corner from where he stood, he saw Miss Carol Lilly. She was bent over in her flower bed. He headed down the sidewalk, wondering: *Bought time for what?* What had he bought time for?

He wasn't sure. But he knew this: If somebody didn't do something there would be trouble. He could feel it.

He went up Randolph Street, toward the Purple Palace to look for Tyrone. He wanted to talk some more. He approached a group of children playing hopscotch along the walk. He walked right through the game, unaware that they were even there.

Down near the Purple Palace, Tyrone was nowhere in sight. Across the street, Henny Penn and some of his boys huddled in a tight knot at the corner of an apartment building. Some knelt down, rolling dice. Others stood around, drinking wine.

Barlowe considered going inside the Palace. He hadn't been in there in quite a while. He could use a relaxing game of cards, or better still, a stiff drink. He would settle for the easy company of people—anybody not connected to that bizarre meeting he had just come from.

Standing out front, he stared longingly at the doorway. A lone man, bug-eyed and morose, sat on the porch in a wooden chair. A brown bag rested between his legs, the neck of a forty-ounce peeking through the top. Ten feet away, on a bald patch of dirt yard, a plastic Big Wheel tricycle rested in the mud. A dazed-looking woman came through the door, her hair askew. She stumbled slowly across the yard.

Barlowe turned around and headed home. On the way, he saw a white man walking toward him with a dog. It was the same white man whose dog had dumped in Mr. Smith's yard a while back.

Short and medium-built, the man had a clean-shaven face that made him look more like a grown-up boy. He carried a pooper scooper now and wore plastic gloves to gather his pet's waste.

As they approached each other, Barlowe noticed the deep blue eyes again. The man looked directly at him, searching his face.

When they were about to pass, the man yanked the leash, pulling the dog in closer.

"Hi."

"Hi," Barlowe said, weakly.

The man's lips parted again, and his blue eyes twinkled, like he wanted to say more.

Barlowe wanted to speak, too, but he had no idea what he would say, even if he could coax a sound from his throat.

As they passed, the man waved good-bye. It was a friendly wave, an awkward extra gesture.

Barlowe wondered what it meant. Did the man know about the secret meeting? What about Sandy? Had she heard about it, too?

What did he care? He dismissed it and continued on.

He reached his walkway and stopped in front of the house, where something had caught his eye. About thirty yards away, at the boundary that separated his house from the Gilmores' place, there was a six-foot wrought-iron fence.

He stood there, baffled. Where did that come from? How long had it been there? Was it thrown up while he was away at work or had he simply failed to notice before?

He walked around back and studied it closer. Beginning at the front corner of the Gilmores' house, the fence wound around to the entire backyard. It was decorative, with pointy ornamental tips on top. The tips weren't razor-sharp, but they were sharp enough to pierce the skin.

He stared, wondering, what was the point? To keep somebody out? To keep somebody in? Or was it put there for decoration?

Barlowe gazed toward the back door of the Gilmores' house, hoping to catch a glimpse of her. What did she have to do with this?

He waited several minutes. She didn't appear.

He thought again about the secret meeting. He thought about Wendell and Tyrone and the blue-eyed white man he'd just passed on the walk.

He moved closer to the fence. With each hand he grabbed the vertical strands and gripped them tight. He stared through the stripes, like an inmate peering through prison bars.

# Chapter 26

Barlowe worked at finishing his last print job for the day. As usual, he was far ahead of the rest of the boys. He had the press running at medium speed, doing a one-color job of twenty thousand sheets. He was feeling pretty good about the day—better than he'd felt since that church meeting. He planned to go home, suck down a few beers and skim through a travel book he'd picked up from the library the week before.

Across the room he saw skinny Franky Doyle, who worked at the press a few feet away from his machine. As usual, Franky was goofing off, stalking a boy named Freddy up a narrow aisle. Freddy ran, and Franky chased, popping his backside with one of the cloths.

Barlowe had returned to his work area and begun arranging printing plates for the next day's run, when Billy Spivey appeared from out of nowhere. His britches hitched up high and jaw puffed with a wad of tobacco, Billy stopped at Barlowe's machine.

"Hey, Barlowe."

"Billy."

"I got a big ol dragon for you to keel."

Barlowe kept his eyes fixed on his press.

"Yeah, Billy? Whas up?"

"They got one a them religious conventions goin on over at the World Congress Center. Alla sudden somebody remembered they need thirty thousand Jesus flyers, on the spot."

He spit in the cup, then smiled a nervous, brown-toothed smile.

Barlowe grabbed more printing plates and checked his watch.

"Thas not good, Billy. Is pretty close to quittin time."

Spivey checked his watch, too. "Yeah, you right bout that. Tell ya the truth it pisses me off. But the boss told em we could do it." He spit in the cup. "You know Mr. Scott. He weren't gonna let no bizness get away."

The foreman checked his watch again and shifted his weight to the other foot. "You can hep us out?"

Barlowe nodded toward Franky, who had just returned to his machine.

"What about him?"

Billy half-turned around. He didn't see Franky, but he knew he was there.

"He goin to a concert tonight. Toby Keith and Reba McEntire. A man cain't rightly pass up on Reba and Toby."

Barlowe hadn't seen the books, but he was sure Franky was paid more than him. Of course it was supposed to be his imagination that there was something wrong with that.

"Can you hep us out?"

Barlowe cranked up the press speed, partly to drown out Spivey's voice. The papers fired faster now.

"Boss said we gotta do it, Barlowe. We may as well face it. It gotta get done."

Barlowe looked up from his machine. "Well, then. I guess it gotta be done, Billy."

The foreman smiled and slapped him across the back. "Thanks, buddy." He spit in the cup, then hurried off.

A piece of paper jammed in Barlowe's press. He stopped the machine and pulled it out. The sheet was crumpled and splotched with ink. It had run catty-corner beneath the plate. He checked the tray up top to make sure the ink supply was strong. He cleaned the plate and wiped down the rollers, then cranked up the machine to finish the job.

It took nearly two hours to complete the convention programs. The press run went without a hitch. When he was done, Barlowe entered the time in his log. He used to treat overtime like he used to treat money: He paid little attention to either one unless he really needed to. He needed both now, so he kept a strict time log, down to the minute.

The job done, he left the shop. He got in his car and pulled away. He flicked on the radio, sank into the rhythm of an up-tempo jazz tune and melted into the traffic flow.

The rush-hour traffic was heavy now, with city worker bees out in force. Women dressed in business suits and clunky sneakers rushed down walkways, toward parking lots. Men wearing cheap white shirts and wrinkled ties headed for the subway line.

He cruised past Woodruff Park, where homeless men who learned to play chess in jail held makeshift tournaments on park benches until the big conventions came to town. Then the vagrants were rounded up like so much cattle and whisked back to jail until the conventions ended and the tourists left.

Driving along, Barlowe wondered if Billy Spivey was trying to mess with his head. He wondered if the foreman was trying to set him up to be fired or get him pissed-off enough to quit.

It made him shift his thinking about working for other shops. In fact, he had recently applied to a shop across town. He might take that job if they made him a decent offer. They might not treat him any better than he was being treated now, but they'd surely pay him something closer to what he was worth. Life being what it was, there likely would be trade-offs somehow.

He stopped at a traffic light. A car filled with white people pulled alongside him in the next lane. He glanced at them, then shifted his attention to the string of folks parading down sidewalks. One man shuffled along in tattered clothes, his dark face a brooding testimony to life's power to unhinge the soul.

Barlowe glanced back at the white people in the car beside him. A woman in the front seat pointed at the derelict, who now sifted through a garbage can. Barlowe could see the woman's lips moving. A backseat passenger flapped his jaws, too. They all laughed.

Barlowe wondered what they were laughing at.

The light changed, and he pulled away. Riding down the street, he thought about William Crawford. Maybe he could ask the old man if he'd accept a lower down payment. Barlowe had managed to save some more money, though there was still a good ways to go.

Gliding along, he felt his spirit soothed some by the music on the radio. It was Johnny Hartman. He cruised and watched the world pass by as he got lost in the lyrics—lyrics about love; love lost and love found. He got so swept away by Johnny Hartman crooning against the backdrop of people walking the city streets that he decided to take the long way home.

Down near Pine Street, whole platoons of homeless women and men lounged in the doorways of vacant buildings, waiting for the next shelter feeding time. Tourists with high-tech cameras hung around their necks walked in tight, nervous clusters, studying maps and keeping wary eyes out for beggars.

Barlowe drove up Peachtree Street, on up by the peep show joints, to the intersection near the Fox Theater. He hung a right onto Ponce de Leon Avenue and went to the Krispy Kreme doughnut place.

It was Wednesday evening. Glazed doughnuts went on sale on Wednesdays. He bought a dozen glazed and a quart of milk, then pulled back onto Ponce, trying to decide which way to go. If he turned left off Ponce he would run into the heart of Midtown, which was mostly white. If he turned right off Ponce, it would take him toward the Old Fourth Ward.

Barlowe turned left. He wasn't ready to go in yet. He rode around Midtown, eating doughnuts and taking in the city scenes. He approached a construction site, where the routine sound of progress drifted his way. It was the persistent knock of hammers against those gigantic nails; the clack of Sheetrock being hastily slapped onto building frames.

A sign out front announced now-familiar news:

**COMING SOON!**
**LUXURY CONDOS**
**LOW $200s!**

Barlowe suddenly slammed on the brakes. A squirrel had run into the street. Caught in the middle of the road, the creature froze, then dashed off and leapt onto a tree trunk nearby. Barlowe turned down a narrow street, lined on both sides with trees and cars. He swung onto 10th Street and drove past Piedmont Park. He went straight through to Virginia-Highland and hung a right onto North Highland Avenue.

On North Highland, the scene transformed into a world of cheery Yuppie clones. Everywhere, there were people, *them*, walking along sidewalks in groups of twos, threes and fours, strolling down happy lanes, some with springy Lab retrievers leading the way.

WASPish and smug, they seemed to be out celebrating life.

**Life. Be in it.**

Barlowe stopped at a light and checked them out. One couple strolled along the walk licking ice cream cones. The woman wore blue leather flats and neatly creased silk pants. She had a sweater draped perfectly around her slender shoulders. The sleeves were cross-tied and hung loosely over her chest, like the models in the L.L. Bean catalogues.

Her companion, a lanky man with moussed-up hair, wore creased denims and a burgundy knit shirt, with penny loafers and no socks.

Barlowe wondered, *Who taught these people how to live?*

People in Virginia-Highland looked like they all had enrolled in the same Life seminars: They married young—right around thirty—remained newlyweds for about eighteen months, then started families. They sprouted apple-cheeked babies (usually one, sometimes two), then traded in their Saabs and BMWs for SUVs and minivans. They settled into homes furnished by Ethan Allen, hired Hispanics to tend their lawns, and traded fitness club memberships for three-wheeled jogging strollers.

Like rickshaws in India, those strollers were everywhere. The side-walks of Virginia-Highland were flooded with *them*, running, panting behind three-wheeled strollers, with wide-eyed, apple-cheeked babies riding high.

Barlowe pulled to another stoplight. Folks sat outdoors at restau-rants, laughing, chattering and drinking beer. In front of him, a pickup truck sat waiting for the light to change. There were bumper stickers pasted on each side of the flatbed door. On the left side, a sticker fea-tured an American flag, plastered below these words:

### UNITED WE STAND!

The truck had another flag, too. A faded picture of the Confeder-ate flag adorned the right side of the flatbed gate.

Barlowe sighed. He couldn't seem to get away from flags. Even when he sat down to watch sports on TV, he noticed them, pasted on the backs of football players' helmets and sewn across their jersey fronts. They were stitched on basketball players' uniforms. Watching the Atlanta Hawks play one night, he spotted tiny flag stickers taped to the bottom corner of the basketball goals—on both ends of the floor!

It was crazy.

Now Barlowe stared at both flags in front of him and sucked his teeth, disgusted. Then, with no conscious thought about it, he released his foot from the brake pedal. The car eased forward, bumping the back of the pickup truck.

The driver, a white man with a long, blond, irreverent mane, poked his head out the window. He flung open the door, spitting and cussing, and started toward the back to assess the damage.

Barlowe got out, too. He walked slowly, fixing a stern gaze on the white man's eyes. When the two men met, Barlowe got right up on him; he got right up in his face.

"You got somethin to say to me, chief?" His fists were balled, tight, ready.

The white man looked in Barlowe's cold eyes and, oddly, thought about health insurance. He glimpsed his bumper, which was slightly dented.

He forced a smile. "Ain't enough damage thar to poke a finger at. Forgitaboutit." He turned around, climbed in his truck and drove away.

Barlowe left Virginia-Highland, too, heading toward home. He took North Highland up through the run-down industrial area and stopped at a corner grocery store. A sign pasted up high on the back wall inside the store announced that the Georgia lottery was up to five million dollars now.

He bought a bunch of tickets. On the way out he thought about what he could do if he won the lottery. He would buy a new house, one bigger and better than the one he was in. He'd buy a new car, too—this time, a foreign brand. And he would take himself on a nice vacation. He had never gone on a real vacation before. He took time off work every now and then, but he never had extra money to go anywhere, except to an occasional baseball game.

He could do a lot of things if he won the lottery. He could even quit his job.

He went back in the store and bought four more tickets.

Heading home, he stopped at a light down near Glen Iris Drive. Just as he was about to pull away, a woman sprang from nowhere and stumbled in front of the car. She waved wildly for him to stop. Barlowe slammed on the brakes, barely missing her thigh. She rushed to the passenger-side door. When he rolled down the window, she poked her head inside.

"I ain't had nothin to eat. I need a ride. Gimme a ride a few streets over."

The woman was brown-skinned, with an oval face that looked like it might have been pretty once. Her hair was thrown back on her head like she had left somewhere in a hurry. Her eyes had the glazed look that he saw in Tyrone sometimes.

She looked wild-eyed, desperate.

Barlowe hesitated, then leaned across the seat and pulled the door handle. She climbed in and slumped back heavily on the seat.

As they rode along in silence, she leaned her head back on the head-rest and closed her eyes. Barlowe stole a closer look. The woman was plump, with meaty thighs that hugged her dirty jeans. She wore a simple gold-colored blouse, with three buttons loose at the top.

He wondered if she was clean.

"You say you need to go a few blocks over?"

"Uh-huh." She opened her eyes, then closed them again.

"You all right, lady?"

"Yeah. I jus got outta jail. I only had money for bus fare home. I'm hongry." She looked at him. "I need fi dollars to get somethin to eat."

Barlowe drew his wallet, pulled out a ten-dollar bill and handed it over.

The woman stuffed it away, quickly. She pointed a finger, directing him where to go. He drove down a narrow street. She motioned for him to turn. He drove a few blocks until the street dead-ended.

"Park here," she said, matter-of-factly.

He turned the car around and parked, then scanned the area. It was a lonely, desolate place. No real signs of life; not even a squirrel or a stray dog walking about. There were a few boarded, abandoned houses nearby; a few others had newspapers plastered across front windows, or battered cars sitting out front.

The woman gazed straight ahead, her eyes not focused on any-thing. She began to rub her breasts. She caressed herself as though she'd forgotten Barlowe was there.

He panned the area again, then peered at the woman. Her eyes were closed.

Barlowe shut his eyes, too. Soon he felt fingers creep onto his crotch. He grabbed the woman's hand near the wrist, but left it resting in its place. His heart pounded, and his manhood stiffened.

*Relax.*

He released his hold on the woman's hand and tried not to think. Sweat beads formed on his brow.

The woman unzipped his pants and leaned down low, moving her hand up and down. Barlowe felt a warm, moist sensation.

*Relax.*

She worked his manhood. He trembled and heard himself moan. He leaned the seat back a little, almost against his will.

*Relax.*

The pressure inside him rose. It rose slowly, then gushed forth. He released, freeing a thousand pent-up tensions in staccato bursts.

When it was over, the woman sat up straight. Once more, she leaned back on the headrest and closed her eyes.

Barlowe zipped his pants. He started the car and drove away.

The woman directed him a few blocks over. He pulled in front of a shabby house, with shingles missing from the roof. Several men stood out front, smoking cigarettes and talking. Before Barlowe stopped the car, the woman leaned on the door. She seemed in a hurry now.

Without looking back, she climbed from the car and rushed toward the house. Barlowe glanced in his rearview mirror in time to see the woman vanish through the doorway. He drove off, eager to get home. He intended to take a long, hot bath and give himself a good talking-to.

He hoped Tyrone was away. He wanted to get a cold beer and sit alone with the lights turned off.

It was dark outside now. He reached Randolph Street and found he could barely get onto his end of the block. A crowd had gathered along the sidewalks, spilling over into the middle of the road.

Closer to his place, the crowd grew dense. He saw familiar faces. Willie and Ely and Amos had drifted over from the Auburn Avenue Mini-Mart; Mr. Smith and Zelda were out there; even Viola and The Hawk had stopped to see what the hoo-ha was all about.

Barlowe pulled to the curb in front of his house. That's when he saw. People stood around, staring at the Gilmores' place. Sean and Sandy stood on the sidewalk, side by side, with their arms folded, staring blankly into space. Twenty feet away, their mailbox had gone up in flames. Smoke billowed ten feet high.

Sirens blared from up the street as a fire engine raced toward the scene.

The fire burned fiercely, its flames ascending the wooden mailbox pole, reaching well beyond the top. Flames flickered and smoke curled and swirled toward the blackened sky.

Barlowe got out of the car and took his place among the people. They watched in silence, the light from the flames reflecting off their faces.

Lapping the edges of the charred mailbox, the flames formed the shape of the old rugged cross.

# PART III

# Chapter 27

For days after the mailbox fire the old folks in the ward sat on their front porches and whispered in solemn tones about how it was a near-abomination that somebody would do such a thing. Despite severe misgivings about *them*, the old folks' Christian faith forbade them from reveling in someone else's misery. And they surely couldn't condone (not outwardly, at least) violent acts of retribution.

But inwardly it was different. Inwardly, the old folks got a certain glee, a twitch, you might say, in knowing somebody put a size-twelve shoe up white folks' ass.

Soon after the fire, word spread through the neighborhood that the Auburn Avenue Mini-Mart had been sold. The next day, somebody flung a baseball through a white family's window.

Later, the old folks sat on their front porches and waved their flags privately. In a curious blend of Christian faith and pagan spite, they cheered the young lions for having the good gall (or bad judgment) to raise such hell.

And they kept a hopeful eye out for more such "developments."

■ ■ ■

As Barlowe stepped outdoors and headed toward his car, a street crew approached with city workers dangling off the back of a truck. Like soldiers leaping from an army tank, they attacked an ancient pothole. They poured in tar and packed it tight, then steam-rolled the spot and smoothed it out until the hole disappeared.

Barlowe muttered: "Caesar."

Mr. Smith called to him from across the street. "C'mon over here, boy, and tawk to me. Tell me somethin good fore I die."

Mr. Smith had gotten get rid of his old car. Now he spent much of his time outside, piddling in the yard.

Barlowe went over and greeted his neighbor. "You see the game last night?"

"I watched the first quarter or so, then turned the dang thang off. I ain't gonna waste time on a team coached bad as that. Life too short for messin round."

"Give em time, Mr. Smith. They'll come around."

The irony wasn't lost on either of them: The younger man preaching patience to the old.

While they stood there, a police cruiser rounded the corner and stopped at the curb near the Gilmores' place. They sat there a moment, spying around.

Mr. Smith studied the policemen and shook his head. "Um, um, um. Place been swarmin wit em."

"Some people glad to see more cops, Mr. Smith."

The old man narrowed his eyes. "Now, *see*. There you go agin."

"What?"

"You know *whut*. Talkin Republican."

Barlowe hunched his shoulders. "What?"

"Don't forget. I went out on a long tree limb for you at that there church meetin. I cain't do that agin."

"I toldja, Mr. Smith. Somethin wasn't right about that meetin. I think Pickerin is a hypocrite. I can't stand hypocrites."

"Yeah, well, sometimes you gotta do wrong to make things right."

Barlowe wasn't exactly sure what that meant. He was about to ask when Mr. Smith leaned over and gave him an elbow nudge.

"Hey. You heard anythin else bout that fie?"

"No, you?"

"Heard they ain't got a single lead. Been a whole week, and they don't know no moe than they did befo."

"Too bad."

Mr. Smith winked. "Maybe it is, maybe it ain't . . ."

Barlowe frowned.

"Shoot," the old man groused. "Nobody was hurt or nothin."

"Somebody coulda been hurt, Mr. Smith. That fire coulda shot cross the grass and caught onto them folks's house."

"Coulda, woulda. It didn't happen, did it?"

Barlowe didn't respond. He looked at the ground, scraping a foot at a stray piece of wood.

"I know what you thinkin. You thinkin a ol man like me shouldn't be that way."

"I ain't judgin you, Mr. Smith."

"You can jerdge all you wont. Don't make me no nevermind. . . . Shoot. I done paid my dues."

They both remained quiet a long moment. Finally, Mr. Smith began to reminisce. The old man looked off into the distance, his rheumy banjo eyes seeing a place and time Barlowe wasn't privy to.

"I used ta work over at the cotton mill, ya know. Worked there for twenny-five years fore they laid me off. The foeman didn't like me cause I looked him in the eye when I tawked to im. Looked im straight in the eye, jus like I'm lookin at you right now. He didn't like that commin from a colored man.

"Him and me locked horns bout somethin one day, and I tole im I weren't scared a him. Told im he put his paints on one leg at a time, jus like me. After that, I knew he was gon come at me first chance he got. And he did. Come to me one day bout a month later and said, 'Bennett, I'm sorry to tell you this, but we gotta let you go.' Thas what he said: 'We gotta cut staff.'

"It woulda been a whole diffrent thang if he had said they were lettin some other people go, but that weren't the case. Looked past all them young white schoolboys and picked me out.

"I had a wife and chilren. I had been loyal to that compney a long, long time."

He swallowed hard. "Me and Zelda struggled for a whole year after that. Lived hand-to-mouf, wit me workin odd jobs for a whole year. We almost lost this house.

"When I got another job, I promised myself that weren't gonna happen no moe. I scrimped and saved every penny I made that didn't go to the house and groceries. Saved my money so if they ever came at me like that agin I could tell em where to go."

Mr. Smith smiled as another sight crystallized. "Soon as I got back on my feet good, know what I did?"

Barlowe shook his head. "No."

"Went out and got me a shiny, red convertible . . . Know that cah you used ta see sittin out chere?"

"Yeah."

"That was it. Bought it from a white man, too. It was used but it was clean.

"Zelda near-bout had a fit when I brought it home. I didn't kere bout her raisin sand. I needed that cah for *me*. I needed that cah for *me*.

"I use ta ride round Lanta wit the top down. It could be fo-ty degrees outside and I'd still have that top peeled back. I used ta like the feel a the wind on my face and bein out in the open while I cruised round. I used ta like the way it made me feel inside. It made me feel like I didn't have so much pressin me down. I could be feelin low bout somethin and I'd get in that cah and drive fast down the street and let the wind blow my trouble away.

"I used ta love the way white folks looked at me when I drove that thang. They looked at me like they was mad as hell. They looked like they was wonderin how I got that cah. They thank they the only ones sposed to live that free.

"Looka here: One day I got a pint a likker in me and got to feelin crazy. I drove that cah up to the cotton mill. It was drizzlin outside. I shoulda had the top up, but that likker was tawkin to me, real loud, so I kept it down. I drove that cah up to the cotton mill wit my nappy hair blowin in the wind and rain. I wonted to show them crackers I was still standin. My pockets was hurtin, bad, but they didn't know. I drove up there in my shiny convertible and pretended I was comin to see how *they* was doin."

Barlowe laughed.

"My ol foeman met me out on the loadin dock. Stood there and chitchatted all nice, like we was long-lost friends. I knew what he was up to. He wonted to know how I got that cah.

"And the whole time I tawked to him, I looked him straight in the eye. Looked him straight in the eye, jus like I'm lookin at you.

"I showed him he couldn't break me. Showed him I'm a man, jes like him. When we finished tawkin, I went and said hello to some a the boys. I could see that cracker still lookin from cross the warehouse when I got in my convertible to leave. I waved good-bye fore I pulled away.

"I know it ruint his day. I bet it ruint his whole week."

Mr. Smith chuckled. "I knew I was gonna be all right after that. I knew they couldn't break me.

"But I still struggled. Struggled for a long time. Yo generation don't know nothin bout struggle."

"Some a us do."

"No you don't," the old man snapped. "You wouldn't know struggle if you tripped over it."

Barlowe was about to argue the point, when Sandy Gilmore's Ford Taurus appeared from up the street, headed their way. Barlowe acted like he didn't notice. Sandy drove past the two men and honked the horn. Barlowe threw up a feeble wave and shifted angles, so that his back faced her house.

The old man eyed him closely. "All that glitters ain't gold."

Barlowe wondered what that meant. He wasn't sure he wanted to know. Besides, seeing Sandy reminded him of something else on his mind. He had been wondering if Tyrone was involved in that mailbox fire.

He pushed it from his thoughts.

"Well, Mr. Smith. I better go. I got some more things to do this evenin."

Mr. Smith smiled. "A fella gotta go when he gotta go . . . She perty?"

"No, not *that*," Barlowe said.

"Well, do whut you need, whatever it is." Mr. Smith turned and started toward his house. "Tawk to you later."

Likewise, Barlowe went in the house and closed the door.

It took only a hot minute to slip into gardening clothes. Barlowe changed and went out back. He picked up a few flowerpots and carried them over to the edge of the yard, near the Gilmores' fence. He set the pots on the ground, kneeled down and began plucking dead and dying leaves.

Minutes later, Sandy came outside, also wearing gardening clothes. She walked straight to the spot where Barlowe worked, leaned down low and began ripping up crabgrass from her side of the fence.

"This stuff is getting out of hand." She kept her eyes fixed on the ground.

"I know." Barlowe didn't look at her, either. "I got weeds runnin long the edges of the house."

"I'm trying to catch mine before it gets too bad." Her tone was tight, not as lighthearted as usual. "Guess I'll get some weed killer for this stuff. It grows too fast; too much of it to pull from between the fence posts every time."

"Yeah," said Barlowe. "Weed killer should do it."

Finally, he stopped what he was doing and looked directly at her. "I'm sorry bout what happened with your mailbox and all."

He hadn't spoken to Sandy since shortly before the fire. Neither she nor her husband had been out much since then.

He wondered if she thought Tyrone was involved.

Sandy looked up, her face flushed red. "Yeah, well I'm sorry about that, too. To tell you the truth I'm sorry about a lot of things. And frustrated. That's it. I'm frustrated."

She flung a clump of crabgrass off to the side. "I'm sorry that my husband and I are so misunderstood around here. And I'm sorry that people can't seem to let go of the past."

She sat up on her knees. "Is there nothing else to think about?" Her tone was almost pleading now. "I mean, will we ever be able to move on?"

Barlowe started digging again. "Maybe not in the way *you* think."

She stared at him. "What?"

"Maybe not in the way *you* think."

"What do you mean?"

He shrugged. "Too much water."

"Water?"

"Too much water under the bridge."

A pained expression spread across Sandy's face. "You— What a morbid view."

He shrugged again. "It is what it is."

At that moment she felt in herself the potential to actually hate Barlowe, right along with the rest of *them*. It startled her to know she could feel that way. It crossed her mind, if only for a flash, and as much as she wanted to, she couldn't deny that she had the potential to hate.

These people were starting to wear on her. How could they reject her? Many times she'd defended them—their peculiar habits and behaviors—in dinner party debates, and now they were rejecting her. It seemed unfair.

"You know what bothers me most?"

"No, Sandy. What bothers you most?"

That was the first time she'd heard him call her name. In the time she had known him, he had avoided addressing her directly. She had wondered if he even remembered her name.

"What bothers me," she said, her anguished pitch rising again, "is I'm sick of people making these sweeping judgments. I'm telling you, it's crazy. It's just crazy, and I don't understand."

Barlowe sat up on his knees and took off his gardening gloves. "These people been out here toilin most a they lives. *You* came in on a fuggin whim. So what don't you understand?"

Sandy yanked off her gloves and slammed them down. She glared at him through the fence.

"Is that what you think? You think I came here on some kind of whim? Who do you think I am?"

"Far as I can see, you just a silly white girl lookin for somethin interestin to do."

Sandy's nostrils flared. *How dare he!* She couldn't believe what she'd just heard.

"Mister, I'm not here on a whim. I'm here because I happen to care. You may not believe it, but I care!" She cupped both hands over her temples and rubbed gently, like she felt a migraine coming on.

"Why do I always feel like I have to prove myself?"

"Calm down," said Barlowe. He looked around. "You startin to make a scene."

Sandy lowered the volume, now speaking through clenched teeth. "I'll have you know this is not something that just started for me. I'll have you know that I've been wrestling with this stuff in some form or another for most of my life."

She sucked her teeth, wondering why she wasted her time.

"You know, I actually feel sorry for you. You're so wounded that you may no longer be capable of seeing the good in others."

That remark pissed him off. He stewed but didn't respond—not because he had nothing to say. He kept quiet for her sake. He knew that if he spoke his mind at that moment, he'd blast her. He'd blast her with so much thunder she might not ever recover. He was tempted to do it anyway, if for no reason other than to crush the arrogance underlying her words: The nerve of her. *She* felt sorry for *him!*

He wanted to let it rip, but he held back for the sake of the thread of a relationship trying to form.

And there was another reason: Hers may well have been the worst case of sincere ignorance he'd ever seen, but at least she was trying. She was trying, which was more than he could say for most of *them*. He couldn't bring himself to torpedo someone who was trying, however clumsy the effort.

Finally, Barlowe held back for his own sake. For reasons that were still a riddle to him, Sandy embodied some vague glimmer of hope; she clung to a vision that reached beyond anything his life experiences had allowed him to see. He sensed his own hope, dim as it was, somehow was tethered to her stubborn optimism. So he kept quiet and peered through the fence, a tangle of feelings tugging at him from every direction, and all at once.

Sandy stared back, wrestling with her own roiling emotions. She thought she saw a subtle smirk creep to the corners of his mouth, but she didn't care. Why should she care what he thought? Why should she care what any of these people thought?

Still, in spite of herself, she felt compelled to explain. "I'm not going to lie. I'm not going to stand here—"

"You sittin." Barlowe smiled, trying to lighten the mood before things got too far out of hand.

"No, seriously." Her tone was tortured. "I'm not going to stand here and try to pretend that I don't have doubts sometimes. I'm human. I have my moments. You can bet that fire has shaken my foundation a bit."

She didn't finish the idea. Her mind raced around in frantic circles. She felt so bothered she couldn't settle down enough to bring cohesive order to her thoughts.

She brushed a hand across her hair and spoke slowly, trying to regain control of herself.

"I'm telling you that me moving out here has nothing to do with a whim or trying to find something interesting to do. The point is, Barlowe, Sean and I are not out here trying to take over."

"The point is," snapped Barlowe, "you don't *have* to try."

Her face turned crimson, like he'd slapped it hard. She gaped at him, processing what he'd said.

He returned the stare. It remained that way for a long moment, them staring at each other, until finally she broke the spell.

"I see," she said, finally. "I see."

Barlowe wondered if she really did see. He wondered if she was even capable of seeing. Now he was pissed again, and so was she. They were fed up with each other and, together, mad at the world.

They both resumed working. She yanked up crabgrass, and he snatched leaves from flowerpots.

Then Barlowe spoke again. "What you wont here, anyway?"

At first she thought he was being flippant. Then she searched his face and saw that he was serious. She stabbed her shears hard in the ground.

"I'll tell you what I want. I want people to accept my husband and me for who we are: We're neighbors. That's supposed to count for something."

"Yeah?"

"Yes."

He studied her a moment like he was trying to search her soul. For an instant his stare, the way she felt him looking through her, made Sandy uneasy. She gathered herself.

"I know who I am. You may not know it, but *I* know."

He squinted. "You one a them liberals, ain't ya?"

"I don't like labels," said Sandy. "Let's just say I'm me."

He bored in some more. "You know what they say bout liberals?"

Sandy's eyebrows raised. "They? Who's they?"

"They say liberals conduct their lynchins from shorter trees."

She grimaced. "You seem to be very morbid today. Do you know what they say about morbid people?"

"No, what?"

He waited while she tried to think up something. She wanted to respond with something snide and witty. She couldn't think of anything, and that frustrated her more.

"Never mind," she said, finally. "I know who I am."

"Okay, then." He looked askance. "Okay. Then that should be enough."

"You don't believe me. I can tell, and I resent it. I resent your whole negative attitude. But that's okay. I'm gonna prove you wrong. You'll see. I'm gonna prove you wrong."

"You do that, Sandy. Prove me wrong."

They fell silent once more. After a while, Barlowe got up from the ground. "I'm done for now. I gotta go."

She was still angry, but not ready for him to leave just yet. The conversation felt unresolved.

"I've got a little more to do," she said.

She hoped he would stay, at least stand and talk until she finished her work.

He didn't cooperate. "Later."

He went in the house, leaving her on her knees, pulling up grass from through the fence.


When Barlowe got inside, he found Tyrone standing in the kitchen, munching on a green apple. He was stationed at the window, gazing curiously outside. Barlowe wondered how long he had been standing there. He got a drink of water and started toward the living room.

"Yo, Unk."

Barlowe stopped and turned around. "Yeah?"

"You bangin that white bitch next doe?"

"No."

Tyrone smiled. "C'mon, Unk. You can tell *me*. I'm your boy!"

Barlowe's irritation showed. "I toldja, no."

"Really?"

"Really."

"So what you and her be out there talkin bout, up at the fence alla time?"

"We talk about the way things are."

"Thas all?"

"Thas all."

Barlowe left the room.

Tyrone looked again out the kitchen window. Sandy had gotten up from the ground. He saw her walk slowly toward her house. He studied the subtle sway of her hips. The hips were really nothing special—he'd seen much better, many times. But they were a woman's hips just the same.

"Shucks," Tyrone said, thinking out loud. "I'd fuck her."

# Chapter 28

Sandy went into the house and headed straight to the bedroom. She sat on the floor and tried to meditate. She tried, but Barlowe's words echoed in her head: *You just a silly white girl, lookin for somethin interestin to do.*

He seemed to think he knew her better than she knew herself. That wasn't possible, was it?

No. He barely knew her at all. He barely knew her, which meant he could not possibly know her heart's desires. In time, he would see her for who she was. He would see for himself. Then maybe he'd apologize.

She inhaled deeply, then exhaled slowly, trying to take herself to that serene place she had gone so many times before. With her legs folded and torso erect, she sat there for the better part of a half-hour, trying to go deeper inward. But she couldn't. Her thoughts shifted from the fire to Barlowe and back again. The fire haunted her almost every night. She tried to push the sight of the flames from her mind. She focused like she had learned to do in meditation class. A few more minutes passed, and she still struggled.

Unable to let go, she decided to submit, to give in to the memory and convert the negative energy to good vibrations.

Fire. Fire was symbolic of so many things. It was a source of warmth and a source of healing. It also was a monster that consumed and destroyed.

Fire. She contemplated its healing powers. The world needed healing, for sure. She inhaled again, holding her breath as long as she could. She exhaled slowly, releasing the fear and anxiety that crowded her chest.

Later, she got a glass of wine and went to the living room to wait for Sean. He'd be coming in from work soon. They had planned to talk.

Despite the meditation, she felt unsettled, tense. For days after the fire, Sean had not spoken a single word to her. It wasn't like him to shut down like that. They had always communicated well until now. Now he walked around the house, silent, brooding, sometimes gazing at her with an icy stare. It troubled her not knowing what her husband was thinking. Tonight maybe she'd find out what was on his mind.

With that thought came a new worry: Exactly what would Sean say? Would he blame her for this nightmare? Would he accuse her of being so wildly idealistic and naive that she was putting their lives at risk?

She was clear about one thing. She would allow for some criticism, but not too much. She wouldn't let Sean delude himself into believing this was all her fault. After all, hadn't they agreed—together—that the move would come with challenges? Hadn't they both decided they were up to the tests, no matter what?

Well, here was the "what" they'd been referring to: a mailbox doused with gasoline and set aflame; a haunting message from neighbors that people their color weren't welcome in the Old Fourth Ward.

This was no time to lose resolve. Sitting in her living room it dawned on Sandy that that was exactly what she saw in Sean: a rapid loss of resolve. He seemed deeply troubled, not to mention punchy and unable to sleep at night.

And now there was this new obsession with security. Since the fire, he had bought a new alarm system, with a motion detector. He'd installed blinding, megawatt floodlights around the house and yard.

And then there was the matter of that hideous fence. She came home one day and there it stood, forbidding entry and exit. She hated being fenced in. She'd protested the fence, then dropped the issue as a concession to his fear. Now she wondered how far Sean would take this security thing.

At night he constantly wandered through rooms in the house, checking the double locks on windows and doors. Just the other day, Sandy had found on the coffee table (maybe he had left it there on purpose) a book about dogs; attack dogs, to be more precise. She fully expected to come home one day and find a snarling Rottweiler guarding the door.

Her Sean appeared gripped by fears that ran deeper than mere safety concerns. She wondered, *What exactly is he afraid of?* She wanted to confront Sean about his growing jumpiness, but decided to leave him be. He was a man. Most men wouldn't tolerate a woman questioning their manliness. She had learned that from watching her father and mother.

But things were getting crazy. Sitting there, Sandy sipped wine and shuddered at the thought that things could spiral out of control. It was a terrible feeling. She wondered again, *How could this be? How could I have been so wrong about the move?*

Then something occurred to her. Other than the family maid, Ethel, she had never really interacted much with *them* before. Sandy knew Ethel before she'd gone to college and studied history and social issues. As a young girl she was too naive to grasp the complexities that surely must have colored Ethel's interactions with her family. Beyond that, she had dealt with *them* only in passing, in controlled settings where they were in the minority.

As an adult, Sandy had never had concrete dealings with black people. She had looked upon them as ideas, as abstract social causes. This new experience was altogether different: living among so many dark, hostile strangers, seemingly opposed to her being alive. She realized now that even after all her study and thinking, she had grossly underestimated the breadth of these people's fear and rage.

She shuddered.

Suddenly, she heard a car door slam. She got up and peeked through the curtain. It was Sean. His back was turned. He leaned over inside the car and stuffed a shiny object into the glove compartment. She rushed back to her seat and waited for him to come through the door.

Sean came in and nodded a silent hello, then headed to the bedroom to change clothes. As had been the case in the past week, his manner was frigid, aloof. In a moment of near-panic Sandy wondered if he was falling out of love with her.

She was anxious about the impending talk. What could she say to put him at ease? How could she apologize without compromising her sense of who she was? And how could she persuade him of the need to hold firm when she wasn't sure *she* was still fully convinced?

Sometimes when she drove through the neighborhood she got an eerie sensation, an intuition, that something bad was about to happen, something worse even than a fire. That sensation passed over her now.

Sean reappeared from the bedroom and went into the kitchen. He returned with a glass of iced tea and sat down on the couch, across from her. He seemed so distant now, so formal.

"How was your day, honey?"

"My day was fine, Sandy. Let's get to the point of why we're sitting here."

She crossed her legs and took another sip of wine. Her throat was dry.

"Okay, Sean. Let's get to the point."

He spoke in a somber tone, like a sheriff who has come to tell a family that a loved one has been killed.

"Look, Sandy, I hope you see now what I see."

"I hope so, too, Sean." She shifted, nervous. "So let's talk about what it is that we each think we see."

"I don't *think* anything," he snapped. "For me it's fairly obvious. We're in a war zone. We've pretty much served our tour of duty here."

She released a pained sigh. "Too much water, huh?"

"What?"

"Nothing. Nothing." She sighed again. "So what are you saying, Sean?"

"I'm saying this is not turning out like we thought it would. This is not 'The Beloved Community' you envisioned. It's time to pull out, move. We can't keep going to sleep at night not knowing whether we'll see another day. That's no way to live. It doesn't make sense, Sandy. We're outnumbered here, about a hundred to one."

"Sean, don't you think you're taking this to the extreme? I mean, you don't think these people intend to kill us, do you?"

He shot her a look that actually bordered on disgust.

"C'mon, Sean. That fire was just a childish prank. It was a bluff from people who are suspicious. These people are afraid. The neighborhood is changing, Sean. Look around. It's changing every day."

"Yeah," he grumbled, "but I need it to be changed a bit more than it is right now. And I surely don't need to be living next door to somebody I think might attack me or firebomb my house." He pointed toward Barlowe's place. "Just my luck. Fucking thugs, right next door."

She aimed an index finger at him. "Be careful, Sean. You don't know that the man who attacked you was involved in that fire."

"The only way I don't know it is that I didn't see the bastard pour the gasoline or strike a match!" He was shouting now. "But I can guarantee you this: I can guarantee you that he was in on it; at the very least he was a lookout! I'll bet you a month's pay he was a lookout for them!"

"Who's *them*, Sean? Who's them?"

"Whoever set that fire! And I guarantee you that it was more than one person. Cowards seldom act alone."

Sandy spoke softly, trying to reassure herself and calm him down. "Be patient, Sean. The policemen told you they would investigate. Why don't we wait and see what they find."

"Why should I be patient? Why should we wait around for something worse to happen? Uh-uh. *You* may be still full of peace and love and light, but not me. My light burned out when they extinguished that fire."

Sandy said nothing. Maybe it was best to let him vent.

"Don't give me that *look*! You know I'm right! You saw what happened! Those people actually booed and jeered the firemen! Fucking thugs! The whole neighborhood's full of thugs and thieves and drunks and . . . I say we cut our losses, Sandy, and get the hell out of here. I say we call that real estate agent of ours, stick a for-sale sign in the ground and see what we can get for our troubles."

Sandy folded her arms and shook her head. She had actually entertained that same idea before Sean came home. Now, hearing him talk this way, hearing the ugliness expressed out loud, produced the effect of cold water splashed in the face.

"We can't do that, Sean. We can't move."

He leaned forward and gawked, incredulous. "Why are you telling me what we *can't* do?"

"Because. If we move it will be an indication of defeat."

Sean leaned back and stared up at the ceiling, shaking his head in disbelief.

"Sandy, you don't understand. I don't care about public appearances. I just don't care."

"Neither do I, Sean. But I do care about how we view ourselves. If we move it would be like acknowledging that we're not who we thought we were; we would be admitting that we have given up."

"For me, that wouldn't be entirely untrue," said Sean. "I'm not feeling very hopeful right now—except that I hope your father was wrong about what he said." (Speaking of her father, they'd invited him—twice—to visit, and each time he'd flat-out refused.) "I hope he was wrong in predicting that we'd never get our money out of this place."

"Sean, you know as well as I do that my father would love it if we moved—"

He interrupted: "And I also know your father would have a frigging fit if I let anything happen to you, all for the sake of trying out some social experiment before its time."

Hearing those words sent blood draining from Sandy's face. "Oh. Is that what you think? Huh? Is that what you think? That this is a social experiment before its time?! That sounds like something my father would say."

Sean refused to dignify the comparison with a response. It was bad enough that her father had been right, after all. No need to let her rub it in.

Sandy continued: "Tell me, Sean. When is it ever time?! When is it ever time?!"

He still didn't respond.

She pressed on, louder. "And if we move, Sean, just where do you recommend we go? Where would we go, back out to the 'burbs? And if we did that, would we be moving forward or stepping back?"

Sandy pounded a fist into an open palm. "No, Sean. There's no choice. We have to stay."

Early in their marriage, Sean and Sandy had made an agreement: Whenever they had an argument, or simply needed to think, one of them would get on the interstate, circle the perimeter and drive and ponder until the temper cooled. Sean needed that now. He needed space, fresh air. He needed to go for a drive and spend some time alone.

Without saying a word, he got up and started for the door.

Sandy called to him. "Sean! Sean! C'mere, Sean! We're not finished!"

He went outside, got in his car and sped away.

On the way down Randolph Street, Sean passed the Purple Palace. He saw Tyrone standing outside, talking with Henny Penn and two other men. Tyrone's arms flailed, like he was embroiled in an argument.

Sean passed the men and eyed them in his rearview mirror. He hated that those thugs were still walking the streets. They had set his mailbox on fire, and there they were, walking around, free, brash as ever. They should be punished, locked up, for what they'd done.

He reached Interstate 285 and shifted into the speeding lane. He reclined his seat and drove, pondering his predicament. For a brief moment, his attention shifted to a classic, souped-up Camaro. It zoomed by. Sean felt vaguely annoyed to see a black guy behind the wheel. The guy leaned down real low with his head propped against the driver's-side door.

Sean leaned back in his seat, too. He thought of Sandy and grunted: "Huummph." He should have known better than to be totally frank with her. He knew she would react the way she did. He knew she would label him, with no regard for the complexities of things. That's how it was with her. Everything was black or white.

Sean hadn't realized that about her when they first fell in love. There were a lot of things he hadn't realized in the beginning. He hadn't even recognized the flaw in himself, his eagerness *not* to see.

They'd first met in college. The first time he saw Sandy she was giving a speech. Sean was on his way to lunch and happened upon a campus rally. Sandy stood on a stage, railing against the evils of the conservative tide sweeping the nation. Her zeal, the passion that she exuded, was alluring to him.

Before then, Sean had given no real thought to the issues she talked about: abortion, genocide, poverty and greed. He had gone to college for one reason: to earn a degree so he could provide more for his family than his father had been able to do when Sean was growing up. And so Sean had focused on the things that mattered most to him: good grades; job prospects; getting laid once in a while.

Sean had always been a good person in a general way, but Sandy in her speech urged students to be more than good people; she urged them to be doers, to demonstrate their caring by getting involved.

The speech was powerful, electrifying. People responded with cheers and a standing ovation. After that speech, Sean became a secret Sandy Peterson stalker. Using his computer skills, he found out everything on public record about her. He tracked her activities on campus, mainly by monitoring the website of an organization she belonged to: Students Against Oppressive Powers (SAOP). He followed SAOP's calendar and began attending its functions. He eventually met Sandy at one of the group's socials. They talked, and he was even more swept away by the dirty blonde with the fiery spirit. After a few more conversations, he mustered the nerve to ask her out.

The week before the date, he crammed as though studying for semester finals. He read the *New York Times* every day, focusing on national and world affairs. When they went to dinner he was at least familiar enough with current events to hold a decent conversation.

Sandy was impressed, even if he was, as he confessed, "relatively new" to social activism. He wanted to learn more, he told her. He cared and wanted to help make a difference in the world.

After that date, Sandy seemed eager to teach him. And so their romance began as two people who shared a mutual concern for environmental issues and social justice. Sean got the girl, and all he had to do to keep the girl was to match her compassion for human beings.

That seemed easy enough. Sean figured that when he graduated and launched a career, he could donate money to various causes; he could even give of his time, maybe tutor some black kid once in a while, if that was what Sandy wanted.

None of that charity threatened to disrupt his goals. Sean dreamed of marrying someday. He dreamed of having children—three, to be exact. He dreamed of owning a home—nicer than the one he'd grown up in.

When they got married after college, Sean knew that life with Sandy meant they would always contribute *to* The Cause, however she defined it at a given time. Never in his most extreme imaginings, though, had he considered that he might be called upon to live *in* The Cause.

He wanted Sandy Peterson, but he had never signed on to suffer. Now it seemed she expected him to do just that, and it didn't seem fair.

Driving along the interstate now, Sean told himself that he had suffered enough already: He'd nearly been robbed; been almost choked to death; had his mailbox set aflame.

Running through the list of transgressions he'd endured, he decided that a change was in order. He couldn't afford to be passive anymore. There was too much at stake; their very lives, for heaven's sake!

Then it came to him: He needed protection. Without protection, something tragic would happen. He could feel it.

After being attacked by Tyrone, Sean had scrounged up an old army knife. Following the fire, he'd shifted the knife to the glove compartment in his car. Now having just seen those hoodlums on the street, looking hardened and ruthless, he wondered, who was he fooling? These people were dangerous. A knife wouldn't be enough against the likes of them.

He shifted his attention a moment and took note of where he was. He had driven a good ways on the perimeter. Now he approached a sign that said *Chattanooga*. He wondered if Chattanooga had these social problems. Probably not. Chattanooga was probably peaceful. Beautiful mountains and country music. Maybe that's where he and Sandy should move; someplace like Chattanooga.

He circled the perimeter once more before heading home. He glanced at the dashboard clock. Nearly three hours had passed. He pulled into the driveway and turned off the engine.

Sitting in the car a moment, he realized he was drenched in sweat. He sat there, sweating and thinking: *Yes, I will get real protection for my wife and me.*

He went in the house and closed the door.

# Chapter 29

Barlowe sat on the supply table and watched the printing press, its engine whirring like a low-speed locomotive. He liked the sound of the press, especially when it was set up right. When the registers were set right on the machine, the paper shot from back to front like bullets fired from a gun. He liked the sound of the paper, too. Each sheet made a sharp snapping sound as it whizzed up front to the cylinder, where the plate pressed the image onto the page. It sounded like a snare drum. *Snap, snap, snap, snap.*

While the machine ran, he collected ink-stained cloths strewn about in his work area. He tossed the cloths in the big laundry basket set up against the wall. He had returned to his press and bent down to restock reams of paper and supplies, when a voice snatched him away from his peace.

"Hi."

It was a woman. She was standing across from him, on the other side of the print machine. She held a manila envelope in her hand.

"I need to have five thousand of these flyers printed by tomorrow."

"Tomorrow?" Barlowe kept his eyes glued to the paper running through the press. *Snap, snap, snap, snap.*

The woman struck an apologetic tone. "I know this is short notice, but the man over there said you might be able to help me. He said you were the best person for a rush job like this."

Barlowe looked in the direction the woman pointed and saw Billy Spivey standing in his office doorway. Spivey hunched his shoulders, implying he had no say in the matter.

Barlowe turned back to the woman. "How many sheets you say you need?"

"I'd like to have five thousand . . . but if that's a problem, I can get by with half for now and maybe pick up the rest later . . . It's just that we want to start distributing these as soon as possible."

Barlowe focused squarely on the woman for the first time now. Her hair was styled in thick cornrows, which flowed back into a bun at the base of her neck. She was dark-complexioned, with very dark eyes, which seemed to take him in fully. She had dimples, which, he thought, complemented her pretty face.

He pointed at the envelope. "Lemme see what you got there."

The woman opened the flap and pulled out handwritten instructions for the flyer she wanted. In near-perfect cursive writing, she had specified the type size and style. Barlowe studied the sheet. It was an announcement for a concert to be held soon at Spelman College. The concert featured a group called Sweet Honey in the Rock.

"I'll do it," Barlowe said, plainly. "I'll squeeze it in somewhere."

"Thank you sooo much." The woman smiled. He noticed a gap between her two front teeth. The gap complemented the dimples, he thought.

"What time do you need to pick these up?"

"*You* tell me. I'll come whenever you say."

He liked the sound of that sentence. *I'll come whenever you say*. He would love to hear those words spoken in another context sometime. They were the kind of words that lately had been missing from his life.

"I'll have it ready by ten."

"Thanks. Ten. I'll see you at ten."

As the woman turned and walked away, he studied her hips, which were accented by a wide, patent leather belt. She wore blue jean shorts that revealed feminine but sturdy legs.

When she had gone, Barlowe leaned down and adjusted a knob on the side of his press. He straightened up and was startled to see the woman standing there again.

"I came back to tell you that I have an extra ticket if you're interested in coming. It should be an excellent show."

"I might do that," said Barlowe. "This contact name on this sheet; is that you?"

"Yes, and you can reach me at that number."

"Will do."

When she left, Barlowe looked at the contact name: Louise Grimes. He looked again at the rest of the flyer. Sweet Honey in the Rock. *Strange name,* he thought. He had never heard of the group. If he went to that concert, he wouldn't know what to expect. It could be a gospel group, or worse, some rap band. He hated rap music.

He finished his print run. He was scheduled to start on another job, ten thousand brochures, but decided it could wait until morning. He wanted to start on the concert flyers right away, to guarantee they'd be ready when Louise Grimes came in.

So he typed and printed all five thousand flyers, and kept an extra one for himself.

# Chapter 30

After the Auburn Avenue Mini-Mart was sold, the store closed in no time at all. Juliette James took the money and moved with her family to Florida. Now there was a big plastic banner flung across the top of the door where the old store sign used to hang:

**COMING SOON: THE CAFE LATTE!**

In the months that followed, the boys next door still brought their chairs outside, like they had done for years. With the store closed, they seemed lost sitting out there near a "No Trespassing" sign. They sat and argued as usual, but in their quiet moments each man chewed on private fears. With little money and few relatives willing or able to take them in, they wondered when the mounting changes in the Old Fourth Ward would swoop down and swallow them.

Barlowe was standing in the front yard, talking with Mr. Smith, when two white men came up the walk. They each carried a yellow legal pad. They stared directly at Barlowe and Mr. Smith with the determined look of Jehovah's Witnesses.

One of the men extended a hand as they approached. "Hi, friends."

Mr. Smith turned and walked away. Barlowe would have left, too, but he was curious to see what the men were up to.

He recognized the men as neighbors. One of them lived on his street. The shorter of the two, the one with the pencil-thin mustache, spoke first.

"I'm Danny and this is Greg. We're part of a team circulating a petition. We'd like to know if you'll be wonderful enough to sign."

"For what?"

The taller man, whose skin was the color of lobster, took a turn.

"We want to create a jogging and bicycle lane on Randolph Street."

"What?"

"Yes, the Murphys—you know the Murphys?"

"No."

"The Murphys live on Howell Street. Anyway, they've come up with a great idea. Some of us are bikers, and we'd like to be able to ride from Randolph Street to the path that leads to Stone Mountain."

He smiled, waiting for Barlowe to acknowledge the brilliance of the idea.

Barlowe grunted instead. "Um."

The shorter man jumped in, pushing his sunglasses up the bridge of his nose. "We've drawn up plans to submit to the Urban Design Commission. We've already checked to make sure there's no problem with the city's historic preservation guidelines."

Then the other chimed in cheerily: "We need signatures from at least two-thirds of the households on the street, to show that this has strong community support."

The sales pitch was disrupted by the squeaky sound of Ricky Brown's grocery cart. Ricky came up the street and stopped right there. He wore dingy pants, a black skullcap and huge, block-shaped glasses, with thick black frames. He had a small radio fastened to his belt, with wires and plugs running to his ears. He wore powder blue earmuffs, to hold the plugs in place.

Ricky glanced at Barlowe's house, then turned to him and shouted, "Look like yo gutters need cleanin!"

"I don't think so, Ricky. Not today."

"I do a good job! You'll love my wurk!"

"Not now."

Ricky turned to the white men. One man pretended to study the names on the petition. The other diverted his eyes across the street.

Barlowe was tempted to drag out the conversation with Ricky, just for the living hell of it. Instead, he gave Ricky a final no, then sent him on his way. Ricky went up the street, stopping midway along the block to pick up an aluminum can.

The white men resumed their pitch: "So. Would you care to sign?"

"No."

"It'll be really nice. We—"

"I ain't sayin yes to everything." The tone was curt, icy.

The men appeared stumped, mystified. *Everything? What did he mean, everything?* They wanted Barlowe to explain, to elaborate on his veiled reference to "everything." But they sensed in him a certain attitude. So they plastered on polite smiles, said good-bye and left, frustrated about the progress of their project, which had been met so far with stiff resistance.


When the men had gone, Barlowe went around to the back porch to get his work shoes. Tyrone's pigeons flitted around in the cage. The birds fluttered wildly, like they were restless, agitated.

Barlowe heard a noise across the way.

It was Sandy Gilmore. She had come outdoors to hang clothes on the line. Barlowe studied her a moment. She was probably one of those folks, he thought, who refused to buy a dryer. *She probably prefers to let her clothes dry in the fresh open air.*

Sandy instinctively felt Barlowe's eyes fixed on her. She turned and looked his way. She smiled weakly and waved. He waved back, then poured some extra birdseed into the tray and waited to see if she would signal that she wanted to talk.

They chatted fairly regularly at the fence nowadays. Through some unspoken agreement, they talked only when Sean was away from the house. In some ways their conversations had grown easier, more relaxed, though they still struggled to get beyond a certain point. Sandy wrestled with ways to unravel the source of Barlowe's leeriness. For him, that leeriness was less about choice than survival. Despite a reluctant fondness for Sandy, his instincts still warned him to beware. She was nice enough, and clearly well-intentioned. Still, nice people like her trampled folks like him all the time, and pretended they never knew they were underfoot.

Sometimes when they talked, Sandy suggested Barlowe was simply afraid to trust. Once, she peppered him with a string of questions, hoping to pull him out:

"What is there to lose in being more open?"

"What," he countered, "is there to gain?"

One day, he actually took an awkward crack at explaining himself. They had been chatting, and in a rare revealing moment he said: "I had a good relationship once."

Sandy perked up, curious. "Oh, yeah? Was she nice?"

"We got along fine on most things, far as I could see. But now I realize I couldn't see so far."

He watched closely for her reaction. She kept quiet, hoping he'd continue.

"Some a our differences came down to her being a woman and me being a man. I couldn't get past all the bridges and walls that came with that. I couldn't get it, even though I wonted to."

"So what happened?"

"After a while, I guess she had to decide whether to keep tryin with me or to cut her losses and move on."

"And what did she do?"

"She moved on."

Sandy shrugged. "Well, then, I guess that was her loss."

"What you mean?"

"As long as someone is willing to try, you've got to be willing to work at it."

"And what if it can't work for reasons that are bigger than botha you put together?"

Sandy gazed at him with that certain look. He recognized it now. It was the look of defiance, resolve, the game face she put on when defending one of her cherished principles.

"You've *got* to keep working at it, no matter what. I believe that. I truly do."

She thought that for once they might reach some accord on something. (Barlowe always seemed to find a reason to disagree.) But his reaction left her more puzzled than before. He looked upon her with a strange, vacant wonder. It was the look of a man standing at the edge of the Grand Canyon, contemplating the vast distance to the other side.

He likely could have bridged at least some of the gap by expanding on the awkward parable that he'd just tried to share. But he couldn't. He was wholly unable to conjure the words to adequately express the profundity of all he knew.

If Barlowe could have assembled the words that reflected his knowing, he might have said something like this: "Between two people with perceptions shaped by realities as alien as ours, some things really are inscrutable; one person's truths can transcend another's language, rendering them utterly incapable of seeing eye to eye."

But Barlowe couldn't come anywhere close to conveying that thought, so he opted out. He muttered, simply, "Never mind. Forget it."

They both rushed to end the conversation after that.

In later exchanges, they took only occasional minor risks. Mostly, they chitchatted about grass and flowers and hornets' nests.

This day, though, Sandy finished hanging clothes and headed indoors without even venturing into small talk.

Barlowe had gone into the yard to rearrange flowerpots. He briefly wondered why she seemed so aloof.

*Maybe she got a lot on her mind.*

He got up from his knees to empty dead plants into the trash. Viola appeared from behind. She was alone, and she looked sickly and weak from lack of food. She cut through the yard on Barlowe's side, trying to appear confident, like she had every right to strut through there.

Barlowe nodded a silent hello. Viola nodded back and continued on until she was out of sight.

# Chapter 31

"Come on, Sandy! We're late!"

"I'll be there in a minute!"

Sean rose from a living room chair, put on his jacket and waited. A sharp pain shot through his head, forcing him to sit down again. He needed aspirin. He had taken aspirin just an hour ago, which meant he'd have to hold off and tough it out—again.

Ever since Tyrone had nearly choked him to death, Sean had not been himself. First he'd been hounded by constant fear. Now he experienced full-blown panic attacks—intense, charged moments when he felt as if he might jump out of his skin.

There was virtually no relief in sleep, either. He had nightmares about intruders. He had visions of *them*, bursting into his home, some choking him to death while others had their way with his screaming wife in another room.

It was horrifying. *Maybe I need to see a doctor*, he thought.

Now Sandy appeared from the kitchen carrying a covered dish. She joined him at the front door.

The Gilmores had been invited to Eric and Katheryn Harper's place, two streets over. Katheryn had framed the invite as an "informal potluck dinner." Sandy hadn't thought much about that description at first. Now it gnawed at her.

The invite came on the heels of news that someone had thrown a brick through the plate glass window of a white couple's house. There had been a burglary at another home after that, followed by a testy civic league meeting that ended in an ugly shouting match.

The Harpers lived on Irwin Street. Their huge home, a hundred-year-old Colonial Revival, with a second-floor dormer window, was widely considered the most fabulously restored house in the neighborhood.

The Gilmores were among the last dinner guests to arrive. After exchanging hellos, Sandy scanned the well-appointed room, noting the sameness in the faces of the people there. Among the guests, about twenty in all, Greg Barron and his wife, Melissa, were there; Danny and his partner, Keith, had come; Sara and Ted Murphy showed up. Blue-eyed Jake Waxman, a bachelor, came without a date. Bill Buckner and his wife, Alice, also dropped in.

Now it crystallized for Sandy why she'd avoided talking to Barlowe earlier in the backyard that day: She was unsure if any of *them* had been invited. She couldn't bear to talk to him and not mention the gathering. At the same time, she wondered why she felt obligated to mention it to him.

Standing in the Harpers' expansive living room, with its glorious wrought-iron stairway winding to the second floor, she shifted uneasily on her heels.

*Relax. You're here. Don't think too much.*

She was distracted by Katheryn Harper. A tall, lean brunette with a full mane of hair cascading down to her shoulders, Kathy gently took her arm and led her in.

"We're so glad you could come." Her voice was warm, sincere. "We've been meaning to do this for some time now."

"Yes," Sean said, smiling. "We should have been getting together all along."

*We? We? Who's we?* Sandy would ask him to explain that remark when they got home.

Eric Harper, a soft-spoken man with sensitive, penetrating eyes, brought them each a glass of wine. He ushered them into the dining room, to an oblong table filled with food. Some guests milled around the table, appraising the various potluck dishes and exchanging favorite recipes: tuna casserole, beef tips, pork chops, lamb stew, etc.

"Aaaahhh! Lasagna!" Ted Murphy cried. "Who brought lasagna?"

Sandy curtsied, smiling.

"God bless you, my dear! God bless you!"

"It's vegetarian." Sean said it as though issuing a warning.

"My favorite," said Ted. "I don't eat meat."

The Harpers directed their guests to the dinnerware. They formed a buffet line and sat around a huge table, where they ate, drank more wine and splintered off into several clustered conversations.

Sean plunged into playful sports banter with Bill Buckner. Sandy was glad to see him so animated.

She was drawn to a chat among women dispensing their takes on books they'd read. She was pleased to learn that Sara Murphy shared her love of poetry, and even did some writing herself. She found Sara quite engaging, so much so that they agreed to keep each other informed about poetry readings around town.

During exchanges, Sandy learned more about some of her neighbors. She discovered Bill practiced civil law; Kathy worked in corporate accounts for IBM. Jake Waxman was a young high school history teacher, and Eric, a therapist, volunteered for Habitat for Humanity, building homes for the poor.

Intriguing people with intriguing lives: perfect for a dinner party.

As they sat in the gorgeous house, with elaborate chandeliers hanging above their heads, it was hard to imagine the conflicts raging just beyond those doors. They all ate heartily and tried to forget.

Midway through the meal, Eric tapped a spoon against a glass. The chatter subsided as guests turned their attention to him.

"Kathy and I want to thank you all for coming out this evening." Eric remained seated, to keep the mood informal. "With all the excitement that's been going on, we thought this gathering would be a good way for us to better get to know one another, to mingle and talk about something unrelated to community problems."

He paused. "We know it's been tough for some of you." His eyes fell on Sean and Sandy. "We just want to say, 'Hang in there.' Things will get better in time.

"With that said, let's just eat, drink and enjoy ourselves."

The dinner guests held up their glasses in a toast. "Cheers!" An awkward silence followed. Kathy Harper, ever the gracious hostess, moved to rescue the moment.

"You heard Eric! Serious stuff aside! No politics or social discourse permitted tonight!"

Having downed her third glass of wine, she was slightly tipsy now. She rose from the table and pointed to the living room bar, where stronger libations were stored. She glided to the stereo, snapping her fingers. "Whaddaya say we party a little!"

Some folks sprang from their seats and danced to the nostalgic rhythms of Diana Ross and the Supremes. Others finished eating, wandered to the living room and gathered around the well-stocked bar. Over the next few hours, every corner of the main floor filled with chatter. Laughter grew louder as glasses were filled, emptied and filled again.

Sandy stood off to the side with a glass in her hand, thinking, watching. She studied the dinner guests, whose boozy faces glowed with gratitude, glee and mostly relief.

Relief from what?

This: The strain that was ever-present at civic league meetings. A white person could hardly make a harmless remark without risk of inviting a rant from one of *them*.

And this, too: Relief from being made to feel guilty about simply wanting to improve the neighborhood.

Relief.

The dinner guests' delighted faces made it clear. A private gathering like this was sorely needed, a time to relax and get smashed—a chance to simply *be*.

Standing there, Sandy realized that she also craved relief. It left her feeling guilty, and slightly defeated. She struggled to reconcile the guilt with the undeniable fact that for once in a long while she was enjoying herself.

Still, she constantly shooed away pesky intruding thoughts: *Maybe they weren't invited for fear they would feel uneasy.* She willed herself to seek distraction. She floated around, dipping in and out of conversations in search of airy banter, or even empty gossip (she hated empty gossip) that might whisk her away from nagging guilt.

She approached one group and heard Ted ask Greg Barron, "How's the petition drive going?"

Greg replied with a sullen silence, prompting Danny to fill in.

"Dead in the water. For the life of me, I can't understand why they were so opposed to that . . ."

"Something's gotta be done," Barron added. He panned the faces in the cluster.

Sandy surmised from the affirming nods that some grim consensus had been reached without a vote. Beyond eye contact, no tally was needed; no more, no less than tacit affirmation of natural kinship bonds.

Determined to honor the hosts' directive to avoid serious talk, Sandy drifted off in search of another cell. Along the way, she passed Kathy Harper, who now was being twirled wildly on the dance floor by the man named Frank. While she flailed and dipped and shimmied, her voice filled the room with ecstatic screams.

Sandy joined Sean in a smaller group, certain he'd be engrossed in shallow conversation.

"I think we're about to turn the corner," she heard someone say as she approached.

"You really believe that?" Alice Buckner's voice was high-pitched, grating. "Or are you force-feeding yourself the optimist view?"

Sean jumped in. He held an empty glass. Sandy could see that he was fairly lit: "I think things will improve once everybody calms down and accepts that this is not personal. This is *not* personal. This is about real estate."

Jake Waxman, his blue eyes sparkling, fired a pointed question. "Is real estate or community the issue here?"

Sean blinked, startled. "Well . . . um, actually . . ."

He avoided looking at Sandy. That was precisely the kind of question *she* would raise.

She sensed the avoidance and cooperated, keeping her eyes averted as Sean rummaged through his head for a coherent response.

Jake stood there, coiled, waiting.

Kathy Harper, now fully wasted, unwittingly rescued the moment again. Flouncing wildly to the beat of a Four Tops classic, she attempted a '50s swing maneuver. She slipped through Frank's outstretched arms and loudly hit the floor. *Splat!*

All eyes shifted to the fallen hostess. The commotion spared Sean, momentarily at least, the strain of addressing Jake's social angst.

Again, Sandy slithered away in search of superficial talk. She spotted some people across the room, holding court near the fireplace. She poked in her head and found to her dismay that they were exchanging neighborhood horror tales. They eventually got themselves all worked up, outraged over the injustices they were subjected to. "Tyrannies!" someone shouted.

Meanwhile, Bill, the lawyer, now blind-high, began misquoting pertinent sections of the Constitution.

Throughout the house, the ranks of the disheartened seemed to swell as the evening wore on. The effects of the liquor dug in deeper, unleashing pent-up resentments that clearly had been mounting for some time now.

Then, when the libations had claimed near-total control in the house, someone, speaking in garbled words and phrases, recalled the stubborn will of Martin Luther King. It was as if King's own spirit had been channeled through those doors to pledge allegiance to their cause.

With the gritty sound of the Temptations bellowing through the speakers, some smashed soul shouted above the music, invoking a civil rights battle cry:

*We shall not be moved!*

Some—among them Sara and Eric and Sandy and Jake—distanced themselves from the drunken pep rally that followed. They each staked out a secluded space and watched in painful silence while the loaded partygoers locked arm-in-arm and sang, kicking their legs way up high in a ragtag chorus line:

*Weeee shall nooott bee!*
*We shall not be moved!*
*Weeee shall nooott bee!*
*We shall not be moved!*

Studying the scene, Sandy thought, oddly, of Barlowe, then homed in on Sean, her staggering husband. Apparently recovered from Jake's affront, Sean had wriggled his way into the middle of the raucous troupe.

It could well have been her imagination, but it appeared to Sandy that he kicked his legs higher than everyone else.

# Chapter 32

William Crawford appeared at the house, unannounced, and started toward the door. Barlowe had been outside working. He caught up with him on the porch.

"Mr. Crawford."

"Oh, hi, son. I was just about to ring the bell."

Barlowe took off his gardening gloves. "What can I do for you?"

"I came to check the water pipes."

"The pipes? Tyrone call about the pipes?"

The mention of Tyrone made the old man's glasses fog.

"No, Tyrone didn't call . . . He here now?"

"No. He didn't come home last night."

Crawford seemed disappointed. "Oh. Well, I need to check the pipes. It's been a while since I checked the pipes . . ."

They went inside and looked around. Barlowe stood over Crawford in the kitchen as he knelt down and checked beneath the sink. He stuck in his head and rattled a few pipes, then came out and stood up straight, smiling nervously.

"They look all right to me. Mind if I check outside?"

"Fine, but wait right here before we go, Mr. Crawford. I got somethin to give you."

Barlowe ducked into his bedroom and plucked up something from a dresser drawer. Crawford could see him scribbling on paper. Barlowe returned with an envelope, which he handed to Crawford.

The landlord looked at it. "What's this?"

"A check for some a the down payment we talked about. I'll have the rest in a little while."

Crawford took the envelope, reluctantly, and stuffed it in his shirt pocket without checking the amount. He leaned against the countertop, wiped sweat from his brow, then turned and headed onto the back porch.

The birds cooed and shuffled around inside the cage.

Crawford turned to Barlowe. He had a solemn look about him. "I need to talk to you about something."

"Yeah?"

"Yes." He dropped his eyes. "I'm afraid you're gonna have to get rid of the birds."

A strange, dry sensation filled Barlowe's throat. "Mr. Crawford, those are Tyrone's birds. You know how he is about his birds."

Crawford held up his hand with the palm open. "Nothing I can do about that. Sorry. It's city code."

"Mr. Crawford, you knew all along about the birds. You were here when Tyrone first brought em in."

Crawford scratched his head and looked away. "Yeah, well somebody called downtown and complained." He turned and stepped off the back porch and onto the ground.

Barlowe followed. "Who called?"

"That's not important, Barlowe. The bottom line is, it's the law. The city says it's a health hazard raising wild animals in town. They could have diseases, you know?"

Crawford went around to the side of the house. Again, Barlowe followed close behind. The old man knelt down and squeezed into a crawlspace. He came out five minutes later, brushing dirt from his pants.

He scanned the yard, like he was searching for something else to inspect.

"Well," he declared, finally, "I gotta go." He took a few steps, stopped and turned around. "I really do need you to get rid of the birds. Tell Tyrone to find em another home."

"Right. Will do." Barlowe seethed.

Crawford made another move to leave, then stopped again and reached inside his shirt pocket. He handed Barlowe the envelope back.

"Wait till I tell you I'm ready to sell. Then we can talk money."

Something about the frigid look on Barlowe's face inspired Crawford to move quickly. He hurried around the side of the house, and made off in his car.

Later that evening, Barlowe sat at a dinner table with his back ramrod straight. The table was lighted with a single candle and covered with a very white tablecloth. The room was dimly lit, intimate. Waiters and waitresses, starched to the bone and heads held high, scurried back and forth to the dining area, taking and delivering orders.

Barlowe panned the restaurant. The diners, well-heeled and sophisticated, were engaged in quiet conversations. He blinked, half in disbelief: He was having dinner with Louise Grimes.

A waiter with a white cloth draped across his arm appeared at their table and handed Louise a wine list. "Madam."

She glanced at Barlowe and turned to the waiter. "We'll need a few minutes to decide."

Barlowe used the opening to excuse himself. Inside the men's room he stared in the mirror. Except for the few times he went to church, he couldn't recall the last time he had been dressed up like this. He wore the gray jacket to the only suit he owned. Earlier that day, he had rushed to the Men's Wearhouse in search of a shirt to match the plain brown pants. The ensemble was no stunning fashion statement, but it seemed appropriate for the occasion.

Now appraising himself, he realized one of the shirt buttons was misaligned. He wondered if Louise had noticed. He reworked all the buttons until the alignments were right. He studied himself in the mirror one final time and returned to the table, where Louise was perusing the dinner menu.

She handed Barlowe the wine list. He concentrated with furrowed brows.

The waiter returned. "Have you decided?"

"I won't be having any wine," said Louise.

"Me, neither," Barlowe quickly added. (What he really wanted was a nice, cold beer.)

Barlowe picked up his menu and began to read. Again, Louise noticed his uneasiness. After a moment, she closed her menu and laid it on the table. She leaned forward and looked into his eyes. "Can I make a request?"

He shifted, nervous. "A request?"

"Yes, a request."

"Go head."

"Let's get away from here."

He looked around. "You wanna leave?"

"Yeah. Let's go. This place was recommended to me by a girlfriend on my job. It's nice, but I'm in the mood for something more casual."

They ended up at Gladys Knight's soul food restaurant on Peachtree Street. The place was crowded, but they managed to get a booth against a wall. Louise ordered the smothered chicken dinner. Barlowe got turkey wings and collard greens.

As they waited to be served, Barlowe stared at her, enamored. At that moment he was recalling the ecstasy that he would always associate with Louise Grimes. It began when Louise arranged for him to get a concert ticket. When Barlowe appeared at Spelman's concert hall and tapped her on the shoulder, she seemed delighted to see him there.

"Hiiiii!!" They sat together.

Barlowe had been to concerts before, but he had never experienced anything like Sweet Honey in the Rock. With no music accompanying them, the black women took to the stage in African garb and sang with voices so strong and clean it sent shudders through him. For two whole hours, they sang love songs and praise songs; they told musical folktales about slavery and oppression.

From time to time, Louise glanced sideways, pleased to see Barlowe so thoroughly enthralled. For him, it was nearly a religious experience sitting in a place where he was surrounded by kindred spirits. He left feeling inspired, hopeful.

He phoned Louise later to express gratitude for inviting him. Then he clumsily asked her out.

Now here they were, on their first official date.

After they had ordered, they eased into the conversational dance. Barlowe could see that, like him, Louise was rusty. After a while, they both settled down.

"Everything about you says 'city girl.'" (That was a line Tyrone might use.)

"Actually, I'm from the country," said Louise. "A place called Waycross, Georgia. You familiar with Waycross?"

"Never been, but I know about it."

"I'm a country girl at heart, but my heart has never been confined to the country . . . Does that make sense?"

"Yeah. I know."

"It's strange," she said. "I could never live there again, but I could never totally leave, either. I go home a lot. I *need* to go. It helps me keep my grounding."

Grounding. That's what he liked about Louise. She had grounding, and a refreshing wholesomeness about her, too; not the nervous, twitchy wholesomeness of young virgins, but the healthy, hydrated look of people living clean.

"I don't go home much," said Barlowe. "Maybe I should go more often, huh?"

"Yes, you *should*, even if home holds some bad memories. At its worst, it's still a kind of compass."

Barlowe smiled.

They talked some more. In time, Barlowe realized Tyrone wasn't hanging around anymore, leaning over his shoulder, whispering in his ear. Barlowe didn't need Tyrone now. Louise was drawn to *him*.

While soul music played softly overhead, a steady stream of people came and left. Barlowe and Louise talked for hours, about his job hunt, their families, houses and, of course, Caesar and That War.

"Please," said Louise. "Don't let me get started about That War."

He was perfectly willing to hear her rant. In fact, he *wanted* to hear it. So Louise ranted, and Barlowe listened. While she talked, it occurred to him that he would never have had such a conversation with Nell. The closest Nell had come to showing the mildest concern about politics was when she'd complained of rising gas prices.

"It's crazy, dumb," Louise was saying. "Sometimes I wanna leave this place."

While she spoke, Barlowe stared adoringly, admiring her dimples. He could hardly believe he was spending time with such a woman. He wanted to tell her that. In a fit of unabashed gratitude he wanted to say: "Where have you been? I been lookin for you, even when I didn't know what I was lookin for."

Barlowe dared not say that, though, for fear that such words, though true, might come off sounding phony, contrived.

He had no idea that nothing would have pleased Louise Grimes more than to hear those words.

# Chapter 33

Barlowe got home late, after midnight. Tyrone was lying on the living room couch. He had fallen asleep watching an old gangster movie. It was a Thursday. Tyrone rarely came in that early, even on weekdays. Normally, he would stumble in late at night, half-high, and go to bed. Then he'd get up the next morning and head to work to get some rest.

When Barlowe stepped in and latched the door, Tyrone yawned and looked him up and down. This new lady was special. Tyrone could tell. Barlowe had gone to the barbershop and gotten his woolly head trimmed. And he had on street clothes instead of khakis.

"Hey, Unk." He yawned again. "How'd it go?"

Barlowe smiled. "Best evenin I had in a long, long time."

"Did you fuck her?"

"Not in a way you'd understand."

Tyrone grinned and sat up straight.

Barlowe started toward his room.

Tyrone turned serious now. "I got somethin I need to tawk to you bout."

Barlowe stopped and waited. "I'm listenin."

"Not now. I'm kinda bummed out right now. Les rap tomorra."

"Lemme know when you ready." Barlowe went to his room and closed the door.

Before falling asleep, he lay in the dark wondering what was on Tyrone's mind. He wondered if it had anything to do with the mailbox next door. It had been a while since that fire. To date, no arrests had been made. Still, it crossed Barlowe's mind from time to time.

The next day, Tyrone came home and went straight to his room without saying so much as one hello. He remained in there, quiet, for a few hours, then finally came back out.

Barlowe was sitting in the living room, reading the paper. He had the business pages sprawled across the coffee table, trying to crack the mystery of stocks and bonds.

Tyrone crept into the room and sat down across from him. His mood seemed low. "Yo, Unk."

"Yeah?" Barlowe kept his eyes fixed on the long list of stock quotes running from the top to the bottom of the page.

"I got somethin heavy to lay on you."

"What?"

Tyrone stared at the coffee table, like something specific there had caught his eye. Then he looked up squarely at Barlowe.

"You won't blieve what happened."

"What?"

"Somebody snitched."

Barlowe folded the paper. "What?"

Tyrone crossed his legs and swung one foot up and down. He swung it high a few times, accidentally kicking the coffee table.

"Some a us left work after lunch to go to a bar. When we got back the supervisor was waitin in the locker room. He had already punched our time cards. Tole us to git out and not come back."

"You got fired?"

"Somebody snitched. I bet not find out who it was."

The gravity of Tyrone's words lowered into Barlowe's lap like a wrecking ball being eased down slow.

"What you gonna do?"

"I'ma find somethin, somewhere . . . You know me. I'ma carry mine."

Barlowe held off telling Tyrone what Crawford said about getting rid of his birds. A man didn't need to take in too much hardship at once.

"You'll find somethin," he said. "You'll find somethin."

Tyrone got up and started toward his room. Barlowe called to him.

"Ty."

"Yeah?"

"I know what you thinkin . . . Don't worry bout this house. It don't matter to me."

Tyrone searched his eyes.

"You don't wont it no moe?"

"Naw."

"How come?"

Barlowe thought about Crawford. The old man had come there fishing, he was sure.

"I'm startin to think that maybe it wont meant to be."

Tyrone breathed a relieved sigh.

"Good. I was startin to worry bout you."

"Why?"

"Crawford had you goin for a minute. He had you jumpin through hoops and shit."

"It was never gonna come to that."

"I don't know. He had you goin."

"Well, it don't matter now." Barlowe thought for a moment. "It don't pay to wont somethin too much. I don't ever wanna get like that again."


True to his word, Tyrone found work in less than a month. In fact, he did better than that. He started his own business, installing sound systems in people's cars. In a stroke of luck he worked out an informal partnership with an Asian businessman at a Greenbriar strip mall.

Tyrone happened to be browsing inside an electronics shop, next to the place that sold gold teeth, when the owner, a man named Kwan Li, sold a customer a car stereo system. Tyrone overheard the customer ask Kwan Li where he could get the system installed.

Li hunched his shoulders. "Everybody ask same question. Tly Cirkit City."

Tyrone took a chance. "Yo." Both Kwan Li and the customer turned around. "I can put that in for you."

Using tools that Li loaned him, he went outdoors and installed the stereo, wiring and all, in thirty minutes. Li came outside and checked as Tyrone put the finishing touches on the job. It turned out to be expert work.

When Li saw the customer's satisfaction, he was sold. He made a proposal after the client left: "You do same for udder customer?"

He didn't want much payment, Li said; only ten dollars for each referral he sent Tyrone.

"Deal."

Kwan Li seemed happy. An on-site installation service could give him a competitive edge on other area electronics shops. He was further pleased to learn that Tyrone was a good worker, and highly skilled. He could install the latest stereos, speakers and amplifiers, and he ran wiring so well it looked like it was factory installed.

Tyrone was happy with the arrangement, too. Just like that, he'd gone from the unemployment line to being in business for himself. He charged between $50 and $100 per job, depending on the work required.

It took no time at all for word to spread about the quality of Tyrone's work. Most of his business came from young men driving big, old American cars with faded paint and shiny rims. They came in seeking high-powered systems driven by lots of bass.

After his first successful month as a legitimate businessman, Tyrone came home one day, ready to celebrate.

"Hey Unk. You wanna come wit me?"

"Where?"

"I'm goin to the nekkid club. They got a real stallion over there, six feet tall! Big ol *juicy* gal! You down?"

"Naw."

"C'mon, man. Is on me."

Barlowe didn't feel like going out. But the occasion called for . . . something . . .

"All right. Les go."

Set in a back alley, the club was located near downtown. Stashed in a smoke-filled basement, it was packed with men and women sitting around tables in threes and fours, smoking, drinking and talking loud.

Barlowe and Tyrone sat at a table near the back. As he sat down and ordered a drink, an odd, satisfied look slid across Tyrone's face. It pleased him to see Barlowe in such a raunchy place. It proved his uncle was no better than him, even though he sometimes acted otherwise.

Tyrone still resented the way Barlowe had embarrassed him in front of Lucretia a while back, lecturing him like he was a child. He acted so straitlaced sometimes it got on Tyrone's nerves. Now here he was, hanging out in a club like normal people.

A waitress came over. Her face was empty, vapid, like maybe she had worked there a tad too long. She perked up, though, when she saw Tyrone.

"Hey, baby boy! Where you been?"

He slid a hand solemnly across his heart, like he was about to recite the Pledge of Allegiance. "Ever time I see you I get a taste for chocolate."

Her mouth twisted into a playful frown. "Whut you wont, boy? Whut you wont?"

"Gimme a scotch, baby. And tell that barman to make it strong. I got problems."

Barlowe ordered a beer—not domestic; foreign.

When the waitress returned, Tyrone stuffed a five-spot in her bra, which seemed to make her happy. He and Barlowe held their drinks high and clinked glasses in a toast. Then they reared back in their seats and soaked up the scene.

The place was cloudy and loud and dark; not pitch-dark, but filled with the kind of faint light that comes through vaguely in disturbing dreams. All around the room, men cheered as a sixty-year-old stripper danced onstage. A bundle of soft tissue in a one-piece swimsuit, she did a tricky three-step number. Wearing street clothes she was an easy guess for somebody's grandma.

Laughing and clapping from time to time, Tyrone and Barlowe watched the old lady carry on. After a while, Tyrone slouched down low, settling in. It occurred to him that, despite their occasional petty differences, he rather liked living with Barlowe. Living with Barlowe made him feel like he had structure in his life, which his life lacked otherwise.

It was strange, though. In all his years growing up in Milledgeville, the two of them had never been real close, not even after the death of Tyrone's daddy, Barlowe's oldest brother. Tyrone was a young boy then, and Barlowe a teenager. Tyrone had thought his uncle was a bit strange. Now, after living with him, he felt like he understood him more. Barlowe was just his own peculiar person, trying to understand how the world worked, and trying to figure out how to make it work for him.

Sitting across from Tyrone, one leg resting comfortably across a knee, Barlowe sipped beer and retreated into his own head, thinking about Louise Grimes.

At some point, one of the veteran dancers, a white woman in a frilly dress, walked close to their table and winked. Tyrone slapped her bottom and grabbed her around the waist. He pulled her in close and whispered in her ear.

There were four white men sitting at a table nearby. When Tyrone grabbed the waitress, one of the men glowered and nudged another.

Barlowe wondered what was being said.

Tyrone groped the white woman and turned her loose. He beamed across the room at another woman, who was finishing a table dance for a few hard-luck-looking boys. She caught sight of Tyrone craving her and sensed another call to duty.

She glided over. "Well, well. If it ain't Mr. Ty-Rone."

"Hey, Chloe."

"Ain't seen you in a while."

He looked at her sincerely and placed his glass on the floor. "I wont you to put yo big toe in my drink."

Chloe giggled and slipped one foot from a stiletto. She dipped a toe and giggled some more. Tyrone picked up his drink and gulped it all. Chloe slid into his lap and pulled his head gently into her ample breasts. She treated him to some lap motion and waved over a friend for Barlowe.

The friend was a real hot looker, with a big, elaborate weave and long, curly nails, painted white. When she walked her flesh jiggled, but Barlowe could see what her shape used to be.

She flopped onto his lap and draped an arm around his neck. "Hey, cowboy."

"Hey." Barlowe lifted her off his lap and away from him. He pressed a single dollar bill into the woman's underpants, which were loose from being tugged a lot. She looked at the dollar, cursed and walked away.

Chloe hung around, though. While Tyrone sought consolation in Chloe's bosom, Barlowe relaxed and took in the scene. Soon he glanced at his watch. Already he was growing bored. After a while, he finished his drink, stood and cleared his throat.

"Ty, I'm gonna head on home."

Tyrone was still lost in Chloe's bosom, which vaguely reminded him of his mama. Hearing Barlowe, he came up for air.

"Okay, Unk. I'll catch a cab. See ya in a li'l while."

He returned to the breasts, and Barlowe walked out the door.

It was late when Barlowe got home. He got out of the car and stumbled toward the front door, looking for his house key in the dark. He moved slowly, his head spinning from the drinks he'd thrown down. He staggered on the sidewalk and stopped a moment to get his bearings.

The moon shone bright, like some gigantic globe light set atop the sky. Light from the moon and a nearby streetlamp bounced off the top of the car, reflecting on the ground where he stood. As he turned toward the house, the moon and lamp lights seemed to shift with his movements. The moonbeams filtered toward a bundle splayed near the curb.

Barlowe thought it might be an old pile of carpet that somebody had rolled up and tossed out for trash. He squinted, straining to see. When his sight adjusted to the darkness, he made out a pair of bony legs sprawled out over the curb. He moved in closer, leaned down and saw part of the face.

It was Viola. She had collapsed to the ground. He tried to rustle her awake. "Hey. Hey. Get up."

She didn't move.

He considered leaving her there, but sprawled out across the curb like that at night, she could be hit by a passing car. He nudged her again, harder this time. "Hey. Get up from here and go on home."

Nothing.

Barlowe turned her over and stared a long moment. Her wig had spilled off, and foam ran from her mouth. A layer of dirt had splattered across one side of her face.

He rushed into the house to get a flashlight. He returned outside and shined the light. He got down on his hands and knees to see if he could hear a heartbeat. None. He checked for a pulse. Now he sat up straight, rearing back.

He spoke to himself out loud: "She dead."

The official cause of death was listed as liver failure, but people in the neighborhood had their own take on what killed Viola. They guessed she died of heartbreak over the mysterious disappearance of The Hawk. He hadn't been seen or heard from for some time now. After The Hawk vanished, they said, Viola's heavy drinking shifted into overdrive. Near the end, she drank so much she could hardly walk. People would find her slumped on the ground, usually somewhere in the several blocks between Davenport's house and the place she'd shared with her man for twenty years.

Viola's body remained at Hogabrook Funeral Home on Auburn Avenue for a whole week before morticians gave up trying to track down next of kin. Finally, she was given a modest city burial.

Davenport and a few of the others showed up, sober. They listened intently as some tired, baldheaded preacher recited a few kind words about a lady he had never known alive. They hung around and watched as city workers shoveled the rich, red Georgia clay onto Viola's grave.

# Chapter 34

The whites arrived early for the neighborhood meeting. They sat up front, arms folded and legs crossed, confident that, finally, the universe was evolving as it should. Moments before the meeting was set to start, the faithful few blacks trickled in and headed directly to the back of the room like they had been ordered there. Once seated, some slouched at the ends of aisles, looking dazed, cross, unsure of themselves.

And for good reason. A civic league election had been held the month before. A new league president was put in place. Now it was official: Power in the Old Fourth Ward had changed hands.

The shift, it seemed, had happened overnight . . .

Worried by apparent signs that they were losing ground, blacks asked the Reverend Pickering to run for the president's seat. Whites didn't have to draft a candidate. Their man, Gregory W. Barron, stepped forward and offered himself.

Before the election, most blacks in the ward had no idea who he was. Seeing the face on campaign literature, Barlowe recognized him right away as one of the men who'd approached him on the sidewalk to press the petition for the bicycle path.

On the day of the election, a blustery winter morning, neighbor-hood blacks mostly stayed home or eased out to buy their lotto tickets or went for groceries. Whites were still a minority in the ward, but they came out in numbers sufficient to eke out a four-vote victory margin.

Soon after the election, the local newspaper ran a story in the Sunday edition, front page, above the fold. Barlowe was one of the first people in the ward to pick up the paper that day. He rose at five, as usual; got a cup of coffee, as usual; and spread the paper across the kitchen table. He grunted, sipped and read some more, then grunted again when he reached this part:

> Gregory Walker Barron, a brash young civic wunderkind, is one in
> a handful of urban pioneers whose forays into the inner city have
> helped bring civilization to a wasteland on the brink.

Barlowe grunted some more, then got on the phone to Wendell Mabry. Wendell read the news story and buzzed Clarence Sykes. Clarence skimmed the article and called Miss Carol Lilly, setting off a ripple of phones ringing from house to house.

Later, the black people of the ward ventured outdoors, yoo-hooing at mailboxes and across rickety fences. They asked each other, and themselves, over and over: If the place was wilderness before *they* showed up, then what have *we* been doin here all this time? Are we, then, invisible? Are we objects, like trees that line the streets? What are we, then? What? Trees?

For weeks after the news article appeared, blacks around there referred sarcastically to each other as "nigger-trees" and called the white folks "pi-neers." They'd say, "A few pi-neers came through here scroungin agin today," or "I'm so sick a pi-neers I don't know what to do!"

Meanwhile, the broader view throughout the city held that the story boosted Atlanta's national image. In media interviews, Clifford Barnes, the newly elected mayor, held up the Old Fourth Ward as a shining symbol of racial harmony.

For his part, Gregory Barron welcomed every bit of the newfound acclaim. A University of Georgia boy with local roots that reached back to the Civil War, he cited the election and news article as proof that he had a real, live mandate to turn the community around. It would start this day, with his first meeting as president of the civic league . . .

Standing before the gathering in a new blue suit, Barron opened the session with a solemn reciting of the Pledge of Allegiance to the flag. (That was Barlowe's cue to go take a piss.) Then Barron launched head-on into his new agenda. He appointed whites to key positions on every civic league committee, including the one that issued the annual Green Thumb Award.

With that move, the meeting assumed the tone and tenor of a football game, with issues booted back and forth by opposing sides. They argued, sometimes vocally, but mostly in the privacy of their heads:

*Why,* the blacks wondered, *do white folks have to come in takin over and changing things? Jee-sus! Who in the hell do they think they are?*

*Why was it too much to ask,* the whites wanted to know, *to clean up the general appearance of the Old Fourth Ward? Why can't we put a stop to those spontaneous social gatherings, where men loitered, drank and played Spades, for God's sake, slamming cards down hard on wobbly tables, cussing and yelling back and forth?*

*As if the rowdy card games weren't bad enough, they hosted front-yard cookouts, where folks hovered around hideous steel drums, barbecuing chicken and ribs, with thick, black smoke billowing forth.*

*My God!*

In an effort to move the meeting forward, Barron formed a committee to study neighborhood commercial establishments. They could start, he suggested, by requiring all businesses to spruce up their premises to comply more fully with historic preservation guidelines.

That proposal drew a quick rebuke from Wendell Mabry, who yanked a dangling toothpick from his mouth. Where, he asked, would mom-and-pop store owners get money for such a thing?

In the spirit of goodwill, Barron appointed Wendell to chair a committee to research the issue. Then he steered the discussion to another money matter: the budget. How, Barron wondered aloud, could precious community dollars be better used? He gazed toward the ceiling, as though waiting for some crystal vision to drop. The people followed the direction of his eyes, straining to see what it was he thought he saw.

"I'm thinking badly needed cosmetic improvements. More streetlamps; maybe concrete pillars, placed at each entrance to the neighborhood."

Mr. Smith cleared his throat, then stood and raised an objection. "We gotta think about the winna."

"What?"

"The cole weatha."

"Oh."

"Ever year, a lotta folks round heah go sometimes thout heat cause they can't ford oil. Usually we donate some a that money to hep em out."

"Yes," said Barron, glancing impatiently at his watch. "Yes."

He moved to the next agenda item, then paused again upon reflection. "Those oil heaters. Don't they create fire hazards?"

Mr. Smith scratched his head. "If you ain't careful, sometimes they catch fie. But—"

"We may want to investigate that."

Something about the word "investigate" made blacks in the room stiffen. It stirred visions of pinstriped lawyers scouring dusty city books for ancient codes banning the things. It stirred fears of the old and the poor floating, slowly and quietly, up shit creek.

As Barron droned on in a throaty voice—he was saying something about his long-term vision now—Barlowe studied him closely. His voice carried no distinct southern inflection, though he clearly was a son of the South. Gone from that voice was the hint of humility that Barlowe recalled from the first time they met. Now the man's tone was cocky, insistent.

Barlowe's eyes remained fixed on Barron, but his thoughts shifted to Louise Grimes. He and Louise were growing much closer. He was thinking that maybe, if things didn't work out here, he could move in with her. That thought was partly inspired by the man in front of him, the man flaunting grand visions that seemed so foreign to him: "We can organize a springtime tour of homes and hoist big, colorful banners on lampposts along both sides of the streets."

The way Barlowe figured, the thought about Louise also was tied to timing—knowing when to fight and when to quit scuffling and move on in life. The time to fight, it seemed, had come and gone.

While Barlowe sat there, wallowing in every regret he had carried since second grade, a dark shadow filled the doorway, just to the right of Greg Barron. The shadow appeared sideways at first, as if the person was talking to someone nearby. Then the shadow turned, and Barlowe could see him flush.

It was Reverend Pickering. Dressed in one of his shiny suits, he stepped into the doorway, drawing all eyes his way. Flanked by an entourage of stoop-shouldered deacons, the preacher walked in, slow and deliberate-like.

Gregory Barron stopped in mid-sentence and watched with open dread as Pickering headed toward a cluster of vacant seats. Then he collected himself and cleared his throat. The next agenda item, he announced, pacing the floor, was a plan to confront "horrendous crime." To underscore its urgency, he directed his new secretary to hand out leaflets outlining his crime-fighting plan. According to the plan, they first would shut down houses of ill repute. Then they would attack rampant vandalism.

When he had allowed the attendants sufficient time to review his document, Barron made his pitch: "The solution is simple. We need private security patrols."

Hearing that, Marvetta Green shot out of her seat, without waiting to be recognized. "We don't need that out here." Her voice was tight, agitated. "We don't—"

Before she could finish, an explosion erupted from the front.

"Oh, *yes* we do!" Sean Gilmore had sprung to his feet. "We can't rely on the police! They're not dependable!"

Barlowe stared at Sean, then peered at Sandy, whose face contorted, pained. After a long, anxious moment, she tugged gently at the bottom of her husband's shirt. Sean brushed the hand away. She whispered something and tugged again. He sat down this time.

All the while, Reverend Pickering sat with his arms folded and stared down at his wingtip shoes. From time to time, he bit his bottom lip and shook his head sadly, as if admonishing the shoes, *I told you so.*

Eventually, the preacher raised a hand. When Barron recognized him, he stood and slapped the anti-crime leaflet against his knee, gazing in exaggerated disbelief.

"Tell me, son. What is *dis*?"

Barron didn't answer.

"Is dis somebody sharin they sense a humor? Tell me so I'll know when to laugh."

Barron struggled, awkwardly at first, to rebound from the affront. Then he remembered the broken windows. He considered the street urchins. He pondered property values.

He pounded a fist into an open palm. "No, you read correctly. This is serious."

Reverend Pickering paused with a long, angry silence that seemed to suck the air from the room. He tucked away his reading glasses and stepped further into the aisle, to give himself more room to operate.

"It's funny sittin here hearin you tawk bout crime," he said, starting in a slow Baptist cadence. "We never knew we should feel so insecure till *you* folks tole us so."

"Nobody said—"

The preacher cut Barron off. "We have always viewed our neighborhood as a ragtag human stew of many parts: part comical, part sad, part noble, wit some crumbs of riffraff sprinkled in." He paused, chuckling. "But now we know better, thanks to you: Dis place is a hopeless den of iniquity, a death trap. Upstandin people should fear fo they lives."

Hearing those words, Mr. Smith and the others in back clapped loudly. A few nodded like they were finally getting their money's worth.

Barlowe watched and listened closely, every now and then glancing up front at Sandy. She sat motionless, paying rapt attention to the preacher. She appeared baffled by his persona, and rattled by the tension in the room.

Beside her, Sean sat erect, sometimes frowning. At one point he scanned the room and met Barlowe's stare. There was a look of vague recognition, confused slightly by the sight of Barlowe away from the backyard.

Greg Barron appeared a bit shaken now, yet determined not to let the preacher hijack his meeting. He pointed at his wristwatch and cleared his throat.

"We'd love to hear all that you have to say on this matter, sir. I'm sorry, but your time is up."

Reverend Pickering shook his head. "Oh, now you wanna invoke time."

"I'm sorry, sir, but time is—"

"Oh, you!"

"Sir!"

"Now—"

"Sir! Sir!"

"Now this is about time!"

Barron was visibly pissed; so pissed that he began shouting: "We don't need your divisiveness in this neighborhood!"

A smile sour as buttermilk spread across the preacher's face. He scanned the room, waiting for others to acknowledge the absurdity of Barron's claim.

"So lemme make sho I got this right."

"Sir!"

"I'm divis—"

"Sir!"

"*I'm* divisive for callin *you* divisive?" Pickering placed a hand on his forehead, feigning shock. "My Lawd! The world done turned upside down!"

Barron hunched his back like a cornered cat and pointed a finger at the preacher. "Well all right, then, sir! We can settle this! We can settle this right now by taking a vote!" He turned and addressed the gathering. "All those opposed to my proposal to hire security patrols, let me see by a show of hands."

The black folks' hands shot straight up in the air.

Barron nodded to the secretary, who recorded the count.

Then, speaking louder, he called for a show of hands from those in favor of his proposal.

Jake Waxman, his blue eyes raging, stood and interrupted. He had been sitting quietly off to the side, and against a wall.

"Wait. I think there's a huge misunderstanding here. Let's talk some more before taking action."

One of the deacons shot back at him: "There ain't no misunderstandin. There ain't none a-tall."

Jake appeared startled, stung by the hostility directed at him. He started to respond, then shrank back, dejected. Without saying anything more, he got up and left the building, followed by a frustrated Eric Harper.

The remaining whites raised their hands, signaling they supported Barron's plan. They voted eagerly—all except Sandy, who rested her hands, palms down, in her lap.

Barlowe watched closely, waiting, as she scanned the room. The others also waited to see what she would do. After a long moment, Barron stepped close to her and leaned over, like he thought she might have fallen ill.

"Ma'am. Did you hear what I just said?"

Sandy glanced toward the blacks in back. Her lips quivered, but no words came out.

"Ma'am?"

She turned and studied the whites nearby. Their eyes scolded her.

"Please, ma'am. We *must* move forward." Barron turned pleadingly to Sean, whose face shone red as a Christmas bow.

Sean elbowed Sandy. She ignored him. He nudged her again.

Finally, she spoke so softly the folks in back could barely hear.

"I, I abstain."

Greg Barron looked again at Sean, then back at his wife. "As you wish, ma'am. As you wish."

Barron consulted the secretary on the count, then announced to the crowd: "The ayes have a clear majority. The security proposal will go forward."

Barlowe sat there, lost, speechless. He looked to the preacher for some kind of response. The preacher remained silent a long moment, staring in wonderment. Then he turned to Barron and curled his lips.

"Boy, you got the devil in you, sho as I'm bone."

Barron cleared his throat. "Sir, I really wish you would refrain from personal attacks. I mean, we *do* have a system in place here."

Pickering nodded and glared at Barron. "Gwon and do what you wont wit yo *system*."

He rose and strutted from the room.

The deacons looked at each other and hunched their shoulders, unsure if he had left for good or simply gone to take a bathroom break.

Barlowe waited for the preacher's return, all the while thinking that now he knew: They needed the reverend. Now he knew. They needed him more than ever.

When several minutes passed and the preacher had not come back, one of the deacons went to check on his whereabouts. He returned and whispered into another deacon's ear. They gathered their papers and left the room.

Soon, other blacks got up and followed, one by one: Mr. Smith and his wife, Zelda; Marvetta and Miss Carol Lilly; Clarence; even Lula Simmons rushed out in a huff.

Wendell Mabry walked through the doorway, mumbling something about taking the matter to the parking lot.

Barron kept quiet. After Wendell left, he nodded, triumphant: "That settles it. My proposal stands."

Now Barlowe remained as the only black in the room. He still held out hope that the preacher would return. Finally, he stood and stared, incredulous, at the white people, whose faces looked to him like big cotton balls lined neatly across several rows. He casually pushed down a pant leg riding up one of his calves. He took his time gathering himself, then headed, as though sleepwalking, for the door.

He reached the front of the room, stopped and aimed an accusing finger: "This is *wrong*! Ever single one a you know is wrong!"

The whites stared at their hands or pretended to study their meeting agendas or counted ridges in the ceiling.

On the way out, Barlowe's eyes met Sandy's for a flicker of a moment. She looked at him and lowered her gaze to the floor.

# Chapter 35

The Cafe Latte held its grand opening on a Saturday morning. The boys shuffled over from the rooming house to see what had become of the place they once knew as the Auburn Avenue Mini-Mart. For months, the men had been curious to know what all the racket and construction noise was about. Now they would see for themselves.

They strolled up the walk and stopped about five feet from the front entrance, noting some of the changes outdoors. There was a newly paved patio area, with lounge chairs and tables scattered about, to create the feel of a sidewalk cafe. On each side of the front entrance were huge shrubs, set in large, decorative flowerpots.

People—mostly friends of the new owner, come to lend their support—milled around outside. A woman with spiked pink hair and black hip-huggers floated through the crowd. Body piercing ran from her navel up to the bottom of a slinky black blouse. The woman stood talking to a man dressed in a jacket and pants, also black. The back of his head looked like a porcupine.

Ely gawked at the woman, fascinated by the silver stud that flicked from her tongue.

When the boys neared, she stopped talking and stared. Her companion spotted the elders, too, and took a few steps in their direction.

"Hi. Can we help you?"

"No," said Amos. "I don't think so."

The man pointed toward the front door. "The owner's inside." He chuckled. "It's the creepy dude with the weird goatee."

"Preciate that." Amos turned and walked away, trailed by his two partners. Once inside, they all scanned the room.

"Looka here, looka here. Much to-do bout nothin."

The grocery store had been gutted inside and redone in somebody's idea of a funky motif. The new place was sparsely furnished, with wooden chairs and tables scattered about. Up front there was an L-shaped counter, encased in glass. Behind the glass were cakes, pastries and muffins on display. Off to the side, against a wall, another counter was filled with napkins, straws, sugar and special coffee spices.

The place was filled with *them*; not a single soul the boys knew by name. The men took their places off to the side and along a wall while people milled around, chatting and sipping drinks with foam running from the top. The faint sound of jazzman Jimmy Smith drifted in from overhead.

The men scanned a big menu written in chalk on a huge blackboard suspended from the ceiling.

"Pitiful," Ely said, grimly shaking his head. "A whole buncha fancy words for the same ol thang."

It amazed the boys to see the transformation of a place that once seemed so permanent. Already, the mini-mart seemed a distant memory, a figment of their cloudy imaginations. The day would come, the men suspected, when no one would know it had ever been.

Eventually, a young man with sun-bleached dreadlocks came over, smiling. He extended a hand.

"Hi. My name is Jonathan. I'm the owner here."

"Hi," said Willie. The two others nodded silent, subdued hellos.

Jonathan sported a thick mustache and a dense but narrow blond goatee. He had the look of an old-time Trotskyite. An apron wrapped around his waist, he wore a plaid shirt and blue jeans underneath.

Jonathan appeared to be about thirty-two, which Amos later said pissed him off. He handed out menus, printed on laminated paper.

"I'll be right back. If there's anything I can help you with, lemme know?"

He smiled and sauntered off.

Amos studied the menu and turned up his nose: latte; mocha; espresso; steamers; frappe; cappuccino.

"Chai? What the gotdamn hell is chai?"

Jonathan returned, his face still plastered with a stupid grin.

"Can I get you boys anything?"

The men looked at each other. They had grown so close they sometimes registered the same thoughts, and at the exact same time: *Boys? Boys? What can this boy get us in a place like this? A place that ain't got no soda crackers and sardines stuffed along the aisles; a place that ain't got no beer and wine in the back; no Vienna sausages on aisle two, or pig ear sandwiches, sold up front.*

*What can this boy get for us?*

"No," said Amos, speaking in a proper tone reserved for whites. "We won't be havin nothin taday."

He handed the *boy* his menu back.

"Fine," said Jonathan, cheerily. "You're welcome to stay and look around."

He smiled, struggling to work through an awkward moment.

"You boys live in the neighborhood?"

"Yeah," said Ely. "How bout you?" He hadn't seen the white boy around, but you could never be too sure these days.

"No," said Jonathan. "I live in Virginia-Highland, but I may be moving over here. This neighborhood is really cool."

*Is cool all right, you li'l sumbitch.* That was what the "boys" thought—all at once.

Just then, Barlowe walked through the doors. The elders were happy to see another dark, familiar face. When he came over, the young proprietor smiled and extended a hand.

"Hi, my name is Jonathan. I'm the owner here."

"Good to meet you." Barlowe looked around.

"You live out here?"

"Yeah. Across the street."

"In the yellow house?"

"Right. The yellow house is *mine*."

"Cool." Jonathan smiled. "Hey, can I get you anything?"

"I'll have a cappuccino blast."

The boys were impressed that Barlowe didn't stumble over his tongue trying to pronounce the name of that fancy drink. Jonathan hurried off to the counter and shouted the order to a worker.

When he was gone, Willie turned to Barlowe and twisted his mouth sideways, to make sure no white folks read his lips.

"Whatever happened to a plain ol cup a coffee? Know what I mean?"

"This *is* coffee, stupid," said Amos. He leaned close to Barlowe. "You can tell he ain't never been nowhere."

Willie aimed an index finger. "I bet I been more places than *you*."

While the two men argued, a green-haired couple strolled past. They, too, were dressed in Goth black from head to toe. They eyed the cluster of black men and flashed tight-lipped smiles, then went outdoors.

"I done seen enough a Halloween," said Ely. "Les get outta here."

The boys said good-bye and left Barlowe standing there. On the way out, they passed a young white man coming in. He also had a Trotskyite goatee. He wore a black beret and dark sunshades that covered half his face. He sported two earrings in each ear and carried a computer bag.

He waved at Jonathan and headed to a corner table, where he sat down and plugged in his computer. He looked comfortable, like he had come to that place at the same time every day for the past twenty years.

Jonathan brought Barlowe his drink. When Barlowe reached for his wallet, the owner held up a forbidding hand.

"No. No. It's on me, dude. I'm glad to be meeting new folks from the neighborhood."

Jonathan zipped to the counter and turned up the volume on a Coltrane number. He closed his eyes and bobbed his head.

Barlowe watched as more whites showed up and mingled easily around the room. They seemed friendly enough. Still, he felt uneasy, out of place.

"Well," he said to Jonathan. "I guess I better go."

Just as he turned to leave, Sandy Gilmore bounced in. She waved cheerily and smiled, approaching the two men.

"Hi."

"Hi," said the proprietor, extending a hand. "My name is Jonathan. I'm the owner."

"I'm *so* glad you're here." Sandy looked around with an approving smile. "This place is great. It's really nice. Isn't this great, Barlowe?"

"Yeah," Barlowe said, dryly. "Great."

Jonathan peered at the two, surprised they knew each other. He frowned, without really meaning to frown.

"I gotta check on the customers. Lemme know if you have any questions."

"No, stay here a minute," said Sandy. "I wanna talk to you. I'm gonna get a latte. I'll be right back."

"No, I'll get it. Stay put." Jonathan rushed off to place the order.

When he'd gone, Sandy and Barlowe stood silently. He was ready to leave. He didn't feel much like talking to her.

"This is gonna be good for the neighborhood," Sandy observed. "This is great."

"You said that already," Barlowe snarled. "You said it. Is great."

Sandy recoiled. "Whoa! Somebody's in a funky mood."

Jonathan returned with her drink and instantly picked up the tension flowing between those two. Bad energy. Bad energy made him uneasy. He rushed off again, pretending to be pulled away by duty.

"I'm gonna head on home," said Barlowe. He took a few steps toward the door.

Sandy followed. "You don't look so well. Is everything okay?"

"I'm good. Got things to do, thas all."

"I'll walk with you if you give me a minute. This drink's too full. I wanna sip it down some before it spills."

Barlowe stepped just outside the door. Sandy stopped directly in front of him. He leaned back a bit, to create more space.

"I like the way they've produced this patio feel," she said, panning the area outside.

Barlowe said nothing. It occurred to him that this was the first time they'd talked in any place other than their backyards. Now they were out in the open, out in public, and he was aware.

"You seem to have a lot on your mind," said Sandy. "You wanna talk?"

"No, I'm fine."

He was trying to recall if she'd ever stood so close to him before. Then it struck him. It was the fence. He had grown used to talking to her through the fence.

"C'mon, what's the matter, Barlowe?"

He opened his mouth to speak, then caught sight of Miss Carol Lilly. She came waddling up, clutching a shiny pocketbook. She was coming to see the new place, too.

On her way up the walk, she gave Sandy a cold once-over. For reasons that weren't completely clear to him, Barlowe hoped she'd join the conversation.

"Hi, Miss Carol Lilly."

She nodded. Only it wasn't a hello nod. It was a nod that said she knew what time it was. A nod that said she had caught him, red-handed, and now she knew. He went *that* way.

Barlowe looked into Miss Carol Lilly's eyes, then climbed into her head and peeked around. He didn't like what he saw.

She brushed past Barlowe and Sandy and went inside. She reappeared five minutes later and brushed past them again.

"Humph!"

She hurried off. As she made her way up the sidewalk, Sandy smiled. "She seems like a nice old lady."

Barlowe grew more agitated. "Whas up with you, anyway?"

Sandy frowned. "What's that supposed to mean?"

"I mean, whas up with all the cheer? You come in here singin bout how great this place is, and you don't even unnerstan."

"What is it I don't understand?"

"Is crazy," said Barlowe. He took a step away from her. "Is crazy."

"What are you talking about? What don't I understand?"

He looked at her, shaking his head. "Where do you get these ideas from, anyway?"

"What ideas? You're not being clear. You're not being articulate at all today."

"Forget it."

"No, tell me." She grabbed his arm. "What don't I understand?"

Barlowe pushed her hand away. "Somethin ain't workin, lady. Somethin ain't workin."

Customers, lounging around, stopped talking and looked their way. Sandy seemed oblivious to the stares.

"Oh, I get it," she said, snapping her fingers. "I know. It's the civic league meeting, isn't it?"

He didn't respond.

"That's what's bothering you, isn't it?"

She could tell from his facial expression that she was right. It was the first time they'd seen each other since the meeting.

Now standing on the patio of the Cafe Latte, Barlowe recalled the session. He remembered the sunken look in her eyes, and the disgust returned all over again. He wanted to get away from her. He turned to leave. She grabbed his arm once more.

"Wait a minute. Tell me what's the matter."

He stopped. "You don't even know what happened."

"So that's what you think, huh? You think I didn't see?"

He said nothing.

She stepped closer and poked a finger in his chest.

"Lemme tell you something, mister. I can see. I can see as well as anybody, including *you*. I saw what happened in that meeting. I knew things weren't handled well. I knew that."

"Then why didn't you say it, then?"

Sandy's face turned red.

"*Say* it?"

"Say what you saw."

She held out her hands, with the palms turned upward, pleading.

"Barlowe, I wasn't running that meeting. What could I have said?"

"You coulda said somethin."

"No, but I *did* take a stand. I abstained from voting, remember? I abstained."

"Yeah, I remember."

"I was on your side. And I wasn't alone. There were other people in that meeting who also didn't like the way Greg Barron handled things."

"Yeah?"

"Yes. They told me later."

"They coulda fooled me."

"There was no need for me to speak up, Barlowe. That preacher made all the valid points. I thought he hit the nail right on the head with some of the things he said."

Barlowe's pitch went up a notch. "Sometimes is more important *who* speaks than *what* gets said."

"How can that be?"

He shrugged. "I don't know. You tell me. Maybe is the only way some folks can hear."

A glint of recognition came to her eyes. She felt like she'd flunked some vital test. For the first time since he'd known her, Sandy appeared at a loss for words. "I . . . I . . ."

He put a hand on a hip. "You *what*? I'm listenin. You *what*?"

Sandy took a deep breath and tried to gather herself. Finally, she covered her eyes with her hand.

He glared. "And you think you so *different*."

"I . . . I . . ."

"Don't you?"

For a long moment, she kept quiet. She just stared back at him.

He waited. Sandy said nothing, which to him said everything.

"You may not be different as you think."

He moved to leave. She grabbed him again. "No, wait. Please. Wait."

Barlowe stopped, aware now that they were making a scene. The people sitting nearby appeared very concerned.

Sandy massaged her forehead, which had begun to ache. "You're right," she said glumly. "I could have said something. And I didn't."

Barlowe wanted to break away. She was staring in his face now with moistened eyes.

Nearby, customers watched.

She dabbed her eyes with a napkin. She wondered if he'd lost respect for her.

He smoldered. But he saw her trying. He saw her trying, so he pulled back from the attack.

Why bother, anyway? Why?

Sandy hadn't finished saying what she'd intended to say, but she had become self-conscious now. When she looked up at Barlowe again, her nose was red, like she had a cold. There were circles around her eyes, like she had been crying. Her eyes had watered but she had not shed actual tears. Barlowe should know. He had been standing there the whole time, hadn't he?

He had. But as with her, there was a brief moment that he couldn't quite account for, a flash of a moment when something passed between them and he actually *wasn't* there. It was like time suspended, however briefly. Then, without warning, the clock started again.

Barlowe looked around, aware again of who and where they were: They were outdoors—out in the open. The sun had set over the rooftops and now lingered, as if awaiting some unburdening of the spirit.

Partly uneasy and partly embarrassed by the intensity of what they felt—some deeply shared anguish over the way things were—neither Sandy nor Barlowe knew what to say. And neither of them could decide which was more unsettling—the discomfort of that moment, or the implications of the scene: the two of them, black and white, standing there, talking that way.

Now actual tears began streaming down Sandy's cheeks. She went back inside the cafe and got two more napkins. She returned, wiping her face.

Barlowe stood there looking at her, mindful of all the white people watching them. Then that feeling came back. It returned to him from the civic league meeting. That feeling like he was about to burst through his skin. Like something inside was about to blow.

He took a deep breath. He had to get away, now.

"Okay," he said. "I understand."

She raised her eyebrows. She didn't believe he was being sincere.

"No. I'm serious." He needed to get away.

Suddenly, Ricky Brown appeared from around the corner, pushing his grocery cart. He stopped at the curb across the street and scooped up two rusty cans from the ground. He smiled to himself, like he'd found two crisp twenty-dollar bills.

"I need to go," said Barlowe. He took another step away from Sandy.

She followed. "I need to be going, too. I'll walk with you."

She sniffled and blew her nose and tossed the napkins in the trash. The two of them walked the short distance to Randolph Street. As they crossed over, Barlowe glanced to his left. Mr. Smith was nowhere in sight. *Good.*

They reached the sidewalk and separated without saying good-bye. Barlowe rushed indoors and beelined to his room. He felt light-headed. He needed to lie down.

Sandy stopped and picked up litter that had been dropped in her yard. Then she went in the house.

She had started toward the kitchen, when a voice startled her. It came from off to the side, in the living room.

"Did you have a nice conversation?"

It was Sean. He had been standing near the window, watching.

"Yeah," said Sandy. "I was talking to the guy next door. I ran into him at the new cafe." She tried to sound matter-of-fact; casual. "You should talk to him sometime, Sean. He's really a nice guy."

"I've tried. He doesn't seem too interested in talking with *me.*" His tone was sharp, accusing.

Sandy turned and walked from the room.

# Chapter 36

It was early morning, a Tuesday. Tyrone spilled out the front door and crept slowly up the walkway toward Irwin Street. Other folks, the working stiffs, filed along the block wearing haggard expressions that dragged their faces in lock-step with their shuffling feet. Trudging along, Tyrone gazed hopefully up at the sky. An orange tint swept across the horizon, ushering in the first burst of morning light. Though slightly cold, it was a beautiful morning. He hoped the weather would hold. If the weather held, he might rake in some extra cash. He needed money, bad.

He reached the bus shelter and waited for the Number 23, which would take him to Greenbriar Mall. As quickly as he flopped down on the long, wooden bench, he rose again, wondering: *Did I set out food and water for my birds?* He strained to recall. Lately, he was beginning to forget things. *Too much worriation. Too much worriation.* He decided not to risk going back to the house. The Number 23 would be coming soon. Maybe Barlowe would check the cage before leaving for work.

Maybe he wouldn't. Tyrone wasn't too sure about Barlowe these days. It could have been paranoia, but he suspected his uncle might be having second thoughts about letting him continue rooming there. With Tyrone losing his old job and all, he hadn't been able to contribute as much to the rent lately.

He felt slightly depressed. A rough stretch of bad luck had blown in on him. Even the bones at the craps tables weren't falling right.

Leaning forlornly forward, Tyrone rested his elbows on his knees. He glanced at his watch. Seven o'clock. The Number 23 was late again. He stood and peered, impatient, up the street and spotted a ragtag army marching his way. As they moved in closer, he made out the frames of two women, surrounded by a bunch of children. The women clasped hands with two children apiece. A fifth child appeared old enough to walk on her own.

The army crossed the street and bailed into the covered bus shelter. Tyrone nodded a greeting. The women ignored him. One child nodded back.

Clothes wrinkled and faces cruddy, the children looked like they hadn't been washed. They each carried a Popsicle, which Tyrone guessed was breakfast. Popsicle juice ran messily down their arms.

The children talked loud, and all at once, shattering the morning peace. The women babbled like children, too; aimless, empty chatter.

The ladies were young, maybe early twenties. They didn't appear to be dressed for work. They wore tight pants; big, fake hair; makeup; the whole nine yards. They resembled the dancers at Tyrone's favorite clubs.

"Bitches," he muttered under his breath. "Bitches."

He thought he might like to have a family someday. He could muster no clear vision of how that would look or feel, but he had accepted the possibility that a family was something he might one day stumble into. He chuckled, tickled that such an idea had entered his head.

Eventually, the anguished groan of the Number 23 sounded from off in the distance. Tyrone stood and paced as the bus, gushing smoke and fumes, limped toward the shelter from up the street. When it reached the stop, he rushed aboard ahead of the army and shot straight to the back. The army piled in and settled noisily up front, near the driver.

When the bus pulled away, Tyrone scanned the handful of people on board. They were mostly regulars: janitors and waiters in hotels downtown. Gardeners and cooks at Georgia State. The unemployed, out on the hunt. And various miscellaneous strays, including people he wanted to keep a distance from.

There was one curious, unfamiliar face in the mix. A woman sat across the aisle and a few rows ahead, reading a newspaper. He couldn't see her face square, but he guessed she was pretty. Even at that angle, she had fine features and an air of prettiness about her.

She had class, too. Tyrone could tell. She wore a business suit, and subtle earrings—not like the gangly hoops tugging the ears of those women up front.

She looked to Tyrone like she didn't belong on the bus. He guessed she owned a car. It was probably being fixed in a body shop somewhere.

From time to time, the woman glanced up from her newspaper, noting people who got on or off the bus. Tyrone watched her awhile, then turned and stared vacantly out the window, wondering what the day would bring.

The bus slugged along downtown, making its way toward the city's south side. It passed the state capitol on Washington Street. A magnificent, gold-domed building, the capitol was fronted with long, sculpted columns and lots of broad concrete steps that led up to tall, majestic doors.

Several old white men in business suits climbed the steps toward the entrance. Carrying briefcases and important-looking folders, they appeared eager, confident enough to run the world.

*Sonsabitches.* That was what Tyrone called them. *Sonsabitches.*

As the bus rolled past, he craned his neck and stared back at the building. It came to him that the capitol was a public building, which meant he could go inside if he wanted. Important business was decided by sonsabitches in buildings like that. Maybe he should go there someday and walk around, just to piss them off.

Downtown, near City Hall, he saw a high-rise apartment building under construction. With all the construction going on in Atlanta, there were plenty of labor jobs to be had. A few times, he'd done electrical jobs on construction sites, but for reasons he didn't want to think about, he never was able to stay with those.

Besides, he had his own thing now, working for himself.

Now the woman in the business suit rose and got off the bus. Tyrone watched her through the window. She *was* pretty, just like he'd thought. She carried a leather briefcase and walked hurriedly toward City Hall.

Maybe he would see her again. If he saw her again, he would say something to her, strike up a conversation, to see how she reacted.

Eventually, the bus reached his stop on Campbellton Road. He got off and walked briskly toward his job site, a shopping center parking lot near Greenbriar Mall. After the first two months installing car stereos, Tyrone had drawn so many customers he had to hire a man to help him out. The new assistant, a guy called Benz, lived a few blocks from the shopping center. On installation jobs, Benz was about as skilled as Tyrone. He did good work, and fast. Problem was, he proved unreliable. Most days he showed up late, and sometimes not at all.

On that Tuesday morning, when Tyrone reached the littered parking lot, Benz hadn't arrived yet. Tyrone was greeted by a man in bifocals, who'd bought a sound system the day before and made arrangements through Kwan Li to have it installed. According to the appointment book, Benz was supposed to install the system at 8 a.m. It was now 8:16.

Tyrone apologized, then proceeded to do the installation, which required wiring the car from front to back and adding four new speakers to the two already in place.

As he worked, another car—a customer Tyrone had booked for *his* first job of the day—pulled into the lot. Then still another showed up.

Hours later, Tyrone was lying on the floor of a Honda Civic, running wiring beneath the steering column, when Benz showed up, sucking on a Budweiser. He leaned down where Tyrone worked.

"Yo. What we got, chief?"

Tyrone kept his eyes focused on his work. "Look out there for yourself and see what we got."

Three customers waited. A fourth had left, frustrated, a half-hour before.

Benz approached a car and went to work. He knocked out the job in twenty minutes, then broke for lunch. He returned an hour later, carrying a three-piece chicken snack and a forty-ounce brew.

He sat atop the hood of one of the cars and ate, tossing chicken bones on the ground.

When he was done, Benz went back to work.

"Yo, Tyrone, you usin your wie cutters?"

"Naw."

"Can I use em a minute?"

"Where yours at?"

"Left em home."

The wire cutters came flying his way, landing on the ground near his foot.

At the end of the workday, when Tyrone had finished his last car, Benz went to him. "Me and the fellas goin over to a bah. You wanna hang wit us?"

Tyrone had gathered his tools and begun sweeping his area of the parking lot.

Benz asked again: "You wanna come?"

Tyrone kept on sweeping. He didn't look at Benz when he spoke. "I done lost two hunnered dollas today fuckin wit you."

Benz stiffened.

"Whut?"

"You ain't shit, thas whut!" Tyrone shouted. "You hear me? You ain't shit!"

Benz shot back: "*You* the one ain't shit! Uncle Tomin for a Chinaman!"

Even in the heat of a moment there are some things you shouldn't say to certain people, even if you believe it's true. Later, as Benz sat in the Grady Hospital emergency room, holding a blood-soaked oil rag to his throbbing skull, he regretted that that morsel of wisdom had not come to him sooner.

For his part, Kwan Li had his regrets, too. He regretted having to end the partnership with Tyrone. And he hated forking over $400 to replace the passenger-side window of a client's car after Tyrone implanted Benz's head in the glass.

Nobody regretted the whole thing more than Tyrone. After the brutal outburst, he ended up right back where he had started—he rejoined the ranks of the unemployed.

# Chapter 37

Barlowe lay in bed after an evening of long, vigorous lovemaking. Louise had fallen asleep beside him. He stared, engrossed, at her TV, which broadcasted bad news, conflict, from around the globe. There was That War going on, half a world away. He watched the latest dispatch and listened with the volume down low: There had been another bombing. More people killed.

On the TV screen, the camera panned to dusty, battered, clay-baked buildings, reduced to smoldering ashes. Clusters of people with contorted faces anguished over the loss of more lives—over the loss of their way of life—as they collected mangled bodies and rushed them to hospitals and morgues.

Standing amid the chaos, a news reporter interviewed a man described as "a high-ranking U.S. official." Dressed in a tie, with his shirtsleeves rolled up, the high-ranking U.S. official assured the reporter, over and over, that Americans were there to liberate.

The camera then cut to a man standing on the crowded street. Bearded and scruffy, the man, arms flailing, pointed to scattered fires raging here and there, a result of the bombs dropped to liberate.

Over and over, the man shouted, in clipped English: "The Americans are occupiers! The Americans are occupiers!"

*Occupiers.*

Barlowe turned off the TV and went back to sleep.



The morning light filtered in through the second-floor window on Ormond Drive and splashed across Barlowe's groggy face. A bird landed on the sill, chirping and fluttering its wings, shaking off icy water from an early bath.

Barlowe gazed past the bird and stared dreamily at the winter sky. It was a Sunday. The morning had come and he felt the kind of contentment a man feels when he's had a good meal and retired to the easy chair to digest his food and rest himself.

Earlier that morning, he had watched through bleary eyes as Louise got up from bed, slid into a sheer black nightgown and left the room. Now he could hear her moving around downstairs. Now there were pots and pans clanging; there was the whiff of bacon wafting in the air and the faint sound of a small kitchen radio playing Mississippi blues.

Barlowe lay in bed, thinking. He felt pretty good about the moment, and even better about the woman downstairs. There was no real reason not to trust the goodness of what he felt. Still, he sensed himself holding back a little.

Something struck him as odd. He had been seeing Louise steadily for several months now and, so far, there was nothing wrong. How could there be a real relationship with nothing wrong? Surely there had to be demons prowling around somewhere behind her dimpled smile. Everybody had demons, didn't they?

So what were Louise's demons? When would they come out and expose themselves?

It seemed almost a law of nature that if she had demons Barlowe wouldn't find out until late in the game, when it counted most. He wouldn't likely find out until after they had gotten married and maybe had their second child. Then demons might appear. He might stumble up on a lifelong gambling habit she couldn't break, or struggles with anger management or a private addiction to prescription drugs.

Everybody had demons, didn't they?

Maybe not. Maybe Barlowe's ship had finally come in. Maybe
Louise was one of the few people in the world passed over by demons.
Maybe there were demons haunting *him*.

He suspected what might be nagging him: He didn't trust life to
turn out right. *Could well be*, he thought, turning over on his side.
*Could well be.*

"Barlowe!" Louise called from the bottom of the stairs. "Breakfast
ready!"

He rolled again onto his back and lifted his head. "All right!"

He climbed out of bed and hobbled to the bathroom to brush his
teeth. He now had his own toothbrush there. It hung on a silver rack,
beside hers. She had given it to him one weekend, without a big ceremony or commitment speech. When he came back the next week, he
found the toothbrush still there, resting in the same slot where he'd
left it. She hadn't taken it down to hide from anybody.

He gazed at himself in the mirror. Did he really think there might
be somebody else sniffing around? Not really. Then he remembered
Nell. Nell proved you never can claim to know anything for sure. She
proved things can up and disappear.

Still . . .

"Barlowe, c'mon! The biscuits are gettin cold!"

He washed up good, went downstairs and took a seat at a small
kitchen table. Wearing fuzzy slippers, Louise stood at the stove with
her back to him, putting the finishing touches on breakfast.

"I got you somethin here that'll stick to your stomach."

"Good, baby. I'm hongry."

He studied her there in that sheer nightgown. It was sleeveless, and
it fell down to the middle of her thighs. He could see through that
gown to the contours of her body. Hers wasn't the shape of a nightclub
dancer, but she was sexy just the same.

Barlowe picked up the morning newspaper from the day before,
which Louise had left on the table. He liked sitting at her table. Just
beyond it there was a sliding glass door with two long windowpanes
that offered a bright, clear view outside. He looked out to the small
backyard, which rose into a steep, tree-lined grassy knoll. Beyond the

knoll was an apartment complex, and a basketball court across the way. Barlowe could hear a ball bouncing. He could see teenagers playing out there. Some ran up and down the court, passing, shooting, jumping, while others stood on the sidelines, shivering in the cold. The morning frost had begun to fade, but he could tell from the way they shivered that it would be a while before the temperature climbed.

Watching the boys it occurred to him that he'd give almost anything to be that carefree again. He'd love to have nothing more weighing on his head than choosing sides for a pickup game.

He shifted his sights back and forth between the teenagers and lovely Louise, standing at the stove in her sheer black nightgown, preparing a breakfast of biscuits and eggs and fried potatoes.

He liked Louise a lot. She had been to college, but she wasn't caught up in the glitz and glitter of such things. She was down-to-earth, wise and calm, even when she was upset. In fact, she was one of the purest spirits he'd ever seen in a woman not married to the church.

As she'd told him on their first date, Louise sprang from a family of simple rural folks. Barlowe actually went home with her once to meet her people, and even went with the family to Sunday service. The family church was so small you could talk across the room without raising your voice. Most of the people there were Louise's kin, and many looked alike. High foreheads and a reddish-brown-to-dark skin tone that testified to blacks and Indians crossing paths.

Sitting in the church service, Barlowe felt the stirrings of something warm and natural. After the visit, he was glad he had gone. It solidified his sense of who she was.

Louise wasn't perfect, whatever that meant. Barlowe was too old now to be concerned with perfect. Still, it somehow bothered him that he couldn't pinpoint some character flaw that proved she was a real live human being.

In their months of dating there was only one habit he could count as anything even close to a vice: coffee. The woman was crazy about coffee. Two cups in the morning were a given. Another cup during the day, a need.

And not just that: Louise was a high-end coffee lover. She drank the gourmet stuff, which required special trips to special coffee stores. She had an expensive, high-powered coffeemaker that percolated like it ran on diesel fuel. She used amaretto and French vanilla dairy creamers, and instead of plain white coffee filters, she preferred the special unbleached brown.

It wasn't just the utensils that brought the obsession through. It was the look in Louise's eyes when she handled coffee. It was the look of the addict measuring drugs.

As vices went, that was about it, about all he could find that might remotely be considered a flaw in Louise Grimes: coffee.

So why did doubt still swirl in his head?

He suspected it was this: The relationship had come too easy. Nothing worthwhile had ever come easy to him. Things that came easy tended to disappear. Like his mama: There one day, sure as the sun; gone the next, like a snowflake melted from the heat of that same reliable sun. His mama's death, which came suddenly when he was a young man, had been enough to make him question whether there was anything in life a body could count as real.

Looking at Louise now, he told himself that he'd be a fool to pass on what he saw.

For her part, Louise trusted what she felt inside. It freed her to fully embrace the time they spent together. When she first met him, she had been in the throes of a relationship drought that had surely gone on longer than God intended. So she was convinced that the romance with Barlowe was a blessing to be savored.

Unlike some of those slick mirages she had suffered in the past, he was an honest, face-value kind of man; worldly wise and tough as nails, yet possessed of a raw innocence, a vulnerability that appealed to her.

Whenever he told her how much he appreciated her, she knew she could believe every word. She had waited two lifetimes to experience this kind of trust. She had no intention of tainting it with fear.

Standing at the stove, she acknowledged that, sure, there were some rough edges to Barlowe Reed. But it was mostly cosmetic stuff, nothing a good barber and manicurist couldn't make disappear.

The bottom line was, he was decent, and she liked him a lot. If forced to frame it in words, she might even have to call it love.

Now she took some biscuits out of the oven. Barlowe got up and went over to help, piling potatoes on her plate. She grabbed his hand. "No, no, no. Too much. What you tryin to do?"

"Eat," he said, smiling. "I'm hongry. I want you to eat with me."

She shot him a suspicious, playful look. "I know what you want. You want me to blow up to two hundred pounds."

"Not hardly."

"Yes you do. You wanna fatten me up like a big, old hog, then you'll leave me for some trim young thing in a blonde wig and spike heels."

"The heels maybe, but not the wig." He slipped his arms around her waist, thinking again about the trip to Waycross. "I'd wont you, even if you were two hundred pounds."

He cupped her face in his rough, ink-stained hands. Her smile stretched all the way across her face, like it had been drawn by a child with crayon on construction paper.

Barlowe tapped her bottom and returned to the table. Louise set his plate down in front of him. They sat there and ate and read the day-old paper, every now and then breaking off to chat about some news item they ran across.

Once, after they had been there awhile, Barlowe looked up at Louise and then scanned the room. At that moment he felt settled, more fully in touch with what life could be. He thought, *Maybe this is it. Maybe she can show me how to live.*

He sat there quiet for a long time. The newspaper was spread wide open, but he wasn't reading anymore.

Finally, Louise broke the silence. "Where do you stand with the house these days?"

He didn't answer.

"You got the down payment money now?"

She had shown him on paper how to save more, and faster, by banking his dollars instead of playing the lottery.

"I'm savin," he said. "I'm savin."

He thought of Crawford. Tyrone also crossed his mind. Tyrone wasn't working, yet he'd come home one day and handed Barlowe $300, cash, out of the blue. He didn't tell him where he got it and Barlowe was half-scared to ask.

Tyrone seemed to be avoiding him these days. Barlowe knew he was spending more time gambling down at the Purple Palace. Not good. Barlowe intended to talk with his nephew about that.

He considered his own job at the print shop. Some days he felt tired and unsure how long he could last.

Louise broke the silence, as if she'd read the flow of his thoughts.

"I'm here for you, Barlowe. I'm here, no matter what." She placed a hand gently on top of his wrist and gave him a reassuring pat.

"Thanks," he said, simply. *Trust it,* he told himself. Somehow he knew now: It was safe to let the barriers down. He looked into Louise's eyes, then reached over and kissed her once.

After breakfast, they went back upstairs and made love some more.

# Chapter 38

Hours later, Barlowe and Louise lay side by side staring up at the ceiling. She asked him again about the house.

"You in or out?"

"I'm in."

"Oh? Last time we talked about it you said you were out."

"Yeah, well I changed my mind."

"Oh?"

He had told her about the civic league meeting, about how Reverend Pickering walked out and didn't come back. Some time had passed since then, but it still weighed heavy on him.

"Sometimes you gotta stay and fight," he said.

"And what are you fightin for?"

He looked at her strangely.

"There's a difference between fighting and just raising hell. You gotta know the difference, Barlowe."

He stared at Louise, looking straight through her. He didn't know what to say, so he got dressed. He put on his clothes and left for home.

When he reached the house, he looked at the spot where he had found Viola's body. Often when he pulled up to the curb, he thought of her. He recalled her frail body lying there that night, stiff as wood.

He thought of how he had touched her skin, and remembered how cold and still it was.

He thought about it again. Viola was dead and buried. He had seen her passing through his yard so many times, and yet she had been a stranger to him. The world was filled with strangers, people working and living close together, with no real sense of who their neighbors were.

A vague sadness swept over him.

He started toward the house, then turned and stopped. He heard loud talking coming from somewhere up the street. He looked north and saw a police cruiser parked crooked with one wheel angled on the curb. There was a commotion, and people dashing toward the car.

He rushed up the street to see what was going on. He came upon two cops standing there. One policeman held Ricky Brown jacked up against the squad car. Ricky stood bent over with his chest pinned against the hood. His wrists were handcuffed behind him. A few feet away, his grocery cart lay on its side, with all his precious junk spilled on the ground.

By the time Barlowe got there, a crowd of spectators had begun to form. In a few minutes, more folks were drawn to the scene. They began grumbling among themselves as the cops prepared to shove Ricky into the car.

One man with wavy hair shouted out to the policemen, "What you arrestin im for?"

The cop, a short, stocky black man, warned him off. "Go on, now. Lemme do my work!"

Nobody obeyed. Instead, more people showed up and began shouting at the cops. "What you doin to im? Let im go!"

"He was out here pokin through these people's garbage." As he spoke, the lawman nodded toward the house in front of them. Barlowe recognized it as one of the new white families' homes.

"Leave im alone!" The demand came from another man standing a few feet back, in the middle of the swelling crowd. "He don't bother nobody! Leave im alone!"

"Mind your bidness," the cop barked. He glanced at his younger partner, who unsnapped his billy club.

More people gathered. Mr. Smith came out, as did bug-eyed Randy from down the street. Amos and Willie and Ely eventually heard the commotion and showed up, too. They all looked at Ricky, then stared at the cops, wondering what to do.

His face still pinned to the top of the hood, Ricky strained to peer up at the crowd. His eyes were wide, terrified, like a scared bird. He seemed confused, stunned that so much fuss swirled around him.

Wendell Mabry appeared, a toothpick dangling from his mouth. He pushed his way to the front of the crowd. When somebody told him what happened, Wendell pointed the toothpick at the policemen.

"That man weren't doin nothin but collectin trash! Once people throw trash in the garbage it mean they don't want it no mo!"

"This is *private* garbage," the lawman barked. "It belong to the people who live here. Now move on!"

Standing near Wendell, one woman hissed, "Trash is *public*, fool! We can tell that by lookin at *you*!"

The cop glanced at his rookie partner. Barlowe could see him thinking, maybe going through the police procedure manual in his head.

People came from out of the woodwork now—from out of their houses or from up the street; some folks passed in cars and doubled back.

Miss Carol Lilly waddled down from her front yard. When she saw Barlowe, she rolled her eyes.

Another man heckled the cops. "Gotdamned Uncle Toms! Out chere protectin white folks' trash!"

The complaint seemed to incite the crowd. Somebody else shouted: "Need to have they asses whupped!"

The idea caught on like a new dance. Two men behind Barlowe whispered. "Rush em fore they grab they guns."

"Look at em! Need to have they asses whupped!"

The white people whose trash was being disputed stayed indoors. They kneeled at their living room windows, peeping through half-closed blinds. People could see them clearly from the street.

Barlowe stood there, taking in the scene, wondering what to do. As a member of the public safety committee, this was his first real crisis. He wondered where he fit into things.

"Move on!" one cop ordered. His partner got on the radio.

Nobody moved. Instead, the shouts continued, now turning into bitter taunts: "You go to hell!"

"Out chere guardin white folks' trash!"

"Need to have they asses whupped!"

Barlowe felt that strange sensation—that tightness in his chest—coming on again. He grew light-headed.

"I done seen it all!" one man near him yelled. "Arrestin somebody for collectin trash!"

"Need to have they asses whupped!"

As the crowd swelled, the younger cop rested a hand on his gun. He looked nervous, agitated.

Henny Penn and some of the boys from around the Purple Palace drifted down. Barlowe wondered how many guns were in that bunch. Other young men and teenagers stood there glaring hatefully at the cops. They were hyped, primed for action.

Another squad car rolled in suddenly and came to a screeching halt. Three more policemen bailed out.

The sight of more cops incited people even more.

"Look at em. Rollin up in here like we sposed to get scared!"

"Need to have they asses whupped!"

Somebody behind Barlowe broke a bottle against the curb and held the jagged edges high. "Let em come!"

Another bottle shattered. "Yeah! Come on!"

Up front, Wendell fussed with one of the cops, still pointing the toothpick in his face.

Barlowe recognized one of the men who'd gotten out of the squad car. It was the precinct captain. He had spoken to him once at a public safety meeting.

Tall and top-heavy muscular, the captain stood erect and faced the crowd. He drew a billy club in one hand and tapped it into the other open palm like he planned to crack some skulls. He scanned the crowd.

"All right! I'm gonna tell ya *one* time! Once! Clear out from here and there won't be no trouble! Go on home and let us do our jobs!"

"Kiiiiissssss mmmyyy blaaacck aaaasssssss!"

The shout came from somewhere in back of the crowd.

"C'mon! Brang it!"

The lawman turned to his troops and nodded. Several officers advanced a few steps toward Wendell and a group of men at the front of the crowd. Barlowe stood there, tension pounding heavy in his chest. He feared what was coming. He had to do something.

He stepped forward, pushing his way in between the cops and the crowd of people edging closer. He approached the captain.

"Officer."

The policeman stiffened. "Get back!"

"Officer, my name is Barlowe. Barlowe Reed. We met before."

The officer looked upon him as though he were diseased. "And?"

"I'm on the public safety committee out here. Can I speak to you a minute?"

The captain kept one eye on Barlowe and the other glued to the crowd. "You wanna talk, you need to go to the precinct commander. I don't do no whole lotta talkin."

"Officer," said Barlowe. He pointed at Ricky. "I know this man. This man don't bother nobody. He just collects garbage round here."

He could see Ricky, his face still pressed hard against the hood, straining to hear what was being said.

"He don't have no right to be goin through people's trash," the captain insisted. "They don't want nobody goin through their things."

"But officer—"

"People got a right to privacy. Thas their right. Unnerstand?"

Then Barlowe lost it. That feeling in his chest, that feeling that had been shoving itself forward for some time now, heaved up and out. Before he could think about it clear, he was talking loud—nearly yelling—arms flailing in the air.

"This is crazy! Don't you see?! Is crazy!"

The cop tried to shout him down. "Hey!"

"Is crazy! Here we are standin out here, arguin over somebody's trash! We arguin over *trash*! Hell, for all you know *we* are trash! Don't you see!? *We* are like garbage to be thrown away!"

"Move on!" said the captain. "I'm tellin you one more time."

"*You* are garbage!" Barlowe pointed a finger in the captain's face. "You can be thrown out, too!"

The policeman took a step toward him, then stopped. The people grew quiet, watching, waiting for the certain blow to the head. The folks with broken bottles tightened their grips. Others squeezed sticks and bricks and clenched their bare fists. The people waited, but nothing happened.

Instead, the police captain remained quiet. He stood there, staring into space, thinking. After a long while, he spoke. He spoke so softly people in the back of the crowd had to strain to hear.

"All right, then. All right. Tell you what." He looked at Ricky. "We'll let im go this time. We'll let im go." He pointed at Barlowe. "But you tell im to stay outta these folks' trash. If we get called again, we gonna do our job. You unnerstand?"

Barlowe said nothing.

"You unnerstand? We gotta do our job."

Barlowe didn't care for the man's tone, but that was less important now. "I understand."

The captain turned around and went to the cop holding Ricky pressed against the car. He nodded. The officer pulled out his keys and unlocked the cuffs.

Ricky Brown stood there a moment, scared and confused. He rubbed his wrists, then turned his grocery cart upright. He gathered most of the trash that had spilled out. Without saying a word, he took off down the street. The sound of the cart's squeaky wheel pierced the tense silence on the block.

Keeping their eyes fastened to the angry crowd, the policemen backed up slowly, making sure to cover one another.

They climbed in their cars and drove away.

When they were gone, some people in the crowd cheered.

"Hot damn!"

"Toldja! Punks!"

"Uncle Toms, protectin white folks' trash!"

Wendell stopped by to give Barlowe a pat on the back. "You tole them sonsabitches good."

Somebody spoke over his shoulder. "We shoulda whupped they ass!"

Barlowe said nothing. He stood there, quiet. The cops were gone and Ricky was free, but he didn't feel so good inside. Something tugged at him, and he had to get it off his chest.

He stepped onto a dirty milk crate that Ricky had left behind. He looked at the crowd. People gazed back at him, wondering what he would say. Folks looked like they expected some kind of victory speech.

Barlowe sensed what they wanted. It only seemed to make things worse.

"You feel good, huh? You feel like we done somethin!"

People looked at each other, surprised by the sharpness of the tone.

"Why you feel so good?" he asked. "You really think we done somethin? Huh? Well, lemme tell you what we've done! We ain't done nothin! Nothin at all! Thas what we done! *Nothin!*"

People looked at each other, then stared at Barlowe, wondering what was wrong with him.

He continued: "You ain't done nothin but make some noise! Thas whas so funny! You ain't done nothin but make noise!"

The people stared, still shocked. What was he saying, and why?

Barlowe shook his head. "We pitiful. Pathetic." He stepped down from the crate.

There was silence. Nobody in the crowd said anything for a while. People stood there gazing at him and shrugging their shoulders as if to say, "Whas the matter with *him?*"

Eventually, Wendell took a few steps toward Barlowe, then stopped. He looked like he was trying to figure out what to say and where to begin.

Barlowe peered into the crowd. He saw Miss Carol Lilly staring back.

Finally, standing amid the gathering, Henny Penn raised a hand. Dressed in a brown suede jogging suit, topped by a leather jacket, he wore dark sunshades. He had on new sneakers, and there was an unlit cigarette stuck on one ear.

"S'cuse me, Slim. That was a nice li'l bullshit speech, but I got somethin to say!"

Barlowe waited.

"I know you a good man and whatnot, but I thought you had more sense than that! You ain't makin no sense, man!"

"You got your opinion; I got mine," snapped Barlowe.

Henny Penn took a few steps toward him. "I don't kere what you say! This ain't our fault! We ain't do nothin! How you gon stand up there wit a straight face and blame us!"

He pointed toward the house where the white people lived.

"What you protectin *them* for?! They don't kere bout you! You can jump up and down all you wont, but it is what it is, bro. It is what it is, and you cain't blame us!"

A few people in the crowd nodded in agreement. Somebody toward the back shouted, "Thas right!"

They nodded and nudged each other, then looked to Barlowe for a response. Barlowe opened his mouth to speak, but he held his tongue. That feeling came back. That feeling in his chest returned, and he struggled to get it under control.

Henny Penn spoke again: "Out chere protectin white folks! I tell ya what! You better be careful! *They* got theirs comin! If you ain't careful, you might git what they git!"

Before he could finish, Barlowe lunged at him. He cuffed Henny by the collar and yoked him once. Henny tried to pry himself loose, but he couldn't. Barlowe's hands were too strong.

After some struggling, Wendell and a few others pried them apart. When he was free from Barlowe's clutches, Henny Penn stepped back and straightened his clothes. A few of his boys closed ranks around him. One of them stuck a hand inside his shirt and peered at Barlowe.

Barlowe glared back. "You got somethin for me?! Huh?! What you got?!"

By now, Henny Penn had collected himself. He shrugged and waved off his bodyguard. "Truth is truth, bro! Thas all to it!"

Barlowe said nothing. He stood there breathing hard, his fists still balled in a knot.

Mr. Smith came over and placed a hand on Barlowe's shoulder. "C'mon, son. C'mon. Don't get dragged into this."

Barlowe scanned the crowd. His eyes landed again on Miss Carol Lilly. He wondered what was going through her tangled mind. Her gaze dropped to the ground.

Other people began walking away. One by one, they departed. A few stayed, waiting to see what might happen next.

"Cmon, boy," said Mr. Smith. "Les go on home."

He steered Barlowe away from the block. Some folks stood back and watched, mumbling among themselves as the two men left.

Somebody shouted after them: "Don't blame us!"

Mr. Smith shook his head sadly. "This is how it always happens. This is how it always happens."

Barlowe said nothing. He kept on walking. Mr. Smith patted him on the shoulder again. "You did the right thang, boy. You did the right thang."

Barlowe kept quiet. He seemed baffled, and a little ashamed. What had gotten into him, anyway? He didn't know. All he knew was things were getting out of hand.

When they reached their end of the block, the old man inspected the sidewalk in front of his home, looking for litter to pick up from the ground. Barlowe said a grateful good-bye and headed up the walk toward his house. He paused near the curb and studied the spot where he had found Viola's body.

*Maybe she's in a better place,* he thought. *Maybe she ain't cryin inside.*

The evening dusk had faded into blackness now. The streets of the Old Fourth Ward were deathly quiet, except for the creaky sound of Ricky's grocery cart. As usual, the cart stopped midway along Bradley Street. As usual, Ricky stood in front of 1712, the modest one-story blue frame house.

There were lights on, and people inside. A man with a thick mustache and slanted eyes parted a curtain and peered back at him. Ricky looked down at his feet, checking to see if he might be standing too close. He pushed the cart across the street, to the exact spot he had marked with a hammer and chisel some years ago.

*A hunnerd feet.* He was safe now. *A hunnerd feet.* They couldn't run him off.

Seeing Ricky move away, the man peering through the window disappeared.

Ricky stood there, staring, barely moving. While he watched, a light blinked on in a side bedroom. Ricky closed his eyes tight and ran his mind from top to bottom, through every inch of that room. He knew the approximate height of the windowsill. He knew the exact location of the single closet. He even recalled the annoying bedroom door, which, set on slanted hinges, always swung closed on its own. The door led out to a narrow hallway and to the other rooms—all warm repositories of Ricky's fondest memories.

Ricky was born in that house. The old folks said the midwife who tended his mama mistakenly left behind a swatch of his umbilical cord. How else to explain his lingering fixation on that place, even after his family moved away?

Ricky was fifteen when his family left for Mississippi. He ran away twice, each time returning to the Old Fourth Ward. After the third trip to Atlanta to retrieve his son, Ricky's daddy gave up trying. He couldn't afford to keep him put.

Old-timers in the ward said Ricky had always been "slow." So it came as no surprise that he had trouble accepting that a new family lived in his old house. One night, the new family, seeing the stranger yanking on their doorknobs, called the cops and had Ricky arrested. A judge ordered him to stay at least one hundred feet away from the house.

Later, Ricky went straight back to the house and stood at the curb. He placed one foot before the other and counted off one hundred times, then marked the spot to establish where he could legally stand.

The people who lived there made peace with Ricky's strange obsession, once some old-timers assured them he was no threat.

Now Ricky usually went past the blue frame house twice a day: once in the morning, when he left the ramshackle outdoor tent settlement he shared with homeless friends, and once in the evening, after returning from collecting his garbage loot.

Mostly, he paused only briefly, as if to confirm the house was still there. This night, after the trauma of his near-arrest, Ricky came seeking the comfort of a familiar place. He stood there for a long while and stared. A single tear filled his eye.

# Chapter 39

After Ricky Brown's near-arrest, relations in the Old Fourth Ward grew testier. Whites there took some of the hardest hits. Bricks were flung through several more windows; a few tires were slashed. An attempted burglary set off a house alarm. And two other mailboxes were set aflame.

The troubles led whites to press forward with Greg Barron's plan to hire private security patrols. When neighborhood blacks bucked the plan, whites hired a company anyway. The security patrols operated much like the paper boy, delivering services to individual subscribers. They provided round-the-clock surveillance at specific houses—numbers 1022, 1271 and 1650 on Randolph Street. Numbers 1220, 2023 and 2409 on Howell Lane. It went on like that for several blocks until most white families were covered.

Whites weren't the only people feeling pressure in the ward. In time, the tension wore on black folks, too, so much so that some began to turn on one another. As more real estate changed hands, blacks began to speculate about who among them would be next to collaborate with the enemy; who among them would be the next to sell?

■  ■  ■

William Crawford came to the house one day to remind Tyrone that it was past time to get rid of the pigeons. Crawford had set a one-month deadline and made sure Barlowe knew it was *his* deadline, too. Tyrone cursed Crawford's name to the highest heavens and refused to speak to him after that. He insisted that he had already begun taking steps to get rid of the birds.

"Look," he told Barlowe one day. "The cage is wide open. They can go free, but they act like they don't even know it. They won't leave."

When he left to take a shower, Barlowe gave it a try. He went to the opened cage door and coaxed one of the birds onto his finger. He waved an arm, hurling the creature into the air. It fluttered wildly, then returned to the cage. Barlowe tried shooing the two other birds away. They flitted to the Gilmores' fence, then returned to the back porch when Barlowe went inside.

Later, Tyrone came out of his room all dressed up. Barlowe sat in the living room, reading the paper.

"Hey, chief."

Barlowe looked up from reading.

"I'm goin to see this honey I met."

"Winn-Dixie?"

"How you know?"

"Lucky guess."

"Nice girl," Tyrone offered. "Real nice. She got religion, too . . ."

Barlowe said nothing. He had noticed something peculiar about Tyrone lately. On Saturday afternoons, he sometimes got dressed up in a suit and tie and disappeared.

Tyrone turned to leave, then stopped in the doorway. Shifting from one foot to the other, he looked like there was something he wanted to say but hadn't figured out how to put the thought together.

Barlowe watched him squirm. "Whas up, Ty? Whas on your mind?"

"I heard about what happened wit Ricky Brown."

"Yeah?"

"Yeah. People been talkin, Unk."

"What they been sayin, Ty?"

"They sayin you been actin kinda strange since that white gal showed up next doe."

Barlowe folded the newspaper. "Whas actin strange, Ty?"

"Actin like you done gone Republican or somethin."

Barlowe nodded and kept his eyes fastened to Tyrone.

"You think I'm gone Republican, Ty?"

"You my unk."

"Yeah, but do you think I'm gone Republican?"

Tyrone shifted on his heels again. "I jus wont you to be careful, thas all, man."

An uneasy silence followed. Then: "Ty?"

"Yeah?"

"What would you think if I wasn't your uncle?"

"I don't wanna get into that, man. I jus wont you to be careful, thas all."

Barlowe stared at him. "I'll be all right, Ty. I'll be fine."

Tyrone went out the door.

Barlowe left the house early for work the next morning. Before he reached the car, he sensed there was something wrong. It was the car itself, sitting out front. Its balance and symmetry seemed off-kilter. He leaned down on one knee, near the curb and inspected the two right-side tires. Then he got up and rushed around to the other side. He cursed and stood there awhile.

All four tires had been slashed. The car rested on its rims.

He looked up and down the street, like he half-expected to see somebody running away. There was no one in sight, except Clarence Sykes. Clarence walked toward the bus stop on Irwin Street, headed to work. He walked with the reluctant shuffle of a man being led to a prison cell.

Barlowe also had to get to work. He had an important print run scheduled. He left the car and trailed Clarence to the bus stop. Somebody shouted to him from across the street. "Yo! Yo! Yo!"

A man dressed in loose-fitting African garb and dark sunshades sat atop a big boom box. "Yo! I got the latest R. Kelly!" He held up a bootleg CD.

Barlowe ignored him and got on the bus.

After work, he caught the bus back home. When it reached his stop, he got off and headed in the opposite direction, away from the house, toward the other end of Randolph Street. He walked the few blocks and stopped in front of the Purple Palace. There were two people, a man and a woman, standing on the porch. They appeared to be arguing.

Across the street, a group of teenage boys played basketball, while older men sat around in chairs, playing Spades. As Barlowe approached, somebody flicked a lit cigarette on the ground, near his shoe. Barlowe panned the card players and settled on Henny Penn, who at that same moment was studying him.

"My *main* man!" Henny lit another cigarette. It dangled loosely from his mouth.

Barlowe nodded. "Henny."

Henny Penn's eyes narrowed. "You gon be makin any pretty speeches taday?"

"Naw," said Barlowe. "No speeches."

"Good. I toldja, I got no use for pretty speeches and whatnot."

Henny dabbed the cigarette, then played a card. He glanced again at Barlowe, then cut his eyes to a pouch resting on a chair nearby. Barlowe took a few casual steps forward and stopped between Henny and the pouch.

Henny tried to appear unconcerned. After a long moment he glanced, almost pleadingly, toward one of his bodyguards. The fellow had turned his back to flirt with a prostitute passing by.

Now there was silence, except for the sound of cards slapping the table. Henny glanced at Barlowe, then frowned, confused by the strange look on his face.

They say a lion wags its tail slightly before it strikes. At that moment, a smile, barely perceptible, formed on the corners of Barlowe's mouth. Henny noticed the smile and shifted uneasily in his seat. He stretched his arms, pretending to yawn. Then he made a move to stand and stretch his legs.

It was too late. Barlowe pounced. In one quick motion, he sprang forward, reached down and smacked Henny Penn across the face. He hit him so hard that Henny's head jerked sideways. Barlowe followed with a flush punch that knocked him out of the chair. Henny Penn spilled to the ground, still clinging to his cards. Both feet shot straight up in the air.

Startled by the sudden outbreak of violence, the other men sitting nearby stood or pushed back from the table, knocking over chairs.

Henny Penn's bodyguard looked at him, awaiting instructions on what to do. Henny moaned, turned over and rested a moment on all fours. He had a bloody nose, and his lip was busted. He flexed his jaw, testing for broken bone. He struggled to get to his feet and slumped back down.

The bodyguard ran over to help. He slid Henny into a chair, then turned to Barlowe. "What you do that fo?!"

Barlowe kept his eyes fixed on Henny. "He knows."

The others stared, content to stay out of the fight. They would have ganged up on anybody else. But they knew better than to take on Barlowe Reed. Conflict with Barlowe might bring more unwanted attention from police. Since the mailbox fires, the cops had been harassing Henny and his band of thugs in and around the Palace.

With some effort, Henny Penn tried to clear his head. Barlowe backed slowly away, keeping an eye locked on him. Henny spread his legs apart and shook his head, still trying to toss off the fogginess. He leaned toward the pouch in the chair nearby.

Before Henny could get to his feet good, Barlowe had already disappeared.

# Chapter 40

More and more, life in the Old Fourth Ward was not like it used to be. Among blacks, the mounting influx of whites was eventually viewed like the notion of death: a grim inevitability that was greatly feared but had to be faced. It was regarded with a certain public acceptance, reserved with private prayers that a divine miracle would let it pass on by.

For Barlowe, life there seemed a bit like a brutal storm closing in: wind pounding violently against windows and doors, trying to burst inside and impose its will.

The storm built momentum when Barlowe heard the news about Reverend Pickering. Out of the blue one day, the preacher called a special meeting of a few select people (Barlowe and Mr. Smith were not invited) to announce that he had dropped his renewed plans for a protest march.

"Not enough fire in people's bellies," he said.

That was only half the story. Word got out that some developer made the reverend an attractive offer, which resulted in the church being sold. High-end townhomes would be built on the site.

The storm didn't subside with the preacher, though. It seemed to gather steam with a sad revelation from Mr. Smith. For several weeks,

Barlowe hadn't seen much of the old man. Then one day he spotted Mr. Smith in his front yard, hammering a stake into the ground. Sweating and breathing hard, the old man's back was turned to the street. Barlowe crossed over, approached and startled him.

"What you doin, Mr. Smith?"

Mr. Smith picked up a black-and-white cardboard sign from the ground and flipped it around so Barlowe could see:

FOR SALE
BY OWNER

Barlow recalled that Mr. Smith had always said you couldn't get him away from the Old Fourth Ward without a solid pine box, sealed with lots of nails. He pointed at the sign. "Whas this?"

"What do it look like, son?" As he spoke, the old man kept his focus on his work.

"Look like you puttin your house up for sale."

"See. All that readin you do come in handy."

"You serous?"

"Serous as a heart attack."

"Why?"

"Cause I'm smarter than the average cracker, thas why."

"That ain't how it look to me. Look to me like you sellin out."

Mr. Smith stopped hammering and glared at Barlowe. "You know better 'n that, boy. *You*, of all people, know better."

"So what, then? What you doin?"

Mr. Smith stood up straight, sliding a hand around to rub his aching back.

"I'll tell ya if you really wanna know."

"Yeah. I wanna know."

The old man explained: "I was sittin in my livin room, readin the paper not too long ago, and some white folks came knockin at the doe. I answered and they axed me how much I wont for my house. I decided to run them crackers off, so I gave em a crazy price. I gave em a price nobody in they right mind would pay.

"Ya know what?"

Barlowe waited.

"They said they wonted to buy it, anyway. Rascals looked me in the eye and didn't even blink. I thought they was kiddin at first. I was gittin ready to run em off. But one a the fellas promised they was serous. I'm tellin you, he looked me dead in the eye and said he had the money. Said it like I was sposed to be blown away, like I was gonna piss my pants soon as he mentioned that much money . . . Know what I did?"

"What?"

"I backed off then. Tole em I was just kiddin. Tole em I planned to die ri chere in this house. Tole em me and my woman gonna stay put and die here together, matter-a-fact, and be buried under the livin room.

"Them crackers didn't even twitch. All they said was for me to let em know if I change my mind. One of em give me a fancy bidness card wit a phone number on it. I put that thang on the dresser, but later on I tawked to Zelda bout it and we got to thankin. If white folks offered us that much money for this li'l ol place thout seein the whole thang inside, then it means the house is probably worf ten times mo. Know what I mean?"

Barlowe nodded.

"So I decided to outfox them coons. I'ma put this thang on the market for a while and see how big a fish I can ketch."

He looked off into the distance, his rheumy eyes seeming to dim a bit. "We cain't stay here noway . . . You seen your tax bill lately?"

Barlowe didn't answer. The tax bill went directly to Crawford.

"Me and Zelda could stay here, but it won't be long fore we start feelin a pinch. We could live real comfortable off our pensions and the money we make from sellin this house. We could move into sisted livin and play bingo twice a day."

"Sounds temptin."

"You bet," the old man said, ignoring the sarcasm in Barlowe's voice.

Looking at Mr. Smith's weary face, Barlowe thought he saw the old man's will starting to bend. It made him mad.

"Mr. Smith, you said you weren't gonna let nobody run you away. You said you were committed to the neighborhood."

The old man closed his eyes and shook his head from side to side. "Hole on, boy. Jus hole on a minute. I was committed to the neighborhood we *had*."

He started hammering again. He finished the chore and began gathering his tools. "If you know somebody black who might wanna buy, lemme know. Tell em I'll cut em some slack."

They both knew the chances of finding a black buyer were slim to none. With neighborhood prices shooting up, poor blacks couldn't afford to buy. And middle-class blacks didn't seem much interested in old houses squeezed onto compact lots. They tended to rush to the sprawling suburbs surrounding Atlanta. They bought newer, bigger homes and posted "Private Residence" signs out front.

When he was done, Mr. Smith picked up his toolbox and started toward the house. "See ya later, son."

Barlowe turned and slowly headed up the walk. It was his turn for community patrol.

Despite cold air outside, and gray skies overhead, the streets were alive. Several stray dogs wandered about. A few old people, wrapped in too many winter clothes, hobbled to and from their homes. Across the lane, a white man stood in front of his house, sweeping the walk.

Barlowe wandered down Randolph Street and ended up near the Purple Palace. Two young men dressed in heavy winter gear stood like sentries on the porch. As usual, the front door was ajar. Out in the littered yard, just a few feet away, a kitten lay dead on the ground.

Barlowe went several blocks in the opposite direction, then cut down a back street and curled around to the Sweet Auburn business district. He stopped in front of the tall, redbrick building that Martin Luther King made famous long ago. There was a blue neon-lighted sign out front, with letters embedded in a large cross: Ebenezer Baptist Church.

He stood there a moment and looked around, like he was waiting for something specific to happen. Then he willed himself to step into the lighted vestibule. He eased into the main sanctuary, past two ancient, white-gloved ushers, and took a seat in the very last pew. He sat there a minute and drew inside himself, thinking.

After a while, he got up and went out toward the courtyard of The King Center next door. He liked visiting The King Center, especially in winter, when the tourist crowds were down. He liked to go and sit at the wall directly in front of King's gravesite and drink in the beauty of the courtyard, which was filled with stocky shrubs and leafy flowers, even in winter. He sat sideways with one foot dangling off the edge of a low retaining wall surrounding the reflecting pool.

A chilly breeze blew in around the pool, sending faint ripples through the water. He looked through the clear water to the floor of the pool, where pennies had been tossed by visitors using it as a wishing well.

There used to be a lot more pennies there. Park rangers now discouraged visitors from pitching pennies into the pool. Homeless people, desperate for food or drugs, were known to wade into the water sometimes to fish out coins.

Staring at the water, Barlowe tried to guess the number of pennies still there. Probably, he figured, not enough to buy a sandwich and a pint. He shivered, then clasped the top button of his coat to keep the wind from whisking down his neck. His cheeks were red from the cold. He stared at King's concrete crypt, mounted on a wide stone platform in the center of the pool.

He wondered, *How did this man do what he did?*

Barlowe had no idea. Nobody he knew had that kind of spunk. Maybe Mr. Smith was right about something he'd once said. Maybe young people nowadays were made from a cheaper metal than those who came before.

While he sat there thinking, a few visitors came and stood nearby, reflecting solemnly at the pool. A woman standing about fifteen feet away closed her eyes and tossed a penny into the water. Barlowe studied her, eyes closed and lips moving as she prayed. She stood still as a statue, facing the crypt with hands clasped together in front of her. Then she dropped slowly to her knees and prayed some more.

Barlowe wondered if she was praying to Jesus or to King. Did she even know the difference anymore? For some, it seemed, the difference had been blurred with time as King's myth continued to grow. Barlowe wondered if a hundred years from now the myths about King would have grown so much that there would even be stories—eyewitness accounts—of King rising from this very crypt.

Was that how it had happened with Jesus? Was he just a good man who was lifted up, deified more and more with each new telling of a tale about him?

When the woman finished praying, she got up and walked slowly away.

It was almost dark outside. Barlowe stood and stepped beyond the courtyard and started down Auburn Avenue. He crossed Boulevard Avenue and passed the old fire station.

Just up the walk, near King's birth home, he saw a woman walking toward him, pushing a twin-sized stroller. Dark and solemn, she appeared to be in her late fifties. The woman's face bore a self-conscious, embarrassed look. As she drew closer, Barlowe glanced down at the stroller and saw two white, apple-cheeked babies slouched in their seats. The babies were strapped in and bundled up, with thick blankets tucked under their tiny chins.

Barlowe's gaze shifted from the woman to the babies and back again. The woman passed, nodded and kept on stepping.

Up farther along the walk, he approached the Cafe Latte, with its tables and chairs out on the patio. The temperature was down to forty degrees. Still, a few white people sat outside, sipping cappuccino and chatting easily.

Barlowe wanted a hot chocolate to warm his insides, but he refused to go inside that place. He turned down a side street and kept on walking.

There were a few more blocks to patrol before he was done. Then he planned to go seek comfort and consolation from his woman, Louise Grimes.

■ ■ ■

It was dark outside when Sean and Sandy Gilmore started home from an emergency potluck gathering. There had been a brutal mugging, leading to more talk of people moving out. Gregory Barron, trying to calm frayed nerves, insisted that things would settle down in time. For some of the folks gathered in the house, those words were only mildly reassuring.

Nobody said it, but fear hung in the air and lingered until the meeting ended.

Walking home afterward, Sean mentioned, for the thousandth time, the need for Sandy and him to sell their house and move away. Sandy strolled along in silence. Now, thinking about the mugging, she began to wonder if Sean was right.

They walked down Irwin Street and turned onto Randolph. They were about a block from home when they heard footsteps from behind. Sean quickened his steps and nudged Sandy to keep pace. She shifted into faster, longer strides, while trying to avoid appearing hurried, afraid.

The footsteps were steady and louder now. The stalker seemed patient, content not to pass.

Sean and Sandy's house came into view, with all the security lights aglow. If only they could reach the radiance of the light, Sandy thought, maybe they'd be all right.

Sean's thoughts raced in another direction. His mind flipped a few months back to the day he walked into a gunshop and asked to see some "merchandise." He needed a gun, he had decided, if for no reason other than to manage his own anxiety, which now seemed to be spiraling out of control.

When he went into the store, the owner smiled and patiently explained the range and power of his deadly stock, taking care to encourage Sean to hold and handle each gun he showed an interest in.

"This here one takes hollow points," the man said, setting a cannon on the counter.

"What are hollow points?"

A city boy. A novice. The man's smile disappeared. He gently took the gun from Sean and returned it to the glass-enclosed case.

"Hollow points will drill a hole clean through a man to the other side, and tear up ever bita flesh and bone along the way," the store owner explained. "It's what I use ..."

After three trips to the store, Sean settled on a plain .32 revolver, which seemed a perfect fit for his smallish hands. The store owner noticed Sean's palms sweating as he tried to follow instructions on loading the weapon and locking the hammer.

Later, Sean spent some time practicing at a local range (he sneaked off whenever Sandy went to her meditation class). Standing in front of the bathroom mirror, he practiced aiming on his own. So on his way home with Sandy that night, he felt fully prepared.

The footsteps behind him seemed closer still. Straining to hear, he estimated there were at least two people trailing. He could handle two. He slipped a hand inside his jacket.

*Let them come. Fucking thugs. Let them come!*

Silently, he began to count off numbers to time his move. One . . . two . . . He had practiced timing himself: One . . . two . . . three . . . now!

In a flash, he shoved Sandy aside. She shrieked and stumbled to the ground. In one fluid motion, Sean drew the gun, swung around and cocked the hammer. *Fucking thugs!*

Sandy turned over, looked behind them and screamed. "No, Sean!! No!!"

Sean leveled the pistol and aimed to fire. He had the bastard right in sight.

"No, Sean, don't!!!"

Heeding his wife, Sean hesitated. He eased the tension in his trigger finger and turned toward Sandy. Before he could refocus his attention, he felt a heavy force pounce on him. The attacker yanked his coat over his head, so that he was trapped, arms and head straitjacketed by his own clothes.

A hand, strong as a vise, snatched the gun and raised it high, preparing to slam down and crush his skull.

Sandy sprang from the ground and rushed forward. "Please! It was a mistake! We're sorry! Please!"

Sean flailed wildly, struggling to disentangle himself. He heard a man's voice growl at him. "You better learn what to do with this . . ." The man tossed the gun to the ground.

In a moment, Sean wrenched himself free from his coat. He straightened up and regained his bearings in time to see that one man, not two, had walked in the darkness behind them. It was no predator. It was Barlowe, returning from his neighborhood safety patrol.

Barlowe stormed up the walk and went indoors.

# Chapter 41

Days later, Sandy was standing at the kitchen sink, washing dishes, when Barlowe appeared in his backyard. She watched curiously as he stood there, staring into space. He headed slowly to the porch, then reappeared. She watched him piddle around, unraveling the hose.

He seemed fidgety.

Sandy dried her hands and went to the front of the house, into the living room, where Sean had settled down to read the paper.

"Sean." She plopped down on the edge of his chair. "Didn't you say you were going to the store?"

He kept his eyes glued to the paper. Ever since the near-shooting, he'd tried to manage his embarrassment by avoiding eye contact with her.

"I wanted to pick up something from the pharmacy," he said, "but I decided it can wait."

She smiled. "Well, actually, I need a few things for dinner tonight."

He looked up at her. "I thought we were having leftovers."

A few beads of moisture formed on her nose. "We can have leftovers tomorrow. I'm in the mood for something else." She tossed him a pleading look. "Please."

He crumpled the paper. "What do you need?"

"I thought I'd make spaghetti, but I don't have sauce."

"Yes we do. I saw some in the cabinet this afternoon."

He went into the kitchen. Opening the cabinet door, he pointed at the spaghetti sauce—a big jar, right up front.

"We need more than *this*?"

"Oh." She looked sheepish. "I didn't see that. I guess that'll be enough."

She moved to the refrigerator now and opened the door. She rummaged around inside and turned to him. "Peppers. We need green peppers, and dressing for a salad."

"Is that it?"

"Yes. I think that's it."

He slipped on a jacket and was out the door. As soon as he pulled out of the driveway, Sandy rushed through the house and went out back. Barlowe was still out there standing around.

"Hey," she said, approaching the fence. "How you doing?"

"I'm doin."

"I was about to start supper. Just thought I'd come out and say hello."

"Hi."

His mood was low. She could tell. She moved closer to the fence.

"Barlowe."

"Yeah?"

"Look, I'm *really* sorry about what happened the other night."

His eyes turned sharp, angry. "I coulda been killed, you know? I could be dead right now."

"I know. I know." The gravity of the incident came back to her. "You have no idea how bad I feel. I think Sean feels bad about it, too."

"I suggest he stay clear a me. I ain't responsible for what I might do."

They both remained quiet, thinking. Then Sandy said, "You've gotta admit things have been pretty uptight around here. There was a mugging, you know? Everybody has been on edge."

Barlowe chuckled. "On edge."

"Listen," she said, "before the other night, I had decided to pull back a bit. I was tired and feeling somewhat overwhelmed by all that's been happening. But after the gun incident I realized I can't pull back now. I'm in too deep—we all are—whether we want to be or not."

Barlowe leaned forward and peered in her eyes, recalling the stories his daddy used to tell when he was a boy. "Men have been killed over the likes of *you*."

Her face pinched tight. "That's not what the other night was about. And nobody's ever been killed over *me*."

"Coulda happened the other night."

Sandy's face flushed. She grew visibly upset.

"Could you handle a man bein killed over you?" Barlowe asked.

"Look, I said I'm sorry . . . Why would you ask me such a thing?"

"Because. It coulda happened."

"No, it couldn't have happened. I wouldn't have let it happen."

He rolled his eyes and shook his head. "The man drew a gun on me. What could *you* do?"

"You're being awfully mean today," said Sandy. "Maybe I should just go back in the house."

She waited, hoping he would apologize. She wanted him to ask her to stay and talk some more.

Barlowe said nothing. He just stared at her.

"Well, I guess we'd better talk some other time," said Sandy.

"Yeah."

She left. Once indoors, she began taking out food for dinner. She busied herself chopping onions. While she worked, she thought about Barlowe. He seemed so troubled, annoyed. She felt tortured, stuck and at a loss. It was strange. She was sure that on some level she was in touch with him, the essence of who he was. At the same time, she had never felt so close to—and simultaneously distant from—anyone before. With Barlowe there was always that wall, ever standing, that she couldn't breach.

She stood at the sink, measuring the range of her conflicted emotions as she ran water into a pot.

Then a voice from behind startled her. "Did you enjoy your little neighborly chat?"

She jerked around. "Sean. I didn't hear you come in." She wondered what time it was. How long had she been outside? Sean had already taken off his jacket and set the store items on the counter. She hadn't noticed the groceries when she came in.

Sean stared at his wife. His face was red, livid. "What is it, anyway?"

Sandy turned her back and began rinsing green peppers. "What is *what*, Sean?"

"You know what. What is it with you and the guy next door?"

"I told you, his name is Barlowe."

"Whatever." He pounded the countertop. "Answer my question."

"We talk, that's all."

He looked at her strange. "About what?"

"About . . . *things*."

"What kind of things?"

"I don't know." She thought for a moment. "We talk about the way things are."

Sean pointed outside. "And what does *he* know? No, lemme guess. He's a nice guy, caring, like you, right."

"Oh, don't be sensitive, Sean. It doesn't wear well on you."

He exploded. "Actually, I've got good reason to be sensitive right now: My neighborhood feels like goddamned Iraq and my wife is suddenly sending me on bogus errands so she can sneak out for intimate chats with the *black* guy next door!"

"Sean, you almost *shot* the *black* guy next door! Remember?"

"Whatever. In any case, there's a lot to be sensitive about."

She stopped cleaning peppers and turned around, facing him. Her eyes were moist.

"What's the matter with *you*?" he asked. "*I'm* the one who should be crying."

She grabbed him by both arms and looked into his eyes. "Sean. You're scaring me."

"Scaring you? How?"

"You didn't even tell me you owned a gun! How could you buy a gun—a gun!—and not tell me?!"

He looked away. "Because. I knew what you would say."

"See? That's what I mean, Sean. I'm no longer sure you're the person I thought you were."

"And I'm no longer sure I *want* to be." He paused, seeming to stumble. "What I'm saying is, maybe I'm not committed to the degree that you are."

She turned her back to him and stared out the window. "I didn't know there were degrees, Sean. I've always thought a person was either committed or not committed."

"I'm committed to the *idea* of what we're doing," he said. "But I don't want to have to work this hard . . . I didn't bargain for this . . ."

"Then you're not committed, Sean. It's as simple as that. You're not committed."

"Well, then. I guess I'm not."

They both went silent, each trying to figure out where to take the discussion from there. They remained silent for a long while, he concluding in his way, and she in hers, that it was impossible to know.

Then Sandy spoke: "You're starting to sound like someone who doesn't care. I've never thought of you as apathetic."

"I'm not apathetic. Maybe I'm just indifferent . . . Is that a crime?"

"It's a crime if your indifference ends up hurting people." She sniffled. "You don't get it, do you? We really are hurting people."

He exploded. "Uh-huh, and they're hurting *us*! Have you thought about that? Huh? We're hurting, too!"

"No, you don't understand . . ."

"Okay," he said, "how about this: We're hurting each other! That sound fair? We're hurting each other! Everybody's hurting! So let's call it even, huh? Let's call it even!"

"But you don't understand—"

He waved her off. "Take it somewhere else, Sandy. I'm tired. I don't wanna hear that crap."

"But—"

"No buts!" He pointed at her. "No buts! These people are hurting us and they're hurting themselves!"

Sandy sniffled again. She pulled a paper towel from a nearby rack to wipe her eyes. "How can you say that with a straight face, Sean?"

"Easy! Look at the bums walking the streets!" He was shouting now. "And what about the drunks? What about that drunk lady who was found dead near the house a while back? We didn't force her to drink herself to death!"

Sandy shouted back, "She might have been depressed, Sean! The lady might have been depressed! Did you ever think about that!?"

Now Sean lowered his voice. "Yeah. She had plenty to be depressed about."

She studied his face. "What do you mean?"

"Her drunk boyfriend, or whatever he was to her. Her drunk boyfriend in jail."

"In jail?" Sandy had wondered in passing what happened to the frumpy man she used to see staggering through her backyard. She had wondered about him when she saw Viola walking through the path alone. "In jail?"

"Yeah. Jail."

"How do you know he's in jail?"

A devious grin spread across Sean's face. He was angry now. And hurt. He felt entitled to be a little mean.

"You haven't seen him around here peeing on the fence lately, have you?"

"No. But how do you know he's in jail?"

Sean picked up a green pepper and tossed it in the air like a baseball. "Because."

Sandy stared, suspicious. "Because what, Sean?"

"Because I took care of it."

"What do you mean you took care of it? What do you mean?"

Sean sensed now that he might have said too much. So what? He told himself that he didn't care anymore. Why should he care? He looked at Sandy, his face a blank page. Why should he care?

"I called the cops on him, that's what."

Sandy's eyes widened, incredulous. "You called the cops on him? When?"

"One night."

"One night, when, Sean? Tell me!"

"It's been a while. It doesn't matter. He probably got out and skipped town or something."

She glared at him, waiting.

"Hell," said Sean, "it wasn't *my* fault. He came stumbling through here, drunk. I looked out the window and saw him out there, in the dark, sitting against our fence. He got up and peed on the fence . . . That's the same guy who sneaked up on me that day. Remember?"

She stared, silent.

"So I called the cops and told them to get him away from us. They came and took him downtown."

"I don't believe you," said Sandy.

"Considering what happened to his old lady, who knows? I might have done him a favor. I might have saved him from himself."

Sandy's eyes grew wider. "I don't believe you."

Sean stepped around her and got a glass of water. "Well, you should believe me. And you should be grateful. Nobody should have to put up with drunk people walking through your yard all hours of the day and night."

Now she was furious. She could hardly believe what she had heard, and coming from her husband at that. Her *husband*!

She started pounding Sean's chest with her fists. "You! How could you bring yourself to do something like that?! I don't believe you! I don't believe you!"

He grabbed her by both wrists, to stop the assault. "Christ, Sandy, what's the matter with you? The man was breaking the law! I'm not apologizing! I'm not apologizing! My life has been hell since we moved out here! I'm fed up with this crap! My nerves are shot! It's driving me crazy!"

She stared at him, squinting. "I'm fed up, too, Sean. I'm fed up, too, with a lot of things—"

She stopped short of blurting it out, but he knew what she meant. Tears welled in her eyes again. She covered her face with her hands and shook her head in disbelief. She turned and rushed from the room.

Sean stood in the kitchen, drinking water and staring out the window. He could hear Sandy in the back of the house. She was sobbing and throwing things around.

He felt lost. He didn't know what else to say to her. Still, he was determined not to give in this time. She wasn't qualified to lead him.

He looked out the window, thinking and feeling lost. He spotted Barlowe across the way. He carried a rake and garden hoe. Sean studied him a moment. He wondered, who was he, anyway?

Sandy reappeared in the living room, breaking his train of thought. She had her car keys and a small purse in her hand.

Sean walked in. "Going somewhere?"

"I'm going *out*! I'm going out for some fresh air! It feels too stuffy in here!" She slammed the door.

"Sandy!"

She got in her car and drove away. She turned left onto North Highland Avenue and headed toward the downtown connector. She planned to take a drive around the perimeter, to give herself room to think, to give herself time to cool down.

She stopped at the red light at Boulevard. A dark, scruffy black man in tattered clothes and long, matted hair sat forlornly at the curb. Beside him was a bucket of dirty water, a bottle of Windex window cleaner and a smudgy cloth.

Sandy had seen him on that corner many times. As soon as she pulled to a stop, the man leapt to his feet and approached the car. She handed him a quarter and waved him off. The man took the money, thanked her and moved on to the car behind her. It was a shiny green Jaguar, with a white couple inside. Sandy could see them in her rearview mirror. They wore nervous, red-faced smiles.

Without waiting for permission, the street man aimed his Windex bottle at the windshield, sprayed and began wiping furiously, all the while smiling broadly.

While the driver kept a close watch on the black man, his companion rifled through her purse for change. Finding none, she ripped out a dollar bill and handed it to her partner. The white man lowered his window, slightly, and slid the bill through the crack. The black man yanked it away and nodded. He stuffed it in his pocket and backed slowly away from the car.

The light changed. Sandy glanced once more in the rearview mirror before driving off. She saw the black man. He reared back and laughed out loud, turning his face upward, toward the sky.

# Chapter 42

Minutes after his wife left, Sean went to his car and sped away. He figured he knew which direction Sandy would take. He got on I-85 South, heading toward the airport. He reached the perimeter and settled into the fast lane, picking up speed. Traffic was moderate, which meant he could have his way on the road.

Eventually, he approached the exit for Augusta. He looked longingly at the cars heading that way. He had been to Augusta a few times on business. It seemed like a decent town; smaller and more manageable than Atlanta, for sure. Probably, he thought, a lot like Chattanooga.

Sean wondered what turns life might offer if he took that Augusta exit and kept on going. It was somehow reassuring knowing a man could change the course of his life with one slight turn of the steering wheel. He thought: *Every person should do that at least once in life. Every person should take off in a direction that offers no resistance or problems; just erase the chalkboard and start all over.*

He thought about that a lot these days. He needed a break from his life. He needed a break, like right now.

By now the speedometer was pushing seventy. He figured he should be able to catch up to Sandy soon. He was more than halfway around the perimeter before it occurred to him how stupid he was. What were the chances of him finding her on the highway? And even if he did find her, what good would it do? She would be driving and he would be driving and there would be nothing he could do but toot the horn.

How stupid. He felt sillier by the day. Each week, his life made less sense to him. He could thank the move to the Old Fourth Ward for that. He could thank the address from hell.

Maybe he should head to Augusta. He could find a hotel and spend a few touristy days there.

Maybe a stiff drink would be better.

He got off at Interstate 20-West and exited at Moreland Avenue. He went to Manuel's Tavern. Inside, he plopped down next to two men seated on stools at the bar. The men wore dirty jeans and leather vests, with bandannas tied around their heads. Bearded and pierced, they looked like they hadn't bathed lately. They spoke in the Georgia hillbilly twang that annoyed Sean so much. *Rednecks.*

Sean cringed and swiveled his stool, so that his back was turned to them. He ordered a scotch and sat there studying his reflection in a mirror that covered the wall behind the bar. He gulped down the first drink quickly and ordered another. A sudden gleam appeared in his eyes, like he had come upon a moment of clarity. At that moment he saw himself as he figured other men had seen him all along—as a wimp, a weak man who let his wife run his life. Maybe he had been unwilling or unable to see it before, but now he was aware: Sandy wore the pants in that house; always had.

Sean recalled the time they spent in Forsyth. Shortly after they moved in, the neighbors on their block held a dinner party to welcome them. They were sitting around the table, talking about the long, stressful commute to Atlanta, when Sandy asked a question that seemed to set them off.

"Where's the nearest subway line?"

The dinner guests around the table searched one another's eyes and sniggered like they were all in on some private joke. Sean and Sandy exchanged furtive glances.

"What's so funny?"

"Well," said one neighbor, Andy Leach. Andy had big horse teeth, which made him look like he had twice as many choppers as everybody else. He chuckled. "You've probably heard this one by now."

"Heard what?" asked Sean.

Andy grinned like a Cheshire cat. "What they call the public transportation system in Atlanta."

"You mean MARTA?"

"Yeah. You know what the letters stand for?"

"No. I don't."

"Moving African Americans Rapidly Through Atlanta."

Andy burst into a belly laugh.

Sandy, disgusted, tried to move past the joke. "In Philly we caught the subway all the time. Actually, I'd prefer to catch the train to work."

"What they need to do," added Sean, "is extend the line out here."

Another neighbor, Mike Scully, chimed in. Mike had moved to Georgia from Alabama decades before, back when, according to him, the state was populated with more "decent folks."

"The problem, you see, is that the subway runs *two* ways." Mike's tone was paternal. "As a general rule, folks out chere don't care much for public transportation." He turned up his nose. "Too risky. Too risky."

Then Scully shot Sean a scornful look and drawled, "I wouldn't have *mah* wive even thankin a catchin a train back and forth to Lanta. The place is like Gomorrah."

Sean's face turned red, defensive. "You don't understand. Sandy is gonna think and do what she wants."

The tone was proud, though the facial expression was unconvincing.

Somebody politely changed the subject, to ease the tension mounting in the room.

That was how it was left at the dinner party that night. It was made clear, especially among the men, that the separation of city and suburb was akin to separation of church and state—and both were preordained by God.

Recalling that dinner party now, Sean took a hard look at himself. He didn't like what he saw: Sandy was the family leader, the head of their household. How did that happen? She wasn't qualified to lead him.

Now it came to him: He had been lazy, too laid back. He'd always left the strong opinions and big decisions to her. As her own father once said, he buckled and bowed too much to his wife. Once again, The Captain was right.

Now, as he recalled that exchange, Sean sat in the bar brooding. He gulped down his drink and ordered yet another. He began to feel light-headed, so that even a gut-bucket country and western tune blaring from the speakers sounded good to him.

At some point, after the third drink, a tall black man and a short white woman entered the bar and sat down in the booth directly behind Sean. The woman was petite, really small, with big, dreamy eyes and dark hair that fell down to her shoulders. The man was thick, with shoulders broad and round as bowling balls.

The biker boys looked at the pair, glanced at each other and rolled their eyes. They finished their drinks and disappeared.

Oddly, Sean thought again about the Augusta exit that he had passed up earlier. If he had veered off that exit, would anybody have faulted him? His life seemed tangled in a Boy Scout knot, and all the confusion stemmed from a simple address. If an address had made that much difference, then a change of address should do the same. Right?

Something else occurred to him. If he were to set out on a new course, could he assume Sandy would come along? Would he even *want* her to come?

Of course he would. He loved his wife, in spite of her risky optimism. He loved her now more than ever. She needed to be reeled in, that's all.

Which brought him back to the moment. He planned to reel her in. He ordered another drink. Against his will, he glanced again in the mirror. He could see the couple sitting in the booth behind him. The man and woman talked and laughed, sharing some private joke. At some point, the black man leaned over and kissed her, pressing her back against the wall.

Sean decided to leave. He paid the bartender. As he rose, he stumbled back onto the stool. He glanced in the mirror. The black man was watching. The man grinned and leaned over and whispered something in his lady's ear.

She laughed out loud.

Sean stumbled past the couple and out the door.

The daylight was fading over the horizon now, moving toward pure darkness outside. Sandy circled the perimeter a few times. Riding along, she thought about her husband: her scared, insecure Sean. She was beginning to wonder if she knew him anymore. In the time since the move, she had learned a lot about Sean, and even more about herself. She thought about something Barlowe once said: "You think you know somethin. You don't know the halfa things."

She wondered what he'd meant by that. She recalled that a college professor had once said something similar, but in a different vein. The professor said there were varying degrees of seeing. Some people walk into a crowded room and take in only the obvious, surface reality. Others walk into a room, he said, and take in ninety percent of what's going on.

So how much of reality did Sandy take in? She didn't know. She was sure she saw more now than ever, though. She picked up things in the neighborhood now—furtive glances, body language—that would have escaped her before. In some ways, Sandy was developing new eyes. But what were those new eyes worth? And what difference would it make to anything?

It all seemed so crazy.

Halfway around the perimeter the second time, Sandy shifted to I-85, headed south. Her car sputtered near the North Druid Hills Road exit. She glanced at the dashboard. Her fuel supply was low. By her estimation, there was enough gas to make it home.

She exited on Freedom Parkway and headed toward North Highland Avenue. It was dark when she approached the neighborhood. She felt tired, drained. She wanted to go home and get in bed.

Driving slowly to preserve gas, she turned onto Glen Iris Drive. There were people, shadows really, out walking the streets. A black woman stood on the corner and gazed hopefully at the car as she passed. One block up, two young men stood off in the darkness, near a tree.

The car sputtered again and made a rumbling sound. Sandy thought: *If I can make these last few blocks. These last few—*

The engine died.

Sandy steered the car to the curb. "Damn!" She turned the key. The engine groaned, but wouldn't catch.

She looked up and around, suddenly aware of where she was. To her left stood the Purple Palace. People went in and out, some carrying paper plates wrapped in aluminum foil. Off to her right, across the street, a group of teenagers played basketball on a portable hoop stationed beneath a streetlamp. Nearby, other people stood around and watched, some leaning against an apartment building, some squatting nearby, rolling dice.

When Sandy's car glided to a stop, heads turned and looked her way. She sat there wondering what to do. A car passed. She looked longingly, hoping the driver might stop to lend a hand. The car disappeared.

At some point, an errant pass sent a basketball bouncing hard off the lamp pole. It ricocheted, then rolled into the street and beneath Sandy's car.

A teenager retrieved the ball. He dribbled it fancily through his legs. Eyeing Sandy sitting in the car, he walked over and cupped a hand against a window.

She sat still, stiff as a pole. The long stem of her slender neck stretched upward as she stared back at him.

He spoke, rapid-fire, so fast she couldn't understand. "Whasamatterlady? Yourcarwontcrank?"

Sandy turned away and looked straight ahead.

Voices called to him. "Milk! Give it up, man! Throw me the got-damn ball!"

The boy called Milk rapped a knuckle on the window. "Lady, youneedsomehelptocrankyourcar?"

Somebody called again for the ball. The boy called Milk flung it back to the group. He stayed there, eyeing Sandy.

"Umtryinahepthewhitelady, man! Cantyouseehercarwontcrank?!"

Some of the boys resumed playing. Others, now curious, strutted toward the car. Some circled around front, near the hood; others drifted around back, inspecting the license plates.

Sandy was growing scared now and, at the same time, embarrassed about her fear. She tried to calm herself. What was there to be afraid of?

She heard the young men talking, whispering. "Maybe she need gas."

The boy called Milk walked around to the driver's side window. "Heylady. Youneedgas?"

Sandy ignored him. She heard someone say, "Ol white bitch. Cat got her tongue."

Sandy thought about the recent mugging. Then she decided she couldn't just sit there. She had to move. Her house was only a few blocks away. She had to get home. She could come back tomorrow with Sean and get the car, but right now she had to go.

Four boys mingled on her side of the car. They peered inside, studying the front seat, the back, the floors, like there was something specific they were searching for.

Sandy inhaled deeply, to collect herself. She exhaled hard, then kicked off her shoes. She had to run. She had to get away.

She slid to the passenger's side, away from the boys. She grabbed the door handle and bolted out. She took off racing, barefoot, down the street, with voices calling to her from behind.

"Hey lady! Lady!"

She dashed, screaming, "Help! Somebody please help!!"

The boys looked at each other and hunched their shoulders. A few chuckled and pointed at Sandy. "Whadda hell wrong wit hur?"

One of the boys opened the car door and checked the front seat. "Look! She left her keys and pocketbook!"

"Don't mess wit it!" another warned. "Don't touch nothin. You take that lady shit, the lawman be comin down. Les roll, man. Les git way from here."

They left, not even bothering to close the door. They drifted off, wondering where that crazy white lady learned to run so fast.

# Chapter 43

On the way home, Sean drove in from the same end of Glen Iris that his wife had taken minutes earlier. Staring through the fuzzy haze of scotch, he approached the Purple Palace. He noticed the teenagers hanging out near the run-down, two-story apartment building across the street. One group played basketball while others stood around in a tight cluster and talked, their hands thrust deep in their pockets.

Sean drove past the green Ford Taurus parked awkwardly near the curb. He went on for a half-block, then slammed on the brakes and wheeled around. *That looked like Sandy's car!*

He pulled in and parked on the wrong side of the street, his bumper nearly kissing the front end of the Taurus. He checked the license number. It was her car, all right. He noticed the passenger-side door flung open. He sat there, confused. *What would Sandy be doing here?*

He leaned back in the seat. The liquor had settled in his blood-stream now. It raced around wildly inside his head. He rested his head over the top of the seat, so that his face pointed skyward. He closed his eyes. He needed to go home, to lie down.

But what about Sandy? He had to find his wife.

He reached in the glove compartment and got his gun. He stuffed it into his waistband and stumbled out of the car, scanning the cruddy landscape, with its decrepit buildings and narrow alleyways. He could hear the teenagers off in the distance, talking loud and bouncing a ball. There were grown-ups walking about, too, out getting revved up for Friday night. Some walked fast, leaning forward, pressing into the wind; others lumbered slowly along sidewalks, coming and going inside houses, standing around, talking—dark faces, out in the darkness, moving about like shadow ghosts.

*Where did all these people come from?*

Until now, Sean had glimpsed only snippets of this gritty world from his passing car. Now he was close up on it; actually, in it. He walked unsteadily to the driver's side of Sandy's car. He leaned down into the opened door and saw that her purse and keys were still inside. He picked up the purse and checked the ID. Even now, looking at his wife's smile staring at him from the driver's license, he could hardly believe she had stopped here. His mind ran the gauntlet of possibilities. He had to find her.

He looked around, hoping to spot Sandy somewhere in the mix of people moving about. He hoped she might appear suddenly on the sidewalk, and in her breezy, naive way, announce that she had stopped to take a stroll.

That was possible with Sandy, wasn't it? That she would pick the most godforsaken patch of real estate in the neighborhood to stroll around and make a point. That was possible with his wife; the good-will ambassador, out among the natives, spreading cheer.

He had to find her and reel her in.

Across the street from where he stood, a steady stream of washed-out-looking people flowed in and out of the Purple Palace. Off to his right, about two doors down, he picked up sudden flickers of light. He saw the outlines of two people standing in the shadows, dragging on cigarettes.

He headed toward the Purple Palace. The front door was cracked. A single yellow bulb illuminated the area. A bent-up kitchen chair lay on its side. A banister with missing railings lined the porch. He guessed she had to be in there. If not, someone in there had seen her for sure.

Two men approached and went into the house. Concentrating hard to steady his gait, Sean followed, looking as conspicuous as any white man climbing those steps at night. He went indoors and entered a long, dimly lit hallway, with rows of rooms split on either side. He detected a musty smell, a mix of stale air and food cooking on a stove somewhere in back of the house. A telephone rang loudly at the end of the hall. A man wrapped in a towel appeared, dripping wet, from a communal bathroom nearby. He picked up the phone.

"Hullo . . . Naw, he ain't here." He hung up and disappeared.

A woman in a slinky nightgown left one room and entered another. Music wafted faintly from some rooms. Muffled voices crept from beneath the doors.

Two men carrying paper plates passed Sean in the hallway. They stared at him and quickened their pace, making their way out the door.

His head reeling, Sean pressed slowly forward and approached a room where there were more voices. He leaned over close to the door and heard loud trash talk, punctuated by the faint overlay of music.

Where was she? Where was his wife?

A glassy-eyed woman appeared from the back and spotted the white man standing in the hallway with his ear stuck to a door.

"You here for Clint, baby?"

Sean looked at her but didn't answer.

"You here for Clint?"

"I'm not—"

"He ain't here."

She was medium-brown, with chapped lips that were two shades darker than her face. Her eyes were yellow in the places that were supposed to be white. Her head was wrapped in a greasy scarf.

"I'm not looking for Clint," Sean heard himself say. "I don't know Clint."

She squinted. "Whut you wont, den?"

"My wife."

"Yo wife?! Ain't nobody's *wife* in here!"

"I know she's somewhere in this house." Sean could hear himself. He could hear his slurred speech.

The woman grew impatient, irritated. "Gwon bout your bidness now, fore I call Big Buck out chere."

She talked too loud. Sean wanted her to shut her mouth.

His head was spinning. He felt slightly nauseous, and his head was spinning like crazy. He was antsy, too. He took a step toward the woman.

"I gotta find my wife."

"Look, I ain't—"

"Move." He nudged her aside. He went to the door of another room and shoved it open. There were three men there, huddled in front of a rickety wooden table. One man held a pipe to his mouth. The other two sat leaning forward, waiting their turn.

"Close the gotdamn doe!!"

Sean calmly shut the door and went down the hall, the scarf-wearing woman trailing behind.

"Who you, the po-lice?"

He ignored her.

"I think you better git outta here!"

He went to another door and turned the knob. The door was locked.

The woman began shouting. "Buck! Buck! We gotta problem!"

Sean moved toward the back of the house and stopped at the last room off to the right. He tapped lightly on the door. The door cracked and revealed a pair of dark, beady eyes.

Sean pushed the door. It creaked open, and there stood Big Buck, a short, squat bruiser in a bolo hat. His fleshy face was gunmetal black. It bore the mark of a nasty slash—testimony to a knife fight in some long-forgotten seaport town. The slash, which ran from his left ear to his nose, served as a stern warning that Buck could take as well as he could give.

He glared up at Sean. "Whatcha need, gray boy?"

"I'm looking for my wife."

Buck clenched his teeth, which made that scar flex. "Yo *wife*?!"

The woman in the greasy scarf leaned over Sean's shoulder, speaking from behind. "I tole him she ain't here, Buck."

Buck bit down on his lower lip. He took a short step forward, preparing to bust Sean's mouth. He hesitated, seeing the man was white.

A white man with a busted mouth might bring more unwanted heat to the Palace.

"I think you best stop ri chere, gray boy. Gwon home fore you get yoself hurt."

Sean was drunk now, and too numb to be scared of anybody. He drew the gun and poked the barrel into Buck's stomach, forcing the big man back into the room.

"Where is she?"

Buck appeared surprised, caught off guard. He took two more steps back so that Sean could see for himself that his wife wasn't there.

Sean scanned the place. The room looked like it had once been a large kitchen. It was lighted by a cheap gold chandelier, hung in what might have been a dining room. In the far corner was a sink with two faucets, flanked by scratched-up countertops. On the wall farthest from the door was a picture of a bucolic farm scene. A young white boy carrying a milk pail ran barefoot toward a spotted cow.

Sean looked around some more. Cigarette smoke hovering thick in the air danced to music playing on a radio. Three women stood off to the side, talking with two men. One of the men nursed a drink. The other held a plate close to his face, shoveling a pile of collard greens.

Two big, round card tables were set up side by side in the middle of the floor. Four people sat at each table, playing poker.

When Sean came in, a few of the gamblers looked up from what they were doing. Others kept their eyes glued to the cards.

Sean's eyes swept over the seated cast. Sitting at one table was Henny Penn, whom Sean had seen around. Then he spotted his next-door neighbor. Even now Sean relived the panic he felt that day, when Tyrone clutched his throat.

Tyrone looked at Sean and blinked, confused. He started to cuss, but Henny Penn beat him to it.

"Who the goddamn hell is *dis*!" He was losing his money, mainly to Tyrone. He was in no mood for distractions.

Big Buck shrugged. "I dunno. The man said he lookin for his ol lady."

Henny Penn turned to Sean, ignoring the gun. "Boy, can't you *see*? Ain't nobody here for you!"

Sean leaned forward a bit. His head swirled so wildly now that he felt like he might puke.

"I . . . I'm looking ffffoorrr my wwwiife! I know she's—"

Henny Penn cut him off. "I'm tellin ya, white boy, she ain't here! Now git the hell out fore you piss me off!"

Sean pointed the pistol at Henny. The liquor had set in stronger, and he wasn't afraid.

"I . . . I'mmm not gggooing annywwherrre without my wwwiife."

People stopped what they were doing and stared at him. Henny Penn stared, too, while easing a hand to the pouch resting between his legs. After Barlowe had ambushed him, he'd vowed to never be caught off guard again. Now wherever he went, he kept the pouch close by.

Meanwhile, Tyrone pretended to keep his eyes glued to the cards while he did some calculating. Counting his own, he guessed there were at least five guns in that room; one pistol likely belonged to Henny. Tyrone didn't trust him, especially not since Henny was losing money.

Tyrone subtly slipped a hand inside his shirt, and waited.

Barely moving his hands beneath the table, Henny unzipped the pouch and slid a finger around the trigger. With his free hand, he pointed at Sean. "Look, boy, I'ma tell you *one* mo time! You got that?! *One* time: go! I'm losin my money here, and you distractin me! Now take this shit somewhere else!"

Sean pointed the pistol at him. "Donn't mmooovve!"

With Sean's attention diverted, Big Buck flipped the light switch, throwing the room into darkness. Then the shooting started. Shots fired from several directions. *Bam, bam, bam, bam, bam! Bam, bam!* There were panicked screams and crashing chairs, as people dived to the floor, scrambling for cover. Bullets rained, followed by more screams and chaos rippling through the house. People in adjoining rooms got dressed, or flushed drugs or climbed through windows. Somebody grabbed a pot of collards off the stove.

*Bam, bam, bam, bam, bam! Bam, bam, bam, bam, bam!*

As fast as it had started, the shooting ended. An eerie quiet settled in. Those who were able beat a path out of the gambling room, scrambling out the back door, into the darkness. Others dashed out front, leaving the rest to fend for themselves.

Minutes later, sirens sounded. Cops arrived and found the Purple Palace nearly deserted. In the gambling room, policemen came upon two men—one black, one white—sprawled near each other on the floor. Life oozed from them in dark pools of blood that merged into one thick puddle.

As one of the men was loaded onto a stretcher, he gasped for breath. Medics who loaded the other man doubted he would survive the trip to the emergency room.

Police fanned out along the block to interview witnesses. Among the people they talked to, nobody saw or knew a single thing.

Barlowe was relaxing at Louise's place when he first heard about the shooting. They had finished a fine dinner of meat loaf, peas and mashed potatoes and settled down to watch an old movie, when the news flashed across the TV screen. A reporter stood at the scene. He tried to appear somber, but he could barely contain his excitement as he raised the mike to his mouth:

"Police are investigating an apparent drug deal gone sour, resulting in a violent shootout in the neighborhood that once was home to the Reverend Martin Luther King . . ."

The Purple Palace appeared on TV. The camera cut to cops flowing in and out of the house.

Barlowe and Louise got dressed and hurried over. Outside, spectators crowded along the walk, beyond the yellow tape ringing the scene.

Barlowe approached a man he knew. "Whas goin on?"

"A crazy white man bust into the Palace and started shootin up the place!"

Somehow, Barlowe guessed Sean Gilmore was involved. When he spotted Sandy's car being hitched to a tow truck, he knew for sure: The worst had happened.

# Chapter 44

Days after the shooting, Tyrone sneaked into the house through the back door. Barlowe had already left for work. Tyrone went to his room, pulled a suitcase from beneath the bed and snapped it open. He yanked open the dresser drawers and hurriedly began packing: underwear, toothbrush, shaver, shoes, socks. He picked one of his best suits from the closet, folded it and pressed it in the suitcase, too.

He had to get away, go someplace far and chill, at least until things cooled down a bit. Who knew? He might go west to California. He had heard good things about California. He'd heard the ladies out there were fine and the people weren't so uptight, like in the South.

He moved with speed and efficiency, every now and then rushing into the living room to peep through the blinds. When he was done, he grabbed the suitcase and left the room. He stopped in the kitchen and returned to the bedroom. In his haste, he had left his gun on top of the dresser. He snatched up the gun and stuffed it in his belt.

Outside, he set the gun on the table, where the birdcage stood. He opened the cage door. The pigeons sauntered forward, waiting for him to extend a finger. He stepped back and shook his head.

"Naw, baby. You on your own now."

The pigeons cooed.

"Gwon." He shooed them off. "Gwon. Get way from here."

He picked up his suitcase and rushed out the door. He dashed, low-running through the backyard and out of sight.


Barlowe came home from work that evening and instantly realized that Tyrone had come and gone. He hadn't seen Tyrone since the night before the shootout. The days that followed had been trying, testy. Every time Barlowe went somewhere, people in the ward looked at him with questions burning in their eyes. Nobody asked outright. People simply told him how sorry they were about what had happened.

"I'm sorry, too," he told them. "I'm sorry, too."

In general, the shooting thrust the people of the Old Fourth Ward into a nervous fit. Gregory Barron called a press conference and demanded that police do more to protect neighborhood whites. Wendell Mabry countered with a press conference of his own, calling for whites to pack up and leave. Mayor Clifford Barnes imposed a curfew, to help cool emotions.

Still, gossip flowed heavy in the streets, with conflicting accounts of what went down at the Purple Palace that night. Barlowe was eager to hear his nephew's version. He went into Tyrone's room and came to the sudden realization that it was unlikely that he would see or hear from Tyrone anytime soon. He looked at the two dresser drawers, which sat open and half empty, and he saw the closet door had been left ajar.

He opened a dresser near the headboard and began sifting around. In the top drawer, Tyrone had stacked a pile of sweatshirts and lined socks neatly along the edges. Beneath the pile, Barlowe found a brand-new Bible, lying open with a page marker. He picked it up and studied the page. Tyrone had marked an asterisk beside a single verse: Isaiah 59:1-3:

Behold, the Lord's hand is not shortened, that it cannot save; neither his ear heavy, that it cannot hear. But your iniquities have sep-

arated between you and your God, and your sins have hid his face from you, that he will not hear. For your hands are defiled with blood, and your fingers with iniquity . . .

Beneath the Bible, Barlowe came upon a handful of Seventh-Day Adventist pamphlets, about fifty in all. Now he knew where Tyrone had recently been spending his Saturday afternoons.

Barlowe chuckled: *Ol Ty. Followed some woman right into church.*

He opened another drawer and found a box of bullets and three reefer sticks. He flushed the joints down the toilet and absentmindedly stuffed the bullets in his pocket.

Before leaving, he scanned the room one final time, half-hoping for a note or some sign to hang on to . . . There was nothing . . .

He went through the kitchen to the back porch. The birdcage was still open, like Tyrone had left it. Two of the pigeons had vanished. One bird stood alone on the Gilmores' fence.

When the bird spotted Barlowe, it flew over and landed on top of the cage. Barlowe reached for the bag of birdseed nearby. Then he spotted the gun. He picked it up and stuffed it in his pocket, wondering if it had been fired at the Purple Palace.

The pigeon ate, then sauntered forward, waiting for Barlowe to extend a finger so that it could hop on board.

Barlowe recoiled and shooed the bird. "Uh-uh. Go."

The bird fluttered back to the Gilmores' fence.

The doorbell sounded, startling Barlowe. He took the box of bullets and placed it beneath the newspaper lining the cage bottom.

The bell rang again, followed by a heavy, insistent knock.

Barlowe went to the front of the house and peeked out front. Two policemen stood on the porch. *Caesar.* Barlowe opened the door.

"Tyrone Montgomery Reed?" The voice was attached to a burly man with pockmarked skin.

"No. I'm Barlowe Reed, his uncle."

The other cop, short and thin, flung him a sideways look. "You got ID?"

Barlowe pulled out his wallet and flashed his driver's license.

"We need to talk to you. May we come in?"

Barlowe stepped to the side and let them enter. The cops sat down and explained why they were there: Tyrone was wanted for questioning in connection with the neighborhood shooting, they said. They repeated most of what Barlowe already knew: One of the shooting victims, identified as James Belton, also known as Henny Penn, was hospitalized, in critical condition. Another man, Sean Gilmore, was about the same. The cops made no mention of Big Buck or some of the other people who were in the room that night.

"We're wondering if you can help us find your nephew so we can find out from him what happened."

"I don't know nothin," said Barlowe.

"Any idea where we might be able to look?"

"No. But I'll be sure to contact you if I find out anythin."

The burly cop leaned forward, to establish that they could speak in confidence. "We hear you and Mr. Belton got into a fistfight not too long ago. You wanna tell us about that?"

"It was nothin. A li'l misunderstandin, thas all."

"That's not what we heard."

"I told you what I know . . . Anythin else you need to ask me?"

The cops scanned the room, like they thought maybe Tyrone might be hiding somewhere. Then: "No. That's all for now."

Barlowe moved to show them the door. Before he touched the knob, the bell sounded again. He opened it, and William Crawford walked in. The old man frowned when he saw the blue uniforms. He nodded a hello, then turned to his tenant.

"What's going on here?"

"Who are *you*?" the thin cop asked.

"I'm the owner of this house; the landlord."

"Can you tell us where we might find Mr. Tyrone Montgomery Reed? He's listed at this address."

Crawford furrowed a thick brow. "Barlowe here should be able to tell you that. . . . What do you want with Tyrone?"

"He's the prime suspect in a shooting—"

Barlowe interrupted, "You didn't say before that he was the prime suspect."

"You didn't ask," the thin cop snapped.

"I'm askin now."

The policeman stepped forward. Barlowe cocked his fists. Crawford shoved an arm between the two.

"Wait a minute. Please, Barlowe. Cooperate."

"I been cooperatin the best I know."

"No problem. We were about to leave." The burly cop aimed a finger at Barlowe. "Be advised. We will be watching this house. If Mr. Reed shows up, we're coming after him."

"Suit yourself," said Barlowe.

They left.

When they were gone, Barlowe remained in the doorway. He wanted Crawford to leave, too. Instead Crawford sat down hard on the couch. He took out a handkerchief and wiped his face.

"Barlowe, what in the world is this about?"

"There was a shootin."

"I *know* there was a shooting. It's been all over the news. But I had no idea Tyrone was involved."

"Seems so."

"Why didn't you call me?"

"Call you? For what? It didn't happen here."

"But it involved somebody *living* here."

Barlowe rubbed a hand wearily behind his neck. "I still ain't sure how much Tyrone was involved. From what I hear it was pitch-black in that room when the shootin started. To tell the truth, they ain't figgered out who shot who."

Crawford listened. When Barlowe was done, he snorted and wiped his face again. "I don't like the sound of this. I don't like somebody I'm renting to having troubles with the law."

"Mister, you rentin to *me*. I ain't had no trouble with the law."

Crawford looked away and shook his head. He hadn't picked up on the hostile tone. "I don't like this. I don't like this at all."

Barlowe shrugged. "Me, neither."

"I can't have this," said Crawford. "I *won't* have it."

Barlowe looked him in the eye. "What are you sayin? You won't have what?"

"I'm saying, young man, that I've had enough."

"Enough a what, Mr. Crawford?" He took a step closer. "Enough a what?"

"I don't do business with people who cause me trouble with the law . . . I mean, the complaint about the pigeons; that was enough." He pointed toward the back of the house. "I told you two to get rid of those birds months ago. Now this . . . Somebody from this house involved in a shootout."

Crawford wiped his face. "No, sir. This is too much. I've got my reputation, and a whole lotta other things to consider . . . Huumph. A shooting . . . I could lose this house behind something like that."

Barlowe stared at him. It was a hard, violent stare. "So what are you sayin, man? Speak your mind."

Crawford rubbed his chin and thought a moment. Then: "This is what I'm gonna do, son. I'm gonna put this house on the open market. If you're prepared to buy at the asking price, then that's all well and good. But if you can't pay what I ask, then, well . . ."

A wry smile crept across Barlowe's face. "That why you came over, to tell me this?"

Crawford said nothing.

"Somebody already made a offer, didn't they?"

Crawford looked away.

Barlowe nodded. "You got a offer on the table. Why didn't you jus say so?"

"Well," said Crawford, "you can't expect me to *give* the house away."

"No. I don't spect you to give it away. Specially not to *me*. I wouldn't buy it, neither—specially not from *you*."

Crawford jerked his head, surprised. He rose from his seat. He was mad as hell. He wanted to give his tenant a good piece of his thinking. But something about Barlowe's body language—he looked tense, taut—inspired him to hold his thoughts.

Crawford stepped to the door and placed a hand on the knob. "So it's settled then." His back was turned to Barlowe.

"Thas right, mister. Is settled." Barlowe stepped forward. Before he could reach him, Crawford rushed out the door and down the steps.

When the landlord left, Barlowe stormed out back, furious. He went into the yard and piddled around in an absentminded, vacant way. He went to the shed and began rearranging tools that were already in their proper place. He looked around for something else to do.

For a while, he just stood there, out in the open, where he could be seen. He needed to talk. He hadn't seen or heard from her since the shooting. Maybe she might show her face.

He waited there a long moment. When nothing happened, he went back to the porch and saw that the lone pigeon had returned to its cage. It hovered in a corner, with the door hung open. Barlowe reached in and extended an index finger. The pigeon hobbled forth and hopped aboard. Barlowe brought out his hand and held it high. He flung his arm, tossing the bird in the air.

The creature fluttered, then flew over to the Gilmores' fence. From its perch the bird watched with interest as Barlowe took the box of bullets from beneath the newspaper in the cage. He carried the cage inside the house and closed the door.

# Chapter 45

The winter months passed, followed by the warmth of an early spring. Barlowe stepped onto the front porch, cradling a big box in his arms. He set the box down and turned to go back into the house, then paused and glanced at the "Sold" sign in the Gilmores' front yard.

Next door, a huge moving van hovered like a hulking dinosaur in front of the house. Its engine idled in a low growl, as two workers hefted an ugly sofa from its massive bowels and headed toward the steps.

A white man, flanked by a woman and two toddlers, carried suitcases up the walkway leading to the house.

Barlowe looked across the street. A few white people had already arrived at the Cafe Latte. They sat out on the patio with their morning papers, sipping espresso.

Barlowe took in a deep breath and rattled off the list in his head: *Tyrone, gone; Viola, gone; the mini-mart, gone; the church is sold, and the elders will be leavin soon.*

*And Mr. Smith and Zelda . . .* Before leaving, the old man had found a way to strike one final, defiant blow. Still, Barlowe would miss him. He would miss him very much.

Looking up and down the street, he spotted The Hawk. Lost in the massive county jail after some temp worker misplaced his file, The Hawk had languished on lockdown for a whole year. He was freed only recently, after the error was discovered.

Now he wandered aimlessly through the neighborhood, mumbling to himself and searching for someone he would never find.

Barlowe went inside the house and got another box. As he carried it down the steps, Sandy Gilmore's green Ford Taurus appeared from up the street. He hadn't seen her in a while.

She got out, waved to Barlowe and crossed the yard. "Hi."

He set the box on the ground. "Hi."

She smiled. It was a weak, embarrassed smile, done more out of habit than feeling.

"I had to make one last stop, to drop off this mailbox key to the people who bought our house."

Barlowe looked toward the Gilmores' old place. The moving men marched back and forth like carpenter ants.

"Have you met your new neighbors?"

"No."

"Their names are Mark and Catherine Squires. Nice people."

"Yeah," said Barlowe, dryly. "Yeah."

Sandy noticed the boxes set at his feet. "Going somewhere?"

"No. Not really."

She looked curiously at the other boxes he'd stacked on the porch. He made no effort to explain.

"So," said Sandy, "what are you gonna do with yourself from here on out?"

"Well." He took a deep breath and released. "For one thing, I'll be startin a new job soon . . . and I got a lady friend over in Grant Park. Me and her gonna travel some."

"That's nice." Sandy's face turned red. He could see her emotions bubbling up. He hoped she wouldn't start crying outdoors. He tried to distract her from her distress.

"Where you gonna go from here?"

"Honestly, I don't know," said Sandy. "Right now, Sean and I need a little distance from town. We found a nice apartment up in Alpharetta.

We'll stay put there until he's fully back to normal. Then we'll see what happens . . . It's a long road ahead—in many ways."

"Yeah," Barlowe said, looking off into the distance. "You right about that."

"We'll have to see where God leads," Sandy declared.

Barlowe said nothing to that.

Now she looked deep into his eyes. Whenever she looked at him like that, he knew she was about to spring one of her probing questions.

"Barlowe?"

"Yeah?"

"You still think I'm just a silly white girl looking for something interesting to do?"

He thought for a moment. "Yeah."

She smiled. "I can't help it. See?" She pinched the white skin on her arm.

"Yeah, I see." He smiled, too.

She looked at her watch. "Well. I guess I'd better go."

He extended a hand. "Good-bye."

She stepped forward and hugged him, tight, and held it there.

Barlowe's eyes danced up and down the street, checking to see if Miss Carol Lilly or somebody somewhere was watching.

Finally, Sandy let go. With the back of her hand, she wiped at tears that had formed in her eyes. She sniffled.

"Barlowe?"

"Yeah?"

"You still think there's too much water under the bridge?"

He looked up the street and saw Ricky Brown. Ricky had parked his Winn-Dixie grocery cart on the sidewalk. He picked up something off the ground and studied it close, like a person reading an interesting book.

"Is a *lot*," said Barlowe.

"Well. I gotta keep trying. I *have* to try."

"I know."

She turned to leave, then stopped and looked back at him once more. She pulled a pen and paper from her purse and scribbled her new phone number. She handed him the paper.

"You'll keep in touch, won't you?"

"Yeah." Barlowe stuffed the paper in his shirt pocket. "I'll keep in touch."

It seemed like the right thing to say, but they both knew he wouldn't likely follow through.

Sandy said her last good-bye and went next door to drop off the key to the newest family in the Old Fourth Ward. Minutes later, she reappeared and rushed to her car. She tooted the horn at Barlowe one last time as she drove away.

He watched the car until it moved out of sight.

He picked up a box and walked across the street. Standing on the front porch of Mr. Smith's old house, which was now his new house, Barlowe looked around. Oddly, he thought about his old girlfriend, Nell. Wherever she was, he hoped she was happy. He wasn't mad at her anymore. He figured maybe he owed her a thank-you note, for lighting a fire under his butt.

He felt at peace with himself now. With Louise he was learning how to live.

He pulled out a key and opened the door to his new house. Before going inside, he peered across the street. The movers, now done unloading, headed toward their truck.

Barlowe's new neighbor appeared on the front porch, carrying something draped across his arms. It was a big old flag. He carefully unfurled it and spread it across the banisters, so that the stars and bars faced the street. The man went back inside and shut the door.

Barlowe looked at the flag and glanced up at the sky, maybe searching for a sign of the God that Sandy had mentioned a few minutes ago. There was a single cloud above, shaped like a big, gray carrot. He studied the cloud. He watched it for a long moment, until a bird came into view. It was a lone pigeon, flying high and away from there, its red tag fluttering in the wind.

# Acknowledgments

Many thanks to the following: Faith Childs, my literary agent, who really got it from the start; Barbara Vance, my lecture agent, who recommended Faith; Malaika Adero at Atria, whose editorial guidance was both judicious and patient; Adrienne Ingrum (the feedback was timely); John Paine, who provided a fresh, incisive eye in the final lap; eternal gratitude, always, to my main man, Jeff Frank, who encouraged me in the beginning.

Thanks also to the people who inspired thoughts and ideas, whether they knew it or not: Warren "Mickey" Drewery, Greg Mabry, Miss Bussey in the Old Fourth Ward, Calvin "Chip" Roberts, Wendell "Cooder" Johnson, Harun Black, Dr. Leslie Harris (thanks for the support), Sharon Shahid, Larry Copeland, Linda Pulley.